A FALCON TAKES FLIGHT

(A BABYLON/PERSIA NOVEL)

KRISTIN SWENSON

PG
B

First published in the United States in 2025 by Pretty Good Books, Charlottesville, Virginia

Identifiers: ISBN 979-8-9989339-2-9 (ebook); 979-8-9989339-3-6 (trade paper)

For Craig

PROLOGUE

*F*amily. Home. What cruel irony that those who lack them can define exactly what it is they're missing. They know the precise dimensions, the shape, color, and textures, the *feel* of a good family, of true home. Countless are the forces that might deny a person these things; singular is the quest to gain them. Only a lucky few do.

ALL HER LIFE, the bastard Amytis had protected her half-sister, the true princess of Media from danger. After all, all their lives, it was to be Mandane who would marry Nebuchadnezzar, king of the greatest empire in the world and thus clinch the treaty with Babylonia that would protect Amytis's beloved wild mountains, forests, fields, rivers, and lakes from the empire's rapacious greed.

But in a final act to protect both sister and land, it had been Amytis who traveled from her home country to Babylon, Amytis who married Nebuchadnezzar, and Amytis who came face-to-face with those powerful elite who could not abide the foreigners whom Nebuchadnezzar had woven into all levels of his cosmopolitan capital.

At the same time that Amytis witnessed the courtier Igliss try to kill her little boy before the child's formal admittance as a prince of Babylonia, she could not have known that hundreds of miles to the north, her father King Astyages was hatching a murderous scheme of his own.

PART I

(MEDIA, CA. 580 B.C.E.)

CHAPTER 1

*T*he magi hurried from the king's bedchamber. Barely out the door, they heard Astyages shout, "Harpagus! Now!"

The king's steward was never far. He rushed in as the magi hurried out. The religious men picked up their pace - away. Only Harpagus seemed able to tolerate the king's capricious rages and demands.

The younger magus shivered and pulled his robe more tightly around him. He glanced at his stout companion, a distant cousin of some reputation within the family.

"You're sure of the interpretation we gave?" the younger asked when they were out of earshot.

To their left, windows punctuating the wall revealed snow-capped mountains just beginning to pink with the pastels of dawn.

"What other is possible? I doubt he needed our interpretation so much as mental bolstering. Don't worry. The gods will what they will. Who knows, maybe they'll finally give the old man his due."

Morning light scattered at their feet. Neither one noticed.

The thin magus shot his cousin a startled glance and looked around. "You mustn't say that. It's treason. And he's not that old, anyway."

"Don't pretend you like him."

"I don't, but -- "

"No one does. Don't worry about it." They rounded the hall and approached a wide staircase. "Anyway, what's he going to do, this king with only daughters, kill his own grandson?" As they went down the stairs, the king's steward rushed past them, heading up.

* * *

KING ASTYAGES HAD WOKEN SLOWLY, his mind slogging out of a troubling vision only to feel the weight of a dread so heavy it pinned him to the bed. There wasn't a sound to break the loneliness of anxiety. No voice, not even the rustle of a caged bird to banish the worry that didn't yet have definition, shape or colors. As it came back to him, he remembered that his daughter Mandane was at the center of it... again. When the king had regained enough consciousness to put words to his fear, he moved to a chair, still in his nightclothes settled a crown on his head and summoned the magi.

"Another nightmare about my daughter."

"Mandane specifically, as before? Or –"

"Of course Mandane," Astyages said. "I said, '*another* dream,' after all."

"Go on, my lord."

Astyages narrowed his eyes at the dour face of the old magus. What would he know? But what options did Astyages have?

The younger cleared his throat in the silence. "That other dream was some years ago, wasn't it?" When no reply came, the magus went on, "You took wise and appropriate action, sir. I believe that your daughter Mandane is now living a long way from here, in... what is it? Well, many miles to the south, a journey that would take a man on horse-- "

"Anshan," Astyages interrupted. "Yes, it's a long way away but still within my reach."

Again the magi shared a look – quick. Astyages's reach was far shorter than he believed. Even he had called the leader there a king.

"The place is Anshan," Astyages repeated. He stared at the pair before him, so highly trained in the arts of astrology, in writing, in healing. But could anyone understand the burden he bore? Everyone thought Media's greatness ended with his father, Cyaxares. Why couldn't they give him, Astyages, even a modicum of the same respect? Astyages tightened his grip on the chair's carved armrests. He would never let down his guard. Oh, the things you have to do, he thought, to hang on when everyone wants to take your throne.

"Yes, right after I had finally taken care of things with Babylonia."

The magi shared a quick look between them. Neither was about to say that it had been Amytis, who had seen to it that the treaty was of equals or Amytis who had clinched it. This was about the other daughter, Astyages, insisted. This was about Mandane.

"In *that* dream," Astyages said, "Mandane peed all over the world." He wrinkled his nose. "Mandane! Disgusting. She let loose a torrent of urine that flooded this city, all Media, and even beyond. It covered country after country. Piss." He shook his shoulders as if that would shake off the image. "Back then, when you gave your interpretation, it was as dire as I could have guessed it would be: that her *issue* would take over this place and more. I acted immediately to neutralize the threat. I found a suitable husband for her, 'king' so to speak of a place suitably impotent and far from here."

Most fathers sought the most prestigious matches for their daughters. Astyages had achieved that with Amytis, he thought. Sure, it didn't happen exactly as he – or anyone – had thought it would. But happen it did. And on his watch. By contrast, the match of this other daughter Mandane to the king of Anshan, was good mainly because it was so *unimpressive*.

Indeed, it hadn't been easy, but he had finally identified a certain Cambyses from Anshan, some 500 miles to the southeast -- a good man his advisors had said, and from a perfectly fine family. Cambyses was called a king, which was good for Mandane's reputation; but the place that Cambyses ruled was so insignificant that the man was in fact inferior to even the most middling Mede. Rumor had it that the king even went by a nickname -- Cam. "King Cam," but still. Astyages hadn't heard of anything happening in Anshan since Assyria had orphaned the region some decades earlier.

At one time yoked to Susa and the powerful Elamite kingdom, Anshan wasn't anymore. Rather, after the Assyrian destruction of Susa, Anshan became irrelevant, as far as Astyages was concerned. It was said that the people there ate wild fruits and *pistaka* nuts. Pathetic. Whatever child Mandane might have in such a place could never be a threat. So, the match was made, and Mandane moved from her father's great palace in the mountains of Media to the plains of Anshan in Parsa far away.

"So, why this? Why now?" Astyages thought he'd neutralized the threat. He'd put her out of his mind. His mind had other ideas. Damn dreams.

"You're sure it was Mandane, and not her sister Amytis, Nebuchadnezzar's wife?" the skinny magus asked. "Amytis has, after all, born a son who could inherit the Babylonian throne."

"*Not*," the older magi shot his cousin a stern look, "that the child ever would. My cousin forgets that Nebuchadnezzar already has a crown prince."

"I didn't forg –" At a blistering gaze from his elder, the young magi shut his mouth.

"The king knows what he's talking about. Please, my lord, when you are ready."

Astyages looked at first one magus and then the other. Finally, satisfied that he had their full – and serious attention – he took a deep breath and resumed.

"This time," Astyages said with a shudder, "I dreamt that a vine sprouted from between Mandane's legs. A vine, all leafy and branching every which way. It spread quickly, covering not only little Anshan, but also all of my Media, even on to Babylon. And it didn't stop there. This horrible vine, it kept on going into lands farther to the east than I could imagine anyone ever going." Across the chair's arms, Astyages's knuckles shone white in the morning light. He loosened one hand, felt for the crown on his head, exhaled, and replaced it, rings clacking against the wood.

"Please, sir. Excuse us for a moment?" the elder magus said.

The king nodded.

The two stepped back, conferred intensely and returned. Astyages leaned forward.

The magi had agreed on a sobering interpretation. The elder nodded to the other, shifting nervously from one foot to the other, to deliver their judgment.

The magus spoke quickly, with as little inflection as he could effect as if speed and a flat affect might appease Astyages. "Mandane will indeed bear a child destined to conquer. He will become king over many people. This dream echoes the last."

Astyages paled at the news.

The magus chanced a quick look at his cousin, who simply lowered his double chin to go on. "It seems," the magus hesitated, "to suggest again that a son of Mandane's will overpower..."

The magus cleared his throat and finished in a rush, "over-power you and take Media for his own, as only part of what would become a huge empire."

Astyages's face reddened with splotchy color, deeper and deeper until it looked like he might explode.

The younger magus stepped his thin frame behind the broad body of his cousin, onto whom Astyages shifted his furious gaze.

"But such details," the elder magus added, his voice placating, assured, "are never definite. For one thing, Mandane doesn't even *have* a child."

"Get out!"

They did, as fast as they decorously could.

Astyages had not told the magi what he had learned the evening before. Mandane was pregnant.

* * *

So IT WAS that the king called for Harpagus, King Astyages's steward, right hand to Cyaxares before him, a skilled military officer back in the day, and the only one that Astyages felt actu-ally granted Astyages the respect he was due. Harpagus now oversaw the royal property and staff. Loyalty and patience, those were the qualities that most defined the man. The first meant the world to Astyages. While Harpagus waited patiently before the king, Astyages formulated a plan.

Finally, Astyages said, "Send to Anshan the order that my daughter must ride immediately back to Ecbatana. Do whatever you have to do to get her here."

I hope she's not so far along that she'll resist my request, Astyages thought. I'd hate to have to force it.

"Add something about how I worry for Mandane, delivering her baby in such a backwater place. In Media, we can secure the best and most experienced midwives for this her first child."

Harpagus didn't mention that Mandane had herself been the

most skilled midwife in Media. Although his wife had become good, Mandane was still and always the best. Instead, he said, "Indeed. I expect that Mandane will be much more comfortable in the palace at Ecbatana, cooled by western winds at the foot of Pointed Mountain."

"Say that, too."

CHAPTER 2

*W*hen they got the message, miles and days to the south, Mandane and her husband were sitting at the rough wooden table. They had finished dinner but lingered on, simply enjoying the late day air across the rolling hills... and each other.

To say that Mandane had been reluctant to marry this man in a place she'd barely heard of (despite the years of tutoring she had endured in preparation to be a queen of Babylonia) was an understatement. If she could have said No, she would have. But Astyages's insistence that the *gods* had decreed it should be so by some dream-vision he'd had the privilege to experience, and she the ever-submissive princess (definitely no Amytis with her bastard half-sister's moxie) insured that Mandane would go along with it. By then, Mandane had finally accepted Harpagus's explanation for why Amytis had done what she did. Over and over again, he had explained why Amytis suddenly posed as the true princess, went to Babylon, and became the one to marry Nebuchadnezzar. "No contact." Both sisters had honored it. So, Mandane had never heard from Amytis herself. She could only imagine the bastard wild-child in the most sophisticated royal court of the world. But Harpagus was nothing if not patient. And finally, Mandane understood that Amytis had not planned it, had not even wanted it. Rather, in a crucial moment, Amytis saw that were Mandane to have gone to Babylon and persisted in the midwifery she could no more abandon that abandon her own breath, Mandane would have been killed. The treaty that was finally to link their nations – Babylonia and Media – *as equals* despite the Astyages's weakening Media would be null and void. Mandane knew that just as she could not turn her back on the work that might have saved Mandane's mother during Mandane's birth, Amytis would do anything to protect Media from whoever might damage its vast wildness. And Babylonia would be first and worst to wreak such damage.

Mandane inhaled deeply. She never would have believed that she could be happy here, in this place – a backwater place by any standard of geopolitical import, wealth, or strength. She never would have imagined herself happy married to anyone other than the most powerful man in the world in the most luxurious of palaces, multiple palaces and servants and jewels and the deference of millions… But here she was. With her feet bare on the home-fired tiles, seated on the plainest of simple chairs, having eaten nothing but what grew mere yards away, in a dress made of linen spun by her own hands, Mandane looked at King Cam, this king to her queen, his wavy hair untouched even by the simple gold band she'd seen him wear only once, and smiled.

Cam ran his finger gently over the soft red swoop of Mandane's lower lip. "Not once since you got here has Astyages taken any interest in you. That alone defies logic. Why now?"

"My father is rarely bound by logic. And he *is* king." She laid a hand across her belly.

"Why did we tell him?" King Cam lamented.

"We were happy?"

Cam laughed, despite himself. "We *are* happy. I only wish I could go, too."

"But the fields need tending, relations between the tribes diplomacy, and –"

"Someone has to eat my cooking!" A woman more square than round, more thick than curvy deposited between them a bowl of plums, so ripe that a bumblebee followed it in and hovered, buzzing above the rim.

Mandane laughed. "And he's just the man for it. I will miss your food, Cook, and can hardly wait for our baby to enjoy it for himself."

"Herself," Cam said.

Mandane, serious again, laid her hand over her husband's. "If this baby is a girl, whatever name you choose for her shall be the name she has."

"Mandane," Cam said, before she'd barely finished speaking.

"Yes?" Mandane said.

"No," Cam smiled. "That shall be her name. It is the sweetest word I have ever heard."

Mandane slapped his hand lightly. Then she wove her fingers into his. "But if this baby is a boy…"

Cam kissed her hand. "You can give him whatever tongue-twisting Median name your heart desires."

Mandane nodded. "I'd like to name him Cyrus."

Cam released her and sat back, a small frown on face. "You never even met my father. And an Elamite name? You never even saw this place before the Assyrians came."

"Perhaps our son will rebuild, will forge that alliance again – Anshan and Elam. It's a good name," Mandane said.

Cam nodded and with a smile. "Yes, it is," he said. "'Bestower of care'. I like that." Then he gathered Mandane into his arms. "Just please, bring her – or him – back to me just as soon as you can."

When the baby kicked hard enough for both of them to feel, they laughed.

"I will," Mandane said. "Clearly this child is eager to be here."

CHAPTER 3

*E*motionally, the trip was easier going from Anshan to Ecbatana than it had been the other way, when as a frightened bride Mandane had traveled to what seemed a rough place distant and little known. Physically, though, this journey was much harder. The baby made her so tired. Every so often, Mandane laid out the tiny dagger that Amytis had left for her and ran her hand over its ornate scabbard, remembering. Amytis, strong and brave. It wasn't much. A cast-off, in truth, from their father who scorned its gold-plate, putting a nick along the iron blade to show its worthlessness to him. More than once, Amytis had saved Mandane from trouble with that blade, small enough for the bastard, no-account girl to wield with remarkable efficacy, wielded to protect Mandane, the true princess. Merely seeing it made Mandane feel safe in ways that had little to do with her environment. And she was safe. Cam had insisted on sending a well-armed escort. But they couldn't make the journey go any faster. Riding slowly it took several weeks.

The route was beautiful, though, traveling north through the Zagros foothills, along mountain ridges, and through green passes. There were enough streams and even cool lakes along the way to quench the thirst of people and animals alike. Predatory beasts were shy in the face of such a company. Once, Mandane spied a mountain lion before it slipped back into the forest shadows. As they approached the palace, its multiple walls slipping in and out of view, Mandane recognized more and more of the outlying hamlets and cottages. She couldn't help but remember the adventures she'd had with Amytis, traveling to the farthest outskirts, anywhere necessary to the homes of birthing women. She couldn't help but remember Spaco, the woman they called "Dog," who could not seem to bring an infant to term. Mandane laid a hand across her belly. She'd seen the woman's grief. How had she borne it time and time again? Mandane couldn't understand. And she wouldn't let herself imagine. Not now.

Mandane made it back to Ecbatana weary but in good health. No surprise, it was Harpagus who arranged to get her, princess of Media returned, settled again in the royal palace. Mandane told Harpagus – he had a way that invited such confidence – that she would name the baby (if a boy) Cyrus. Then she swore him to secrecy on the matter. He would keep her secret, she knew. He wouldn't have kept such a job if he couldn't. For his part, Harpagus wanted to tell her all about his own baby. Their only, and just born, Harpagus knew beyond a shadow of doubt that his son was more a prince than any could be. But it wasn't his place to share. And although Harpagus was as important a person to the king as any, he was still a servant. And his son had no place in the palace other than that.

In the following days and weeks, Mandane gave herself over to the ministrations of Astyages's court staff and enjoyed her father's surprising excitement over this new grandchild. The entire palace, indeed the whole region, seemed to delight in her presence and state. Mandane was certain that some of it was merely relief that Astyages had something positive to focus on. And focus he did. Meanwhile, weavers created swaddling robes of the softest linens and wool and laid out golden bands and medallions to cinch and pin the folds in place. Son of a barely-king, he was nevertheless grandson to a grand empire and darling even before he was born.

Still, Mandane missed Cam. And despite the finery of the Median empire, the ministrations of teams of people, and the pleasures of the world that passed through the crossroads at Ecbatana, every day, every moment of every day she missed the rugged simplicity of Anshan. But time passed. One day, her time would come. Mandane focused on her one, true goal in the meantime: to bring a baby back to King Cam in Anshan.

Mandane coached the midwives who would attend her. None was better than Mandane. Ever since Kara, the slave who raised Amytis and Mandane, told them that it was baby Mandane's birth that had killed her mother, Mandane had been determined that as long as she could help it, no mother would die like that. She had done such work for as long as she could remember. She wasn't always successful. But she was the best of anyone. So, even while Mandane hoped for a straightforward birth and a healthy baby to bring home to Anshan, she also steeled herself for the worst of what she'd seen, and not only in childbirth.

The most terrifying to her was how some new mothers – and there was no predicting it – could suddenly lose any shred of interest in the world, their newborn included. The vacancy in their eyes, the tears at best – suicide at worst – haunted Mandane. Well, she had promised. And she realized, with surprise, that she wanted it for herself. More than anything, she wanted to bring this baby *home*. For that is what Anshan had become for her, and she wanted that for this child of hers. Yes, Mandane would bring this baby back to Cam, the first of many children she hoped they'd raise in Parsa together. And when the pains of labor finally began, Mandane tucked beneath her bed the gold-plated dagger that Amytis had always carried to protect Mandane, the dagger that she could not take with her to Babylon but insisted at the last moment that Harpagus give to Mandane herself. Courage and strength. Mandane would need all of it now.

The birth was long and difficult. Mandane was barely conscious when a midwife finally pulled the baby from her. The new mother fell asleep before she had a chance to see her robust son wrapped so fetchingly in the brilliantly colored robes fixed with gold.

Of course the midwife immediately told King Astyages: "A boy!"

Astyages summoned Harpagus.

* * *

"BRING THE BABY TO ME," Astyages said.

"With pleasure."

When Harpagus returned, cradling the tiny bundle gently in his long arms, Astyages refused even to look at it. "Take it away."

"Excuse me, sir?" Harpagus withdrew the infant. He looked down at the baby's newborn face and bewildered up again at the king.

"Was Mandane still sleeping when you left?" Astyages asked.

"She was indeed, sir."

Astyages laid a bejeweled hand on Harpagus's arm and squeezed it tight. "Kill him. In the mountains... you know how the gods demand it –"

Shocked, "Of the dead, sir," Harpagus blurted. "But this boy is ali-"

"You heard me." Astyages snarled. He dug his fingernails into Harpagus's bicep. "If you fail me in this in any way, I will ruin you in every way." Astyages loosened his grip. "Now. What happened is this. In her sleep, Mandane rolled over and smothered the baby. We spared her the torment of discovering it herself by removing the infant immediately."

Harpagus, his eyes wide, swallowed hard.

"When it is done," Astyages narrowed his eyes at the faithful steward, "show me the body."

As Harpagus rode from the palace, the tiny form swaddled close to his chest, it became clear to him: he couldn't kill this baby. Loyalty, yes. But to whom? The whole thing sickened him. He'd never felt as close to the princess Mandane as he had to her half-sister Amytis, but this was the true princess's son, a baby that she and her husband, a king, had eagerly awaited. There was no way Harpagus could kill this child.

Someone else would have to.

CHAPTER 4

*T*he opportunity appeared even sooner than he'd hoped. Harpagus had hardly passed through the second of the city's walls before he came upon a man, sitting idly while a flock of sheep grazed the hillside around him - a palace slave, tending the crown's animals.

Harpagus dismounted, careful not to jostle the sleeping baby tucked under his tunic.

Seeing Harpagus approach, the man stood. Even from a distance, Harpagus could see that the man's skin was weathered, his hair dark brown with the faintest bits of gray. Yet he rose without leaning on the rugged staff he held in thick fingers. Tough to tell his age.

As Harpagus drew up his horse, the shepherd slave began to bow, the details of his face hidden. Harpagus let him. What he asked would benefit from the sense of a command.

The baby moved against Harpagus's chest. "Something I need you to do," Harpagus said.

The man straightened.

What was it about him? Harpagus thought, then focused again on the task. He could feel the infant's soft breath at his neck. For a moment, Harpagus hoped he'd say, No, this man who looked vaguely familiar. For an instant, he hoped maybe the shepherd would protect the baby like he protected his sheep – from wild animals and any danger. But no. Harpagus shifted the baby roughly, fully prepared to hand him over. Astyages made good on his threats. Harpagus hardly dared imagine the horrors that king would visit on him. The baby had to die. And Harpagus had to prove it.

"Do you know a far, high place, exposed to the weather, to the wild things there?"

The man nodded.

Harpagus opened his shirt. "Take this there," he said and thrust the baby at the man. "And leave it."

The man's mouth dropped open in disbelief, then snapped shut again as he took the infant. His eyes traveled between the soft, tiny face and Harpagus's fierce one.

"Then, in three days' time, meet me here..." Harpagus said as he remounted, "with what's left of the corpse."

The man said nothing.

Harpagus studied him until he was sure the man would follow through. Nevertheless, he added, "If you fail," Harpagus said, his voice severe as a spring storm, "the baby will still die. And you will wish that you had died with it."

The man nodded. "I know a place -"

"Don't tell me," Harpagus said. He whirled his horse and rode without looking back.

He had almost reached the inner city walls when he remembered: Mithradates. That man had once been a favorite of Astyages's. The king had kept the man close, hungry for the popularity Mithradates, nicknamed Mit, so easily commanded. But the man was popular for his candor. Mit was the embodiment of truth. And that's what finally got him expelled, reduced to a shepherd slave. Mit had refused to say that Astyages was thought to be a greater king than his father Cyaxares before him.

Such a thing was simply untrue. Everyone knew it; only Mithra-dates would say it. Harpagus wished he felt better about this stroke of good luck. For the man would surely kill this offspring of the palace that had so disgraced him. Harpagus stopped his horse abruptly, jumped down, and vomited in the grass. Still shaky, he wiped his mouth, remounted, and rode for home.

CHAPTER 5

*H*arpagus's wife, above average in every way, was not there when Harpagus got home. She was in the country, some miles out from the outermost city walls, tending to the difficult birth of a shepherd slave. The woman was too old to be getting pregnant, too old to be giving birth, by Harpagus's wife's opinion. But no one had asked her. And this couple were desperate. How many children had they conceived? And yet not one living child. The woman, Spaco, was believed to be a seer, skilled in reading the sacred stones. Years ago, when she was just a girl, she had read that one day she would have a son. Not only that, but she believed that he would change the world. And nothing that happened could convince her otherwise. So here she was, pregnant again.

Harpagus's wife knew the tale, and she knew that interpreting the stones was an art. Maybe someone else would have read them differently than Spaco. Whatever the case, Harpagus's wife was here to help. The best midwife, the king's own daughter, had returned to Ecbatana but was in no condition to attend another woman's birth. So, Harpagus's wife did what she could. She had brought her own child along, still a baby himself, young enough to strap to her back, young enough to stay put while she tended to other things. And this woman's childbed was not easy. Nor was it quick. Yet, for all that labor, for all the pain and all the hope, this infant, too, was stillborn. Crushingly full term, the baby was perfect in every way except for this: the little boy had never drawn a single breath. His mother wept with a grief as pure as it was deep. Life was so uneven.

As Harpagus's wife cleaned the tiny body, she said with the kindest of voices, "I can see your little boy even now, feasting at a gold and silver table in the underworld. He is playing with his brothers and sisters and all the many children who died before their time. That's what we believe, where I come from. Can you see him with me?"

But Spaco's grief was beyond such comfort. She waved to the midwife to give her the newborn corpse. "I'll hold him," she said, "before I send him on in fire."

That was not the tradition of this place, and not the tradition of the midwife's people; but each to her own, Harpagus's wife thought. If it gave the woman peace... She wrapped the baby in the faded rags of royal cast-offs that Harpagus would bring home from the palace from time to time. At Spaco's insistence, she laid the cold bundle on the woman's heaving chest. Then she turned away. Then, any tenderness aside, Harpagus's wife yanked the Pazuzu amulet off its hook on the wall and holding it by the eagle-like talons, thrust it into the undyed linen sack she kept for that purpose, head first – its face half snarling dog, half hissing cat – then around the wings, the man-like legs and snake-penis. "And take that demoness Lamashtu with you back to your dank and windowless world," she said as she pulled the string shut. "You failed us. Now let this poor woman rest."

CHAPTER 6

*A*s soon as Harpagus heard his wife's voice – the words didn't matter – soft and low, singing to their own little boy as they approached the house, he burst into tears.

When she saw Harpagus, ordinarily so cool, so measured in his affect, Harpagus's wife rushed toward him. "What is this about?"

She took their son from her back, which made Harpagus weep even harder. He clutched their infant so tightly that the little boy began to cry. Harpagus's wife eased the child from Harpagus's hands and brought him to her breast. She pulled a chair close to her husband and stroked his arm until he had recovered enough to explain.

But before he could, there was a knock on the door. Husband and wife exchanged a look. Harpagus swiped his eyes and rose to open it. Two men in the palace's official armor (Astyages had insisted) stepped inside, their faces grim. "Dispatch from the king," one said.

Harpagus began to tremble. How could he explain?

"The princess birthed a child, a boy. But he's dead."

As his wife exclaimed "No!" In the distance, the sound of public wailing rose.

"The princess," the man went on, "when told the news – that she was the cause – pulled a dagger from under her bed. She killed herself."

Harpagus covered his mouth and stumbled back into the chair, stunned. Of course he knew the former bit of news – and these men were simply telling the story around; but Mandane also dead?!

"Poor girl. Poor babe." Harpagus's wife ushered the men out. She shifted their baby to her other breast and hurried back to Harpagus. "I understand now. That's why you were so upset."

"No," Harpagus said. He put his head into his hands. "That's but the half of it." He looked up at her with tormented eyes. "Hear me out." And so he told her what had happened. As he spoke, Harpagus's wife went from disbelief to anger to an urgent anxiety.

"Get up," she said.

Harpagus swiped at his eyes, then did as she commanded.

"Go back to that man. Stop him!"

"But I can't," Harpagus said. "If the baby is not killed, who knows what Astyages will do to me... to us!"

"Do you know that settlement, not far – maybe two miles west of here... The slaves' cottages, maybe three or so – shepherds. The ancient one – a garden, fruit trees..."

Harpagus nodded.

"This morning, I delivered a baby there. Stillborn."

Harpagus's eyes widened with understanding.

"Find that man, get the baby, and meet me there. But hurry!"

When Harpagus's wife detached their son from her breast, he began to cry. Bouncing up and down, she put him to her shoulder, and patted his back.

"Go!" she said to Harpagus, who was frozen in place.

She bundled their son back onto her back. Only when she

flew out the door, did Harpagus move. "The corpse," she called back as she ran. "They're going to burn it."

* * *

WHEN HARPAGUS'S wife burst into Spaco's door, Spaco instinctively clutched the body of her baby, dead, to her chest. Harpagus's wife bent over double, trying to catch her breath, her own baby wailing from the hill of her back. Harpagus's wife held up her hand to Spaco to wait, wait until she could speak. But first, she laughed. She smiled and to Spaco's horror, laughed. But her laughter – relief – evaporated when Harpagus darkened the door. Alone.

"He was gone," Harpagus said. "I skirted the land to the north and west – the pasture is rich up there. And leads into the mountains, of course. Then I retraced to the southeast. A great big circle. But I couldn't find him anywhere."

Harpagus's wife straightened. Their baby fussed. While they talked, Harpagus untied their son tenderly from his wife's back. Neither noticed when Spaco walked out the door.

It was the sound of sheep that brought their attention back to the place where they stood, this tiny house in the foothills of the Zagros's white-capped mountains. They rushed outside to see Spaco and Mit, each holding a swaddled babe, talking urgently to one another. When Mit saw Harpagus, he paled. Even the sheep went silent.

Behind him, Harpagus's horse stamped a foot impatiently. Harpagus's wife took his free hand. With his son on the other arm, Harpagus walked toward the shepherd couple.

Spaco said, "My husband, Mit. But you have already met."

Harpagus nodded. He looked at the baby Mit held – the bright clothes, the fine fabrics and golden bracteates, such contrast to the faded rags that bound the other infant's cold body.

"She would have named him Cyrus," Harpagus said. "Only I know that. And now you."

Harpagus's wife looked deeply into the face of the live baby, this baby born a prince. Then she looked at Spaco. She looked at Mit.

"I can see the resemblance," she said.

Harpagus cleared his throat. "Three days' time," he said.

Spaco swallowed hard, then nodded.

CHAPTER 7

*J*ust because the decision was clear didn't make it easy.

Inside their hut, "Harpagus will return," Mit said. "I have to show him ... "

Spaco nodded. She bowed her head to the lifeless infant in her arms, kissed its cold brow, and laid it on table worn smooth with the tasks of farm life conducted there, the thousands of meals they'd shared at it. Mit laid the other infant, red-faced and bawling with hunger now, out next to their son and gently stripped him of his palace finery. Even when the bawling infant quieted on Spaco's plump breast, and Mit's throat ached at the sudden joy the sight brought to him, he would have done almost anything to avoid the rest of it. Almost.

Mit turned to the baby on the table. Tenderly, he unbound the tattered rags from his dead son. Then he redressed the blue and stiffening body in the finest fabrics his rough hands had ever felt. On the cold body, he refastened every golden bracteate, smoothed each wrinkle. When he was done, he held the baby high for Spaco to see.

"Our son, a prince."

And when Spaco had nursed the new baby, now warm and dry in clean rags, she handed him gurgling happily to Mit. "I give you your son," Spaco said.

* * *

IN THE MORNING, Mit carried the dead boy into the mountains, hiking an old route that he knew would take them far away. When Harpagus had told Mit to leave the baby in the wildest, most remote place, the shepherd slave had known immediately the perfect spot. He arrived there late in the day. He clambered up the last steep bit -- several feet of rocky outcropping -- careful to keep the baby, swaddled in a wide cloth across his chest, from jostling. As if it were alive. Breathing heavily, Mit stood up tall. He inhaled deeply. He smelled the juniper, the crush of leaves becoming soil, the mineral-edge of a breeze off the mountains' cold slopes.

The smell of pines, of height and heaven filled his head. Below his feet, cracks in the great, broad rocks harbored tiny white flowers. Wind, ever blowing up the cliff heights, buffeted the trees below so that they whispered constantly in whoosh and shush. From there, he could see places so distant he could hardly imagine them. And he nodded, satisfied that he had chosen well.

As the sun dropped away, Mit fell to his knees. "This," he said, his voice husky, to the still bundle before him, "is a good place. The pure wind, the sun and rain, will take you and care for you. The gods as they live in and through the wild things will make you fly. You will root, and you will bloom." He laid the baby, a tiny multi-colored bundle, on the rocks. The shepherd man, whose child would grow into the same enslaved state, looked deeply at his little boy. The pieces of gold that he'd carefully refastened, each pin and band accounted for, caught the last bits of light and shot bright beams back into the air. Mit picked his way carefully down the ledge into the waiting woods below. He prepared a temporary camp and settled in. Wild birds came, hungry, and left satisfied. And at night he heard the soft padding of shy beasts making their way to that rugged place.

Three days later, Mit climbed to the spot where he had left the infant corpse. It took some time, but he was thorough, careful to regather the bundle, now tattered and torn, careful to leave nothing of what the others had left behind.

* * *

HARPAGUS atop his horse watched the shepherd approach across the verdant hillside where they had met. He grimaced. The whole business sickened him. Between Mandane's suicide and the king's façade of innocence slashed through with genuine grief, the palace atmosphere these days was taut as the gut strings of a lyre.

The men exchanged not a word. There was nothing to say. But as Mit watched Harpagus ride back to the palace with what was left of a newborn body, he silently willed for this child peace in death, all peace forevermore. Dead for dead, Mit thought as he turned for home, and life for life.

The shepherd slaves raised the once-a-prince as their own, and they called him Bartatua, "with far-reaching strength."

CHAPTER 8

*T*he secret remained. And like some buried rubbish, out of its deep darkness, it enriched the lives of its keepers. Harpagus increased in the king's favor; Spaco and Mit took joy in a child, the only child, that they could call their own; and Cyrus grew up and into a life he didn't know had been so narrowly won.

For all that the boy Cyrus knew, he was Bartatua, son of shepherd-slaves who were themselves born into service to the palace. Like them, and like generations of people before, he learned the skills of husbandry and herding. He adapted to the demands of the palace, kept his head down, and enjoyed the extras that were their own after satisfying the king's wants and needs. Cyrus also learned that Spaco had a gift for seeing what was invisible to everyone else, seeing truths; and from Mit, Cyrus learned the value of calling a thing what it truly was.

Cyrus experienced the capricious nature of the gods, who might at their pleasure or whim assault the region with bitter cold in temperatures reaching fifteen degrees below zero, or in the summer steal the energy of people and animals alike with a wilting heat. He was grateful for the warmth of woolen coats and leather trousers in winter. With the leather that Mit tanned behind their cottage, Spaco made high lace-up boots for him like his father's to protect their feet from rough terrain. For the most part, though, the region around Ecbatana was comfortable, a good place to live. Naturally well-watered, the region easily met the daily needs of gods and men.

The palace animals that Cyrus learned to tend with Mit grew fat on the meadows' rich grasses. And Spaco kept a small garden with a variety of vegetables and herbs including chickpeas, oregano, spicy greens, and onions. Buckwheat-type shrubs near the cottage yielded a substance in the fall that Spaco put to use sweetening ground pistachios in a rich confection. Her mother before her had planted fruit trees that grew to produce apples, plums, and pears. In a normal year, grain was easy to get in trade with the slaves and citizens who planted acres and acres of wheat and barley. These farmers prided themselves on growing wheat of such quality that its reputation brought traders from far away.

Ecbatana controlled a corridor through the rugged Zagros Mountains that connected Mesopotamia in the west to the Iranian highland's traders and beyond in the east. Inhabitants called it "The High Road" and marveled at the strange ways of foreign merchants with exotic goods that passed through their land, even if they could not afford such luxuries themselves. It seemed to the boy Cyrus that merchants from all over the world passed through his home. Other people, too, other than native Medians, called Ecbatana and the lands around it home. Some, people from the confederacy of Israel, for example, had been settled there by the Assyrians over a century earlier.

At an elevation of 1800 meters, Ecbatana was still only half as high as the rocky snow-capped peaks that towered over it. Just outside the city, nestled on the eastern slope of the Arvand Range, fertile fields rolled away to the east. As the years passed, the boy tending animals along the far periphery learned the mountains' paths punctuated by lush meadows and shady woods and became skilled in defending the flocks from predators – jackals, wolves, mountain lions, and more that lurked in the shadows.

Also peppered throughout the landscape were the world's most desirable horses. Some said it was the grass they ate that gave the animals such extraordinary size, strength, and speed. Some said it was the gods. At least as famous as its wheat, the region's horses -- an exceptionally large breed called Nisean – benefited indeed from rich pastures, a temperate climate, and a culture of equestrian knowledge unparalleled in the world.

When he was out with the flocks or hunting for his family, Cyrus delighted in seeing the horses. To watch them run or even simply graze across the landscape lifted his spirit and gave wings to his imagination. But Cyrus knew better than to get close to them, even if they had let him. Like everything else, the horses belonged to the palace. And the palace was not his. So, one morning, when he heard the steady clomp of horses' hooves just outside their cottage, while it was still the earliest hour of a new day, Cyrus followed his parents to the doorway and stepped outside to see what important people those prized beasts bore.

* * *

THERE WERE TWO OF THEM, a man dressed in the clothes of the palace and with a sword on each hip, and a woman whose demeanor was regal even though she wore no jewels and sat the horse as if she'd been riding all her life. Harpagus hadn't been back to the shepherds' cottage since he'd left the slave couple, each holding a newborn - one alive, one dead. That was nine, almost ten years ago. Now, each of them – Harpagus, Mit and Spaco – looked from the woman on the horse to the boy in the doorway to the woman, Amytis, again. Cyrus had never seen his reflection, so he didn't know what they did: he and the strange woman had the same eyes - strikingly sharp and all around them, a lining dark as kohl.

There was something else, too. Amytis stared at Cyrus. Although Amytis's horse danced nervously beneath her, she didn't notice. Even as it stepped this way and that, her eyes stayed on the boy. Still staring, she dismounted, passed the reins to Harpagus, and stepped forward as if in a daze. On the ground, she was smaller than Cyrus had thought. Her hair, long and light brown, was streaked with all sorts of other colors, he could see now, now that she stood so close. Cyrus held his ground. Even when Amytis bent to his face, even when she reached a finger toward his mouth, he stood still. Amytis touched Cyrus's lower lip, then, traced her finger along the full swoop of it.

"Mandane," Amytis whispered. In wonder, she turned back to Harpagus. "He looks like Mandane."

"They call him Bartatua," Harpagus said.

CHAPTER 9

After they had left, the little boy Cyrus peppered Mit and Spaco with questions. The shepherd slaves answered very few. Yes, those people came from the palace. No, they weren't the king and queen. But. That woman, Amytis, was the primary wife of Nebuchadnezzar, king of Babylonia.

"Yet she was born here," Spaco said, "the bastard daughter of King Astyages."

Mit cleared his throat.

"It's quite a story." At Mit's warning look, "What?" Spaco said, "A little bit couldn't hurt."

And so she told the rapt little boy about how the woman he had just met surprised everyone some fifteen years earlier by going to Babylon to insure that the terms of a treaty protecting Media were in place and then marrying Nebuchadnezzar herself in order to confirm that it was so. Spaco told how the woman Amytis, who as a girl – Mit laid his hand over Spaco's; she adjusted the narrative from detailing the bastard's status – had never been one for the trappings of royalty, was now married to the most powerful in the world. And she had a son who was even now visiting Media for the first time. Word was, Mit added, that Amytis's son, nicknamed Bushu, loved this wild place even more than all the luxuries of Babylonia could provide. Neither of them said that the woman had had a sister, Media's true princess, a girl prepared to become Babylonia's queen. A girl named Mandane. And of course they didn't tell Cyrus that nine years ago, almost ten, that girl – then a young woman – had returned to Media to birth a baby, a boy who everyone thought was dead. Everyone except a few... and now one more.

"Will I see her again?" Cyrus asked.

"She and her son are leaving today to go back to Babylon, back to where in order to keep the treaty, Amytis must live," Mit said.

"Until Nebuchadnezzar dies," Spaco added.

* * *

AFTER AMYTIS HAD GONE, Cyrus talked of little else than the palace. He had so many questions. Mit and Spaco answered what they could without revealing more than they should. It wasn't easy. So, some months later, after the lambs had come and had been weaned, when it came time for Mit to take them and the best of the fleece that Spaco had spun to the palace, Cyrus said, "Let me go with you, Pop."

"No!" both Mit and Spaco answered at once.

Their response was so quick, and so vehement, Cyrus said, "Why? I've shepherded the flocks by myself for years. And we won't be gone long, no longer than we've done for autumn pasturing, right?"

The shepherd slaves looked at each other. They could hardly explain that the king at the palace wanted him dead, had wanted to kill him as an infant. How much worse would it be, could it be now?

But Cyrus was incorrigible. And neither one had ever been

able to deny this child, this wonder of a son they thought they'd never have, anything that he wanted so badly.

"Let me consult the stones," Spaco said. "They will tell me if it's a thing for the child good or bad."

Mit and Cyrus watched Spaco walk deep into the woods until she disappeared out of sight. Then, they waited.

When Spaco returned, her face was troubled. Mit let himself exhale, certain that she would tell the boy that the gods had said he should not go to the palace, not this year. Maybe not ever. But what she said was, "They say it's fine. The boy will be all right, if he goes."

Cyrus whooped for joy. Mit looked at the sturdy boy, so happy. He took Spaco's elbow and led her back outside.

"What if they're wrong?"

Spaco grimaced. "The stones are never wrong. Our interpretations might be, but not the stones. I tried and tried to see other interpretations. It was clear." She hung her head. "I don't want him to go, either."

"We'll come back as soon as we can," Mit said. Spaco smiled at the effort. She knew that he would. He always did. Mit hated the palace.

* * *

GETTING READY TO GO, Cyrus was so helpful that he was in the way. Spaco laughed despite herself. When he and Mit had done everything necessary to go, Spaco slung a water skin over Cyrus's shoulder and pushed a satchel of food – fresh cheeses, sweet fruit, and hearty bread – into his hands.

"Two things you must remember," Spaco said. She took Cyrus's chin in his palm, looked into his dark eyes. "One, don't say anything about meeting Amytis and the king's steward. They merely happened to be passing by. There was nothing special in it, and there's no sense in telling anyone. Do you understand?"

Cyrus nodded. "I won't say anything about it. I'll remember. What's the other?"

Spaco released his chin and looked to Mit.

"When we're there, we'll use a different name for you. The king is… sensitive," Mit said. "Everyone knows that Bartatua means 'With far-reaching strength.' It wouldn't do to use that in front of King Astyages."

"Will I see him?"

"Probably not. I never do. Still, it's better this way."

"What's my name to be, then?"

Mit and Spaco exchanged a look.

"We'll use 'Cyrus' instead," Mit said. "It's unusual around here. And even if Astyages knows its meaning, 'One who bestows care' is more fitting of shepherd slaves such as you and me."

When they said no more, "That's it?" Cyrus's face was as eager as only a ten-year-old's could be.

Mit straightened. He looked at Spaco. She nodded.

"Let's go!"

Spaco laughed, ruffling his hair. The curls had come in, tight and thick, when he was just a toddler. She'd long ago given up trying to manage them and simply tried to keep it cut. She hugged Cyrus tightly to her chest, pulled his cap down over his head, swiped her eyes, and stood again.

"Your boy is ready, Mit!" she said.

Mit accepted the bundle she'd prepared for him, put on his hat, and followed Cyrus out the door.

"May the gods guard your way," Spaco said to them, just as she had every time that they left with the animals to pasture, just as each did when another went away.

"And yours," Mit and Cyrus replied.

Spaco waved at them - a big man and a small boy - each getting smaller, until they were out of sight.

CHAPTER 10

*a*s Mit and Cyrus passed through Ecbatana's walls, one after another after another, it became clear that there was no risk he would say what he shouldn't. Cyrus said nothing at all. When he wasn't ogling the massive structures, he was staring at the diverse swath of humanity that passed through the gates. Ecbatana, at the cross-roads of east-west travel saw merchants from all over the world, from the Mediterranean Ocean to the west as far east as India. And now, especially, people from the greater empire of Media, which itself comprised all sorts of disparate peoples, and beyond flooded this capital city.

Only when they had gone as far as they would and stood waiting to deliver their goods, did Cyrus break his silence. He wasn't the only child around. So when Mit was called to bring the lambs and the spun fleece and the most beautiful, fat sheep they had raised, Cyrus remained behind, in a corner of the courtyard where children played games. Unlike home, where the children Cyrus knew and played with were similar to him, here, there were all sorts of children – from those who lived in the palace city to those who had come from far away to deliver what the crown required. And in this particular place and this particular time, they rubbed shoulders, mostly boys. But there were a couple of girls, too. It took only moments for Cyrus to acclimate. He was having a grand time.

* * *

AFTER A WHILE, as sometimes happens, the children that Cyrus had joined decided to play a game that mimicked the ways of the adults they watched. It was one of the court officials' children who suggested playing "palace and kingdom." The boy who suggested it proudly reminded the others that not only was he the oldest one there, almost twelve; more importantly, he was the son of Artembares from a family long established among the Medes and a regular friend of the real king's.

"That's Artembares, my father," the boy said. Again. In truth, even among the boy's family friends, no one knew the boy's name. He was so like his self-important father that they simply called him Junior. "So, of course," Junior said, "I should be king."

The declaration had a dampening effect. No one moved to do anything else. When Junior glared from one to another, the littler ones looked down and shuffled their feet.

After a strained silence, a knob-kneed little boy said, "I think Cyrus should be king."

Seeing Junior's face flush with anger, Cyrus said, "Let's vote. Anyone who wants to be king, or that someone else suggests is in the running. All right?"

"Sure," a few said. The others nodded, all except Junior.

"Names?" Cyrus asked.

No one spoke.

"Any others for king?" Cyrus asked again.

"This is ridiculous," Junior muttered under breath. "Just vote, for gods' sake."

"All right," a wiry youngster said. "Who's for Junior?"

Junior's hand shot up. He glared around the group, trying to catch the eye of others, anyone else. None of the children raised their hands. One or two caught his glance, winced and shrugged.

"For Cyrus?"

All of the others raised their hands, some timidly at first. "Cyrus! Cyrus!" one called from the back. The others joined in. "Cyrus! Cyrus! Long life to King Cyrus!"

Junior's jaws clenched. Cyrus leaned against him lightly. "It's just a game," Cyrus said.

CHAPTER 11

"All right. Gather around," Cyrus said. "There's much to do in this land of ours, and you're just the ones to do it. Who are the experts?" With a little encouragement, each child named their favorite things to do. All except Junior. One by one, Cyrus assigned roles and tasks, which they dashed off to accomplish. Builders stood with their imagined styluses, plotting out where houses should go, with how many courtyards and rooms. Then they staggered around with their imagined materials -- heavy clay, lumber, and stone -- preparing the sites. There were blacksmiths taking orders and hammering invisible shoes over here, play-cooks stirred and served over there, and priests officiously waited on the gods in imaginary temples around the square.

Cyrus appointed the two boys who had first spoken up to be his bodyguards and clothed and armed them with the imaginary best. A third he discreetly instructed should be a spy, mingling with everyone and looking out for disobedience and insurrections. To the smallest child, a little girl, Cyrus assigned the task of messenger, shuttling between the others delivering news and instructions. Each had a job to do.

Cyrus assigned a particularly prestigious post to Junior --
army general -- charging him to organize the military and report
back on the training and status of the troops (all imaginary, since
the others were busy with different things).

Junior said nothing, his jaw clenching and unclenching.
Cyrus's play bodyguards shifted their feet. Cyrus walked away.
His bodyguards followed him, looking back over their shoulders.
Junior's face was blotchy red.

Cyrus went about his own business as king, which he soon determined was only interesting in action. He got tired of sitting and
pretending to eat and drink. Instead, he wandered around checking
on the others, listening to their plans, and instructing where he felt
some direction might be needed to keep the game alive.

Meanwhile, Junior hadn't budged.

The little messenger girl grabbed Cyrus's hand and said something, shy and under her breath. He bent down. "What did you
say?"

"The spy told me to tell you that Junior isn't doing his job, sir,
my lord, sir."

"Thank you. Will you please tell the spy to bring the general
to me?"

"Yes!" she said and ran off.

She returned a short time later. Behind her, the spy and a boy
playing blacksmith pulled Junior along between them. It took yet
another, pushing Junior from behind to get the boy to face Cyrus.
They released Junior in front of Cyrus, who took a seat on a
broken block of limestone. The little girl ran up to Cyrus and
placed on his head a vine that she had tied into a misshapen
circle. She bowed, grinned, and ran back behind the boy spy, who
-- it happens -- was her older brother.

Cyrus's smile disappeared when he looked at Junior. "I trust
you, General Junior, to get our troops in order. As I commanded
earlier."

Junior stood still.

"When you're done, we'll talk strategy."

Junior muttered something and crossed his arms over his chest.

"Is there a problem, General?" Cyrus said.

"Yes, there's a problem. You're nothing but a stupid slave."

Cyrus sat still as the stone of his makeshift throne.

"Why should I serve you?" Junior spat at Cyrus's feet. "Your father's worthless, and your mother's a whore." Then, he turned to go.

"Seize him!" Cyrus said to the two boys serving as bodyguards.

They grabbed hold of Junior, who struggled vainly against them.

"Bring him to the dungeon."

The boy guards looked at each other, then at Cyrus.

"Over there!" Cyrus said and pointed to an alcove in a wall across the street.

Cyrus hopped down from his limestone slab. By now, most of the other children, hearing the commotion, had left off their tasks and come to see what was going on. They followed their king to the "dungeon."

"What are you going to do?" Junior asked, his lip curled up so that his nostril wrinkled. "Have me flogged?"

"I gave you an order," Cyrus said.

"Yeah, and I disobeyed, if you can even call it that. You're a nothing, slave-boy. While I become rich and powerful, *for real*, you'll still be lying around with sheep." Spittle flew from Junior's mouth. "Go ahead. Be king. I dare you."

Cyrus nodded to his friends, the two bodyguards. "Flog him." They raised their eyebrows and dropped their jaws. "You know." He softened his tone. "In play. Something soft."

First one and then the other untied from around his waist the ropes that served as belts. Their makeshift swords -- slim, flat sticks -- clattered to the ground.

"Such disobedience will not be tolerated in my kingdom," Cyrus announced with an official air.

"Hey!" Junior said, pointing to the children's belts. "Those things are dirty."

"Remove his robe," Cyrus said.

The spy boy pulled Junior's robe back from his shoulders.

"Five lashes," Cyrus said.

The guards flung their rope belts back, swinging like dead snakes, then threw them forward - thwap, thwap, - against Junior's back.

"Ow!" One of the ropes left a thin pink mark along Junior's right shoulder.

"That's two," Cyrus said.

The boys drew back again. Even flinging as hard as they could, the ropes landed like string against Junior's shoulders.

"Four," Cyrus said.

But already Junior was in tears. And even more furious for it. "That's enough!" he said.

His mouth pinched, "One more," Cyrus said.

The children were silent, looking from the high-born boy, son of Artembares friend of King Astyages, to their king in play. Cyrus's arms hung at his sides.

He nodded at one guard. "I said five."

The last lash landed with a final soft thwap and swish.

"Release him," Cyrus commanded.

Junior ran off.

The remaining children stood staring at Cyrus. Their toy props lay scattered about. No one moved to pick them up, and no one moved to leave.

Cyrus scanned their faces. "Loyal subjects, brave men... and women," Cyrus added smiling at the little girl, "You have done good work today. Each one of you is important to our beloved nation, and I value your contributions. I am sorry that our work was interrupted in this manner. But there is trade to be conducted, a city to defend, and a feast to be prepared. So, back to your work!"

The air popped with high voices as the children resumed their play.

Meanwhile, Junior ran toward home.

CHAPTER 12

$\mathcal{A}$s he got closer to his father's great house, Junior's steps slowed. He stopped. He wiped his face carefully. And when he was sure that his eyes weren't red and his story clear, he and walked the rest of the way.

By the time that Junior arrived home, his complexion had returned to normal. By then, he had put a swagger into his stride. With effort, he turned his mouth down just so, exactly as he had seen his father do when dealing with inferiors.

"Well, look who's home," one of the servants said when he pushed through the door. Then, seeing Junior's expression, she added, "my lord."

"Is my father home?"

"I think he's in his room, sir," the servant said.

Artembares was hunched over a small table discussing something with a slave from the palm plantation when Junior walked in. The boy said nothing but stared at them from the doorway.

Artembares dismissed the slave.

"What?" he demanded.

"Something happened today."

"Well?"

"I went into the plaza near the palace."

"Spit it out."

"I was going to play with some kids there, but they --" Junior's voice broke. He stomped his foot, and great red blotches rose again on his face. "They made some stupid slave boy king, and when I refused to go along --"

"They did what? Why not you?"

"I refused to play."

"Good." Artembares turned back to his table.

Junior cleared his throat.

"You're still here?"

Junior squared his shoulders. "That stupid slave had me flogged."

"No."

Seeing that he had his father's attention now, Junior warmed to the story. "A whole bunch of them held me down, while others slashed at me with whips!"

"No!" Artembares got up and spun Junior around. "Let me see," he said as he pulled Junior's robe from his shoulders. Artembares peered at his son's back. The same pale skin as always. He stepped back, still looking intently, then looked closely again. Maybe a few pink lines... But. He turned Junior to face him again.

"A slave, you say?"

"One of the king's herders, I think. He was awful!"

"Come with me," Artembares grabbed his son's arm, hurried Junior out of the room and straight to the palace. "The king should know about this. It's shameful, it is. Shameful. A common slave," he muttered as they walked the halls toward the throne room.

"You're hurting me," Junior said, squinting at his father's fingers digging into Junior's soft bicep. "And I'm hungry."

Artembares looked down as if just seeing him and let go of his arm. "Well, walk faster."

Junior shuffled along next to his father trying not to bump into him as Junior pulled his robe back into place.

* * *

KING ASTYAGES WAS JUST FINISHING his afternoon audience when the door guards announced one more case.

"Artembares, how are you? And this is your son? So big." the king adjusted himself in his throne, scratching his bottom.

"Since you ask, my lord. I am a bit distressed," Artembares said.

Astyages sat back.

"This is indeed my son, a fine young man, as you can see. The matter concerns him."

"Oh?"

"One of the palace slaves, a herdsman from the mountains brought his son into the city today. The boy took it upon himself to be king. That's right, a slave! And he wasn't pretending to be you, my lord, but king of his own empire as though you didn't even exist. Well, my son refused to go along with it, refused to bow down to such a lowly piece of dirt. And," Artembares paused, "It pains me to say this, though it's nothing compared to what my son endured. That boy had him flogged. A slave, with the help of a lot of other boys – young men – mind you, beat my son as if to teach him a lesson. I felt you should know, my lord. For if such a thing goes unpunished, imagine what other inferiors will think that they can do!"

Astyages leaned forward. "Not me, you say? He was pretending to be king; but not me?!"

"Yes, sir. But the problem is with my son."

Astyages's face was all dark clouds. He sat back again. "Boy, show me where they hurt you. Is that the robe you were wear-ing?" he asked as the boy removed the outer robe, a fine linen weave as clean as new.

Junior looked at his father, who nodded at him. "Yes, my lord."

"I see. Turn around."

Junior turned. The king strained to make out the faint pink lines. "How terrible, and humiliating, I suppose," the king said. Then, noticing the streaks of red along Junior's upper arm, he said, "But the ones who held you were even more cruel."

Junior glanced at Artembares.

Artembares cleared his throat. "Only the strength of many, a whole gang of them, could hold my son still for the beating. Imagine, a slave thinking that he could do such a thing to a citizen!"

"Put your robe back on, boy."

"Pretending to be king..." Artembares said, "as though you didn't even exist." He shook his head at the grave offense.

To a waiting guard, Astyages called, "Fetch that herder who brought animals in this morning, and bring his son, too."

CHAPTER 13

*A*styages's men found Mit at the temple's corrals where he had left the last of the animals. Cyrus was with him. The guards said nothing more than that there was some trouble with the boy and both were required in the king's audience hall. As they walked toward the palace, the wrinkles that ran through Mit's forehead deepened. He looked hard at Cyrus.

"Some boy got mad during our games today," Cyrus said.

"Tell me," Mit said quietly.

Cyrus told just enough for Mit to figure out the problem. They passed through the columned hallway.

"Let's keep it a minor incident. Apologize – "

"For what?"

"You hurt the boy's feelings, right?"

Cyrus looked down at his feet. "I suppose," he muttered.

"Let's hope that's enough," Mit said as they approached the heavy door. "You remember the two things, yes?"

Cyrus nodded.

When the guards opened the doors to announce their arrival to the king, seated on a gaudy throne at the far end of the room, Mit removed Cyrus's cap and then his own.

"Shepherd slaves, my lord," the guard declared.

Mit exhaled. Their status was so low that they didn't even merit names.

Heavy woolen tapestries covered what windows the room had. Thick tallow candles cast the only light there was. Weak. Just as Mit remembered, relieved for once at the relative darkness. He kept his head down, looking only at the heavy stone floor beneath him. Mit missed the staff a guard had taken from him.

"THAT'S THE BOY, ALL RIGHT," Junior said, when Cyrus stepped up next to him.

"I'm sorry," Cyrus said.

"Insolence!" Astyages roared.

Cyrus started in surprise.

Mit put a hand on Cyrus's shoulder and made a show of bowing low, hoping not only to appease the king but also to keep Astyages from identifying him. Cyrus followed suit.

"My lord," Mit said, his head still down, on one knee. He elbowed Cyrus.

"My lord," Cyrus repeated, glancing at Mit to do like he did.

Then Mit stood again and Cyrus beside him.

"Slave boy," King Astyages said, "come forward."

Mit inhaled sharply. Cyrus glanced at Mit. His head still down, Mit nodded once to do as the king commanded.

Astyages glared at Cyrus. "Did you, the son of such a father..." A single gesture made Mit painfully aware that Astyages not only did not recognize him as Mithradates, he did not recognize him as a person of any value at all. "... dare to inflict injury on the son of one of our foremost citizens?"

"I apologize for hurting his feelings."

From his place to the side, Artembares leapt forward. "His *feelings*?! You, impudent brat, you and your lowlife gang beat my son without mercy."

Cyrus's eyebrows shot up. He glanced back at Mit, who furiously shook his head to say nothing.

Astyages leaned forward. "Explain yourself."

Cyrus said, "We were just playing. It happened that the other children made me king as part of a game. I played along, giving orders and –"

Behind him, Mit cleared his throat.

Cyrus adjusted. "The others did what they were told, but not Junior. He ignored what I said. Refused. So I had him punished."

"You 'had him punished,'" Astyages repeated, hushing Artembares who huffed, eager to fill in with his own allegations.

"Play-punished," Cyrus said. "Like a king."

Again, Mit cleared his throat.

"My lord, like you," Cyrus said. "If it is right to punish me for this, then here I am."

Astyages studied the boy before him. He frowned. "Come closer," he said.

As Cyrus stepped forward, Mit dared to raise his eyes the tiniest bit, watching and wishing that he could pull the child back and flee for the hills of home. He held his breath. Astyages leaned forward, staring at the boy's face, staring at Cyrus's mouth. "Artembares," he said, not taking his eyes from Cyrus, "Leave. And take your son with you."

"But –"

"Guards!" Astyages shouted. He pointed at Cyrus. "Take this child next door."

Mit stood helpless as Cyrus stepped between the king's guards through a small door that shut behind them.

Then, Astyages told the guards to leave the room. King and slave were alone.

CHAPTER 14

*B*ack home, Spaco packed. It was all she knew to do. Why, for whom, and where weren't questions that the stones had answered. Maybe it was unnecessary; maybe she had that part wrong. But if she were correct, she wouldn't have much time. The details would reveal themselves in their own time. Time. How come it felt so slow when one waited? And where had the past ten years gone? It seemed like yesterday that she had let Mit remove the baby they had made, yesterday when she greeted him coming back. "Your son," she had said.

The thing about Cyrus, Spaco thought, as she folded a blanket up tight, was how ordinary he was. Every day, he seemed like a miracle to her – calling her Mama! – and every day did what any other infant, toddler, little boy, boy would do. Crying, laughing, complaining, pleading, joking... Mit raised him well, and she'd like to think she had a part in that, too. He certainly wasn't wanting for love. But the love the child gave to them in return, the ordinary needing and trusting and relying and learning of a child with a parent was Cyrus's with her and with Mit. It was love, and Spaco knew it. And oh, the confidence he had. Gods forbid you told him he wasn't enough – big enough, old enough,

... - of some thing or another to do what it was he wanted to do. He would try that much harder. Like any other child. If there was anything extraordinary about Cyrus, it was how very ordinary he was.

Spaco worried. Of course she would. But she trusted that he would be indeed be all right. The stones had said that it had been fine to let him go with Mit to the palace. As for the rest of what she'd seen in the sacred stones... Spaco turned to the sheep, made sure they were each accounted for in the holding pen, had plenty food, plenty water. And the dog whose whole purpose it was to guard them, too. Ever-vigilant and never far, Moth watched Spaco's movements, accepting them as usual, so long as they were in service to the flock. "Watch them well," Spaco said. The dog didn't blink.

* * *

MIT HAD BEEN CONCERNED that Astyages would recognize him as the man who had refused to proclaim a false greatness for the incompetent king. But it was clear that Astyages couldn't see past Mit's humble state. It wouldn't have mattered. Mit was utterly focused on Cyrus's well-being now, getting the child back, and getting the both out of the palace that was nothing but trouble for him.

"My lord, please," Mit said. "The child didn't mean any harm. He —"

"How old is your boy?" Astyages asked.

"Ten years, my lord." Mit kept his head down.

"Where did you get your boy?" Astyages said.

Mit looked up, then.

"And from whom?"

Mit paled. He stared at a crack in one leg of the king's throne as if its very emptiness might give him an answer. And he knew he could only say one thing. Mit took a deep breath and looked directly into the king's small eyes.

"He is my son. I got him from my wife, who is his mother."

"I'm not sure I heard what you say." Astyages thin voice was thick with threat. "You do realize that if you lie here, all manner of bad things will happen to you and to the woman and boy also. Now, tell me how that child –" he threw his hand in the direction of the door through which Cyrus had disappeared, "came to be the son you claim he is, even though he was *not* born to your wife."

Mit closed his eyes. The stones, he thought. Spaco, let the stones be right. He opened his eyes again. "Ten years ago, while I was in the field, tending the sheep…" Mit told how Harpagus had charged Mit with killing the newborn infant. "I didn't know it then, but at the same time, back at my cottage, my wife had gone into labor. It wasn't her first birth; but we had no living children. That baby, too, was born dead."

"So you switched them," Astyages said.

"Yes." Mit's worry evaporated, and a strange sense of calm took its place.

His eyes on Mit, suspicious - the man's equanimity, Asytages summoned Harpagus. The steward was at the door in an instant and fast approaching.

When he saw Mit, Harpagus's feet hitched for an instant before regaining his stride.

Harpagus bowed deeply before Astyages. "My lord," he said.

"Exactly how," Astyages said, "did you treat the baby, my daughter's, whom I handed to you those years ago?"

Harpagus started. He looked again at the herdsman, then shut his eyes in a long blink.

Finally, "My king," Harpagus said, "when I took the child, I wrestled with how both to obey and not later to be thought a murderer by your daughter or you. What I did was this: I passed the child to this slave and told him that you had ordered it to be killed. I gave him explicit instruction to place the child on a desolate mountainside and to stay there until it was dead. I threatened him with terrible punishments, if he disobeyed. And I commanded him to show me what was left of the body, when it was done. He did. That is how the business… and the child… ended."

Astyages let the statement hang. Then, "You both tell me the same thing." Astyages nodded slowly. "I suppose it's true. Though it didn't end. The child is here."

"Guards!" Astyages called.

"My boy!" Mit exclaimed. He couldn't wait any longer. If Astyages had wanted to kill Cyrus at birth and now discovered him alive, would he kill the child now? He couldn't bear it.

Astyages glared at him.

"The child. Cyrus. Please, where is he?"

"He's fine," Astyages said. "Unhurt, if that's your concern."

Mit exhaled in a burst of air. He trusted Spaco. And Spaco trusted the stones. As for Mit, surely that's why Astyages called the guards. Astyages would have Mit killed. The knowledge calmed him in a peculiar way. There was nothing more he could do.

But when the guards entered, Astyages called for them, not to slay Mit; but rather, "Watch these two," Astyages said and hurried from the room.

CHAPTER 15

*A*styages knew where to find the magi. They'd be mumbling over star-charts in the observatory. He didn't particularly like the room – round spaces had no hierarchy, no front and back; top and bottom. And that feeling of the gods looking down, seeing him, judging... the whole thing was uncomfortable. But the boy, and a play-king besides, now *that* made him even more uncomfortable. Astyages wanted answers, and he wanted them now. He couldn't imagine waiting while guards or runners or whoever he could summon would come first to him, then to the magi, and the magi finally to Astyages. Better he went himself.

Astyages was out of breath when he reached the doors. He flung them open and strode inside, Harpagus close behind. Seeing him, the magi scattered to the perimeter of the room. Astyages strode into the center. He dismissed all the magi but two – the same two who had, a decade ago, given him their interpretation of the dream. The older, the stout one was stouter. And older. The younger had filled out a bit. He shifted on his feet.

When it was quiet, Astyages reminded the men, obviously

nervous, of the vision they had parsed for him ten years ago. "Have you ever questioned that interpretation?"

"No. It was the right one," the elder answered without hesitation. "If he had lived, the child would have become king."

"Well, he did live," Astyages said, which set the elder back on his heels. He stepped closer to the door, not that that would have helped. Then Astyages told them everything that had happened – the children choosing Cyrus "What kind of a name is that?" for their king; about Junior "Artembares's boy. A bit soft. Nevertheless"; and the flogging "hardly a beating. But again. A nobleman's son?! And the way the boy stood before me –"

"Junior, my lord?"

"No, this 'Cyrus.' He was so... so... Ordinary. His father... well, the shepherd slave who posed as his father confessed to the whole thing."

While the magi conferred, Astyages continued to mull over what he'd seen. "Extraordinary," he muttered.

The younger coughed into his hand. Regaining Astyages's attention, he said, "We've reached a verdict, sir. Unanimous. In fact, it's perfectly clear."

"Go on," Astyages said.

"If the boy is alive, then he's already been king." The magus grinned and swiped his hands together twice. "Done," he said. But seeing Astyages's confusion, "Your dream has been fulfilled," he said slowly. "The boy commanded a kingdom. Of children. For a few minutes. He won't be king again."

"My lord." The older magus stepped up. "It's always hard to judge the seriousness of a vision such as yours." He lifted his shoulders. "They can be quite trivial, as this indeed is."

Astyages squinted at the effort of putting it all together. Then his face cleared and he said, "I've been thinking the same thing."

The magi shared a look and visibly relaxed.

"The boy has already been king of as vast an empire as he could imagine," the younger said.

"Indeed, your vision was resolved as a small matter. We aren't worried about it."

The younger nodded vigorously.

"You shouldn't be, either. Besides, what's that you said about the boy – 'Ordinary'? Think about it. He's been a slave. The son of slaves, shepherds, no less. Hardly king-material. He'd never measure up."

"Not like you," the younger said, bowing deeply, "my lord."

Astyages nodded. Satisfied, he hurried out of the room.

In the presence of the guards, Mit and Harpagus hardly looked at each other. They couldn't know for certain that each had reached the same conclusions. They were hardly going to reveal that they knew each other, that Mit was the same Mithradates who had been thrown out of the palace, his reputation muddied by Astyages's accusations of treachery and lies. Neither stood to gain anything by reminding Astyages of it. And remarkably, so far anyway, he hadn't seemed to recognize Mit, hadn't thought him worthy enough even to ask a name. Additionally, both of them hoped that Astyages wouldn't ask for the kind of details that would reveal Harpagus's knowledge of the switch of infants, much less that Harpagus had not-so-subtly suggested that Mit and Spaco raise Mandane's baby as their own. Mit had briefly considered volunteering the information, but to what end? It wouldn't do any good and only cause yet another person, Harpagus, more harm.

Besides, Mit's mind was on Cyrus. He clung to the thread of hope that Spaco had given to him – her confidence that Cyrus would be all right, going to the palace with Mit as he had. Cyrus had been alone before, and even in danger, before. But that was in the forest and fields, among wild animals. Whatever threat they posed was pure and true, according to the natural laws of which they were all a part, the sophisticated interplay of beings that kept order in the world. Wild, when it came to animals, was far principled than the wildness of humans. Where was Cyrus now, and with whom doing what to him? Mit clenched his teeth, made fists of his hands. Gods, Mit hated the palace.

What each man *did* know, each for his own reasons, was that their futures – welfare, happiness, life itself – was in the hands of a paranoid and capricious tyrant. So, when Astyages blustered back into the room, after each had bowed, demonstrating whatever obsequious gesture might placate the king, Harpagus stood still as stone while Mit twisted his hat so tightly that if it had been a living thing, it would have died on the spot. Mit clamped his tongue between his teeth. He was so desperate to know about Cyrus – an innocent in all of this - so tempted to demand his release that he tasted iron. As for Mit's own welfare, he hardly thought of it.

Astyages sat, adjusting his ample behind against the down-filled cushions. "Do you know," he said, looking from one man to the other, "I'm glad of it, glad that the boy survived."

Mit exhaled audibly, and the color returned to Harpagus's face.

"What I thought had been done to him – declared dead at birth and removed so suddenly! – upset me a great deal," Astyages went on. It was easy for Mit and Harpagus to hear in the wheedling tone of his voice see that the content of his speech was for the benefit of the guards, the only others in the room. "And that my daughter accused me and then took her life was hard to bear. Aside from that, things have turned out well." Then, he turned to Mit, nodded toward the door through which guards had taken Cyrus. To the herdsman's astonishment, he said, "Why don't you go, join the boy?"

Astyages didn't have to ask twice. Mit dipped his head and fairly flew through the door, opened just in time for his stocky body to pass.

"Follow him," Astyages said to the remaining guards.

CHAPTER 16

*W*hen they had left, Astyages turned to Harpagus. Astyages's voice was steely. "Listen carefully. This is the story we shall tell: We had thought that the baby was dead at birth. We gave it to this slave to expose before burial; but when he got home, his wife found the baby to be alive."

"Yes, sir," Harpagus said. "Very good."

"That's not all," Astyages snapped. He leaned forward. "Make sure that everyone knows, so wicked was this couple that they dared to raise the child as if he were their own, as if they would never be caught. That is what you shall tell everyone, including the boy."

"Yes, sir."

"But I did catch them."

Just then, a voice at the side door requested admittance.

"Enter," Astyages said.

The door opened with a crack. Mit stood struggling between the two guards. He had kicked the door open, cracking the heavy wood with the sole of his foot.

Mit roared, "Where is he?! Where did you take my son?"

What Astyages hadn't said when he reentered the throne

room was that after he spoke with the magi, on his way back to confront Mit and Harpagus, he had stopped to see again this boy, the child that still lived. Ordinary indeed. And dirty. Hardly a prince of Media, which was all fine and good. Astyages would go through the motions, but the child would never amount to much of anything. He had decided to integrate the boy into palace life. Astyages didn't like to think that he Astyages would one day die; but he knew it. And surely having an heir would play well on his reputation for the rest of his days. That the child wouldn't amount to any kind of leader wouldn't be his problem; he'd be dead.

So, what Astyages hadn't told Mit when he released the herdsman from the king's audience was that Astyages had already directed that Cyrus be brought to princely quarters and made appropriately presentable. Cyrus would stay.

Astyages tolerated Mit's outrage with infuriating calm. "'*Your* son'? No. This Cyrus is belongs to me."

Mit growled through his teeth. The guards struggled to contain him even as the knowledge that he couldn't prevail against Astyages wearied Mit's muscles and weighted his bones.

"The boy will grow up here as he always should have," Astyages said. "Already, he is beginning to understand how treacherous were those little people who manipulated his boyhood, made him believe that he was a mere slave. 'Theirs,' at that. Already, he is beginning to see the truth of his fine lineage and how horrible his life was and would have been if that wicked couple had succeeded in their vicious plot."

Mit's face, red with effort and anger, nevertheless registered everything Astyages said. He knew how futile it would be to dissent. He and Spaco had no leverage. What's more, now that Astyages knew the depth of their love for the boy, he had more power over them than they could ever counter. He had Cyrus's health and well-being in his hands, and neither Mit nor Spaco would do anything that might lead Astyages to hurt Cyrus.

"Now," Astyages said, "Count yourself lucky, the recipient of my benevolent mercy, that I won't keep you here, won't even kill you here." Then Astyages's anger got the better of him. "Get out!" he shouted.

Harpagus stepped quickly to the side as the guards dragged Mit, still fighting, toward the audience hall's double doors.

The only thing that kept Mit from raging through the palace, throwing open every door, mowing down whatever or whoever stood in his way to find his boy was knowing he would be identified. Harpagus wasn't the only one who would recognize him. If there was any hope of getting out and getting Cyrus back, Mit had to keep his head down now. Leaving was the hardest thing he had ever done.

As the guards tossed him through, Mit shouted back, "Cyrus will always be my son! My son, Bartatua!"

* * *

BARTATUA. At the name that rang of strength, the king sucked in his breath. Only the doors closing behind Mit spared the herdsman from a sudden violence. Astyages trembled with fury. Finally, recalling his victory over that nobody-slave brought the king back under control. It was he, Astyages, who had the child. Astyages would play this for all it was worth. When he had regained his composure, Astyages sat back. He lifted his arms and threaded his fingers behind his head. "So, all's well. And I have a new prince in the palace. Fine indeed."

Noticing that Harpagus was still there, Astyages dropped his hands. He considered the steward. Then he smiled broadly, his crooked teeth yellow in the dim light.

"This," Astyages said, "is surely cause for celebration. The baby we thought was dead, returned to us – a boy! Fine indeed. Cause for feast. We have fresh lambs after all, fattened by the youth himself. Perfect. I do want to sacrifice to the gods. Surely they deserve honor for saving the boy. And you, as do you."

"Sir," Harpagus said, wary. But he dipped his head once in acknowledgment.

"After all, without your actions Cyrus - 'care-giver,' the magi said his name means - would not have come to be among us here in the palace, his rightful place."

Harpagus wasn't sure how to read Astyages's tone. So he remained still.

"Yes, a special celebration," Astyages said, "and you an honored guest. At my table."

Harpagus started with surprise. He was a servant, after all. Important to the king but never invited to dine at the king's table. His eyebrows lifted, and he smiled despite himself.

"And my wife?" Harpagus asked.

"Don't get greedy," Astyages reprimanded.

"Of course," Astyages said. "Of course not." He squared his shoulders. "It would be my honor, sir. I agree - cause for celebration."

"As for the child's training, clearly he hasn't had the proper influences," Astyages said. He narrowed his eyes, thinking. "Why don't you send your son to meet the newcomer here? Playmates for the day."

It was more than Harpagus had ever dared to hope. His son, a guest in the palace. Playmate of a prince?! Harpagus bowed deeply. "As you say, my king. It would be my pleasure."

Zubaba, an old army friend of Harpagus's was waiting for Harpagus when Harpagus emerged from the king's audience hall. "I could swear I saw Mit earlier - Mithradates. It's been years. Did you know he was here?"

Harpagus pulled up short. "I can't imagine,..." he said, then shrugged. "But maybe."

CHAPTER 17

*A*styages was happy to learn that soon after he had commanded that Cyrus be removed from the room adjacent to his audience hall, one of the guards had preoccupied the boy with a tour of the stables. Cyrus had no idea what had transpired with the shepherd slave who had raised him. Now, Astyages was ready. He summoned for the boy to join him.

When Cyrus arrived, the king met him with a smile. "Sit, boy, and enjoy."

Cyrus stared, unsmiling, at him.

Astyages gestured to a couch and table heaped with delights that Cyrus had only seen carefully guarded in the marketplace.

Cyrus looked away.

"It is important for a prince to take boldly from life's greatest pleasures." Cyrus shook his head. "Such enjoyment makes us more lordly," Astyages went on. "Pleasure and luxury eases one's mind. They exalt a person. Work, on the other hand, makes people small and low. Try some." It was not an invitation. It was a command.

Astyages held out a candied cherry. Cyrus took it, put it into his mouth.

"Sit." Astyages nodded to a plush seat. "I have a story to tell you."

Cyrus sat.

"Many years ago, ten to be precise, my daughter the princess Mandane gave birth to a baby. We were all so sad, because we -"

"*What* was her name?"

Astyages's eyes flashed. "Don't interrupt, boy. Manners." He lowered his voice again. "As I was saying, Mandane..." Astyages held the name, "had a baby, a boy that we believed to be dead. It was so upsetting that the poor dead thing was removed immediately."

But Cyrus was hardly listening. He was remembering rather that woman who had visited the cottage in the early-early morning not so long ago. How she had knelt to his face, staring at it; how with a feather-light fingertip, she had traced the line of his lower lip. How she had whispered that word. Mandane. Cyrus looked at Astyages, his mouth moving... King or no, he seemed slippery somehow, not entirely solid in some way. It made Cyrus doubt his words. But. Mandane.

"Well," Astyages went on, warming to what he thought was Cyrus's full attention, "The shepherd slaves that you learned to call Mother and Father –"

"Ma and Pop," Cyrus corrected.

Again, Astayges's anger flared. Again, he choked it back. What he had hoped to further string out in a dramatic story, he finished in a violent rush. "They stole you. They lied. They are wicked, wicked people. And you'll never see them again."

Cyrus's eyes filled with tears.

Astyages jumped up. This was not the way he'd intended things to go. He paced across the floor, then sat down again. "I suppose it's... disappointing," Astyages said, "to learn bad things about the people you thought were your parents. But everyone said that your mother, your *real* mother, the princess was a lovely woman." As it came out of his mouth, Astyages realized that that was actually true. Everybody loved Mandane. She was dignity and grace personified. Sometimes he liked that; sometimes he didn't.

"And my father?"

"Oh!" Astyages's eyebrows shot up. "Well. He is a king. Kind of. Not grand. Not like this." Astyages thrust out his chest, its breast of heavy embroidered brocade and draped with jewels from the empire and merchants from faraway lands.

Cyrus was not impressed. Instead, "I want to go home." Never before had Cyrus had this feeling, this nameless want, the horrible lack of place, the kind of place that transcended geography. The place that was home.

"But you *are* home."

Cyrus's face was unreadable, stricken and blank.

Astyages prayed for patience. But the gods weren't listening. His voice rose, "That hovel in the middle of nowhere is slave-stuff, and those people lied to you. You should be happy that we finally found you and –" Astyages heard himself shouting. The boy had shrunk back away from him. Astyages stopped. He pursed his lips, and then he leaned in so close that Cyrus could smell the sour cheese on his breath. "You should know that that man, your 'Pop,' left without you."

"What?!" Alarm dried Cyrus's tears.

"He's gone. It's true. Now, if he was your true father, if he hadn't been lying to you, defrauding you of the royal lineage that is your rightful due… if he *cared*, would he already be halfway back to the hovel where he lives?"

Cyrus jumped up. "He didn't! He didn't leave!"

"He did. Ask anyone. Many people saw him go – out the door where he confessed, down the hall of the upper porticos, and straight outside. Guards confirmed that he passed the last of the city gates just moment ago.

"Mandane," Cyrus said, melting back into his chair. "She was my mother?"

CHAPTER 18

*A*s swiftly as Mit had left the palace, as disheveled as he now looked, and even with his hat pulled down over his head, there was one who recognized him, a certain Zubaba, who back in the day had commiserated with Mit over Astyages's poor management of the empire that Astyages had inherited. Harpagus had been a part of those furtive conversations, too. But for Zubaba, descended from Elamites taken by the Assyrians before Cyaxares defeated Assur, it was Astyages's disregard for the diverse tribes, nations even, that composed the greater empire of Media, Astyages's willful ignorance of generations-long ways of managing land and society that he found so exasperating. He had kept such criticisms to himself; but Zubaba had always respected Mit for the man's straightforward honesty, though he'd warned Mit more than once that it could cost him his position, if not his life. So, to see Mit – he was sure it was him – back in the palace was striking. That Mit seemed so unhappy about it, from the hurried manner of his exit, was no surprise to Zubaba at all.

Mit made his way home, feeling the absence of Cyrus's chatter with a terrible sadness. He dreaded Spaco's questions, her anger and grief. What could he tell her? How could he tell her without her heart breaking into a million pieces like his had? Even after many miles, he had come to no conclusions, had found no way except by reporting every detail of this most awful day. His feet scuffed the road. He watched them turn – oh, habit – off onto the wooded path that would lead to their cottage. He watched his feet step over the rocks and roots so familiar to him. But there was no boy beside him, no boy waiting ahead to lift Mit's heart, to lift his head.

Mit had slumped so completely in his walking, was so lost in the horrible thoughts replaying over and over and over again how he came to lose the only child they had ever had, that when a hand seized his elbow, Mit leapt into action. He grabbed the arm, prepared to flip the bandit onto his back, but –

"Mit!" It was Spaco. She called his name with quiet urgency. That's when he noticed how laden she was. Mit took the heaviest parcel from her back. She straightened only to look back, furtively. She pulled him off the trail. "The stones," Spaco said. Then, "Where is Bartatua?" But as soon as the question was out of her mouth, she covered it with her hand. Her eyes filled with tears.

Mit said, "He is fine. He is all right," just as you said. He needed her to stop crying, needed to know he could tell her what he must.

She brushed her eyes and waved him to stop. "Not now," Spaco said. "We must go. We have to leave this place – fast and far." She tugged Mit's arm.

But he wouldn't move. She pulled more urgently, more desperately.

"But the animals."

"They're fine. And –" Spaco's eyes were wide with terror. "Someone will be there soon."

Still unsure, Mit nevertheless gave in to her pulling. He followed her first reluctantly at first, then faster and faster.

Spaco explained as they went. "There was more to the reading than I was prepared to say then. Like I told you, the stones were unequivocal: It was fine to bring our boy to the palace; he would be all right." She stopped and bent over with the grief of remembering. "I wish it had been different. I wish I had never asked, that he had never asked to go at all." She straightened again. "But I do believe that he will be all right."

Mit swung his head in a slow shake. "I abandoned him there. Our son, in a nest of demons."

Spaco laid down her burden then and took her husband into her arms. "You raised a strong boy, a resilient child. The best thing we can do for him now..." She hoisted her pack again and set out. "Is to get as far away from here as possible."

CHAPTER 19

*H*arpagus was so relieved at how the king had taken the news, and thrilled at the honor of dining with Astyages that he could hardly contain himself. As soon as he had delegated afternoon duties, he hurried home, barely containing his steps to a respectable walk.

Harpagus's wife was more measured in her excitement over the invitation that Astyages had extended. "You've never needed such attention before," she said.

"If you'd seen the king," Harpagus said, "you'd understand. Astyages was delighted that the child is still alive." He was disappointed that his wife didn't share his relief – and pride that her husband would be so honorably recognized. "If he hadn't been, he would have killed the boy on the spot. You know how Astyages is."

Harpagus's wife nodded, "But he *was* clear, deadly clear, when the child was an infant that he couldn't abide the boy's survival."

"Be that as it may, he seemed to like what the boy had become, a natural leader," Harpagus said. "I think he's proud."

Again, Harpagus's wife nodded. Maybe so. But she wasn't entirely convinced.

Just then, their own boy ran in. And the pride that Harpagus had attributed to Astyages was his a thousand times over. It never failed. As soon as Harpagus laid eyes on his son, he felt he might ignite with joy. Only ten years old, the boy was tall for his age, tall like Harpagus, though he looked like his mother. Harpagus glanced at his wife. Her face was bright, too, the lines softened at the sight of this, their only child.

Harpagus called the boy close. He wrapped an arm around the child's narrow waist and said, "The king has a new young visitor, a prince, the king's grandson. You'll hear all the details later. But the best part: King Astyages wants you to meet the boy." Harpagus didn't see his wife's smile disappear, the softness turn hard. Instead, warmed by his son's quick grin, Harpagus said, "He wants you to help the child feel comfortable at the palace, to help him fit in better than he does right now." Harpagus hugged his son tight. "You and this Cyrus might even be friends!" He released the child. "Now, go straight to the palace. They're expecting you there. Hurry! And remember, be obedient and respectful."

Harpagus watched his son, dashing off, with pride. Who needed more, when one had a child this perfect? He imagined how this alliance could serve the boy. Perhaps his son would become an elegant, quick-witted courtier, dressed in the very best, laughing and feasting at leisure, instead of a palace servant like Harpagus, important as his position was. But when he turned back to his wife, his reverie evaporated.

Harpagus's wife sat frozen, her eyes wide. Finally, she found her voice. "Why didn't you tell me this?"

Harpagus looked at her for the first time. "But... I'd thought you'd be pleased," he stammered. "Our son, at the palace."

"I don't trust him," she said, shaking her head.

"Oh," Harpagus leaned back. He laughed. "They're boys. They'll figure it out. And if you had seen this Cyrus, heard –"

"The king," Harpagus's wife said. "I don't trust the king."

* * *

WHEN IT WAS time for dinner, all the guests were served mutton.

"Yes," Astyages declared beaming through wine-wetted lips, "From the very animals our dear prince – he gestured to Cyrus, small and quiet at the far end of the table – raised himself!" Astyages took a swig from his golden rhyton. "But never again such lowly work!" he roared and laughed. "A toast!"

The guests responded with enthusiasm.

To Astyages's right, there at the king's table, Harpagus was already into a second rhyton of wine. His cheeks were rosy with the treat. He'd heard the king complain that this year they'd only gotten the sweet white stuff; something happened to the grapes that rendered the best – his favorite red. Harpagus didn't care. It was all so special. He had never before actually *sat* at a king's feast, actually enjoyed what would otherwise compromise his excellence at prompt and efficient attention, since he was always at work in the palace. At the toast, he drank deeply, and raised his cup to the sober little prince, way over there.

When the meat came, heaped both boiled and roasted upon his plate and by the king himself from a special basket of cuts earmarked only for him the guest of honor, Harpagus tucked in with pleasure. It was grand. As they ate, the king reported what a nice time Cyrus had enjoyed with Harpagus's son, whom Astyages himself had sent on his way only a moment or two ago. Harpagus savored the news, the fantasy it fed of his son a noble-man, higher than Harpagus could ever dream. Indeed, he savored everything – the luxury of relaxing while others ran around making everything just so, the happy air of the empire's elite rejoicing in the vitality of a prince they'd thought long dead, and the food – so well prepared, and so much!

When to his left, Astyages thought that Harpagus had eaten enough, the king asked Harpagus if he'd enjoyed the dinner.

"Very much," Harpagus replied, his voice slurred, but still

carrying every bit of dignity he'd ever cultivated, maybe more so proud and satisfied was he.

The other guests, too – even those dignitaries at the king's table – were so deep into the pleasure of the feast, that no one noticed the king direct Harpagus to lift the top off the basket at his feet, the basket from which he had been served. Harpagus grinned and bent to do so, turned his head to the side, and threw up everything that he had eaten. Harpagus retched and retched until his sides convulsed with the effort. For there in the basket, soaked with the blood of meat, lay the hands, the dear feet, the head...!"

As it happens, Harpagus's son never saw Cyrus at the palace. A eunuch had met the boy at the gate and led him around to the kitchen courtyard with instructions to wait there. It was the king himself who had showed up. Alone. He greeted the boy, pulled out a slaughtering knife, and cut the child's throat. Astyages dismembered the small body then turned the parts over to horrified cooks with orders that some pieces were to be roasted and others boiled. And if anyone ever said anything, if he ever heard anything of this ever again, he would do the same to each and every one of them. To a person, gaping mouths slammed shut. And they had turned to their grisly task.

At the table, Astyages leaned close to Harpagus's ear. "Do you know the meat you've eaten?" he asked, his voice barely audible over the chatter and laughter of a crowd oblivious to the horror.

Harpagus straightened, his face grey as stone. He wiped his mouth with his sleeve.

"I do indeed," Harpagus said. His eyes were dry, empty. "Everything that the king does is pleasing," he said in a voice absent any hint of the flesh and blood that gave meaning. Harpagus blinked, but the man was gone. He floated above the scene and watched without emotion, the tableau of horror. From there, Harpagus watched his earthly body fill with a dark and viscous desire for revenge.

CHAPTER 20

*S*paco and Mit traveled paths they knew well... until they didn't. Then, they followed a valley they knew ran mostly south from Ecbatana. Thanks to the stones, Spaco believed that they had gotten a head start on anyone from the palace whom Astyages might have sent after them.

"But would he?" Mit asked, when paused at a stream to drink.

"You tell me," Spaco said. "You know the man better than anyone. Better than he knows himself," she added with a wry grin. Then serious again, "But the stones said to go."

They decided to climb to the ridge line, use the jutting boulders for cover if necessary, but to reach an elevation that afforded a long view back the way they'd come. It was a scramble. Finally they reached a small, treeless plateau across the ridge. Shielding her eyes, Spaco oriented herself. Then she pointed. From the direction of the place they'd run, a thin line of smoke rose into the air.

"And what do the stones say now?" Mit asked.

Spaco gave him a long look.

"You left them."

Spaco nodded. "I have to trust that when I need them again, they'll be there. For now, we're on our own."

They looked out again, from this elevation for any evidence of pursuers. Seeing none, the pair slowed. In truth, they couldn't have gone any faster. And they couldn't go much farther.

It was Spaco who observed, "That we're just a couple of old slaves, and with no children is a good thing right now."

"But we do have a child," Mit said. "Should we just leave him with that tyrant?"

"Yes," Spaco said. "We should, and we shall. You said it yourself. There is nothing that we can do to get him back. Not now."

"Nothing?"

"You know there isn't."

They walked on in the silence of that knowledge.

The fall of night finally gave their aching bodies permission to stop.

"Did the stones say anything more?" Mit asked when their simple cloth shelter was in place and the evening's bread and cheese almost gone.

Spaco shook her head. "Not yet. But," and for the umpteenth time she said what they had volleyed between them all day.

Mit finished the sentence with her "… he would be all right."

They never tired of hearing it.

Later that night, while the stars kept their vigil through dark trees overhead, "Maybe Astyages will send the boy to Anshan," Mit said, staring up at the cloth above, his head in the palms of his hands.

"Then let's go there," Spaco said, her voice heavy with sleep.

"It's a terrible long way."

"Tomorrow," Spaco mumbled, "toward Parsa, Anshan."

Back at the palace, Astyages got a full report: The animals were each accounted for and had been redistributed among neighboring palace slaves. And yes, "The hut is fully burned. The roof took quickly. We kicked in the stone walls. Didn't take long. But the couple – nowhere in sight."

"Forget them," Astyages said. "They'll be food for lions soon enough. Oh, and no need to tell anyone – not Harpagus, not leastwise the boy."

They nodded. It made no difference to them either way.

In the distance, golden jackals howled.

* * *

WHEN HARPAGUS'S wife met him at the door, frantic with worry, and peppering him with questions about their son's whereabouts, Harpagus was like a mechanical thing. When she wouldn't be ignored, he finally faced her. He put his hands on her shoulders. What she saw silenced her. Where intelligent eyes had sparked with life, she saw only a depthless black. Vacant. And dry. She let the weight of his hands lower her onto a chair.

"Our son is not coming back," Harpagus said. "He is dead."

And when she began keening, he walked out the door. Harpagus walked and walked and walked. He didn't remember where. He didn't remember how far. But when he returned, it was light again. Another day. He straightened his clothes, he straightened his back and shoulders, and he walked back into the palace. He had not wept a single tear.

No one except Astyages and Harpagus knew what had happened there in the banquet hall. Harpagus's wife never spoke to him again.

CHAPTER 21

*A*styages, blind to Harpagus's simmering rage and resentment seemed to believe that what he'd done evened the score somehow, that Harpagus's disobeying the king's order to kill Mandane's baby was justly punished by killing Harpagus's son. And now, bygones were bygones. So, he assigned Harpagus to oversee Cyrus's training. On this, Astyages and Harpagus agreed: the boy would fail. Astyages couldn't bear the possibility that Cyrus might surpass him in any of the areas that distinguished Median royalty, never mind that the magi had reassured him that the child would never be threat. As for Harpagus, there was only one acceptable outlet for his rage. He hated the boy.

Time and again, Cyrus sought to escape the confines of the fortress that was Ecbatana's palace, to run back to the cottage where he'd known a purpose and love that he'd never thought to doubt, never questioned,... until now. He simply could not believe that they had deceived him like King Astyages and Harpagus said. And yet. That incident with the woman from Babylon, Amytis... It did ooze a slick of doubt into his mind. It was hard to ignore with the constant drumbeat of a story from the king and his horrible steward. One way or another, he had to ask them. But Cyrus never got farther than a few yards in any direction. He was under constant surveillance. Finally, he saw that there was no way forward except to submit to the training that Harpagus dictated. And it was hard indeed. Harpagus made sure of it.

To Cyrus, Harpagus said in the low, acid tone he reserved for just for the boy, "You'll never amount to anything, never come close to the excellence of children born here, raised here." In this, Harpagus pushed aside – it was years ago – the memory of little girl, bastard daughter of the king yet so dear to Harpagus. "Better you should give up now than get hurt."

Despite the fury that Cyrus could see so clearly in the steward's dark eyes, Harpagus never lifted a hand against the boy. He didn't have to. The training took care of that. Javelins, arrows, hand-to-hand combat, Cyrus was cut and stabbed and beaten every day. And every night, Cyrus went to sleep alone, in a cold room rudely furnished, Cyrus's little-boy muscles aching, his body bleeding from more wounds than he could count. Despite all this, Cyrus did not give up. He would not give up. So, Harpagus drove him harder. And if Harpagus's heart ever angled to compassion or worse, to imaging his own child so subjected, he recalled to himself that it was this child who was the death of his own.

Harpagus took Cyrus to the stables, where before he could learn to ride, Cyrus picked stones from horses' hooves, curried their coats, and mucked the stalls. Here, among the horses into which Harpagus had thrown him, he was stepped on, kicked, and bitten. Still. Cyrus had been around animals all his life, domesticated and wild. And he'd watched these animals. Magnificent, strong, smart… but prey, like the deer, the mountain goats, and the sheep. So, it wasn't long before he learned his way around the beasts, not long being thrown from their backs every which way before he began to learn to sit a horse, no matter its demeanor.

* * *

ONE DAY, while Harpagus watched Cyrus sit a horse that bucked, then reared, then leapt and twisted from one side to the other, Zubaba happened by. Harpagus's attention was so completely on Cyrus, alternately resenting and admiring the boy's success that at the sound of his friend's voice next to him, he jumped.

"Reminds you of Amytis, doesn't he?"

Harpagus spun on Zubaba. How dare the man evoke Harpagus's favorite in such a context? "No!" he said sharply. "They're nothing alike."

Zubaba's eyebrows shot up. He took a step back, hands in the air. "Okay," he said, backing away. "I was just... walking by."

Harpagus scowled and turned back to watch Cyrus. And Zubaba stopped – to watch his friend watch the boy. In the next moment, the horse, which had planted all four feet and hung its head panting, leapt again. It worked. He flung Cyrus like a rag doll, who smashed against the wall. At Zubaba's exclamation, Harpagus turned. Harpagus's expression was stony, unreadable. Zubaba shook his head at Harpagus as he watched the little boy tentatively pick his body up from the dirt and limp back toward the stables into which the horse had disappeared.

When Harpagus met Cyrus there, the boy was not with the horse who had thrown him, a horse who stood nonchalantly chewing hay from the bin in its stall. Harpagus huffed. He knew it: at any opportunity, Cyrus could be found in the stall of an ugly little mare. The horse, a youngster still, was the accidental brood of an Egyptian merchant's stallion. The Nisean mare who bore her couldn't have looked more different from her filly. It seemed the foal hardly grew but remained small even full-grown. The horse was undersized despite an enormous appetite and aptitude for sleep. Spindly, with a splotchy coat. And rather than bearing the strong, arched nose of Media's chargers, this horse's nose, nostrils always flaring was dished, hollowed out, almost as if it had been punched between the eyes. It acted like it.

Never broken to the saddle, she resisted the pedantry of Astyages's finest trainers, actually crippling one who, so frustrated by her refusal to charge a wooden dummy, had thought to beat her into submission. Cyrus saw how the mare thrust her head up and out each time another horse passed by, her huge eyes following its progress with what looked to him like a haughty sense of superiority. No one rode her, or even tried, now.

Seeing Harpagus, Cyrus spared the man the trouble of reprimanding him but limped his way to the other horse and despite its injury to him, began brushing it out.

In the face of the challenges Harpagus threw at him, and in the face of the smooth assurance King Astyages gave that Cyrus needn't try so hard, needn't worry himself over the knowledge and skills of a palace-born prince, despite both the king and the steward reminding Cyrus of his humble upbringing... or maybe because of it, to the dismay of both Astyages and Harpagus, Cyrus excelled. At everything.

CHAPTER 22

*I*t was time, Astyages and Harpagus agreed, for Cyrus to experience his first lion hunt.

It was an easy sell. Ever since his training began, Cyrus had been looking forward to his first hunting expedition on horseback. That's what he'd said, anyway. In truth, Cyrus hoped a hunt would give him the chance to run... and actually get away.

Even if he were caught at the cottage, he had to see Mit. He had to see Spaco. Had they really stolen him away, deceived him all those years? Mit, who had impressed so strongly upon Cyrus the importance and value of truth, no matter who does or does not recognize it. Cyrus wanted their answers. He needed their answers. Besides, for all his fury-fueled bravado, Cyrus was still a ten-year-old boy. And until he'd come to the palace, all he'd known of adults – even in their teaching him and challenging him and making demands of him – had been kindness, respect, and love. He missed with a throat-aching, gut-hollowing force the only parents he'd ever known.

So, when Harpagus said, his eyes narrow with the antipathy that still cut little Cyrus's soul, that the boy had been approved for a hunt, Cyrus cheered. Even when Harpagus said that it was to be a lion hunt, Cyrus acted like there was nothing he had more hoped to do. Yet he knew a palace lion hunt was nothing like the hunting Mit had taught him to do, the quest to end an animal's life for their own in such a way as to preserve the delicate balance of the complex whole around them and honor the fact of a life independent of their own. A palace lion hunt was nothing like that. Ever since Mit had told him how such things worked, Cyrus hated the idea of it, hated everything about it.

The leaders in war and hunting had been preparing for weeks. Astyages himself walked Cyrus through the dungeons to impress upon the boy the extent of it. Men whose sole job was to have the palace ready for such an invigorating spectacle of prowess and hierarchy, had caught hundreds of wild animals from the surrounding forests and fields and kept them in terrible cages to be released on the day of the hunt. It wasn't only lions but also cougars and boars, wolves and golden jackals of course. Cyrus steeled himself against responding, against showing any reaction or emotion as they walked the damp tunnels along wide aisles. Also there: the crown's dogs - animals raised for the hunt and the hunt alone – howled and roared in their cages. The dogs, their ribs showing past muscled shoulders, were fed just enough to be strong yet hungry. Cyrus hated it all.

More than one person remarked with surprise about Cyrus's inclusion in the event. No one dared ask the obvious: What was the king thinking to invite a boy, much less *this* boy – the long-lost prince – a child, and one who had had so little training for such a dangerous if exciting undertaking?! After all, young men – *men* – and in military training, no less, strove extra hard against one another in fierce competition. Sure, it was a great honor to be selected to join the king and his nobles in the hunt. But it was an honor ostensibly reflecting ability. Each man sought to prove himself worthy. But make no mistake: a lion hunt was a dangerous thing. Neither Harpagus nor Astyages remarked on it except to say that although Cyrus had been in the palace only a matter of months, he had developed skills beyond expectation. That much was true.

* * *

EARLY IN THE morning of the hunt, hunt officials transported the caged animals -- lions, foxes, and wild boars among them -- into designated forests some distance from the palace. Then, while the king and his party mounted their horses armed for the expedition, the caged beasts, desperate to be free again, were released. Hunters would drive them out into the countryside, where the riding was good. Although the game was varied, and each animal posed its own challenges, the largest and fiercest beasts were prized above all.

On the day of the hunt, the palace was as busy with frenetic energy as Cyrus had ever seen. He hoped it carried over into the event, the better to slip away. So, when Astyages pulled assigned to ride with Cyrus only a couple of demonstrably elderly men – friends who made clear that they'd leave all honor to other hunters; they'd like nothing better than to amble together and chat the day away – Cyrus rejoiced.

Astyages ordered Cyrus, with Cyrus's "guards" start at the front with him, the king. Or rather, with Astyages *and* the discreet team of elite warriors who had the honor of spending the day with the king. Everyone knew their heads remained atop their bodies only insofar as Astyages remained unhurt. And victorious. It was a heady moment.

"Don't you worry, little sir," one of Cyrus's escorts said to him as their horses shifted, eager to spend the nervous energy they'd built up. "Just stay with us." He gave Cyrus a kindly smile and nodded to his partner, who did the same. Cyrus returned the grin.

When the king gave the signal, the hunt began.

And they were off. The horses lowered their haunches and

sprung forward. When he saw Astyages and Harpagus with him head into a stand of oaks to the east, Cyrus directed his mount, a stubborn if strong charger west toward a dark copse of pines.

"What ho, child," he heard behind him.

And then the elderly pair were at his side. Cyrus looked from one to the other. They all had to slow, as they entered the woods. And Cyrus decided he had misjudged them. A little. They were old, yes. But these were men who had been raised for this sort of thing. Experience would keep them with him, no matter what. For a while. And the day had only just begun. So, he slowed until they'd caught up and rode alongside.

"Eager to get your arrow into a tawny hide, aren't you?" the chatty guard asked Cyrus.

Cyrus swallowed, then nodded, hoping it was convincing.

"Well," he glanced at his companion then back at Cyrus, "you should know. Killing a lion is ... not for all of us."

Cyrus looked at him then.

"It's the king's prerogative. You see, his killing them demonstrates not only royal strength, courage, and cunning but also - and most importantly - his ability to protect the populace and maintain order in the face of unrestrained ferocity." The man had warmed to his description.

It was up to the other, then, to add, "And when it comes to this king... It's best if you aim to kill something different, something smaller. A fox, say. Or a rabbit."

"Yes, a rabbit would be fine."

The whole thing, another charade to boost Astyages's pride and reputation, almost made Cyrus want to shoot a lion. Almost, but not quite.

"There!" Up ahead, an opossum humped its way toward a leafy elm. Cyrus pretended to fumble for an arrow.

"Ah, let it go, the poor beasty," his guard said. Clearly, they'd been instructed to let Cyrus take at least the first shot at anything.

Cyrus looked at the sun, the angle of the shadows the pines' trunks made across the forest floor. Spaco had taught him how to orient himself, and he'd been not far from here with Mit and the animals before. He was confident that the cottage lay to the west. And pretty certain that it was still some ways away. Though his skin itched to run, he'd been caught too many times. He'd have to be patient. Cyrus slowly stepped his horse to point in that direction. The others came along. They walked their horses at a meditative pace through the pine woods and into a forest of hardwoods. The men had taken to talking. Well, mostly the one. The other maintained companionable responses. Cyrus barely listened. Instead, he imagined all the different ways his reunion with Mit and Spaco might go. In each one, they were happy to see him.

Cyrus got his break when a band of other hunters rushed down on them.

"Which way did it go?" a wiry young man, his eyes wild with the thrill, demanded of Cyrus's companions.

They looked around quickly. "What, what was it?"

The rest of the man's companions had arrived and clustered loosely, their horses snorting and stomping the ground.

"A lion, grandfather!" the young man said.

The old men looked at each other, eyes wide.

Suddenly, somewhere back in the direction from which the others had come, a crashing in the brush, then the sound of stones tumbling down hill made everyone freeze. For an instant, as if as one, the group collectively held its breath. Then, they exploded. In a great cacophony of shouts and whinnying, thundering hooves, and crashing branches, everyone rushed toward the sound, Cyrus with them. But he saw his chance. It was chaos, and just enough for Cyrus to peel away. Before the old men could miss him, Cyrus galloped his horse directly west.

Cyrus had barely made it a quarter mile when, out of a break in boulders just up the bank to his right, the thicket parted, and a golden-eyed lioness leapt out, directly into his path. His horse screamed and planted its feet. Cyrus's mouth dropped open. He forgot everything except the reality of this huge cat as from a flat-out gallop, his mount slammed to a stop. Cyrus sailed over its head. By time Cyrus slammed to the ground, the horse was long gone. But the lioness remained. And her smoldering eyes were unblinking in their fix on him.

Cyrus scrambled backward, his heart beating wildly. His hands shook as he ripped the bow from his back. He whimpered in fear as he groped awkwardly for the arrows in the quiver on his back. The lion stepped a dinner-plate sized foot forward. Then another. As she walked, her scarred flanks rippled with anticipation. Her tail flicked right, the left, then right again. She moved without hurry, ever shifting her unblinking eyes from the little boy in front of her. Cyrus threaded an arrow into the bow. But his hands shook so badly that it fell to the ground. He left it there. The lioness ran her pink tongue over her whiskered muzzle as Cyrus pushed his heels against the ground, scrambling back farther as he fumbled to draw another arrow. The cat was only twenty yards or so from him now. When Cyrus shot, it was without aim, without any of the skill he had worked so hard to learn. The arrow swerved so far to the lioness's left that she didn't even break stride. The next was close enough to make her twitch. But she didn't stop. Finally, Cyrus got to his feet; but his legs trembled so violently that he couldn't run. It was just as well. The lioness gathered herself to pounce. In that moment, Cyrus was no different than any other small, soft defenseless creature. He was simply an animal facing the agent of his death. He froze.

Then, just as the lion unfurled her muscles in a magnificent leap toward the little boy, Cyrus was catapulted to the left, the wind knocked from his frame. The granite body of a warrior, Zubaba, had slammed him out of the lion's path even as it drove an arrow that found its mark. They fell – boy, man, and lion – into a heap. When the wounded cat turned her razor teeth in fury on the human cause of her fear and pain, Zubaba drove his sword straight into her throat. She died in a great coughing gush of blood. That's when Cyrus screamed. And he screamed with every breath he could draw, he screamed, overcome with a panicking trauma. Zubaba heaved the lion's carcass off of them and lifted Cyrus to his feet. Finally, after the reality of his survival set in, Cyrus's screams turned to hiccupping sobs. The man, whom Cyrus did not recognize, held him. When the group, including the two men assigned to stay with Cyrus came roaring into the clearing, Cyrus had regained some composure. He wiped angrily at his eyes while they took in the sight: a lion, impaled by a warrior's sword within feet of the little prince, and a single man standing on the ground beside them.

No one said anything. Then, Zubaba sighed. He withdrew his sword from the lion's throat, wiped it in the tall grass, and slid it back into its sheath.

"There are a couple of ways that this could go," he said. "Before you decide, remember that this boy here is the king's grandson. And each of us were..." He looked long and hard at the old men, "... recently with him." They nodded. Each understood. "I suggest that unless one of you..." He pointed his finger around the group. "... would like to claim this kill for yourself..." No one moved. Zubaba nodded. "We leave the animal where she lies. Let the wild carrion beasts gain something from this whole business."

"But what if someone else were to come upon it?" the wiry young man asked.

"Such as the king," a companion added.

Zubaba looked up at the sky, and the old men with him. The sun was low, nearly touching the peaks of the mountains that would soon swallow it. Already, the brightest of the night's stars blinked.

It was one of Cyrus's escorts who said, "They'll be headed back to the palace by now."

They all stood around silently, nodding, another moment or

two. Then, a few of the young men dismounted and approached the lion. Awed by the beast, even in death, they quietly dragged her body off the path, into a sheltered space between two boulders.

"It's a good suggestion," one of them said.

And that was that. Slapping shoulders and regaling one another with recollections of the hunt – they had several animals among them – the other hunters rode off, headed back to the palace.

Cyrus took a long, weary breath, and began to walk after them.

"What's this?" Zubaba said, untying his horse. "How about a ride?"

"I fell off my horse." Cyrus hung his head. "Harpagus taught me, 'You've got to accept the consequences.'"

Zubaba scowled. "It appears you've learned something else, too. Perhaps even more important." Zubaba bent to look Cyrus in the face. "Three things. No matter how good you are, everyone falls," he said. "What matters is that you get back up again." He hoisted Cyrus onto the saddle in front of the quieter of his two elderly escorts. "And accept the help you need."

CHAPTER 23

When Harpagus had agreed with Astyages that they'd include Cyrus in the lion hunt... and go light on whatever might preserve his health and well-being, he hadn't exactly wanted Cyrus to die. He hadn't thought about it in those terms. But when Cyrus returned as full of life as ever and threw himself back into meeting and surmounting every challenge Harpagus put in his way, gaining strength and agility and skills and knowledge that set him on the way to surpassing any nobleman's child, Harpagus couldn't shake the thought that his own son could have done, would have been even better. It clawed at his mind, obsessed him. It fed the fire of resentment Harpagus nursed against the boy until he couldn't bear it.

When a group of merchants from Bactria came to the palace to deliver and trade luxury goods, Harpagus saw an opportunity he wouldn't let pass. Traveling under heavy guard, these men from the east bore whisper-soft pelts, golden jewelry, and creamy blue lapis lazuli on the rolling backs of camels. Seeing them, Cyrus was transfixed. Harpagus watched Cyrus approach the largest man, probably the merchant guard in charge.

Cyrus had never seen animals such as these. They were the

strangest pack animals he could have imagined with their fantas-
tical faces and great humped backs. When he got close, a man
raised his hand for Cyrus to stop, to stay back. Cyrus didn't
understand the man's language but the gesture was clear. So he
waited. And stared. For the man was almost as captivating as the
animals he tended. When he raised his hand, first to Cyrus and
then to seize the harness of the camel, his flowing sleeve dropped
away. Tattoos covered the man's arm in deep black ink. The lines
were as twisting and smooth as his muscles and veins yet
followed a pattern different than anything found in nature. Cyrus
couldn't make out the image exactly. It seemed like a lion but
bore a striped tail and a mane that swirled and soared like a great
wing over his wrist and forearm. Cyrus stayed where he stood
and watched until unburdened, the camels plodded after their
keepers into the wide jousting arena. Acres of field, where
warriors honed the skills of combat, it was empty for the season
and overgrown with grass and twiggy shrubs.

So, when Harpagus set Cyrus to his regular training and then
dismissed himself "to attend to urgent matters of the king," Cyrus
made his way back to those animals. Cyrus didn't think anything
except how disappointed he was when Harpagus denied Cyrus
the choice of a spirited mount. Harpagus had insisted rather that
Cyrus conduct his training on the dullest most docile horse in
the stable, a horse used more these days for its calming influence
on the others than for anything else. That way, Harpagus
thought, no one could blame for Harpagus for what was about to
happen.

The camels were out of sight over a small hill at the far end of
the arena, when Cyrus entered with his old nag. He was so intent
on approaching the fascinating beasts that Cyrus didn't see
Harpagus reappear at the hill's crest. They walked past the
jousting bales and targets, obstacles and jumps and climbed the
low hill. At its top, Cyrus's mount caught wind of the strange
animals. The horse flared its nostrils, tossed its head and stopped.

Frustrated, Cyrus drove his heels into its flank, spurring it reluctantly forward. Just then, a bull camel in the back, raised its head and screamed alarm. The camels charged.

And something in Harpagus snapped. Harpagus watched, in now excruciatingly slow motion: the horse pitch and turn, Cyrus fall to the ground, Cyrus rise, his eyes wide in terror, the camels – a great cloud of dust – stampeding toward the boy. And Harpagus saw: A boy. Ten years old. A child who knew nothing of Harpagus's pain, nothing of crimes committed in his name, only that he had been ripped from the only parents that he had ever known. Inside of Harpagus, something broke, and a great and awful love poured out. Suddenly he saw that not only was this boy innocent of everything Harpagus had held against him, but also and most searingly that if Cyrus died, his own son's death would have been in vain. It was a chilling realization that galvanized Harpagus such as he had never been before.

So, as the animals thundered their heavy bodies on enormous feet toward the child in their path, Harpagus launched himself forward. His long robe flew out behind him as he ran. He ran in front of the approaching herd, and when his long arms caught the boy up, stumbling briefly under the weight, it wasn't only his robe that fell under that camel's right forefoot. His own foot was crushed on impact. Harpagus didn't notice. He didn't care. Cushioning the boy with his body, Harpagus fell to the ground and rolled rolled rolled out of the way of the crazed animals.

When the camels were past, Cyrus wriggled out from Harpagus's arms. He stood and braced himself for the reprimand that was sure to come. Harpagus rose to his knees. Ignoring his broken foot, he sat back on his heels.

And he wept.

"I am sorry," Harpagus said. "I am so sorry."

How could explain to this little boy how hard it was for Harpagus, how every moment Cyrus was near, Harpagus bled with the thousand cuts of his own son's absence, the horror of his grisly end?

He couldn't. So he said simply, "I am sorry."

Cyrus shifted on his feet.

"I will take you back to the cottage, back to the couple who raised you."

Cyrus's eyes opened wide. But his feet remained planted.

"I cannot let you stay there," Harpagus said. "But I will bring you. And you can see them, know them again."

Cyrus threw himself into the steward's arms.

Harpagus held the little boy's body tight. And let him go.

CHAPTER 24

hey left the following day. On their way out of the inner courtyard, Harpagus explained what had happened. "Unless they've been specifically trained to it, horses are utterly, uncontrollably terrified around camels." He looked over to see that Cyrus understood. "It's something to keep in mind."

Cyrus nodded. He had more questions about the camels and the traders and yet more about the diverse peoples that passed through Media. Harpagus answered Cyrus's questions as well as he could. But as the palace walls dropped away behind them, Cyrus's attention turned more and more toward home.

Finally, Harpagus simply rode quietly beside the little boy. Maybe one day he would find a way to ask Cyrus's forgiveness. Meanwhile, Cyrus had more to say than Harpagus could ever imagine had been in him. Cyrus chattered happily recounting stories trivial and bold about his life with Mit and Spaco. He talked almost all the way to the cottage. As they grew nearer, though, as they rode past the fields where Cyrus and Mit would take the flocks, past the places where Spaco showed Cyrus the best foraging for materials, medicine, and food, without sign of their flocks, of Mit, or of Spaco, Cyrus grew quieter and quieter.

For his part, Harpagus began to wonder at something his own injury hadn't made space to consider. When they entered the place where the cottage had been, Harpagus slumped in his saddle. "No," he said under his breath. "No."

Cyrus leapt from his horse and let out a wail that rang from the far cliffs.

The cottage was in ruins, the animals long gone, and only charred remains scattered about. Cyrus ran inside the broken walls, fell among the weedy undergrowth, and began to dig wildly with his hands. Madly, he flung bricks and stones, clods of dirt, dashing from one area to another, searching and searching for the remains of the people he loved. Finally, he lifted his face to Harpagus. Tears streaked the dirt across his cheeks and chin. His eyes were wild.

"Where are they?!" Cyrus keened.

Harpagus lowered himself from his horse, pulled the crutch from his saddle, and hobbled up to the ruined foundation. He shook his head. "I don't know, child. I don't know."

"What happened to them?!" Sobs shook Cyrus's thin ribs.

Again, Harpagus shook his lean head. "I don't know. I wish I did." He limped slowly among the ruins. "No one ever told me," Harpagus said. "But they are not here."

They stood there among the remnants of a different life – a life over and gone – in silence. Time passed – a lot, a little, it was hard to say. Finally, Cyrus sniffed. Once. Then, he walked back toward his horse, and to Harpagus's surprise, remounted.

"Let's go," Cyrus said.

Uncertain, Harpagus nevertheless got back on his horse. He waited for Cyrus to say something more – to shout or rage or accuse or cry – readied himself to chase the boy should Cyrus take off in grief and anger, but the boy simply turned his horse for Ecbatana. At a walk, they headed back toward the palace. The only indication that the scene affected him was that Cyrus seemed to have lost his fire. The boy who had risen to every challenge with a fierce determination rode now with rounded shoulders and a slack back. He let the horse follow its inclination for home at whatever pace it chose. Harpagus kept a watchful eye. Cyrus didn't seem even to notice to him there. And when they entered the inner palace gate, Cyrus let the horse plod straight to the stables. He went through the motions of unsaddling it, picking its hooves, currying its coat, and loading hay into the manger of its stall. Harpagus kept a close eye as sent away a groom to care himself for his own mount alongside Cyrus. Only when all his duties were done, did Cyrus take any initiative. And it was simply to go to the stall of mare he loved. She nickered and nuzzled his curly head as Cyrus balled himself up at her feet. Harpagus left them there.

HARPAGUS WAS STILL BROODING over the incident when he passed by Zubaba on one of the airier of the palace's long halls.

"You don't like the boy, do you?"

Harpagus stopped and shot Zubaba a wary look.

"Seems you hate him." Zubaba shrugged. "Almost like he's done something to you."

Harpagus sighed. "I did." He dropped his head, shook it slowly. "Hate him. Now... well, you're right – he's just a boy." Harpagus didn't say out loud the truth that always landed like a punch at the back of his skull: Harpagus's injury wasn't by Cyrus's hand. "Still. It's true, I'd rather he be far from here."

Zubaba studied Harpagus. He remembered that Harpagus had had a son about Cyrus's age. He nodded. That was enough.

"I hear the king wants to send him away," Zubaba said, "down Parsa to live with his true father,

Harpagus lifted his head sharply. This was the kind of news

he was used to having before any other. But since the king had assigned him to the tutelage of Cyrus, he wasn't as closely privy to Astyages's thoughts and demands. He wasn't complaining, just observing.

"It's all Media, anyway," Zubaba said. He smirked. "As Astyages is fond of reminding us. Anyway, if that's the case, I'd gladly be among those who escort him to Anshan..." Zubaba shot Harpagus with a grin. "Put in a word for me?"

"You'd like to go, wouldn't you?"

"I've never seen it - Elam," Zubaba said, "though it's all I heard about as youngster."

Harpagus made note that he'd pay the king a visit, see if what Zubaba had heard was correct, that Astyages planned to send the boy away, down to Anshan.

It was. For months, King Astyages had tried to downplay the little prince's popularity, temper the reports of his success, but they only grew. It annoyed him. So when Astyages told Harpagus that he was thinking the child really belonged with his father, down there in Parsa, Harpagus wasn't surprised. And when Astyages declared that a single guard would be sufficient - "It's not as though he'll travel with riches. Any more armed guards would only draw attention and violence," Astyages said – Harpagus had just the man.

CHAPTER 25

*C*yrus took the news of his departure – "It's a more suitable place for you," Astyages had said smoothly, "more the kind of place you're used to" – as Cyrus took everything these days. With a weary stoicism. Frankly, the little boy was tired. The wrenching grief of losing Mit and Spaco, the chronic questions he bore that none but they could answer, and the disorienting cold that palace life had been for him sapped his vitality. He was exhausted. Where he lived, and with whom... it just didn't matter to him anymore. He was tired.

Once it was determined that Cyrus would go, Astyages softened toward the boy. He had a gift he wished to send with Cyrus, he said. Harpagus led the king to the stables, where Astyages would, of course, find Cyrus. He was rarely if ever anywhere else.

Astyages summoned Cyrus from the stall and reached into his ample embroidered robe. "A gift for you."

Harpagus stared as Astyages produced the very dagger with which Mandane had killed herself.

"It belonged to your mother," Astyages said as he transferred it into Cyrus's hands. The small scabbard was ornate as the golden hilt of its dagger. Cyrus looked up in surprise. He'd never had anything near so fine as this.

"Metal workers from Ziwiye gave it to your grandfather King Cyaxares some years ago. You can have it."

Cyrus drew out the dagger, small enough to fit his hand perfectly. Despite Astyages's apathy, he admired the thin blade, polished to shine like the sun. Cyrus ran his finger along its edge and gasped quickly to see a bead of blood. He hadn't felt a thing. He slid the blade back in. As he sucked his finger, Cyrus turned the scabbard over and over peering at the embossed decorations that covered both hilt and sheath. Along the scabbard's length, winged beasts - some with the bodies of lions, others bulls -- strode in a magnificent line. Where the hilt met the scabbard, both sword and sheath bore images of winged men guarding a central tree. At the scabbard's top, on the golden flange punctured to hang from a belt, a single stag lay, its legs tucked under its muscled body. From the top of its head, all along its back ran a rack of curled antlers.

"Thank you," he said.

Cyrus didn't need to be told that this was an item to treasure, but Astyages told him, anyway.

"Take care of it, and don't be stupid," the king said as a servant fastened the scabbard to Cyrus's belt.

"When I leave, may I take the horse?" Cyrus asked Astyages.

"Don't be silly, boy. You need a horse one can ride... and fit for the prince that you are," the king said.

"But what will become of this one, sir?"

"Who knows? She's good for nothing."

"If she's so useless, why not send her with me?"

Harpagus sucked in his breath, prepared for Astyages's outburst at the show of insolence.

And Astyages did look hard at the boy. But what he saw was a ten-year-old, dead set on rescuing a doomed underdog. Too soft.

With such sensitivity, Astyages concluded, the magi were right: the boy would never be a threat.

"Fine," Astyages said and thought no more of it.

When Astyages had left, pleased with how things had gone – it wouldn't be all bad if the cursed dagger brought ill luck to the child as well – Harpagus crouched down in front of Cyrus.

Harpagus took the boy's hands, still holding the weapon, into his own. "There is an evil history in this pretty thing," he said. "But as with everything, that's not the only one. After good King Cyaxares had died, the dagger found its way first into the keeping of your aunt, Amytis."

"The woman I met..."

"Yes, not long ago," Harpagus said, "though it seems forever," he added, his eyes dark and troubled. With a shake of his head, Harpagus dismissed that and smiled. "Amytis wore it every day. She guarded your mother's safety again and again with nothing but that tiny weapon, her strength, and..." Harpagus tapped Cyrus's temple lightly. "... her wits."

Cyrus returned Harpagus's grin.

Harpagus stood. What would Amytis think now, he wondered, remembering that miserable day when she had realized that not only her sister's well-being but Media's entire future depended on her. Harpagus remembered the rough bastard Amytis thrusting that dagger into his hand before the Babylonian entourage drove her away, the dangerously ambitious Igliss at its head. Harpagus had worried mightily over her. Harpagus looked at Mandane's son before him. This was different. No reflection on the child, but Harpagus was glad enough to see him go.

So it was that with only a single escort, Cyrus left the lush palace of Ecbatana wearing the loose trousers of a Median rider atop the black Nisean charger Astyages had chosen from the royal stables. Plodding along in tow was the nag that Cyrus loved so much.

CHAPTER 26

*A*s they passed through the last of the city's walls, Cyrus looked back. Past the palace with its silver and gold topped walls his eyes went to the mountains behind. A thick veil of falling snow obscured their craggy peaks. Soon such blizzards would reach the capital and confound the roads. He faced forward again. South to what – he didn't know. Here, in the only land that had ever been familiar to him, sour cherry trees had already begun to drop golden leaves. He'd always loved this time of year. Clusters of sumac in the valleys and hillsides abandoned their modest green to turn a reckless red. Wild sheep watched from craggy heights while finches, geese, doves, and falcons busied the air in migratory flight. Maybe he'd see them again in a place that might be home.

Neither King Astyages nor Harpagus knew that Cyrus and Zubaba had already met. As far as the king was concerned, Cyrus would have a single escort – who it was mattered not a bit. (If the gods determined the boy should live, they'd see to it. Though he'd put more stock in the bandits along their way than he would in the gods.) As for Harpagus, he remembered his friend's request, knew that Zubaba was eager to see the region from which his ancestors had come. Since he had discovered that he couldn't bear the idea of the boy's death any more than he could bear the boy's presence, all that mattered to him was that Zubaba was a good man... and an accomplished war veteran. For now, Harpagus wanted Cyrus to be safe. If Cyrus could have only one escort, Harpagus would have chosen this man, whether Zubaba had wanted to go or not.

"Of course it's best they travel with little," Astyages said when even he had to admit it looked strange to send away this grandson whom Astyages had declared so widely he was delighted to have found, strange to send him away and with so little, from grand Ecbatana to Parsa, of all places. Word was that Parsa in recent years had gone from poor to desperate.

"A band of two with few possessions will be less likely to draw unwanted attention than a crowd seeming to transport the wealth of kings," Astyages said.

No one remarked that the boy's mount alone would tip him off as a child of means.

But the king was firm. What's more, he instructed Zubaba to take the shortest route. Rather than follow the Royal Road west to Bisitun and south from there through Susa, a long but safe passage, he had instructed Zubaba, "Go directly. Follow the eastern edge of the mountains south. You'll be in Anshan before you know it."

Hearing this, Zubaba very nearly said No. The whole reason he'd told Harpagus that he'd take the journey was because he wanted to experience Susa and the region around it, the Elamite area of his family origins. But Zubaba was in too far at this point. Besides, he figured that if they made good time, if he got Cyrus to Anshan more sooner than later, he could take that longer route on his way back.

What no one said of Astyages's directions but everyone knew: they'd have to take their chances with the Kassites in Luristan who made no pretense of clinging fiercely to a semi-independence. It was widely said that they lived in caves like wild animals and off of whatever they could find... or steal. Their fine metal-work, especially the bits, bridles, and accouterments for outfit-ting horses, exquisite with such sophistication as to adorn the crown's own mounts was distinctly at odds with their brutal reputation.

* * *

In fact, it wasn't only the Kassites who resisted submission to Astyages's Media. It took only two days' travel, still within the area of the Busae, and only a fraction of the distance they'd have to travel, to encounter people whose allegiance to King Astyages was thin. As they entered a cozy village, Zubaba kept an eye out for the kind of outbuilding that would provide a bit more warmth and shelter than the small tent they carried. The sun was gone, and the air whispered of winter come early to the mountains.

They rode in single file. Even with Cyrus behind him, Zubaba had seen more than one person they passed take a long look at Cyrus's horse – the good one – with what might be suspicion or might be envy, then look away again. It had been the same the day before, even when they'd only just left the last of the city's walls. It was clear that no one imagined that the child could be the thought-dead-prince-returned, much less heir to the Median throne. At best, he was the son of a decorated warrior, or so was the appearance of the man that traveled with him.

And anyway, these people didn't seem to need what modest resources Cyrus and he might have with them. Indeed, from clothes to houses to the animals and crops they kept, the people of this area seemed to be doing just fine. Zubaba stopped in front of a sprawling house. Its cedar-shingled roof had not yet weath-ered to gray, and the walls were newly painted wood, like the palace (though not painted in silver and gold) that they had left behind. If he had to guess, Zubaba would have said the material was cedar or cypress. Like the palace. He dismounted and handed the reins to Cyrus.

They'd hardly exchanged a single word – Cyrus and Zubaba – in their journey so far. When Cyrus had emerged from the palace stables riding the heavy black charger that Astyages had insisted he take, the haughty little mare behind, his heart jumped again to recognize that his guide was none other than the man who had saved his life during the lion hunt.

But rather than returning Cyrus's quick grin, Zubaba acted as if he'd never met the boy. Cyrus's face fell. First (and worst) Mit and Spaco, too, lying to him about whose he really was; Harpagus, who had been so curt and even cruel now inexplicably gentle, almost kind; Astyages, who had proclaimed such delight over Cyrus's arrival never showed it again, not even when Cyrus proved to be far better at everything than Astyages expected of him now seemed he couldn't get rid of Cyrus fast enough; and finally this man who killed the lion that would have torn Cyrus to pieces and given him such encouragement too, acted as if they'd never met. Cyrus bit back tears and lifted his chin. Now he knew. It didn't matter where they sent him. He'd go anywhere they said that he should. He belonged nowhere and had no one.

For his part, Zubaba was simply preoccupied – by the logistics of travel through country off the main roads, rugged country where he'd never been, to deliver a boy whom anyone might like to take and not only for the reward. When he wasn't worrying over the route or their appearance or, frankly, why the king wanted to be rid of Cyrus after so recently "finding" him, he was rehashing memories. The good ones, the tales of pride in the illustrious history of his ancestors gave way to the more immediate. Memories he thought he'd buried lay in a shallow grave. In his own melancholy, Zubaba hardly noticed Cyrus. Even when they stopped for the night, he spoke only to instruct the boy in helping with the tent and their simple food before the intensity of the day overwhelmed them both and they slept. Cyrus was up early, which suited Zubaba, who wanted to make this trip fast. So, they'd hardly spoken.

And now, Cyrus saw that it was better that way. While Zubaba stood at the door of the house, from around the barn, two men appeared, engaged in conversation as they walked. Over the shoulders of one man hung skins of wine. Cyrus cleared his throat. Zubaba turned. They both watched as the man with the wine stopped and transferred them to the other who in turn dropped the clink of metal into his hand. A sale. Seeing the travelers, they men parted ways, and the one trotted forward.

"Travelers, on our way from the city to the south territories," Zubaba said by way of explanation. "Getting a later start than we'd hoped. We were hoping to stay ahead of the weather ..." He gestured to a cloud-bank, rosy-gray in the light of the setting sun. "... I wondered if we might – my boy and I – spend the night in your barn."

The man shrugged. "It's all the same to me." He paused.

The man studied them – his eyes resting, of course, on Cyrus's horse. "On second thought, better you should come inside." He helped Zubaba lift their few belongings from the horses' backs. and said to Cyrus, "Boy, bring the animals to the barn – the near stalls – you'll see what I mean when you get there. Then come straight in."

Setting down his load, "I'll help get the horses settled," Zubaba said.

But the man had laid his hand on Zubaba's shoulder and the grip said that he wouldn't. "It'll only take him a minute. Good to learn responsibility at any age like that.

The man dropped his hand.

Cyrus turned away disgusted. Adults. He didn't wait for Zubaba. He could do it himself. Gods knew, Harpagus had tasked with far more and far worse.

Cyrus heard the man say, "I had a boy myself, a son, grew into a fine young man."

"Is he here?" Zubaba asked.

"Killed." The man's voice broke. "We've been battling a group of Arizanti just over that valley. It's been years now."

"But –" Cyrus turned back, "aren't they all Media?"

The man shut his mouth and narrowed his eyes at Cyrus. Cyrus could see there'd be no answer forthcoming. He left with the horses.

CHAPTER 27

*T*he barn was dark but smelled clean. Like the man said, there were empty stalls near the door. Cyrus got the horses settled, helped himself to fresh hay, and left the animals there. It was dark, spooky, toward the back of the barn. So Cyrus left their tack just outside the horses' stalls and walked back to the house. The man had said to come straight in, so Cyrus opened the door and stepped inside. It was quiet, the rooms he could see were empty.

It hit him – he was small and alone and farther from anywhere familiar than he'd ever been. Cyrus took a step forward and then another. Finally, "Zubaba?" he called.

"Out here."

Cyrus exhaled in a rush of air and hurried toward the voice. Through a back door, the men sat an open table.

"Zubaba is it?" the man asked.

They had been drinking. On the table was food – simple but nice. Cyrus sat.

Zubaba nodded.

"It's an Elamite name, yes?"

"That's home," Zubaba said.

The man suddenly grinned. He whacked Zubaba across the back and said, "For a while there, I thought – coming from the city, a horse like that, your boy assuming 'we're all Media'..." He mimicked Cyrus's voice from earlier. "I almost thought you were from the palace. Here." He took Zubaba's cup and with a flick of his wrist tossed out the wine. He did the same with his own. On the ground, the wet glistened in day's last light. Then the man trotted off. He returned with a flask from which he poured fresh wine – red, the kind of red wine that Astyages had said wasn't available on account of some problem with the crop. Zubaba took a sip and lifted the cup appreciatively.

"Very nice," he said. And the next morning, when Zubaba peered into shadows at the far end of the barn he nodded and said, "Uh-huh," like it was no surprise at all to find rows of wine barrels behind stacks of hay.

Only when they were well on their way again, did Zubaba explain.

"The territory of Media is vast. Your great-grandfather like his father before him ruled it well. Not everyone was happy giving annual tribute to the palace in Ecbatana, but he was fair about it. He made sure he knew what was happening throughout the empire, which made it easier to exact appropriate taxes and things like that. King Astyages on the other hand... Listen. Family is a strong thing, tribal identity,... It's hard to explain but no amount of wishful thinking or dictating, or even force of arms..." His voice trailed off, searching for how to say it then tried again. "If people don't see a common connection..."

Indeed, the farther they traveled, the more Cyrus saw what Zubaba stumbled to explain. Media was not so unified an empire as his grandfather made it sound. Rather, significant areas (especially those out of easy reach) were governed by their own king-like leaders. His own father Cambyses was called a king, for example. Astyages wouldn't have married Mandane off to him had that not been the case. The different peoples were willing enough to pledge allegiance and support to Astyages, if the need arose – if forced or more strategically to invest in armed backing against other bigger powers. But they retained a degree of independence that Astyages refused to admit.

Finally, Zubaba summed it up. "We all just want to belong," he said.

That, Cyrus already knew.

CHAPTER 28

They missed the storm that threatened on that third day. It passed them to the west. But Zubaba hurried them even harder in the days that followed. It had gone well with the Busaean man, sharing his roof and table; but they might not be so lucky with all the people they met. Zubaba determined they'd keep to themselves even as they traveled the more difficult route. It snowed one night, but the tent held fast, and the horses' coats still kept out the chill. But when the northern skies threatened a true blizzard, Zubaba elected to pick their way down off the ridge to a lower elevation and take what shelter they could find in a narrow valley with southern exposure. He planned well. And they got lucky. Or found favor with the gods. By the time the next big storm, raging a blizzard only miles to the north and up the mountains, came down from the peaks, it was a slushy rain that passed quickly. They were wet but the temperatures were mild. And nothing seemed to stop Zubaba from pressing on.

Cyrus thought about what Zubaba had said about the different tribes, even his own father Cambyses – "king" of a region that Astyages considered vassal to Media. Cyrus didn't know if his father paid tribute like the tribes they'd passed through. Maybe it had a special status because of Mandane. But if that was a bit vague, Astyages *had* made clear that every one of the regions he claimed (and there were many) was categorically inferior to Media. Astyages never passed up an opportunity to remind that he, king of the Median empire, was the king of kings.

Related, but inevitably personal, Cyrus thought about family and home. Specifically, the absence of it. As the miles passed and the days, too, Cyrus couldn't stop thinking about all he'd lost. Over and over again, his mind returned to how the life that had seemed so rich in its simplicity was ripped away and scattered like so many dry leaves. The passing of time and miles did nothing to diffuse Cyrus's brooding over Mit and Spaco. He simply had to accept that they really had pretended Cyrus was theirs even though he wasn't. (How else explain the mysterious visit of Amytis and Harpagus, especially Amytis's recognizing Mandane, his real mother, in Cyrus's face?). And that called into question all of their affections for Cyrus, each example, each memory, he turned over and over. And it called into question every lesson from and every interaction he'd ever had with them. Add to all that the shattering blow, still raw and wounding afresh each time he thought of it – that Mit had left Cyrus there in the palace, alone and scared. The man he'd learned to call Father had finally abandoned Cyrus like he was nothing other than an animal of the palace herd that Mit and Spaco had raised to deliver one day. Never mind that his experience with the only blood-family he had, Astyages, had been distant and cold at best. Cyrus knew he should trust him – Astyages was his grandfather, after all – but Cyrus never could.

When his thoughts grew bleak with loneliness and disorientation – where, indeed *what* was home for him, anyway?, not that he could quite name the question like that - he fingered the scabbard at his side. That alone leant a shred of comfort. There was no reason Astyages would lie that it had belonged to his mother. And there was no reason Harpagus should lie that before that, his aunt Amytis, the woman who had looked so long – and yes! lovingly – at him those months (that seemed years) ago had wielded the tiny weapon in regular defense of Mandane, the princess that people loved. Mandane, Cyrus's real mother. Mandane, who was dead.

As they rode through the mountains that angled south, mountains that Zubaba said would give way to hills and then to land wider than Cyrus could ever imagine, Cyrus turned these thoughts over and over. And he stared at the back of a man whose drive was all for home. Whenever they resumed their travel – after a break (always brief), or in the morning (always early), his face glowed with a yearning eagerness for home that made Cyrus's absence of it only that much sharper.

* * *

THEIR TRAVELS HAD BROUGHT them well into the mountains of the northern Luristan region. The road had narrowed to a path, and the travelers began to wind their way along a precipitous edge. To their left, the path dropped off into a boulder-strewn ravine. To their right loomed the high wall of a mountain face interrupted every so often by wadis - the now dry valleys of what ran with snowmelt in spring. As usual, Zubaba took the lead. Cyrus followed on the heavyset black charger that had proved a worthy mount indeed. The small mare picked her way daintily, bringing up the rear on a tether behind.

Suddenly from a narrow wadi up ahead, two men on sturdy ponies flew out from behind dense shrubs and stormed down the hillside, scattering rocks as they went. Long swords conspicuously hung from their sides and clattered with the flurry until the men pulled to a stop directly in front of Zubaba. Zubaba pulled up and Cyrus stopped behind him. The men wore dark cloths wrapped over their heads that partially concealed the faces beneath. Cyrus's heart pounded in his chest. Bandits.

CHAPTER 29

*T*he last of the rocks the men had loosened tumbled across the path and sailed off the cliff to their left. The horses whinnied in alarm. Cyrus looked back. His little mare met his eyes with a wild look of her own. There was no retreat. Looking forward again, Cyrus urged the black charger to move. It was useless. They both knew it. Cyrus's mount tossed its head, eyes rolling at the hostile strangers and the lethal cliff face. It stamped its feet.

"Be still," Zubaba hissed.

"There are taxes for traveling this road," one of the men facing Zubaba said. "Just give us the gold you're carrying."

"We are poor travelers, only me and my boy, trying to get home."

The man laughed and gestured behind Zubaba to Cyrus. "Yeah, I don't think so." His companion took up the joke.

"Listen. We can do this quickly, and no one gets hurt. Or..." He let it hang.

"I see," Zubaba replied evenly as he loosened the purse from his belt. Cyrus gulped. It was all they had.

"I trust that you'll find what is required here." Zubaba tossed it lightly toward the man.

He caught in one hand and opened the sack greedily. The other peered over his shoulder.

"It will do," he said. "But barely."

"And only for you," his companion said. The other nodded, grinning. "How about the boy?"

Cyrus's mouth went dry. His horse stepped nervously.

"The boy carries nothing," Zubaba said, keeping his voice steady. "He's a child. I'm merely his grandfather's friend, returning him home."

They looked closely at Cyrus, then back at Zubaba and grinned. "Merely a friend, you say. Uh-huh."

To Cyrus's surprise, the men turned away. They stepped their ponies back into the narrow sluice through the cliff. But as soon as they were out of the road, and before Zubaba and Cyrus could move ahead, they turned around again. The spokesman dismounted. He stepped to the side of the path. Then he waved Zubaba forward. Cyrus exhaled with relief. Maybe they really would let them pass. Zubaba stepped forward cautiously. They let him go. Cyrus urged his horse to follow.

But no sooner had Zubaba had passed in front of him, than the man stepped out again, directly in front of Cyrus, blocking his way. The man grabbed the black horse's bridle. The horse threw up its head in alarm. The man didn't care.

"Pretty horse..." he said low, close enough for Cyrus to smell the sour onions on his breath "For a pretty boy."

"Leave the child," Zubaba said. His voice, steady until now, wavered with desperation and the impotency of his demand.

The man ignored him. His eyes, red-rimmed and yellow where the whites should be, held Cyrus's. He transferred his grip on Cyrus's horse into his left hand. With his right, he grasped Cyrus's boot. Cyrus whimpered as he slid his hand up the boy's leg hungrily, tightening his grip as he went.

Cyrus released the reins – slack, with the man gripping the bridle. He gritted his teeth, reached under his tunic, and with a single motion drew the little dagger from its scabbard. Before the man could protest, Cyrus sliced the blade deeply across the man's leering face. So sharp was the knife's edge that it met no resistance, cutting through beard, skin, muscle and vein, straight through to the bone. So swift had been the motion that Cyrus's hand kept going. And he lost hold of the tiny weapon. And while the man dropped his hand from Cyrus's leg, howling in pain, to bring it to his bleeding cheek, Cyrus watched the dagger plummet down the cliff below.

"Give me this horse!" the man roared, fumbling for his sword while hanging onto Cyrus's horse's bridle. But the blood ran too fast to free a hand. He clung to the bridle. "Be off, you brat!"

There was only one thing to do. And Cyrus did it as fast as he could. He slid down, on the opposite side of his horse from where the man stood, onto shaky legs. He slipped quickly into the slender space between the cliff face and his horse's flank. The man, still shouting without words, jerked the black horse forward with one hand. Horrified, Cyrus watched his mare, still tethered, step forward and roll her eyes in terror. Before he could think any further, Cyrus loosed the saddle to which she was tethered, grateful for all that Harpagus had demanded Cyrus perform every task.

So, when the man led the charger into the wadi, the saddle dropped off from behind it and onto Cyrus's thin shoulder. The man glared at Cyrus, but he let it go. And with it, the ugly little horse to which it was attached. Awkward under the weight of the saddle, Cyrus nevertheless hurried the mare ahead to Zubaba and safety. As he passed the narrow valley where the man had gone, Cyrus glanced up into it. He shivered, heart pounding. The man looked back at Cyrus between bloody fingers with hate-filled eyes until with the clatter of hooves he'd retreated into the wadi and out of sight.

CHAPTER 30

*C*yrus was so furious with himself for losing the horse but especially the dagger that before he could think otherwise, he snatched the scabbard from his belt and threw it over the cliff. Zubaba shook his head and moved on, a chastened Cyrus on foot behind. Each of them looked around and back frequently. But although there was endless activity - a herd of mountain goats scrambled the sides of the next wadi; for a time, a hawk circled and screamed overhead; and every so often a pica dashed from its sunny ledge into the crevice of boulder fields – Cyrus and Zubaba seemed to be the only humans around. Each lost in thought, they didn't talk.

Zubaba was disappointed in himself. No, it was worse than that. What had happened back there called into question his very identity. And he was so preoccupied with it, so angry with himself that he had forgotten the child behind him. Cyrus figured that Zubaba was as angry at Cyrus as Cyrus was for failing to keep the two most valuable things he'd taken from his former life. So Cyrus stumbled on. He shifted the saddle to the other shoulder and took comfort from the steady breathing of the little mare. In and out she blew warm air, her muzzle just behind his neck. After a while, Cyrus's legs had quit shaking from fear, but with the weight of the saddle, provisions too, on his back, they couldn't hold out for long.

So, when the narrow path crossed a true stream, running clear with fresh water, Cyrus stopped. He watched Zubaba, his body moving with the steps of his horse, go on. Cyrus could not. He shed the saddle on creek's edge, took off his shoes - the soles wearing thin, and sighed to feel the water wash over them. The mare drank long and deep. Cyrus cupped water in his palms and did the same. Suddenly, the pounding of horse's hooves startled them both. Zubaba cantered back to the stream and leapt from his horse. "What are you doing?!"

Cyrus was too tired for the man's anger. He'd lost his own some stretches back. Sustaining that anger and disappointment took more energy than he could muster. "Resting and drinking," he said.

Zubaba dropped his head. He waded through the creek, lifted Cyrus, and set him atop his own horse. Zubaba gathered Cyrus's things and the mare's lead. Then he hoisted the empty saddle onto his own back and set out walking.

They walked in silence. After a time, Zubaba flagged. He tripped. He kept going, doggedly, but longer still and it was clear that he was exhausted.

"How far is it?" Cyrus asked.

Zubaba stopped, turned around and considered the boy atop his horse. Then he smiled sheepishly. He dropped the saddle and shook his head. "Too far to walk."

* * *

CYRUS DISMOUNTED, and while the horses browsed, they rested in the long shade. When Zubaba spoke again, it was as if he were talking more to the horse than to the boy.

"Before the Assyrians attacked Susa, my people and yours

were closely linked, though geographically separated by the foothills of the Zagros. The lowlands of Elam and the highlands of Anshan were allies, united under a single monarch, the 'King of Susa and Anshan.'" Zubaba looked up then.

Cyrus was listening. Intently. Zubaba had said, my people and yours, as if Cyrus actually had somewhere he belonged, some*one* to whom he belonged. And he ate it up like a boy starved for far too long.

Zubaba sighed and stroked his horse's thick neck. "Yet when we, the Elamite people of Susa suffered devastation at the hands of Assyria, your people in Anshan or Parsa or however we call it... didn't."

"And that made you angry?" Cyrus asked. "I mean, because my people..." He wrapped his tongue around those two words, savoring them like a sweet. "... Got away without being hurt?"

Zubaba shook his head, No.

"It was how. And why," Zubaba said. "I had been raised to think that you Anshanites were cowardly and solicitous."

Cyrus clammed up, confused.

Zubaba said, "During that great conflict – Assyria versus Susa and Anshan, an elder of Anshan made a great sacrifice. In a critical moment, he gave up something very precious in order to protect his people. It wasn't solicitous or cowardly, the way I'd learned to interpret what he did. It was smart and brave... and at a terrible loss to him. That man's name was Kurash – "

"Cyrus," Cyrus said in a hushed voice.[1]

Zubaba nodded. "Same as yours. We don't know for certain whether or not he was king. But probably. And we don't know whether or not you two are related."

"But maybe," Cyrus said tentative with hope.

---

1. "Cyrus' emphasis was on Anshan: not Persia, and not Elam" (Waters, 289). People continue to debate the linguistic heritage of Cyrus' name -- and if he was born with it or took it when he became king.

Zubaba nodded. "Maybe." Well, Kurash sent not only conciliatory tribute to the Assyrian king Ashurbanipal. He also sent his son -- his eldest, Arukku -- to be held in Nineveh at Ashurbanipal's pleasure. It worked. Ashurbanipal did not destroy Anshan."

"And Arukku?" Cyrus asked. "What happened to him?"

Zubaba's face was pained. "We don't know.[2] Anyway, back there, when I handed over the purse without any fight at all and you fought and lost a that dagger, never mind the horse, it made me question what I'd assumed about your people. And mine."

But Cyrus didn't care about what had happened back there with the bandits. He didn't even care about the dagger anymore. What Cyrus cared about was that maybe, just maybe, somewhere up ahead, he had real family. Somewhere he belonged. For the first time, Cyrus cared whether they stayed or went. And for the first time, he cared where.

"Well how are we going to get there?" Cyrus asked.

Zubaba looked up from his brooding. The boy's bright interest, his happy eagerness to move on was like an absolution. They looked from each other to the mare, sleeping at the end of her tether, and back to each other again.

---

2. Waters, Parsumash 293.

CHAPTER 31

*N*ot far from Cyrus, the little mare slept, her head low, eyes closed and snoring lightly. At the end of the tether, she stood one hoof on tiptoe, the hip relaxed.

"She's never worn a saddle?" Zubaba asked.

Cyrus shook his head.

Zubaba looked at the road that lay ahead, then back at Cyrus. He shrugged. "Let's hope she's smart."

"Oh, she's smart, all right."

"Smart enough not to take a saddle so far," Zubaba muttered. "Without a bridle, we'll have to keep her tethered to my horse." Zubaba lifted again the saddle that Cyrus had slipped from the back of his stolen mount. "But at least, if we do this right, you can ride." He nodded at the horse. "Lead her here to me."

Not certain it was a good idea, Cyrus screwed up his mouth; but not seeing otherwise – Zubaba was in charge, after all – he did. She woke drowsy and docile to follow Cyrus. But when they got close to Zubaba, she squealed and reared up.

Zubaba gritted his teeth. "Hold her steady."

But Cyrus had already led the horse away.

"She doesn't want to," he said.

"But –"

Cyrus ignored Zubaba. He brought the horse next to a large rock and kept her in place while he scrambled up the rock's side to stand, almost level with the horse's back. To Zubaba's astonishment, the horse stood still as Cyrus leaned over her back, easing himself slowly until he was draped over her back like a sack of goods. He lay like that, his arms and legs draped over her speckled flanks. The little horse bobbed her head a few times, nervous, but didn't move her feet. After a while, after she had relaxed again, Cyrus slid back down to the ground.

"I used to do that with her," Cyrus explained, "in her stall at the palace. She felt good on my belly on and chest." Cyrus gestured for Zubaba to give him the saddle, get on his own horse, and go on ahead. Away.

Reluctantly Zubaba did. But he rode slowly and after a few yards stopped again. He turned to see the boy, carrying the saddle again, leading the horse. Exasperated, Zubaba started to dismount. They couldn't walk the whole way like this, not switching places, not at anywhere close to the pace they would need to keep.

But once again, Cyrus stopped him with a hand. Zubaba gritted his teeth but complied. Cyrus led the mare forward past the stream. When the path was once again a narrow ribbon – rock wall on the left, drop-off to the right, Cyrus stopped and stepped to the side of the mare. She threw her head up. Cyrus spoke softly to her and leaned against her flank. He ran his hand, soothing, down her neck. Then, as slowly as he could manage, Cyrus eased the saddle onto her back. At the unfamiliar weight, the horse pranced and snorted. But with nowhere to turn and Zubaba ahead, the little mare held her ground. Still talking softly to her, Cyrus tightened the girth.

Zubaba approached prepared to take the tether before Cyrus

mounted. But before he reached them, Cyrus tied off the rope in makeshift reins, and as the mare switched her tail and shivered her skin, Cyrus grabbed her mane and swung lightly into the saddle. She spun her small muzzle back, flared her great nostrils over his boots, paused, exhaled heavily, and then as if it had been her idea all along looked straight ahead, tail high. Holding only the tether harness for her head, Cyrus urged her forward. Zubaba let out a low whistle and walked on.

* * *

WHEN THE MOUNTAIN path gave way again to a road wide enough to travel side by side, and the mare walking as calmly under the saddle as if she'd been born to it, Cyrus drew up next to Zubaba. He cleared his throat.

"In the palace... Did you know my mother?"

Startled, Zubaba looked over. The little horse's head was high. Her bright eyes were more alert than she'd ever looked along their travels. Cyrus's small frame sat atop her in perfect proportion. Cyrus's face held a wary eagerness.

"She was perfect," Zubaba said and the wariness evaporated. Zubaba relaxed into the telling. "You know that she was the one, true princess of Media, raised with every refinement the palace could muster."

Cyrus bobbed his head up and down, yes.

"And instruction, too," Zubaba said. "She was smart. Everything about her growing-up was to prepare her for life in Babylon. *She* was supposed to marry Nebuchadnezzar. With that, a parity alliance – a relationship of equals – between Media and Babylonia would be fixed, which became ever more important for Media especially. Anyway, it was a deal Nebuchadnezzar's father had made with Astyages's father."

"Cyaxares. I remember learning that."

"Well, you might not know is that even while your mother mastered all the things expected of a princess destined to be queen of the greatest empire in the world..." Zubaba glanced over at Cyrus. "Don't tell your grandfather I said that." Zubaba brushed a fly from his horse's shoulder. "... Mandane had a passion for healing, a particular kind of women's healing. And she was very good at it. The best. Unfortunately, the Babylonians believe – strongly – that such healing belongs to the gods. Hence, to the priests. Their priests. And the consequences of presuming to such work, if you're not a priest, could be deadly. That's what Amytis –"

"My mother's sister. The bastard."

Zubaba slammed his mouth shut and stared. But Cyrus was nonplussed, simply stating facts. Zubaba chuckled and nodded his head. "Amytis learned that not only would your mother be in danger if she went to Babylon, but so would the treaty on which Media's well-being depends. Amytis saw that, and so she went instead."

Cyrus was quiet. "I met Amytis," he said. "Once. She came with Harpagus to our –" He stopped. "... To where I lived with Mit and Spaco."

Zubaba nodded. "I heard what happened..." he said and briefly repeated the story that Cyrus had been told – how Cyrus had been thought dead at birth, and Mit and Spaco had taken him, pretending his was their own. He paused. Then he said, "I knew Mit."

"You did?"

Zubaba nodded. "From a long time ago. He actually worked at the palace."

He had Cyrus's attention now.

"He angered your grandfather the king. Rather than kill him, Astyages forced Mit out and into the service that you did with him." He shook his head again. "Mit was always such a truth-teller..." He looked at Cyrus – "that's what got him into such trouble"

– then faced forward again. "So, how he lied about you – you, of all people…" Zubaba shook his head. "I can't understand it."

They walked on quietly for a time.

"He was the only father I knew. Pop." Cyrus's voice broke. "And I wouldn't have wanted another."

Zubaba sighed. It fit with what he knew of Mit. It pained him now to see how quickly Cyrus's bouncy enthusiasm had given way to melancholy. When Zubaba had volunteered to make this trip, he, who had no children, had lived the life of a soldier – warrior and military man – hadn't considered the fact that his only companion would be a ten-year-old. With a lot of questions. And grief.

He didn't think it would bring up grief of his own. He kept it to himself and said instead, "They say your real father, Cambyses is good man."

Cyrus looked over at him, quickly, eagerly.

"So," Cyrus said. "Am I part Mede and part -?"

"Anshanite?" Zubaba finished for him. He considered. "Yes," he said. "But it's a little more complicated than that. For one thing, as you know, your grandfather King Astyages sees even Anshan as *part* of Media." Zubaba grimaced. "Sort of. Nominally – in name, though even he recognizes its independence. Besides, it's so far from Ecbatana that…" Zubaba could see that he'd lost Cyrus.

Cyrus ran his hand under his horse's mane. She nickered. "But my people…" Cyrus prompted.

Zubaba nodded. "In Anshan, there are at least two different kinds of people – Elamites and yet more tribes whose origins are related to Medians. You'll see when you get there. The greater region is called Parsa and includes mixes of both kinds of people. In Anshan, people speak mostly Elamite -- my native language. But don't worry," Zubaba said, "you'll also find people who speak a language like we know from Media. And I bet you'll learn Elamite quickly enough."

Cyrus looked ahead and let himself imagine what it might be like – for people to know who he was – in a good way – as one of them. He let himself imagine his father – like Mit in all ways but one: Cambyses was a king. Already it felt different than Median royalty. He had no idea how different it would be.

CHAPTER 32

$\mathcal{I}$t had been a hard day, and the night didn't look like it would be much easier. As they trekked the western slope of the Zagros range, Zubaba kept his eye on a thick bank of clouds that hung just this side of the ridge they followed. It was sure to open up soon, and they'd be in the thick of it. There was no getting ahead of it. What's more, they had little left by way of the provisions the palace had sent with them. Hunger made the situation even worse.

So Zubaba counted it a stroke of luck when a rustle in the leafy woods ahead revealed the tawny rump of a small deer. He loosed his bow from the side of his saddle. In a flash, the deer was off. Three others, invisible before now, leapt to join it in swift retreat. One crossed the path just in front of Zubaba. In a single swift motion, he had retrieved an arrow, strung it, aimed, and let fly. The doe tumbled forward in the brush. Zubaba leapt from his horse, and ran to it, struggling to rise. He slit its throat and began to dress it. By then, Cyrus was beside him. To Zubaba's surprise, Cyrus worked efficiently by Zubaba's side, tugging away the organs that Zubaba's knife revealed, and shifting the body to drain its blood away. Mit had taught him well indeed.

While they worked, Cyrus said, "What kind of a bow is that?" he pointed with his chin to where Zubaba had laid it. The frame revealed several different materials – wood but maybe other things too – melded into a single, graceful piece crowned at each end by a carving in the shape of a duck's head.

"It belonged to my father." A shadow passed over Zubaba's face and was as quickly gone. "You're right. In Ecbatana, I used the weapons assigned to me, the ones that Harpagus trained you to, not unlike the ones that you used with Mit, I'm sure." He wiped his hands, retrieved the bow and laid it into Cyrus's hands. It was lighter than it looked. He ran a hand up its side. And so smooth. He ran a finger over the black inset of the duck's eye and handed it back.

Zubaba laid it down carefully and returned to skinning the deer. "The style is particular to my people, the most famous archers in the world," Zubaba said. "It seemed right to bring along." Then, his voice suddenly husky, "back to where it all started." He straightened brusquely, the task done.

* * *

THEY SET up their little camp close by. Zubaba wanted to roast the meat before whatever those clouds held doused what fire they needed. While Zubaba prepared a fire, Cyrus busied himself in the woods nearby. He returned with knobby roots. "Spaco showed me," Cyrus explained, seeing Zubaba's suspicion. He thrust them under the coals, prodded them once, and after a time, nudged them back out.

With the horses lightly hobbled and the tent tied between sturdy green branches, the venison dripping clear fat from browning flesh, they were as ready as could be. It was a feast. Cyrus's tubers were soft and sweet with the meat. They had fresh water from a near stream. Zubaba was grateful for the wine he'd slipped from the Busaean man miles back. With all those barrels

– and none of it going to the crown – he'd never miss it. He'd probably spilled more in the evening before, all drunk and singing, swinging his arm this way and that.

A low roar in the treetops announced the coming wind like a crier. Big spattering drops fell at an angle and drove man and boy inside. At the crack of thunder, the horses whinnied in alarm. Cyrus went to the tent flap. Zubaba pulled him back and let it drop.

"She'll be all right. They won't go far."

Cyrus wriggled from his grip, lifted the flap and looked outside. Indeed Zubaba's horse stood steady, and Cyrus's mare had sidled up close – on the protected side.

"Smart all right," Zubaba said into his ear. Cyrus could hear his grin.

Back inside, each nestled on a linen-topped pallet of brush and leaves, Cyrus said, "Until we met that man – with the barn, the wine – I thought that you were from Media. That Ecbatana was your home."

Rain drummed against the skin of the tent. In the distance a long roll of thunder rumbled and echoed off the mountain.

Zubaba sat up and crossed his legs. Whether it was the wine or the dark or the storm or simply the eager audience of a child, Zubaba's tongue began to tell things he thought he'd buried long ago.

CHAPTER 33

"*My* father was one of the elders of Elam," Zubaba began. "He fought in the great wars." He paused. "I envy you a father as good as Mit," he said bitterly.

"Did he do a bad job in the war?"

"No," Zubaba said. "War did a bad job on him." He took a deep breath. "I told you a little already – about the Assyrians... that damn Ashurbanipal. But there's more. Much more."

In the quiet dark, Cyrus didn't have to wait long.

"Before the Assyrians, before Ashurbanipal," Zubaba said, "our capital, Susa, was the most glorious you could ever see, ever even imagine. I loved to hear my father tell of it. When my father spoke of Susa, Susa before the war, he was gracious and proud. Not angry or sullen and mean." Zubaba let himself savor those precious moments of good memory. "But inevitably," he went on, "it would come around to Ashurbanipal."

"The king, right?"

"Yes," Zubaba said. "It's from my father that I learned what Ashurbanipal had done to Susa and to its people. When his Ashurbanipal attacked, it was with the strength of a world behind him. Impossible to withstand, though every Elamite troop did his best to do so. He plundered Susa's great wealth, of course, taking silver and gold, weapons, gems, even fine furniture and equipment.

"Susa's queen," Zubaba said with a long exhale, "was forced to entertain the king in his palace garden at Nineveh while the severed head of an Elamite king, Te-umman, swung from a nearby tree."

If Zubaba heard Cyrus gasp, it didn't matter.

As it was, he was lost in the recounting. "Ashurbanipal carved that image into the palace walls," Zubaba said. "He bragged about his cruelties, his brutality. 'I devastated Elam,' Ashurbanipal said, 'scattering salt and poison on the land. Their kings' daughters and sisters I took. Anyone I wanted from the families of the kings, officials chiefs, and generals... I took.'"

"Is that how your father ended up in Media?" Cyrus's voice seemed small in the dark, the rain lashing the sides of their tent, Zubaba's own voice rising with emotion, like the thunder across the mountains.

Zubaba said simply, "Yes." The sound of Cyrus stirring on his pallet, the smell of wet earth and fire ash, dampened to mud kept in this place. Zubaba said, "As you learned, it took a coalition of Babylonians and Medes to bring Ashurbanipal down. But that was still decades in the future."

"... when Cyaxares made that deal with the king of Babylonia, right?" Cyrus said.

"Yes, that a princess from Media would marry the crown prince of Babylonia. But that was still in a future no one could imagine, not least those assaulted by Ashurbanipal and his troops. My father, for one." Zubaba sighed. "Ashurbanipal claimed that from Susa he took 'People, male and female, children and adults, as well as every useful animal, countless as grasshoppers. I carried them all off to Assyria.' Of course, some died in the process."

A break in the wind made Zubaba's sudden silence especially

full. Cyrus waited. What was there to say in the face of it? The rain tapped more gently now, straight onto the peak of their shelter. Miles away, a peal of thunder died away in the night.

When Zubaba spoke again, his voice was low, resigned. "Some of those who died along the way from Susa north to the cities of Assyria were my father's family - his first, and as far as I could tell, most beloved. All of them, his wife and their children, too."

"But you survived?" Cyrus asked.

"Different wife, different children." Zubaba said. "There wasn't any 'me' then, not yet. And by then, he was a different man."

"Anyway." Zubaba sniffed. He ran his hands briskly across the tops of his thighs. "Of those still alive after the horrors of assault, Ashurbanipal didn't actually take everyone. He admitted as much, the liar, in his own words. Oh, it was terrible, catastrophic, and enormous the affect he had on Susa. And elsewhere. Plenty enough to seed his boasts with truth. But never enough as far as he was concerned. He claimed to have 'carried them all off.' But he didn't."

Cyrus could hear the grim smile on Zubaba's face. "Never had he captured the Elamite king. Never. Apparently it was too great a truth to deny. So, finally Ashurbanipal said it himself: that the Elamite king 'returned from the mountains where he had been hiding... and settled again. Of course he laced it with pride in the horror he caused. He said the king settled 'in grief, in that devastated place.' Still, for my father and others who had fought, who had lost so much, who had been forcibly removed to dwell as exiles in their conqueror's cities, it was small comfort, a bitter comfort, but comfort nonetheless: That the Assyrian lied about Susa's utter destruction."

"But what about you?" Cyrus asked.

"Me?" Startled, Zubaba looked in the direction of the boy. "I wasn't there. My father remarried. Much later. And even after I was born, I was there, in my father's world, only as audience to his lament, only as ... my father couldn't help his despair, couldn't control his rage. It took me a long time to understand, longer than the years he lived. Humiliation and grief are a terrible combination."

The wind had passed, and the rain outside was light. But Zubaba talked on.

"After Susa's defeat, only the desire for vengeance gave him purpose. So, when he learned that the Medes were planning an attack on the Assyrian capital of Nineveh in alliance with the Babylonians, he left us to join in the fight. Few people know that a ragged band of Elamites, my father included, signed on with the Medes to keep fighting.

"He had a new energy when he came home, a bright intensity fed by vengeance realized. One of his best moments, my father told me, was when the victorious troops stormed through the great palace at Nineveh, with no one to stop them. They passed what stood for beauty and truth... they passed the *lamassu*, those massive winged guardians part man, part bull without marring their serene faces or stone bodies. But when my father and his Elamite friends saw the wall carving of Ashurbanipal's garden feast, they took hammers and swords to it, defacing the image of the king and his royal retinue that Assyrian artists had labored so carefully to construct. They smashed in the only visages of their enemies that they could – images cut in stone.

"Victory hardly eased the painful memories, though, and even after his vengeance was satisfied, my father was eaten by the shame of his city's destruction. There had been no way to withstand Ashurbanipal, from all that I learned later. But that didn't matter to him. What mattered was that his home, the place he loved beyond love, the place that informed everything right and good for him had been violated beyond his imagining. Seventy years ago, when Ashurbanipal assaulted Susa, his troops went into the hidden groves, where only the initiated were allowed. They tore open the secret places and burned everything. Ashurbanipal forbade people to make offerings and boasted that he had made the deities powerless ghosts. My father was thirty years old. History demarcates such battles by days, months, or years; but they raged in my father for the rest of his life.

"Like I said, he settled in Media, took a Median wife (my mother), and served out his life in Astyages' army. I was born in Ecbatana, where on his better days, the best days I ever had with my father, he told me stories of Susa, stories of home. His eyes would go long and soft with remembering. That's when I knew it was safe to come close. I wanted to hear everything and over and over again. One thing, I could never quite imagine but have longed to experience for myself is the sweet taste of the water there. My father said that out of all the wonders of Susa and the spiritual richness of its sacred places, his favorite thing the simple and serene river Choaspes, something that he said even Assyrian filth couldn't defile. 'There's nothing like that water for its sweetness anywhere in the world,' my father would say. He drank from it every day." Zubaba's voice trailed off.

From the corner, Cyrus was quiet. Asleep, Zubaba figured. He rose quietly and lifted the tent flap. The rain had stopped, and the clouds moved on. The horses stood quiet in the moonlight, his horse's chin resting on the little mare's withers.

"I bet you wish we were going that way," Cyrus's voice sifted through the darkness.

Zubaba nodded. "One day." Then he turned and let the flap close again. He shook off the melancholy that had settled in his shoulders and face and said, "But we'll get you to Anshan much faster this way. To your father, to home."

Zubaba couldn't see the furrow that wrinkled Cyrus's brow or know the halting hope he held in his chest, the hope of family, the hope of home.

CHAPTER 34

*I*n the glistening new morning, as they resumed their southerly trek, Zubaba was happy to tell Cyrus that in the decades since Assyria's destruction of Elam, and Anshan's diminishment, both had had opportunity to recover. "I don't know the details about Anshan," Zubaba said. But they must be similar. After all, your father sent his one true princess there to marry your father, its king."

"So tell me about Susa, then," Cyrus said, "about Elam, whatever you can."

Zubaba nodded. "Over time, we came back -- smaller and weaker of course, and more a collection of bands than a unified nation. That's what I've been told, anyway. It wasn't enough for my father, who died before much if any restoration could take place. Besides, although Elamites such as he stayed on in Media, the Medes don't really deal with Elam now. It's just as well."

"What about those sacred places?" Cyrus asked.

Zubaba raised his eyebrows. The boy hadn't been asleep after all. "Well," he said, "It takes a long time – with both tending and restraint – to foster the growth of things like trees." They walked in the thick of tall trees, even now. Zubaba looked up and around at them, seeing them differently now. "I'd never much thought about what makes a place sacred, though," he admitted. "But I'm pretty sure that you can't just say it is to make it so. It takes time. A long time."

"And people have to notice, too," Cyrus said.

Zubaba laughed. "Something like that. Yes, I suppose so. As for Elam, they did rebuild temples for the gods. Probably the most important is Inshushinak. I'm not sure if his reach extends into Anshan. Anyway, my father spoke of him with longing, wishing that Ashurbanipal's Assyria fell within his range. You see, it's Inshushinak who weighs the souls of those who died. They – we – even call him 'the Weigher.' Inshushinak sees to it that justice is done – if not in this life, then in the next. Close to him is Lagamal, who dwells in the underworld. Now that one - Lagamal or Lagamar - does have an Assyrian reach. 'No mercy,' they call him.

"There's also a new temple for the goddess Pinigir, mother of the gods, with brilliantly glazed bricks. And I hear that they hope some time soon to restore the old palace."

"He never left," Cyrus asked, "the king, right?"

"Such as he could be called after Ashurbanipal laid waste to the place," Zubaba nodded. "And it's true that the king's officials, such as they are, remain. The administrative system of the Elamite kingdom was complex and multifaceted. That makes a thing much harder to undo. As time goes on, it becomes clearer that Ashurbanipal's victory was partial indeed. And life has gone on there, regardless."

* * *

IN THE DAYS THAT FOLLOWED, Cyrus was so full of questions for Zubaba about the region, Susa and Elam and about Anshan, of course – more than Zubaba could answer, that the man sometimes welcomed the stretches where the mountains forced them into single file, forced them into quiet again. Still, he enjoyed recounting what he could and Cyrus didn't care if he told the same things over and over again. And after they'd traveled for about ten days, Zubaba pointed to a high peak about 50 miles to the west. "That's Yellow Mountain," he told Cyrus. "the highest peak. About 100 miles on its other side is Susa."

In the coming days, traveling now through territory that had all been part of old Elam, they encountered no particular trouble, even as they passed through regions whose inhabitants proudly claimed affiliation with different chieftains and territories. Although they kept their interactions superficial and brief, they met Turukians, Markhashites, Kassites, and Ellippians. Zubaba remarked to Cyrus that it seemed there existed nothing like the central government that had defined Elam in the great days that Zubaba's father recounted. And apart from an occasional mansion in the Median style, there was little evidence of influence from the palace at Ecbatana. Cyrus found it refreshing, if foreign, and tried to soak it all in – closer and closer they were to his people, his home.

As the mountains tapered into foothills and those into broader stretches of flat, Zubaba regaled Cyrus with stories and descriptions of the bounty and variety of beauty and food that he would find in and around Anshan.

"Up north, in the mountains in and around Ecbatana, the growing season is short," Zubaba said. "Since it was all you ever knew, I'm sure it all seemed normal. And enough."

It was true.

"But here? The sun shines longer and warmer than ever could up there."

Cyrus let Zubaba's cheer infect him.

"Even now, in autumn, you'll see fields of all kinds of delicious grains, vineyards that produce massive amounts of grapes, and all sorts of other fruits besides. They get multiple harvests of vegetables each year, and lush fields fatten animals over more months than not. People herd flocks of sheep and goats, like you did. But there are all sorts of cattle. You'll see," Zubaba said. "Not as many horses as in Media. But you knew that, already. Watch for the ducks and geese. They're cultivated and wild, too. Some we'd never see around Ecbatana. And oh, the saffron. You think you've seen it..."

And Cyrus had – the little purple flowers whose spice only the palace ever tasted. The labor of harvesting its tiny threads plucked from the flower's center, only a few for each bloom, was extraordinary. It traded for gold among the merchants passing through.

"Great fields than you can imagine. They should be blooming now. They say the land looks like it's blanketed in purple snow."

As the pair got closer, Cyrus kept an eye out for these things.

Meanwhile, "Anshan," Zubaba explained, "is the name both of the city where Cyrus's father had his palace and of the general region in the fertile Kur river basin." Located on a high plain between foothills where the southernmost reaches of the Zagros Mountain chains give way to undulating wrinkles of land, Cyrus would come to see the region's remarkable fertility aided by many delicious rivers. "It's hard to beat," Zubaba said. "Even I, who has a special loyalty for the Susa of my people, have to admit. Anshan is without peer. Cooled by the mountains and warmed by the Persian gulf about a week's ride to the west, you're going to love it there."

For his part, Cyrus already did. The time and travel had let him leave behind some of the pain and betrayal that had worn at his young soul ever since Astyages had "found" him and taken him into the palace and whole new life. The loss of Mit and Spaco would never go away; but he saw the futility of wishing for his old life back. He told himself that had a father – a true father – and with time he came to believe that Cambyses, the father who awaited him, was indeed "a good man," as Zubaba had said.

Whatever the case, Cyrus thought, he had this place, a place he had already begun to love. When he lived in Media, in the cottage outside of the city, he had never felt he lacked for anything. He lived with the cold, the ice and snow simply a part of life – and the weather that had made the task of caring for the palace flocks an endless one. He had appreciated the mountains and all the wild things that grew and thrived among them. He had loved that land. And he still did. But, ah. Cyrus took a long breath. This was nice.

The sun was long and warm on his shoulders. Cyrus liked the way he could see for miles. He could see the long colors of the sky at sunrise, track clouds and birds and the changing light all day. He loved the brilliance of the land's sunsets offset against the rolling hills in all the colors of green and gold. And at night, to lie on his back and see the stars – so many! Without the rocky mountains blocking half his view from the verdant valley where his Median cottage had lain, he could see for himself the constellations that Zubaba pointed out twinkling across the sky.

* * *

THE RUGGED MOUNTAIN range that they had followed south slowly began to give way to softer hills until they came through a pass that entered a high, flat valley. Zubaba was eager to turn around and head for Susa, eager to see the land that he had heard so much about. Besides that, he was eager to collect the sum Astyages had promised him for seeing Cyrus safely to Cambyses in Parsa. But as the pair grew closer and closer to Anshan and the place he'd leave the child, he had to admit: he'd grown fond of the boy. He had seen Cyrus's excellence in the tutelage to which Harpagus had put him. And he knew that Cyrus had struggled to reconcile the loss of everything he'd known and loved to adjust to a completely different life in the palace at Ecbatana and then to be torn from and sent to live in the far less sophisticated and luxurious region of Parsa. It was a lot for a ten-year-old boy. And yet.

Zubaba glanced over at the Cyrus atop the horse who loved the boy with a singular devotion, loved only him. The child would be a prince here and one day king. Could it be, Zubaba wondered, that within this child who belongs nowhere, whose lineage is mixed and fraught, the gods have placed their *kitin*, with all its mysterious, numinous power? Special or not, Cyrus would indeed become leader of lands that bordered and bled into the territory that Zubaba always felt was his own.

So, in the evenings before sleep, Zubaba reiterated all he knew he helped Cyrus design and fashion a bow similar to his own -- crude, but with hints of every characteristic that lent excellence and beauty to the Elamite bow. And he approached the time they had remaining with a greater sense of urgency that Cyrus know about the Elam that once had been, about its relationship to Cyrus's new Anshan home, and about the New Elam that still could be.

They were close now. Assured of the bounty that awaited them, Zubaba and Cyrus finished what provisions they carried. Almost there. Cyrus looked and looked, eager to see the marvelous land of purple snow. And then they were there. Exactly thirty-five days after they had left Ecbatana, Zubaba drew them up to a stop. They had arrived on the high steppe where Anshan stood. Low foothills interrupted the plains around. Streams cut through from the north. But there were no crocuses blooming.

Neither said a word. Zubaba stared across the broad plain, toward the city that he knew had to be the place, the site of the capital and Cambyses's palace. Except for the rumble of his empty stomach, Cyrus was quiet beside him. Neither had expected to see a sprawling city or many-walled palace such as that in Ecbatana. But of the settlement ahead, some five hundred acres, judging from the remains of a modest encircling wall, there was no high palace, no particularly grand building at all. What was there, even from a distance showed disrepair. But perhaps most striking of all, there were no vast acres of diverse grains. There were no rows of grapevines to cover the hillsides, trees heavy with fall fruit, or people tending flocks and herds along the plains. A group of ducks troubled the air overhead; but they were wild, and their squawking sounded like alarm.

CHAPTER 35

$\mathcal{C}$yrus looked his question, filled with anxiety and dread, at Zubaba. Zubaba did not return his gaze. The man was clearly as surprised - and dismayed - as Cyrus. Where both had expected a vibrant community of people tending and enjoying a beautiful and fertile land, they saw only a few people stooped and moving slowly among acres and acres and acres of drooping flowers such as neither had seen before.

Finally, Zubaba took a deep breath and raised his eyebrows. "Let's get ourselves cleaned up," he said with a forced brightness, nodding to a small river that cut a valley across the way, "and ready you for your grand entrance." He chucked Cyrus's cheek lightly with a fist. "Mandane's son returned!" Zubaba said. "They'll be happy for certain to have you here."

They dismounted. Zubaba had insisted that Cyrus keep fresh a final change of clothes. Harpagus had explained – they were to be his best trousers and tunic, carefully packed for just this moment. After they'd bathed north of town as well as they could, Cyrus folded his soiled and dusty clothes and drew on the clean – a burgundy tunic of the lightest wool and trousers cut from skins so thin and soft they might have been parchment. He tucked the ends into his boots and groaned. They were so dirty. He slipped the boots off again, pulled a swath of loose fabric from his bag, spit on it, and rubbed them as clean as he could. Finally, he drew from the bottom of his sack a black panther pelt that Harpagus had insisted he take.

"Put it over your shoulder just so," Harpagus had told him. "And tuck it into your belt there. That, child, is the clothing of a king."

Fully dressed, Cyrus stood.

Zubaba grinned and nodded his approval.

Cyrus said, "It's ok?"

"Ok?!" Zubaba said, "My boy... Excuse me. My lord. You look every bit the prince that you were born."

"Thank you," Cyrus said, looking down, smoothing his tunic and brushing his trousers. "I'm nervous."

"Hey," Zubaba said, squatting down so that he could look Cyrus in the eye. "You have nothing to worry about. You are the long-lost son, son of the king, returned. You needn't be anything else. Everyone will be overjoyed to see you." He straightened up and scratched his head. "Astyages did send the news of your, um, discovery, did he not? And that you'd be coming to Anshan?"

"Yes. At least that's what Harpagus told me."

'Well, then. Like I said, you've got nothing to worry about." Zubaba clapped the child on his shoulder. "I hope you're hungry! I know I am," he laughed. "Prepare yourself for feasting ahead."

Cyrus stood still, staring at his horse. He looked up at Zubaba, who could not read the sober look on Cyrus's face.

"Let me hoist you up." Zubaba said. "The less you walk, the cleaner you'll stay."

"Do you think that we should groom the horses first?"

"No, I do not." Zubaba led the mare up next to Cyrus. He held out his hands, laced together, and nodded to Cyrus to step into them. "I think that we should go."

Cyrus hesitated. Now that they were here. And that the place was so different than what he had expected – than what he had anticipated – Cyrus wasn't sure he wanted to go forward. But. Where else was he going to go? He took a deep breath, stepped into the sling of Zubaba's hand, and swung up into the saddle. His horse gave a little snort and pulled her head up and down against the harness – no bridle, no bit – that neither Cyrus nor Zubaba had ever replaced.

"See, your little friend is eager to get to her new home," Zubaba said.

When Zubaba had mounted and they had urged the horses on at a slow walk, Cyrus said, "We are near, right? I mean, that's the city just up ahead?"

"As far as I know, yes."

"Shouldn't someone come to meet us?" Cyrus asked. "Even just to see who we are, and why we're coming?"

Zubaba didn't have an answer. So he said, "I don't know. But that doesn't mean anything. There are a thousand reasons – good reasons… Maybe it's so peaceful here that they no one worries. And maybe everyone is busy…"

Neither had the heart to speak what he really thought.

PART II

(PARSA, CA. 570 B.C.E.)

CHAPTER 36

The flower heads were large, their petals papery, white on the rims and gradually pinker as they yielded to a black center eye. Green tufted bulbs bent over like shy children. Here and there stood spheres of hard pale green seed pods. Cyrus and Zubaba rode slowly toward the city's mudbrick walls, silently through the pearly pink field, crushing flowers under the horse's hooves.

"Poppies," Zubaba said. "I've heard..." He leaned over his horse's neck to look more closely. Many of the seed pods bore straight scars, nicked in shallow lines. He shook his head slightly, frowning, and said again, "Poppies."

Even after they'd entered the city gates, no one approached them. In truth there were hardly any people there at all. Apart from furtive eyes ducking behind doors or the occasional person pushing a cart or hustling a child along, they talked to no one. And no one talked to them.

They rode the final stretch slowly and straight up to the palace's gate. Still, no one came to meet them. Finally, just when they decided to enter anyway, a young man hurried out from around a corner. He bent to catch his breath. When Zubaba explained who they were, he straightened again, his face bright with delight.

"Oh, yes, right! The name's Martiya." He put a hand to his chest. "Member of the guard." More quietly he added, "In training for it, anyway... Upadarma's son." Bright again, he said, "You can dismount, here. Follow me."

As they crossed the threshold, leading their horses, Cyrus turned back. One of the gate's great doors hung askew. And the stone on which it turned was cracked wide open. Cyrus and Zubaba walked slowly even when Martiya jogged ahead.

After passing through the modest walls, the central palace lay straight ahead. It sat up a little higher than the other buildings around but nothing like the ostentatious monument that marked Media's throne. The street was very quiet. Martiya had disappeared around a corner. Cyrus sidled closer to Zubaba.

Zubaba walked straight and tall, looking neither left nor right. But Cyrus took it all in. A flash of motion from a near doorway drew Cyrus's eye. He could have sworn a child had been there moments before. Again, a flash of movement, the hem of a woman's robe? Suddenly, a skinny cat darted between Cyrus's legs. Both cat and boy yelped in surprise. Cyrus's horse snorted as the cat dashed away.

Finally, from a dark doorway in the palace wall, Martiya reemerged with a sallow-faced man.

"My father, Upadarma, the palace groom," Martiya said by way of introduction. The man approached, a limp hitching his steps. To both Cyrus and Zubaba's surprise, Cyrus's horse didn't put up any resistance when the man took the reins of both horses with a sober nod and walked away. Cyrus watched the narrow haunches of his mare disappear, stirring up dust around her hocks like the fringe on a skirt. Cyrus looked up at Zubaba, who shrugged with a grin. Cyrus relaxed just a little. It must be a good sign, a sign that yes he really did belong here.

That's what he told himself. But the shock of seeing no crops or activity like Cyrus had imagined and the undeniable poverty of the palace itself left Cyrus feeling numb with despair. Only the thought of his father, his real father King Cam, meeting the man everyone said was good – Zubaba was sure of it – kept Cyrus's feet moving forward. They didn't regain the bounce they'd developed in the preceding days. But he did recognize a happy anticipation in his belly.

The main palace entrance was marked by double doors. Slender with the bright energy of youth, Martiya pushed lightly on wide clay knobs and swung open the doors. As he strode past, again Cyrus noticed their disrepair. Knobs fired in the shape of rosettes and set into tiles with raised petals in each corner, they must have been beautiful. Once. But the glazing, chipped and cracked, had dulled. And some of the squares had come loose from their setting, fallen out and broken on the ground. Cyrus stepped carefully over the shards and through the double-doors.

They walked into a small, rectangular room - the palace's entry hall for public audiences. By contrast to the palace in Ecbatana, it was tiny and almost completely bare. Cyrus scuffed his toe against the ground. Its floor was only dirt.

A rough wooden bench ran along each of the hall's short sides. Martiya motioned to them to sit there. "If you'll just wait a moment..." he said and then was gone again.

Cyrus stared. Who could sit at a moment such as this? he wondered.

CHAPTER 37

*T*hey waited and waited. Cyrus had to relieve himself but straightened his back and tried to be still. Finally, just when the boy considered asking where he might pee, he heard movement from the door that led inside the palace. The scuff of shuffling feet brought an old man, gaunt and grizzled, leaning on the arm of broad man, grizzled in the face, but tender in the circumstance.

"King Cam of Anshan," the man announced, which made the king start with surprise. Then they continued their slow march forward, the strong man matching his footsteps to the king's.

Cyrus stared in dismay. Was this decrepit man his father?

When Zubaba elbowed him in the side, Cyrus saw that Zubaba had stood. Cyrus rose slowly to his feet. Then he followed Zubaba's lead and bowed.

The only thing distinguishing the old man as king was a thin tarnished band of bronze or gold, uneven in thickness, that ran around his brow. When he had jumped, it had slipped, and now hung at an angle, nearly covering one eye. A thin line of spittle hung from the corner of the king's mouth. Cyrus stared, fascinated with disgust as the line of spit widened at the base until its tiny ball dropped, and the line fell back against the man's stubbled chin.

Cyrus caught his breath. The old man didn't seem to notice.

Despite Zubaba's discrete cough, despite his shifting on his feet beside Cyrus, Cyrus stared. Back in Ecbatana, in that grand palace, Cyrus had finally seen his own face. He had looked into a mirror for the first time. So it was that now Cyrus could see that this man and he had the same square jaw, the same arc of a strong nose, the same high chest. He felt sick. Suddenly he smelled the acrid scent of urine. Cyrus whimpered. His face flushed red. But it wasn't him. It was the king. Cyrus watched, horrified as the king's robe darkened at the front.

The guard whispered something into Cam's ear.

The old man nodded and mumbled, "My steward... you... rooms."

At least that's what Cyrus thought he heard.

The guard opened his mouth to say something to the travelers, then appeared to think better of it, pursed his lips, and helped the old man back out. The pair disappeared in a kind of stumbling dance through the same doorway they had so recently entered.

* * *

"THAT'S MY FATHER?" Cyrus's voice was laced with panic. He looked up at Zubaba with wide eyes. "Was that King Cam? My father Cambyses?" His tone rose until it bordered on hysterical.

Zubaba grimaced. He laid his arm around the boy's shoulders. Cyrus turned into him then, burying his face in the guide's tunic. Then, as the boy sobbed, Zubaba smoothed and patted Cyrus's shoulders. They stood like that for a long time, until Cyrus's sobs petered out. Still, the room was empty. No one – not steward, or guard, or even groom – had arrived to lead them to their rooms.

Finally, Cyrus looked up at Zubaba, wiped his eyes, and said, "I have to go."

Zubaba looked down and shook his head. "This is where you're supposed to be," he said.

"I mean…" Cyrus crossed his legs.

"Oh," Zubaba said. "Come on," and they walked out the way that they had come. The street was as quiet as the hall. Zubaba thrust his chin toward the wall across from the palace. "This is fine, my lord."

The boy's thin line of water was the only thing that moved on the dusty street.

"Don't call me that," Cyrus said.

"What?"

"My lord."

"I just thought… now that you're here."

"Here?" Cyrus said. He closed his eyes tight and shook his head.

"Okay. Well. We have to go back in. I'll ask that man where we might find the steward. And something to eat."

Cyrus had completely forgotten his hunger. Given how his stomach felt now, full of knots, it was hard to imagine he could ever eat again.

"Things will look better when we've eaten and drunk," Zubaba said.

Cyrus only nodded and followed Zubaba back out the way they'd come. The doors were still open, just as they'd left them. Suddenly he stopped. Cyrus stood on the threshold, utterly defeated. "I miss my parents," he said, "Ma and Pop."

Zubaba turned the boy to face him and knelt down. He inhaled through clenched teeth. There was no easy way to say this. "This is the only parent you have, Cyrus," Zubaba said. "He may not be what you wanted or what we expected, but he is your father, and he is a king." Cyrus looked down. "And you are the prince who will succeed him." Zubaba shook the boy's shoulders gently. "Listen to me, now. You cannot think of what you were. That is over and done. Focus on who you are and will become."

"But back home…" Cyrus's voice broke. "With Spaco and Mit, I…"

"Shh, shh," Zubaba said. "This is your home now. You must make this your home. These are your people here."

Cyrus swallowed hard. How could he explain? He didn't have the words. Home was gone.

"And remember that they are related to my people. The culture of Elam, of Susiana and Anshan is a rich one and the people fine and strong. You and I have only just arrived in this place. There is much more to learn about it and about your life here. It will be better."

"I want to see my horse."

"Your horse!" Zubaba grinned. "How she walked away with that groom… She is fine. We'd know if it's different."

Cyrus's stomach growled again. He bit his lower lip, set his jaw, and nodded. Zubaba dropped his hands, and Cyrus walked back through the door.

CHAPTER 38

$\mathcal{A}$s soon as they entered the audience hall, the guard who had brought Cam hurried through the far door where they'd last seen him escorting the frail king away. He strode up to them, bowed deeply to Cyrus, and said, "Welcome, my lord."

"Thank you," Cyrus said softly.

"The name's Nahhunte," he said. A heavy lock of hair dropped over his right eye. He pushed it back with rough hands, then swung them gesturing around the room. "Sorry to say there is presently no steward of the palace. I'm it, I guess. I'll show you to the rooms where you'll be staying. You can stay wherever you like, of course," he added, correcting himself. "But we did prepare a suite for you for the time being. I hope you'll like it well enough. Oh, and if you want to settle your guide in another part of the palace --"

"It's Zubaba. He'll stay with me," Cyrus said.

The guard looked relieved. "This way, then."

"The king's quarters," Nahhunte gestured to the rooms adjacent the audience hall. "Except for this one." He slowed outside a door like all the rest. "It was Shahbanu Mandane's – your mother, the queen," Nahhunte said softly. "All but closed off after she died.

No one... well, almost no one has gone in since." Nahhunte cleared his throat roughly and led on.

They passed through another door. It led into a short hallway, flanked by two small rooms. Through the hallway, they stepped into a large rectangular courtyard open to the sky. A covered corridor ran around the courtyard's perimeter. The timber roof was supported by columns, which stood at graceful intervals all around. In the fresh air, with the big sky above, Cyrus stopped and took a deep breath. He felt the tightness in his chest loosen a bit.

Nahhunte said, "This courtyard, whose corners point in the four cardinal directions, is the central piece of the palace, itself built on a foundation hundreds of years old. Your mother... Mandane..." He spoke her name tenderly. "She liked it here." The guard looked around as they did. "Nice isn't it?" Without waiting for a reply, he added, "Well, apart from the trees and shrubs," he gestured to the twiggy collection struggling to survive. "And the pool, I guess. Things have gotten a little..." His voice died away. He didn't need to finish to the thought. The scene spoke for itself.

Green algae nearly covered the surface of a small central pool. The space hinted of past beauty. But once-ordered pathways were overgrown, and the plants scraggly. Clucking guinea hens and skinny chickens wandered busily about, pecking invisible grubs and seeds.

"And the chickens." Nahhunte tilted his head, studying them as if the sight were entirely new. "Shouldn't be in a palace court-yard, should they? Funny the things you see differently." He paused. "Anyway, the courtyard defines the shape and layout of the entire complex. This corridor makes a nice transition from outside to inside and cools the suites around the perimeter. Yours is this way." Nahhunte walked to the northeast end where he slipped through a doorway. He poked his head back out. "This way."

Cyrus and Zubaba followed the guard through an empty

room and then entered a small square room set with a wooden table and two wooden chairs right in the middle. A long, shallow dish was set in the middle filled with dusky green sprigs dotted with tiny pale blue flowers. Cyrus walked up and looked closer.

"Rosemary," the guard said. "Cook put it there. She's very... Well, you'll see for yourself soon enough.

"Now." Nahhunte planted his feet, facing the table and the door through which they had just come. "To my left is a room for the guide, Zubaba. Besides a bed, you'll find a basin and a pitcher of water for drinking or washing. You probably saw the river coming into town. We are never short of water, though it does require some effort to get it here. Nothing for you to worry about. To my right, the prince's quarters, for the time being anyway -- a bedroom and two small rooms connected to that. In one, washing tools and whatnot. In the other, a chest of drawers and a rack on which to keep your robes. I think Cook put some citron in there, too. Keeps the moths away and smells good, too."

"Oh, I know them," Cyrus said. "We do, or did, the same in Media."

Nahhunte smiled revealing teeth so crowded they overlapped. "Through here," he gestured behind him and then followed his arm out the far door. To the right was another small, empty room and through that, a latrine. A simple hole in the floor surrounded by beige ceramic tile served for a toilet. He pushed back the hair that had fallen over his eye again. "Well, that's probably enough for now. Unless you have questions?"

Zubaba and Cyrus looked at each other. It was hardly a kingly palace. They looked back at him and shook their heads.

"No? All right," Nahhunte went on. He looked around. "Martiya should have brought your things from the horses." Then, seeing their few bundles stacked neatly in a corner, "I hope you'll find everything that you need. Look for me, if not. And, let's see..." He brushed his right hand absently over his head. "Oh! Dinner. Your father is eager to share your first meal here together," he said, as if willing that it should be so. "We have dinner in a long room attached to the kitchen. You can find it by going straight back to the courtyard." He turned and pointed. "Take a hard right. It's in the west, northwest section of the palace. And... well... do try to arrive when the sun dips below the southwest corner of the palace. Easy to see from the courtyard. Cook is quite particular."

"Thank you," Zubaba said. "We'll be there."

CHAPTER 39

*C*yrus walked into the rooms that the guard had said were his. The bedroom was larger than he had expected. In the far wall to his left were two windows that looked directly onto the corridor running around the courtyard. Shutters pulled back on the inside let a breeze into the room. Like the rest of the palace, it was sparsely furnished. But it was clean. Against one window was a tiny tile-topped table. A round stool was pushed neatly underneath. On the table was a ceramic bowl filled with fresh sweet lemons. Some had leaves, which were still bright green. Cyrus picked one up, its thin skin smooth in his hand, its weight comforting. He bobbed it up and down as he peered into the empty courtyard, tossed the lemon into the other hand, and let it roll off his fingers back into the bowl. It released a sweet smell that evaporated almost before Cyrus noticed.

A wooden palette raised the thick ticking of a mattress off the floor. Posts on each corner of the bed rose several feet and supported slim horizontal beams on which linen curtains hung nearly to the floor. Cyrus looked more closely. Into the posts were carved twining vines. Streaks of green paint hung on in random patches and streaks. Most had chipped away, but Cyrus could make out pink and white areas that must have been flowers. Two pillows rested on the end abutting a wall. An undyed linen sheet lay folded neatly at the other end. Cyrus perched on an edge. A waft of lavender rose up. The linen covering was thick and seemed to enclose a filling of hay or maybe it was pure lavender flowers. The scent was strong but lifted straight away.

Cyrus sat further back and leaned against his hands, looking up. Rectangular holes, each a few inches square, dotted the opposite wall high against the ceiling at regular intervals. Cyrus noticed similar cut-aways along the floor on the courtyard wall and opposite. These were covered with wooden panels carved into a fine mesh.

"Air in, snakes and scorpions out," Zubaba had told him about this. Cyrus shivered.

He walked into a small adjacent room. The washing table was covered in tiles glazed white with blue swirling through like the sky on a cloudy day. Some of the tiles were cracked, and a gouging chip marred the side against the wall. But again it was clean. Besides the empty basin waiting for water and the rough clay pitcher that held it, a small wooden bowl sat filled with herbs and pastel, thumb-scooped rose petals. Cyrus suddenly missed the mother he had never known. It was a surprising and strange feeling, but not unpleasant.

Cyrus's mind darted to Spaco and Mit with a twinge of guilty betrayal. The cottage was always clean and tidy, but Spaco would as soon have thought to decorate it as she would have thought of riding a charger to the moon. Cyrus poured water into the basin, leaned in close, and splashed it up over his face: once, twice, he ran his hands down over his eyes, three times, he wiped his eyes then his chin as he raised his head and reached for a rectangular linen cloth, neatly stitched around the edge in the same undyed thread, and lifted it to his face. He held it there, feeling the wetness soak through. He pressed it against his eyes. His breath pushed the cloth away from his mouth and pulled it back again.

"Ah, good. I see you're cleaning up."

Cyrus jumped.

Zubaba stood in the bedroom. "Nice room. And I'm guessing that your clothes and things are all put away. Mine were. I appreciate that. Anyway, good to see you found the water. The sun is getting close to its dinner spot. You can see from here." He walked over to the little table at the window. "Are you ready?"

Cyrus didn't answer. Ready didn't matter.

CHAPTER 40

They walked slowly through the rooms and back out into the central courtyard. Heavy blocks of shadow cast from the walls darkened much of the space. Cyrus stopped and squinted his eyes against the spindly shrubs, the chickens, the foul pool. A bird squealed overhead, startling the boy into looking up just as a hook-nosed vulture flapped its ragged wings and disappeared over the wall. The hens' clucking escalated in distress.

Cyrus walked on, Zubaba beside him. Cyrus tripped on the legs of a broken old bench. It sat, partly hidden by the broken limb of a tiny tree. He caught himself before Zubaba grabbed his arm. Cyrus choked on a sob. Zubaba said, "I think it's this way," putting his arm around the boy's shoulders. Zubaba guided him along a paved pathway, barely discernible for the weeds and dust that had accumulated over it.

Cyrus shrugged off Zubaba's arm, sniffed, and said, "I think I can smell the way, now." He looked up at his guide with a wan smile.

They passed through a door midway along the northwest side of the corridor. A few steps in, they caught a glimpse of the kitchen through another door to their left. A fire flared up, making Cyrus jump, then disappeared as quickly back into the stove, where a woman stood with her back to them. Sweat made her tunic cling to a broad back. Her gray hair was collected into a knot on the top of her head. Wisps stood out at random. She brushed the back of her hand against her forehead and hollered to someone just out of sight, "the bread! Get the bread! And cover the cheese, by the grace of the gods. Would you rather feed flies than a prince?"

"It's best not to look too closely at what's happening in there." A low voice said.

Cyrus and Zubaba started as if caught spying and walked toward Nahhunte. As they went, Cyrus peered back into the kitchen. Long pale strands dusted with a fine powder hung from a high wooden dowel off one wall like a dozen dozing snakes.

"How did you find your quarters?" Nahhunte looked at Cyrus.

Cyrus tore his eyes away. "Fine, sir."

The guard laughed. "Don't 'sir' me, my lord. You're the 'sir' here. You and your father the king, that is. Speaking of which, just go through that door there, and you'll find the dining hall." He hesitated. "The place where we eat."

Cyrus knit his brows and nodded at him.

"I'll fetch Cam."

Cyrus looked up at Zubaba, who shrugged. They walked on as Nahhunte had directed and entered at one end of a long room. Two chairs were pulled up against the wall of the door they passed through. The other chairs, ten, were set around a single long table. Another tall table, on which were two heavy pitchers, stood pushed up against the near wall on the left. The room was most peculiar.

Only half of it was a room; the other half was a covered patio. No wall or door separated the two. Cyrus walked forward as if in a daze and entered the light of the setting sun. From the far end of the table, he could look directly outside. In the foreground was a tidy little garden of herbs, vegetables, and flowers. Along its far edge, a few fruit trees stood like brave sentinels --lemon and lime trees were bright with fruit, a showy pomegranate sported brilliant orange flowers and leather-skinned fruits. Beyond the distant, crumbling, city wall the great orange ball of the sun hung just above the horizon. High clouds caught shades of apricot and pink. The Zagros foothills to his right, toward the north, had turned a purple-green. A breeze lifted the pale linen runner from the side table and whistled through a wide door near it.

"You call this chopped?" a voice blared through. "Now hurry up. I won't have fronds of dill slapping the poor boy's chin. And have you shelled the pistakas? Remember, *chop* them! Little pieces. Little, like the pebbles in your head."

"Hey-ey!" he heard a protesting voice answer and crack in its register. Then the door swung shut.

Cyrus turned to look for Zubaba's reaction and saw Upadarma limp in. Martiya followed close behind. They bowed to Cyrus then stepped aside. Behind them, Nahhunte appeared with the king on his arm. Cam wore the same slim band around his brow, but it was polished -- gold -- and he was clean-shaven this time. Still, his steps were halting and his free arm waved erratically with each step, lending him a disheveled air despite the bright robe and clean shoes. He looked behind every so often, as if expecting someone. But there was no one else. Zubaba bowed to him and Upadarma and Martiya followed suit.

"Come here, boy," the king said in a querulous voice, looking at Cyrus.

Cyrus stepped forward slowly.

The king dropped the guard's arm and immediately stumbled. He caught himself and straightened. "Closer," he said.

Cyrus stepped forward again. He began to bow but Cam reached out, cupping Cyrus's chin and lifting his face. The king wobbled, making Cyrus's head bob and turn a little. They stood like this for a long moment. Cyrus still didn't move when the king wobbled again, more strongly this time, pulling the boy's head this way and that. Zubaba stepped forward and without thinking took the king's other arm to steady him. No one stopped him. They were staring at the king, transfixed.

Cam slowly ran his index finger over Cyrus's lower lip, tracing its full swoop.

Cyrus watched the king's eyes fill with tears. They dropped down his cheeks in two lines that caught the light of the setting sun.

"Mandane," Cam said. "Like Mandane." Suddenly, his face clouded, and he pulled his hand back from Cyrus's face. "But not her." His voice grew louder. "Not her!" His swung his arm awkwardly. Cyrus ducked. "Liar! Thief!" Spittle flew. "Guards!"

Nahhunte stepped up swiftly and seized Cam' free arm. Zubaba grabbed the other and glanced with wide eyes across the king's head to the guard.

The guard spoke quietly but firmly into the king's ear. "This," he said, "is your son. This is Mandane's son, long lost whom we all had thought was dead. It is no fault of the boy's, my lord. Now, he has come to us from far away. He has come home. Your son is home."

Cam slumped against the men's arms, and Cyrus backed away quietly, exactly as Mit had taught him should he chance upon a wounded animal.

Nahhunte nodded to Zubaba and gestured with his chin to the table. Together, the men led the decrepit king to the near end, pulled out the chair, and eased the old man down. The guard motioned Cyrus to take the seat to the king's left with a view out at the softening sky. Cyrus shyly pulled the chair as far from his father as he could without drawing attention to it. Nahhunte sat to the king's right. The others quickly took places around the table.

Cyrus had been hungry before. He and Zubaba had shared a small breakfast at dawn. It was nearly the last of their supplies, and they hadn't hunted or stopped to gather the nuts that clustered on the trees they passed. Zubaba had been so confident that there would be a great feast on their arrival that they had simply hurried on. That breakfast seemed ages ago. Yet now Cyrus didn't think he could ever eat again. His stomach was all tight and tangled.

CHAPTER 41

They didn't have to wait long. From a wide door behind
the table where Cyrus sat, a boy two or three years
older than Cyrus, his face spotted with acne, hurried out carrying
a tray. Limpid steam rose from small bowls in thin wisps and
quickly evaporated in the breeze. Cyrus looked across at Zubaba,
who couldn't hide his disappointment. An insipid soup would be
just the kind of thing people would eat in such a place, his
expression suggested.

The boy – "Cook's nephew," Nahhunte explained, "doesn't like
to speak" – zigzagged down the table starting with the king, then
to Cyrus, on to Zubaba, and then the rest, setting small bowls in
front of each person and in front of the four empty chairs, too.
The soup looked cloudy and thin. The king raised the bowl to his
lips and shut his eyes. The guard nodded to Cyrus to do the same.
The others waited, so Cyrus made as if to drink like his father
had done.

The broth crossed Cyrus's lips with a nutty aroma. He sipped
then swallowed, lowered the bowl, and sighed. A little salty, but it
had substance -- meaty and redolent of bread -- lightened with

something green. He drank again deeply. Soft beans -- white, red, and tiny brown lentils -- rocked to the bottom of the bowl. Finely chopped herbs of the brightest green floated to the top. Suddenly, Cyrus stifled a shriek. He pushed the bowl away, nearly spilling it. There, swimming inertly in the remaining broth were opaque, beige strands - long white worms?! He looked up just as Cam fished them out with his fingers and dropped them into his mouth, sucking and smacking his lips.

"Welcome, Prince!" A ringing voice saved Cyrus from watching it all again. The stout, gray-haired woman from the kitchen stood in the doorway, her hands on her hips. She grinned at Cyrus as she strode forward and pulled up the empty chair to his left. "May I, my lord?" she asked. She sat heavily, not waiting for an answer. Her nephew quietly took another of the empty chairs. Cook drank from her bowl, smiled at Zubaba over its rim, and set it down.

"Wine!" Cam said. "Where is the wine? Bring wine!"

The cook's smile evaporated from her face.

No one moved.

"It's coming, my lord," the cook said, her face grim.

Then, the woman grinned. She put a thick arm around Cyrus's shoulder and pulled the boy toward her, dragging him half out of his chair in a strong embrace. Cyrus found his face squashed up against her bosoms. "Oh, child." She pushed him away, studying him, "It is good to see you. Just like your mother," she said. "And your father, too. That nose! No messing with you."

She leaned forward, pushing Cyrus back against his chair so that she could face Cam. "Looks like you, too, King Cam!" she shouted toward the old man.

Cam nodded, preoccupied with retrieving a fat red bean from the bottom of the bowl.

"Like you and your beautiful bride!" she shouted again. The king ignored her. She turned back to Cyrus, "Did you find everything in your room to be all right, clean, comfortable? Do you like it? Enough air? We can change anything. But is it all right for now? Do you like it?"

"Yes, ma'am," he said when she took a breath.

"Oh, my!" She said, sitting back, her mouth wide in exaggerated astonishment, revealing a few missing molars toward the back. She looked around the table. "Manners! This child has manners." Then she leaned toward Cyrus conspiratorially and said, "That's a good thing in a prince. It's a good thing in a king."

Nahhunte explained, "It was Cook who put the special touches in your room."

She waved her hand. "Nothing. Such small things. I hope it's pleasant enough."

"Yes, thank you," Cyrus said.

"The r-r-r-rosemary is from our kitchen garden out back," Cook's nephew said as he finished his soup.

Next to him, Nahhunte leaned back and listened as if in surprise.

"The herbs and roses, too," Cook's nephew continued. "And the sweet lemons come from what's l-l-left of the palace orchards."

Nahhunte looked at Cook, who raised her eyebrows and shrugged. He laid an arm across the back of Cook's nephew's chair and said to him, "It's nice to hear your voice, child." To the others, he said, "Gets a bit stutter-y when he's nervous."

The boy's face flushed and he dipped his head with embarrassment even as a small grin lifted the edges of his mouth.

"Rosemary means loyalty." Cam spoke, his voice clear and true, then licked his fingertips and looked longing at the bottom of his empty bowl.

"He's right, of course," Nahhunte said. "Cook was here when your mother came as a shy young bride to Anshan. And even after your mother..." He bit his lip.

"I want wine!" Cam shouted, bringing a fist down on the table.

Again, no one moved.

"In time," Cook said to the king.

The guard went on, "Even after we knew that your mother was dead, Cook refused to leave. She turned down a lot of suitors in her younger years. Loved your mother, she did. The most prominent chieftains of the region still try to woo her away to work for them..."

Cook flapped her hand at the guard, "Shush."

"But she won't go -- says she'll take care of this family as long as they'll have her. Until yesterday, that was only King Cam." Nahhunte smiled. "And he can't seem to get rid of her."

Cyrus involuntarily looked down into his bowl with its spooky strands.

"She makes all the ordinary, traditional things," the guard went on. "But she creates new things, too. Like this. He reached into his own bowl and drew out a strand. "She makes these from the wheat that grows well around here. The grain makes poor bread. They say you have to mix it with others to get a rise. Cook took that as a challenge. She grinds it very fine, or rather her nephew does," he said nodding to the quiet, pimply-faced boy, "and somehow turns them into these long pieces of dough. They are delicious." He nodded to Cyrus's bowl.

Cyrus tried not to grimace as he reached in and pulled one out.

"Works best if you kind of dangle it like this," the guard tilted his head back a little and lowered the strand into his mouth. He chewed contentedly. "Go on," he said, the words muddled.

Cyrus did. The flavor was subtle and rich, infused with the flavors of the broth, beans, and herbs, but with a delicate taste all its own. He reached in for more and quickly finished the noodles. His hunger had returned. The bowl was so small. He picked it up and sipped the last few drops.

"You like it?" Cook asked.

"Yes, ma'am, very much."

"It's delicious," Zubaba added.

Cook nodded, her heavy chin alternately flat and round like a ball of dough kneaded against her neck. "Now," she said, turning to Cyrus. "Tell us! How did this come to pass?"

Cyrus looked at her blankly.

"How did you come to be alive, all this time, and now here?"

Even Cam quit his restless fidgeting to hear the story.

Cyrus put aside his thoughts of the soup and began to tell what he'd only just learned himself. No one noticed, so enrapt they were, when the king quit listening and began craning his neck, looking around expectantly. It was just as well.

Cyrus told them of his years with the slave herders as good ones, that even if they had kept him for their own, they were good to him. Zubaba said nothing to contradict him. How much Cyrus missed them, he didn't share, nor how confused he felt about their hiding his identity from him. It was finally an account filled with praise for Mit and Spaco, whose name he explained means "dog." Years later, Cyrus would hear it whispered among the lands of Anshan that he had been saved from exposure by a real, wild dog. She, a formidable beast with strong white teeth and a gray-black coat, had suckled and raised him. It was too good a story to dispute.

In the silence that followed, Cook gestured to the pimply faced boy to pick up the bowls.

Cyrus wrapped his hand around his bowl. "Is there more?" Cyrus asked quietly.

"Hah!" Cook's breasts bounced. "Is there more?!" She looked at Zubaba, who ducked his head. "Oh, child," she said. "I knew I'd like you. There is more, all right."

Cyrus loosened his grip on the bowl and let the boy take it away.

Cook stood up from the table. Her eyes went to the doorway and her entire demeanor changed. It was as if she had risen several feet, a tower of fury. "Oh, no," she said, looking over

Cyrus's head to a newcomer beyond. In an instant, her smile had transformed into a terrifying glare. "Not for you. Don't you even think about it!" she called.

The object of her anger was a man, red-faced with bloodshot eyes. He stood, one hand on the doorframe, and swayed. "Aw, shut up," he said, letting go.

CHAPTER 42

*P*ropelled on unsteady feet, the newcomer made his way to one of the two empty chairs, the one with a bowl of soup still waiting. He pulled the chair out slowly, concentrating hard as if he were fetching a burning lamp brimming with oil.

"You're late!" Cook yelled even as she nodded fiercely to the boy to remove the soup. Before he could, the man swiped for it. He hit the boy's arm sending the warm broth hurtling to the floor. Somehow the bowl didn't break. The boy hurried the tray away into the kitchen.

"Ack!," Cook exclaimed. "Lucky to get anything, you are," she said as she bustled back into the kitchen.

When the boy returned with a linen rag to mop the spill, "Tell her not to poison my grub," the man said. Then with a cruel laugh. "If you can sp-sp-sp speak."

He looked around for others to share in the joke. No one did. The man's eyes stopped on Cyrus. Cyrus froze in the man's piercing glare. The man leaned over Cook's empty place, his face inches in front of Cyrus's. Cyrus cringed at his foul breath.

"So here's the little lord, the prince returned." The man made a show of bowing, his forehead hitting the table. He looked long at Cyrus with hard eyes and then sat back in his chair. "What's in that pitcher, there?" the man demanded, pointing to the tall table against the wall.

"Wine!" Cam said. "Bring the wine. Let's drink."

"As you command, my lord," the man slurred loudly, getting up.

"That," Nahhunte said to Cyrus, "Is Sadeghi. Or so he says," Nahhunte added in a low voice. "Though he's anything but."

Honest, Cyrus remembered. That's what the name Sadeghi means.

They watched as the man peered and then lowered his nose into the tops of the pitchers, sniffing first one and then the other. He grinned at the second, grabbed it, and stumbled back to the table, sloshing as he went. Purple liquid landed in soft splats on the floor.

"Cups. Who forgot the cups?" he roared. "Cook!"

"Sit, Sadeghi," Nahhunte said with quiet intensity. "The cups will come in time."

"No cups?! Well, my king," Sadeghi said, resting his elbow on the corner of the table, leaning in to Cam, his rear end to Cyrus, "Looks to me like this is one great big cup. Fit for a king, if you ask me," he said, contemplating the pitcher. He held its rim up to the king's lips and tipped it back. Cam swallowed and reached for the pitcher. Wine ran down his chin and soiled his tunic like weak blood as he took great gulps.

The guard stood up and led Sadeghi forcefully back to his chair.

"Sit," Nahhunte said in a low voice, "and stay there."

Sadeghi stuck out his lower lip and then brightened as the kitchen door swung open again. Cook's nephew balanced a plate on his arm -- fresh sliced cucumbers flecked with dill. In his hand was a shallow basket of fragrant flat bread piled high. In the other hand, he held a wide dish heaped with fresh herbs and tiny purple and white onions, their long green stems blending into the herbs like tiny spears. Sliced radishes peeked red out of the mix. He placed them in the middle of the table and rushed back into the kitchen.

The old groom, who had sat still and quiet as stone until now, jostled his son, who leapt up to help. Martiya returned with a tray of shallow drinking cups of pale blue glass, two small bowls each containing a tiny mound of rock salt, and another larger filled with snow white yogurt. He set out the salt and yogurt, distributed the cups, and returned to the kitchen.

The other boy deposited a steaming platter of eggplant cooked with plump dark raisins and chives, glistening with oil, and a shallow bowl of chickpeas swimming in a yellow broth with the delicate fragrance of saffron. The youths returned again, one carrying a large wooden-handled carving knife, a double-pronged spike, and a carafe of sesame oil, all of which he set down next to Cyrus. In Martiya's hands was a broad plate of chicken pieces braised with onion, plums, and lemon, all sprinkled with parsley.

"Mmmmm," Zubaba hummed. He inhaled deeply, "A feast, a real feast,"

"Not yet," Cook said, entering the room just then. "This makes a feast."

In front of Cyrus she lowered a platter on which a spit-roasted leg of lamb lay nestled in a smoky red sauce redolent of pomegranate and fig. A streak of bright green paste ran in a line down the meat's length. The whole was surrounded by roasted garlic cloves and rosemary sprigs.

"I see you found the wine," she said, pursing her lips and shaking her head at the late-comer. She retrieved the other pitcher. "Water," she said, shifting the tray of bread and plate of eggplant to make space on the table.

"Wine," Cam said, holding up his cup. "This calls for wine."

Sadeghi apparently overcome with a drunken weariness since he'd sat down merely stared at his plate. And swayed lightly.

Cook pulled up her chair next to Cyrus. "For the prince," she said, reaching for the pitcher that was passing on the other side of the table. She poured a splash of wine into the bottom of his cup and then filled it with water. "And for the king." She took Cam's cup and did the same. Cam's face reddened. He sputtered. Nahhunte swiftly exchanged his own empty cup for the king's cup and poured the king a full cup of wine, undiluted. He looked across at Cook and shrugged. Cam took a long drink and settled back, quiet again and apparently satisfied.

Cook huffed. She stood up at her place, glared at Sadeghi. Cyrus had thought that she was a large woman. But when she stood next to him like this, he could see that she was only a little taller than him. Stout, yes, but not huge and definitely not tall. But the disgust she felt for Sadeghi was palpable. So when she reached for the knife and spike next to him, he leaned back and away as far as he could and watched while she drove the spike into one end of the meat at so hard that she would have sent it off the platter but for the knife she held stabilizing it at the other end. Cook withdrew the blade slowly. Then, holding the leg in place with the spike, she carved rosy strips of meat from the leg with the other. Cyrus's mouth watered as he watched the strips of meat fall away under her expert hands.

"All this?" Cyrus said, "for us? It looks really, really good."

Cook's mouth twitched. She set down the knife, wiped her eyes with her wrist, and resumed carving. She sniffled then chuckled. "It's good to have you home."

CHAPTER 43

The food dispersed quickly onto individual plates. For a while, the only sound was the brush of a platter on the table, request for this or that, and the smack of lips and wordless grunts. The old groom cleared his throat. "That's some horse you have, my lord."

For a moment, everyone stopped eating. The guard and Cook's nephew looked across the table at each other, eyebrows raised. Nahhunte resumed eating.

"Is she all right?" Cyrus asked.

"Fine, my lord." Upadarma shared a look with his son.

Zubaba said, "I hope she hasn't been any trouble."

"She's got spirit," the groom said. He looked at all the faces watching him, reddened, and bent his head over his plate again.

Cyrus stopped eating and looked at Zubaba.

"The stables are heavy mudbrick," Martiya offered. "Which is good. We left her with a pile of good hay, which she took to like,... like Nahhunte to Cook's food."

The guard looked up, his mouth half full. "What? What?!"

* * *

CYRUS ATE FROM EVERYTHING. Cook saw to it that he didn't stop until he couldn't take another bite. The chair at the far end of the table, facing Cam remained empty, but the plate in front of it filled with every dish that passed. Cook leaned over and whispered to Cyrus, "for your mother. We always set a place for Mandane."

"She must eat, too," Cam said loudly. Cyrus noticed that the king's own plate had hardly been touched.

"Hears better than he lets on," Cook muttered, digging into the sauce under the bare lamb bone with a strip of spongy bread. "Indeed, my lord," she replied loudly.

When the light faded, Cook's nephew lit oil lamps around the room and on the table. Then, he and Martiya, with a heavy sigh, began to carry away the ravaged dishes. Cook disappeared back into the kitchen.

Cam, who had been drinking steadily, began to cry, softly at first, big round tears tumbling down his cheeks and shirt. Snuffling loudly, he put his elbows on the table and his head in his hands. Cyrus looked around.

"I'll take him," the groundsman said and stood unsteadily. He walked to Cam, holding the top of each chair as he went. He put a hand on the king's bony shoulder and said in words slurring and blurring together, "Come on. I've got some.... Make you feel better." Cam, his eyes red and swollen, looked up like a hopeful child and hiccupped on a final sob. The two men wove slowly out the door. Cyrus remained seated like the others.

Pretty soon, Cook returned, the boys close behind. She carried a platter heaped with pastries -- airy cylinders of crispy fried pastry coated in honey and sprinkled liberally with chopped pistachios and sesame seeds. One boy held small plates. The other carried a bowl of cut melon, pomegranate quarters, sweet lemons, and grapes. Cook noted the empty chairs, shook her head, and returned to the kitchen for two clay pitchers of rose water. Their sides were damp with the slow evaporation that made the water inside refreshingly cool. They passed the fruit, and each person reached for a sticky pastry.

Zubaba took a bite, set it down, and licked his fingers with obvious satisfaction. "We have been looking forward to this, the boy – Prince Cyrus," he quickly corrected himself, "and I since... Well, it's been a long journey."

Flames from the oil lamps flickered as a slight breeze passed through.

"This is a special day," Cook said. "A special day indeed." But the sadness in her tone was unmistakable. No one followed her remark with cheer or even a smile.

"It's not always like this," the guard said. "Don't get me wrong, Cook does amazing things with what we have; but don't get used to so much meat, so much... everything. The past years have been hard."

Cyrus thought of Spaco's small garden, the extraordinary moments when they were allowed a tiny bit of the meat they raised. He understood that. But at least there he never doubted that he was wanted, that he was loved. The pastry in Cyrus's mouth turned to dust.

"We'd best get back to the animals," Upadarma said, pushing his chair back. Martiya stuffed a last bit of pastry into his mouth and stood up, too.

Zubaba left shortly after, exclaiming that he was so exhausted that if he didn't get up right then, he would have slept at the table all night.

Cyrus watched him go. His mind was far too busy for sleep.

CHAPTER 44

"*N*ot quite what you imagined, my lord?" Nahhunte asked after the others had left.

Cyrus swallowed hard. "Not quite," he said.

"Tomorrow morning, your father will be better. Nighttime is hard for him."

Cyrus thought of their introduction, when Cyrus had first laid eyes on his father. That was midday. He swallowed hard. Cyrus wiped his hands on a linen swath of napkin, the fabric pulling against his sticky fingers. He looked over at Nahhunte. "Does he even know who I am?" Cyrus asked.

The guard reached for a lemon. "Until mere months ago, King Cam never knew you were alive much had he imagined ever seeing you before now. It'll take some time." He peeled the fruit absently.

Cook pushed her chair back and lifted her feet onto Cam's now empty chair.

"Who was the other man, the man who led him out?"

"Oh, gracious. Sadeghi?" Cook rolled her eyes.

The guard sucked on a slice of lemon. "That's the grounds-man." He grimaced – at the fruit's sharp tartness or the declaration it was hard to tell. "He takes care of the palace lands and gardens."

"Fat lot of 'care,'" Cook said.

"He's not very diligent," Nahhunte said, "as you may have noticed."

"'Not very diligent?!'" Cook exclaimed. Leaning forward and stabbing at the air with a plump finger, she said, "he is worse than that. He won't do anything except tend those damn flowers, and he's very pushy about it. I had to work very hard, threats included, to convince him to let me keep the kitchen garden. Recently, though, he even tried to take that." She settled back, her cheeks red.

"But," the guard said, "he is your father's best friend."

Cook huffed.

"He gives the king relief," the guard said.

"And made him into a blathering old fool," Cook said.

"Careful," the guard said.

Cook turned to Cyrus, who had been watching their exchange, words tossed like a hot stone between them. "Your father was an intelligent and handsome man, full of energy and ideas, when I first came to work at the palace. And when your mother was here."

Cyrus looked up, hopeful.

"There were a lot of us here then. You would hardly recognize the place – so busy, nothing chipped or broken, fresh paint and the gardens and orchards so lush. We had a full stable and fat flocks." She gazed off above Cyrus's head for a moment. "Don't get me wrong, Upadarma and his son do a good job; but there's only so much a man and his boy can handle, especially when they have to drive the animals so far now to reach grazing ground."

"What happened?" Cyrus asked.

Cook and the guard looked at one another. Then she fixed her gaze, kind and sorry, on Cyrus. "Your mother died." She took a deep breath. "After that, and the news that the baby - you, too, - was dead, from all we knew -- King Cam was devastated."

Nahhunte nodded. "When he first learned of it, your father was like some wild onager caught in a horse pen. He couldn't accept that your mother had killed herself, and so far away. She had been happy here. He couldn't understand it. None of us could. And it made him wild. But after a while, the rage burned out. Then it was like he turned against himself. He began to just wither away. He would hardly speak or eat, and every night, when he should have been fast asleep, he wandered in the gardens."

Cook nodded. She set her feet on the ground again and pulled her lips together tight. "That's when Sadeghi came along. He said he's from an area not far from here -- north, northeast -- though no one knew his family. Said they were all killed by some fire that he alone escaped. Told us he didn't need pay, only room and board and the authority to make decisions about what to grow where. He said he'd start with a small section, and if King Cam were pleased, he would take control of more.

"Well, by that time, a lot of the staff had left. It was too depressing to be here. Besides, your father didn't want to change anything. So, work at the palace petered out," Cook said.

Nahhunte said, "The city emptied but for a few hearty – or helpless – souls."

"We haven't seen a rainbow anywhere near here for years. It's as if Manzat has forsaken us." Cook added.

Seeing Cyrus's confusion, Nahhunte said, "Goddess of prosperous cities... It's just as well, we can't support many residents as it is. And it's easier to protect the king... his privacy... his reputation, this way."

"As for the surrounding areas..." Cook inhaled deeply, then exhaled shaking her head.

"The tribes have withdrawn. Like Cook, I can't fault them for exercising whatever independence they can." Nahhunte raised his eyebrows and lifted his shoulders. "As far as the palace goes, we all do several different jobs around here. As you saw, I'm one of two guards, part-time for the entire city. Thank goodness it's small – "

"And mostly empty," Cook added.

"Martiya and I exchange responsibility for the city and palace. We each serve as a kind of steward for the king, too."

Cook said, "But mostly you."

"He's learning." Nahhunte waved off the compliment. "Anyway, King Cam agreed to the man's idea. A trial of sorts. Sadeghi went to work first on a small section of the palace land just outside the gate." The guard shook his head. "Your mother would never have let it happen."

"I should have stopped him then and there, king's orders or no." Cook narrowed her eyes. "That man, calling himself a groundsman, tore up the small almond and plum trees that were just coming into fruit. Then he planted those damn poppies – the flowers you saw when you arrived. Everywhere. Sure, there's a prettiness about them; but pretty like that doesn't feed people. I use as many seeds as I can in cooking. But a body can't live on poppyseeds. And food wasn't Sadeghi's intention for them, anyway. Not at all."

Nahhunte nodded. "Sadeghi's main interest was – and is – in the tiny tears a seedpod sheds when nicked with a sharp knife. It's a laborious process, but he scrapes that gooey nectar off and sells it -- poppy milk, opium. It's a drug. It all started here, the insidious spread of poppies where so much else used to be, when he first offered it to King Cam. 'It will make you feel better he said.'"

"That's all he need to say," Cook said. "He's hooked and completely dependent on that slimy man. And now look at the place. Well, you saw it," she said to Cyrus. "That's all there is around here. Sadeghi sells the stuff for a lot of money, ostensibly to support the palace." She huffed and shook her head. "He always has enough for King Cam."

"It calms your father," Nahhunte said. "It really is the only thing that can make him relax, forget his pain, and even sleep. Wine helps; but this is much more powerful."

"The trouble," Cook said, looking out into the dark night, "is that it addles his brain. I'm not sure which is worse -- the grief or the medicine. Besides, your father has become so enamored of the stuff that he can't separate his love for the opium from the man who provides it. Your father essentially adopted..."

"King Cam has given Sadeghi power outside of these gates equal that of the crown," Nahhunte said.

"He says that the tribes are happy about it, that they see the benefit, even if I don't. He says they understand that with these poppies and the money they bring, we can rebuild Anshan's strength and ensure the best defense. Against what – I don't know. And I for one don't see improvements. Not for anyone." Cook sat back and crossed her arms.

"Sadeghi deals with the tribes, handles all the communication, tribute and such, like Cook said. And they're doing it – this move to transition lands away from traditional subsistence methods of farming in order to raise more and more and more poppies for the opium they sell. Oh, there have always been faithful families in the region, people who bring 'gifts' of food and such to the king. Still are. But listen. Tribes are tribes. And ever since your mother died, the palace doesn't provide any kind of central support, none except to act as middleman in the opium trade. Some tribes are better than others at controlling the lawless. But they get no help from here. So, they don't think they owe anything. I can't blame them."

"We don't hear much," Cook said. Then, "Oh, poor child."

Head on his arms, Cyrus had slumped over the table, fast asleep.

Nahhunte shifted Cyrus into his arms. "Good night, Cook. It

was a wonderful meal," he said softly, his breath ruffling Cyrus's tousled hair.

"Good night."

The boy's arm dangled and his head bobbed lightly as the guard carried him across the moonlit courtyard with steady steps. Nahhunte peered into Zubaba's room. Zubaba was stretched out on top of his bed, fully clothed, and snoring lightly.

Nahhunte laid Cyrus down on the boy's bed. He removed Cyrus's shoes, loosened his belt, and fluffed the pillow beneath his head. The guard stood for a time over the sleeping boy, watching the rise and fall of his chest, his long eyelashes fluttering. He drew the linen coverlet up to Cyrus's chest. "Gods grant you good dreams, little prince. Goodness knows, your waking won't be easy."

CHAPTER 45

*C*yrus woke in the night. His heart raced. He tried to remember where he was… Some room in the palace at Ecbatana? Then he recalled his arrival with Zubaba to Anshan, and the stress of the evening came back to him. He threw off the coverlet and swung his legs over the side of the bed and got up. He would tell Zubaba they must return to Media. He couldn't stay here. But then he sat down again, hard.

The realization hit him: there was nothing for him in Media, either. The cottage had burned to the ground. He couldn't return to Spaco and Mit. They were gone. He pulled his legs back up and curled his body around itself. For all he knew, the people who had raised him with such love were dead. Besides, all that, his grandfather King Astyages had been determined that Cyrus should leave Ecbatana. And when he thought about the Median king, it became clear as a summer stream: He didn't trust Astyages. He couldn't go back.

Cyrus tried to tell himself it was okay. It would be okay. His father might be crazy and weak, but merely pathetic. The others, except that groundsman anyway, weren't bad. Plus, this was supposed to be his real home, his real father, his real self – prince of Anshan, whatever that meant. The dried lavender in the mattress beneath him rustled softly and lent a sweet smell to his pillowed head. Finally, despite himself, Cyrus fell asleep again, the night air wafting cool through the windows.

* * *

CYRUS OPENED his eyes to see Zubaba sitting by the courtyard window. He sat up, threw back the coverlet and reached for his trousers.

Seeing him approach, Zubaba smiled and pulled another chair up close. "Did you stay up much later last night?"

Cyrus thought about telling him what he had learned, about Sadeghi and the poppies and tribes and all that. But it was fuzzy in his mind. Plus, what's the use? Cyrus thought. Zubaba would soon leave him just like everyone else Cyrus ever cared about. So he merely shook his head.

Zubaba mistook Cyrus's melancholy for sleepiness. "That food," Zubaba said grinning. "Everything. I barely remember returning to the room. Next thing I knew, it was morning. Sorry. I meant to come back, bring you along."

"That's okay," Cyrus said. He pulled a tunic over his head.

"Someone left keffir, melons, and bread on the table over there," Zubaba gestured to the little room they shared. "I can fetch you some here."

"That's okay," Cyrus said again. He sat.

Zubaba leaned forward. "I checked on the horses -- they're fine." He scratched his head, bewildered. "Your little mare seems to have found a friend. Maybe you'll come to the stables with me this morning, and I can show you."

"Sure."

Zubaba buttoned his lips. He slid his chair to face the little boy.

"Listen, Cyrus. I need to begin to head back today."

"I know," Cyrus said flatly. "I knew you would leave. And you said you wanted to get started, visit Susa. "

Zubaba nodded.

"So, you should just go, go visit your people." The bitterness was hard to miss.

Zubaba inhaled sharply through his nose. He brushed the tops of his legs, as if they'd gotten dusty. "Look –" Zubaba reached into the pouch at his hip. "I was going to give this to you when I left. But why not now?" He withdrew a scrap of parchment. "While you were sleeping, I wrote down the name and neighborhood of a certain Elamite, Huban-ahpi in Šullaggi. He lives about midway between here and Susa. Or did. They were an important family. I don't know if they still are, and I don't even know if they are still in that neighborhood or still intimate with Susa. But, here." He spread it out for Cyrus to see. "If you ever travel that way, bring this document. It's written in Elamite. You'll learn the language soon enough. Ask for them, introduce yourself and tell them that I – my father's name is on this sheet, too – sent you. Tell them that you and I are friends."

Cyrus looked at the paper without touching it. It's true, he couldn't recognize the writing at all. He dropped his head.

"Listen. You will be fine here," Zubaba said.

"But will I?" Cyrus asked. "And what does that even mean." Cyrus's voice rose. "Just look around."

Zubaba sighed. "Whatever the case, it's where you live."

"But that doesn't mean I belong here." Cyrus twisted the ends of his tunic in his hands. "From what I can tell, I don't belong anywhere." He bit his lip.

Zubaba crouched in front of Cyrus. He took the boy's hands into his own. "You've got to make the best of it. I'm not sure how. I really don't know." Zubaba shook his head, at a loss. "But it's yours. This place." Gently, he lifted Cyrus's chin, looked the boy in his eyes. "And this life. Yours." Zubaba stood.

Suddenly, Cyrus threw his arms around Zubaba's legs. "Please don't go."

Zubaba embraced him and then extricated Cyrus's arms. He bent to the boy, tucked the parchment into a pocket in Cyrus tunic, and patted it. "Remember: some people you can trust." He straightened again. "Come with me to the stables. I think you'll be happy with what you'll see."

Cyrus wiped his eyes and followed Zubaba out the door.

* * *

UPADARMA MET them at the stable doorway. To Zubaba he said, "I've saddled your horse, sir. And Cook packed you provisions for your journey." He patted a bulging sack tied tight. "Oh, 'morning, my lord," he said, when Cyrus stepped out from behind Zubaba.

"Hello."

Zubaba said, "I told the prince that his mare had found a friend."

"See for yourself," the groom said, limping away down the aisle.

The stable had a dozen stalls, six on either side of an aisle, but only three were occupied: one by Zubaba's horse, one by Cyrus's, and one by a sway-backed bay with rheumy eyes. The bay's shoulders were rubbed bare in two matching patches and jutted out no less for his hanging head.

As Zubaba stepped into his horse's stall and began to tie his sack to the saddle, Cyrus took in the sight. The walls that separated the stalls went to the ceiling or should have. Several were broken open in broad cracks or missing boards. On many, there were no doors.

"A bit rough," Upadarma said, reading Cyrus's mind. "Your little filly didn't help things." He led Cyrus to one of the broken stalls, pointing to a splintered door. "She's got her own ideas about things, huh? Lucky thing my boy jumped. Made it to the loft just in time."

Cyrus knitted his forehead, concerned. It was quiet now. And there was no sign of his horse. But Zubaba grinned at him.

Upadarma walked to another stall and peered over its door. "You wouldn't think it to see her all calm like that right now. But when we first put her in here, and I made a move to go, that little horse raced 'round the place, kicking and biting at everything in sight. It was mayhem, I tell you. Mayhem. Until Old Avery ambled in. Here, have a look." He gestured to the space.

Cyrus got up on his tiptoes. But it was too high. The old groom lifted a misshaped bronze pail and tipped it upside down in front of the door. Cyrus stepped up and looked over. On a pile of fresh hay, his horse lay, legs tucked under, her head resting on a forelock. A billy goat -- brown with white splotches, a great barrel belly, and skinny legs -- lay in the curve of her legs, his long nose resting on her cheek. His eyes were closed. A bit of pink tongue stuck out between thin lips.

"Your girl took one look at that homely goat and settled right down," Upadarma said softly. "It was he who got her into the stall she's in now. The door's a bit flimsy, but long as he's around, don't seem to matter." He gave the door a little rattle to demonstrate.

Seeing them there, the horse snorted, her eyes white and rolling, and scrambled to get up.

"Hey, it's me," Cyrus said.

The goat fell away awkwardly, bumping its head against the horse's knee as it struggled to stand. The horse planted her feet and dipped her head at the goat, unmoving until it had its legs underneath it. Then, she looked at Cyrus, blew out her nostrils and nickered lightly.

"A friend, indeed," Cyrus said. "I envy you," he added quietly.

Zubaba rejoined Cyrus. "Things are all in order for me. I guess this is goodbye."

Cyrus swallowed the lump in his throat. He nodded once.

Zubaba swung into the saddle. He held his mount still and looked Cyrus in the eye. "Remember what I said. And keep that document safe."

Cyrus nodded. He watched Zubaba turn. Then to Zubaba's retreating back, a sight that had grown so familiar to him over the long miles they traveled, one behind the other, Cyrus called out, "May the gods guard your way."

"And yours, my lord, and yours."

As Cyrus watched Zubaba's form grow smaller with the distance, he saw the groundsman picking his way through the poppy fields. The scraping knife he wielded and the tin cup at Buhari's side caught the sun in explosions of light. Cyrus's hand went to the parchment in his pocket. "Some people you can trust," Zubaba had said. He didn't have to say, "Some people you cannot."

CHAPTER 46

For a long time, Cyrus did little else than sleep. He spent long hours lying in his bed, in the stable, on a hillside, under trees... He spoke only when spoken to, and even then, not always. But he didn't rage. And he didn't cry. He was past all that. Cyrus had gone to a place inside himself, a wound so great and gaping that he simply fell in. And even as he stared up and out, eyes open to the world around him, inside he was wandering like a ghost untethered from its body and the stuff of life.

"Cheer him up," Cook said to her nephew, but he only looked at her with baleful eyes. It was no use. And not only because speech came so hard to the boy.

They all tried – Nahhunte with his gruff ways and the groom's son Martiya, not so very much older than Cyrus. But no one could rouse Cyrus to interest or activity in anything. Not even his horse. Upadarma almost regretted the way that she had settled in. Cyrus rarely went into her stall. He'd go out when roused from his room but merely moved in and out of the orbit of his little mare. It was as if he had become an old man as soon as Zubaba had ridden out of the gates. He'd lost too much. And the one who could give him what he so badly needed, King Cam, wasn't as good as gone. Worse. The frail king was a walking reminder of all that Cyrus lacked.

As the weeks went on, Cook took to saying, "Don't pester the boy. He'll come out of it. In his own time."

Truth was, they were busy. With such a skeletal staff, there was too much to do. Thankfully, Sadeghi was scarce. It was harvest time, and he wanted to account for every gram of every pod of every seedhead over the hundreds of acres he had pressed into cultivation. Whole teams of people were enlisted in the work. They came from all over Parsa, driven by need. And they worked desperately, if badly. Sadeghi drove them mercilessly and punished them for their errors and inefficiency. He paid them in opium. Cook complained that no one kept the feasts.

Even when traders from Babylon showed up at the gates, where Cyrus lay on the bench that he and Zubaba had used, and with big news: Nebuchadnezzar's beloved crown prince had died and Bushu, the half-Median prince was now next in line for throne... Even when the conversation happening around him – between Nahhunte and a young Babylonian merchant – reported that Cyrus's aunt Amytis stood to be the next Queen Mother and she with Bushu were all but ruling Babylonia since Nebuchad-nezzar had gone crazy with grief, it didn't shake Cyrus from his stupor. With disinterested eyes, he watched the Babylonian buy a block of opium. And with disinterested ears Cyrus heard him tell Nahhunte that while it brought great money, he never used the stuff. His father would kill him, "... if the stuff itself didn't. 'Waste of money, waste of life,' that's what my father says," the young merchant reported.

Through it all, Cyrus in his depression and despair was a silent presence, all but inert. Then, and for months on end. In fact, it took until the following spring – specifically Sadeghi's looking to prepare those vast fields for planting – to finally, violently, crack the inertia of depression and wake Cyrus up.

* * *

IT WAS AN ORDINARY MORNING. Roused by Cook, Cyrus wandered toward the stable - a perfectly ordinary thing. From the kitchen, Cook watched him go. And her nephew, working nearby to build a trellis for the beans, saw Cyrus lie down as usual on a short bench, as if the walk were too long to make in one trip. Like Cyrus had done countless time before. Clouds came and went overhead. Nearby, birds busied themselves on the last of the herbs' dried flowerheads. They flitted nervously, daring to dash in for a seed or a bug. Not that it mattered. Cyrus was just another stone.

Then he heard it. From the stable, a piercing cry and a great crash.

Cyrus sat up with a start. It was his horse. In terrible pain. Another cry, and Cyrus dashed toward the stable doors, toward the sound. As Cyrus ran in, he collided with sour-faced groundsman, storming out. Cyrus tripped over a low pile of discarded building materials – the product of a tear-down from before his time. Before he could recover, the man grabbed Cyrus's arms. His fingers wrapped clear around Cyrus's thin biceps.

"Get that demon under control," Sadeghi hissed through clenched teeth.

From the stable darkness, Upadarma pleaded, "easy, easy!"

Another crash.

Cyrus wriggled against the man's grasp. It was futile. "What did you do to her?" Cyrus's voice carried more passion than it had he'd felt in months.

"I didn't *do* anything," the groundsman said, pinching Cyrus's arms even tighter. "I just walked in to have a look at the new horse."

Upadarma's voice from the stable was low and soothing.

"My horse," Cyrus said.

Sadeghi narrowed his eyes. "That's the king's horse," the

groundsman said, "same as any in the stable. And all she does is lie around. Same's the boy who brought her."

"What's it to you?"

Sadeghi released Cyrus with a push of his hands and stepped back. Sarcastic, "Now, where are those princely manners?"

Cyrus rubbed his hands up and down his arms and glanced toward the stable door. It was quiet now; but Cyrus was not.

"What do you want with my horse?" He had found his fight. But it didn't look good. Cyrus was but a boy, after all, and Sadeghi a man. A man who commanded power over the king himself.

Sadeghi slapped dust off his robe in rough strokes. "The king's land requires a lot of work. Ochre, there," he nodded to stable and the ancient bay it housed, "could use some help. And that little mare has energy to spare. I'll see that she uses it." From the discard pile next to the stable, he bent and picked up a stout piece of lumber. He turned it over in his hand. Along one side, the exposed ends of rusted nails poked through. The groundsman hefted it with a grin.

Cyrus didn't think. Before Sadeghi could walk back through the stable doorway, Cyrus stepped between him and the door. Sadeghi turned. At half the man's height, and with empty hands, Cyrus was hardly in a position to stop him. But.

"The mare is not for plowing," Cyrus said. Cyrus squared his stance and blocked the way.

Sadeghi scoffed. He tossed the piece of lumber to the side. "With proper breaking, she'll do just fine." He seized Cyrus under his arms and tossed the boy aside. Cyrus fell with a thud. Eyes narrow, he got back up as Sadeghi retrieved the nail-studded wood.

A voice from behind Cyrus stopped them both.

"I believe the prince said that the mare is not for plowing."

It was Upadarma. The old man limped his way out of the

darkness. In the doorway, he straightened his bent back as well as he could.

The groundsman laughed and rolled up his sleeves. Transferring the lumber from one hand to the other, he measured the crippled man with his eyes and the small boy beside him and grinned at the prospect of sure win. A hand on his shoulder pulled him around. The grin disappeared.

Nahhunte stood facing the groundsman, not so smug anymore. Martiya and the Cook's nephew, still panting from his dash to get the others, flanked the guard on either side. The stand-off, only a moment, felt like a year.

Upadarma broke the spell. "I'd best check on the horse," he said and hobbled his way back inside. Cyrus followed him in.

Sadeghi jerked his shoulder out from under Nahhunte's hand. He tossed the lumber back onto the discard pile. "This isn't over." Sadeghi said with a growl and strode away.

* * *

SURE ENOUGH, after Cyrus had visited his horse, after he had talked with Upadarma... and talked... and talked with old man about the little mare and all things horses and goats and stable life in the palace at Anshan... After Cyrus had helped Upadarma tend old Ochre's wounds – they were significant indeed – and ease the workhorse's aches and pains... After Cyrus had admired with Upadarma the heavy steed that Sadeghi had introduced... "To accomplish my considerable duties, responsibilities of travel and trade," Sadeghi had told Upadarma, justifying his purchase as somehow critical to the well-being of the palace and of all Anshan, of all the tribes of Parsa,... After the sun had moved past the southern sky and into the west and Upadarma had retired to the little house he shared with his son... Sadeghi returned.

When Cyrus stepped back out of the stables – alone, Sadeghi was waiting for him.

Cyrus stifled a cry of surprise. The groundsman was unarmed. Cyrus looked quickly toward the pile of junk and whatever might serve as a weapon to level the uneven ground he shared with Sadeghi. But Sadeghi followed Cyrus's eyes and positioned himself between the boy and it. Cyrus's heart pounded. He saw that the sun had dropped nearly to the point where it would touch the southwest corner of the palace wall. Everyone would be gathering at the dining hall. Sadeghi stepped closer. Frantic, Cyrus looked around for a safe exit.

But the man was solicitous. He tipped his head to the side and turned his mouth down in a falsely sympathetic frown.

"Must be hard for you," Sadeghi said. "To come all the way here." His voice was soft and smooth. "New place... and so strange."

Cyrus swallowed hard.

"No mother." Sadeghi shook his head in sympathy.

Despite himself, Cyrus eyes smarted.

"And to find a father who..." Sadeghi's eyes probed Cyrus for the raw spots, the wounds. "...doesn't even want you."

Cyrus felt his eyes fill and his nose sting with the truth of it.

"Must be hard."

Despite himself, Cyrus sniffed, then bit the inside of his cheek.

"It can be better," Sadeghi knelt before Cyrus and held the boy's red-rimmed eyes with his own. "I can help you," he said in a tone sweet as the honey Cook drizzled over her pastries. Sadeghi smiled. "I have something that will take all your troubles away."

Quietly, "Opium," Cyrus said.

Sadeghi smiled even wider. "Smart boy. Now –"

"Late!" From across the yard, across the kitchen garden and the ruined courtyard, Cook shouted at them. "Lazy and late, I should have known!" Cyrus's eyes flew open wide. He darted out and away. It was the worst infraction, he knew.

But Cook's indignation and fury was for more than tardiness.

She'd seen what transpired and ground her teeth in helplessness. Except to intervene like this, there was nothing she could do. And when after dinner Sadeghi led King Cam away "to help him to feel better..." And Cyrus got up with them... When Cyrus told the others not to follow but to leave him alone, Cook hung her head. There was nothing she nor any of the others could do. To a person, they slumped in defeat. It was a royal edict, after all.

CHAPTER 47

*A*s Cyrus followed his father and Sadeghi, he recalled what had transpired at the marketplace. Despite his depression at the time, despite the disinterest he'd felt in the merchant's report and exchange with Nahhunte, Cyrus was a child. And as a child, he had taken it in. Cyrus had seen. And he had heard. All of it.

Concerning the recent turn of events in Babylonia, neither Cyrus nor Nahhunte understood the significance of that shift, how singular it was. They did not know the opportunities it presented. Nor the danger.

Cyrus didn't know that he had met Amytis in Ecbatana on the final day of the only visit she had ever been able to make back to Media, the land of her birth. It was a land of wild and wilderness that she had loved so completely that she gave up everything – living out her days within it – in order to save it. It didn't concern Cyrus. And it didn't concern Cyrus that she had come to Media with her son, her only son Bushu nor that he had been so captivated by it that he told his mother that he wanted to forfeit his right to the Babylonian throne in order to return there.

Cyrus did not know that although Bushu was indeed a son of

King Nebuchadnezzar's, a prince, it was never expected that Bushu would become king. Babylonia already had a crown prince. Never mind that he was mentally erratic, frail; that prince was a man born to a *Babylonian* woman, Nebuchadnezzar's first wife and Queen Mother. And it was he, Ean (Eanna-sharra-utsur), who stood to inherit the throne. Anyone who was anyone in Babylonia not only expected that it would be so; they wanted it to be so. Ean was, after all "pure" Babylonian. And there were too many foreigners there already, foreigners in respectable, even powerful positions, no less.

After all, every time that Nebuchadnezzar conquered another country, another people (and there were many), he took their best and brightest back to Babylonia, especially its capital city, to enrich the empire's everything. Literacy and the mastery of diverse languages enabled communication across the empire's reach; engineers and architects created the most impressive structures; artists of all kinds made everything even more elegantly functional and beautiful besides. Only Nebuchadnezzar's building projects rivalled his military conquests. And all of it screamed to the world that Nebuchadnezzar's Babylonia was without peer. The trouble, in the eyes of a broad swath of Babylonia's elite, was all those "Other People." The trouble was that Nebuchadnezzar employed the artisans and intelligentsia of people who did not "come from" Babylonia – people who had different traditions, different languages, different foods, and different gods (though they'd better make a show of elevating Babylonian deities above all others), people who did not look like them.

So, the prospect that the son of the Median woman Nebuchadnezzar had married in order to make good on a treaty that had lost its luster for Babylonian interests (and actually compromised efforts to capitalize on the natural resources *and* trading prospects of those wild lands to the north) might become king of Babylonia was just too much. The possibility was one that people such as Neriglissar (Igliss) of the esteemed Nur Sin family and son-in-law to Nebuchadnezzar, a man who would be regent should the *Babylonian* crown prince (continue to) be incapacitated, could not abide.

And yet.

Here they were. As it had happened, at the very moment when Bushu and Amytis were traveling back to Babylonia, planning Bushu's forfeiture and happy return to Media (Amytis could follow when Nebuchadnezzar finally died) – the Babylonian crown prince Ean had died by his own hand. With that, Bushu became crown prince and Amytis the queen mother. And Nebuchadnezzar became immediately and utterly immobilized by grief. So, Bushu and Amytis agreed that in order to keep the empire on an even keel (and Igliss from using Nebuchadnezzar's weakness – and Astyages's too – as opportunity to start cutting trees and mining Media), they would accept the crown's responsibilities. Until Nebuchadnezzar was back on his feet.

It got ugly.

But that's another story. As far as Cyrus was concerned, as far as Cyrus's life had taken him down to Anshan and into his own crippling grief, Cyrus heard the young merchant's report on recent developments in Babylonia – that Cyrus's aunt and cousin had ascended to positions of power that no one had thought they would ever encounter – as if they had no bearing on him. And he had heard how the opinionated young man accepted his father's adage about opium: waste of money, waste of life as if it had no personal relevance. But he remembered it all. He had no idea how significantly they would affect him. One he wouldn't encounter for a while; the other, immediately.

As Cyrus followed his father following Sadeghi back to the rooms that leaked the sweet smoke, he remembered merchant's father's warning. His own father was living proof.

So when they reached the door, "No thank you," Cyrus said to Sadeghi.

"No? No?!" The groundsman's fists clenched at his sides. He took a deep breath, and let his finger fall open again. "You don't even know how..."

"I do, and I don't want any."

Sadeghi narrowed his eyes and inhaled deeply through his nose. Then, "Have it your way," he said.

Cyrus watched his father grasp Sadeghi's hand. He watched the king shuffle, eager and gracelessly into the dark and stifling room, then disappear.

In the doorway, Sadeghi turned. "Let me know when you change your mind," he said to Cyrus. "It's going to get a whole lot harder for you."

CHAPTER 48

*I*t did get harder. The groundsman made sure of it. In the worst of it, the man cooed and stewed his way into convincing Cam to order the training and use of Cyrus's horse for plowing in his precious poppy fields. There was nothing that Cyrus, or anyone else could do. King Cam had commanded it himself. Using every means at their disposal, the staff delayed the mare's training as long as they could. After exhausting all the options, they could put off the inevitable no longer. King Cam (in practice, Sadeghi) insisted that the mare be broken to the yoke and put to use. Tomorrow. King's orders.

The staff gathered to figure out how to protect the boy from what was sure to send him back into the near-catatonic state they'd suffered through for so long. This time, given the certainty of damage to the singularly spirited mare that Cyrus loved – the only living being that connected him to Media and (though still once removed from) the life of innocence he'd had there, the only one who had been able to jar him from the sadness that sucked the life from his soul – they feared they'd lose Cyrus forever. Losing Cyrus, they'd lose any hope for the future of Anshan and Parsa.

They couldn't force him, not their prince. But they could talk to him. It was decided the best one to do so was the youth Martiya. After all, Martiya was groom as well as steward and guard. He was closer to Cyrus's age than either Nahhunte or old Upadarma, he could keep calm better than Cook, and he didn't stammer like Cook's nephew when he got nervous.

And Martiya was nervous.

So, when Cyrus declared that he was going, that had to present when Sadeghi broke the mare, Martiya said, "But you don't have to be. My father will be there. And Old Avery, too. So will I. You know that we will do our very best to keep her calm."

"She won't be calm."

Martiya nodded. They both knew that he couldn't argue with the fact. "But," he said, "we will not let Sadeghi hurt her."

Cyrus gave Martiya a look that was almost pitying. "Trying to make her will hurt her. That's just the way it is. The least I can do is be there."

Martiya sighed. "But what good is it for you to get hurt?" Martiya asked.

"For me to get hurt, *too*, you mean?" Cyrus said.

Martiya hung his head.

Training would begin the next day.

* * *

THAT EVENING, over a dinner of Cyrus's favorite, most comforting foods, the groundsman stood. He banged his cup for the table's attention. When he had it, he faced Cyrus.

"Some news, little lord." Sadeghi gave Cyrus a tight-lipped smile.

Seated next to Cyrus, Nahhunte pulled his chair closer to the boy. Quietly, Martiya set down the platter he had held. Cook slipped in from the kitchen, her nephew following. They sat without a sound.

"Returning from the far fields north of here, I encountered some Ellippians who reported that your Median guard, the man who had delivered you here..."

"Zubaba," Cyrus said, dread lacing the quiet pronouncement.

"Yes, that's the one. Well. It pains me to report..." Sadeghi said, though nothing in the man's visage suggested pain; on the contrary.

The other adults around Cyrus (all except Cambyses whose head lolled in sleep) looked nervously, desperately at the boy and at each other. They were helpless to stop it.

Sadeghi went on. "Some men, Cossean raiders from the mountains, just east of Susa, intercepted your... Zubaba."

Cyrus listened, stone-faced.

"One of them rode a fine black Nisean charger. Yours, once, I understand. Apparently, they didn't get all that they wanted. One of them had a fresh scar, deep across his cheek. They wanted vengeance. And..." Sadeghi inhaled long and hard, then exhaled in a great sigh of performative resignation. "... They cut his face into ribbons before sending his corpse on to Ecbatana."

When the groundsman was done, he waited. Everyone waited. Even the birds of twilight were quiet. However it was that Sadeghi had truly gotten this news, however it had actually happened and whether Sadeghi had been complicit in it or not, the details – the horse, the scar... It was true. Zubaba was dead.

Cyrus looked at Sadeghi, looked without emotion at the man's squirming hatred and said simply, "Did he get to see Susa?"

Sadeghi stammered. This was not within the scope of reactions he'd expected. "I – I don't know."

Cyrus nodded. Then, he slid his chair back from the table, and without a word, he walked out. When Sadeghi made a move to follow, Nahhunte stood. With the fire in his eyes, all he could do was shake his head. Sadeghi sat again.

So it was that they all let Cyrus go. That horse was their only hope.

When Cyrus opened the stall door, Old Avery made room. Cyrus laid his hand on the mare's speckled shoulder. He leaned his forehead against her neck. Then he picked up a grooming rag. Slowly, from her funny little forehead with its swoop in the bone, to the round of her hip, Cyrus ran the cloth over her warm hide. Over and over, over and over, all evening and into the night, until the horse fairly shone.

When he finally emerged from the stables under the midnight stars, it was impossible to tell whether or not Cyrus was aware of the eyes of Cook and her nephew sitting in the courtyard watching for him, of Upadarma and Martiya watching from the narrow window of their house, or of Nahhunte standing vigil beside to door to Cyrus's room. He simply walked straight to his bed and turned his face to the wall.

* * *

THE NEXT MORNING WAS OVERCAST. Clouds moved in off the distant hillside and hung heavy over the steppe.

"Good," Sadeghi said. "We won't have that damn sun in our faces."

There was no wind, no rain. No storm to compare to the day.

Cook watched Cyrus go.

And then she threw herself into the labor-intensive work of shaping complicated pasta. She would prepare diverse fillings and toppings. She would mince herbs, mince meats, mince beans, mince nuts. She would mince everything. And her nephew had never been more eager to help.

Meanwhile, when Upadarma and his son could find no more daily tasks to delay them, they made their way to the barn, Martiya walking even more slowly than his limping old father.

To their dismay, Cyrus was there. Of course. They'd held out a hope that neither had the will to deny. That maybe, after last night, and in the last minute, Cyrus had realized that he wouldn't be able to bear the strain of witnessing this last of the beings from Media whom he loved broken. But now, with the child's anxious face watching their approach, they couldn't pretend any longer.

And there was Sadeghi, all ropy limbs draped over the bars of the paddock fence, a smug smile on his drug-pallid face.

It was Cyrus himself who led the little horse out of her stall, the goat hustling along behind, and into the paddock. He stroked the mare's muzzle, spoke softly to her, and then turned the rope of her lead over to Martiya. Cyrus positioned himself as far away from Sadeghi as he could... without having to look at the groundsman. It would soon be impossible, of course.

But even before Martiya had stepped out of the barn, carrying with him the yoke and its long reins to the paddock, Nahhunte appeared. With Cambyses. Sadeghi frowned. Nahhunte gently but firmly led the frail king to a spot next to Cyrus against the fence.

Then they began. It was awful. The mare shrieked merely to see the equipment Martiya bore. She reared up on dainty hind hooves and paddled the air, fierce and afraid. And so it went. Cyrus wept while Upadarma and his son struggled to hold the horse -- rearing, kicking, and biting -- against the Sadeghi's grittooth efforts to approach her with the harness and yoke. Old Avery was helpless to stop the assault, helpless to calm his friend and added a hoarse, coughing bellow to the ruckus.

Meanwhile, beside Cyrus, Cambyses shuddered and swayed and moaned in distress. Only Nahhunte kept him upright.

It ended in defeat. For everyone. Except Sadeghi. The whole thing had so upset the king that it turned him even earlier to the pipe.

The next day was the same, but worse.

And the day after that.

And every day Nahhunte led King Cambyses to the site.

Despite the king's obvious distress and how it pained the stoic guard, he saw to it that King Cam witnessed everything.

On the fourth day, when the mare frothed and charged and was in every way out of her mind before they'd even the reached the paddock, the groundsman produced a terrible prodding spear along with the whip that had already drawn so much blood.

"The king has a request," Sadeghi said. "Noble sir?" he prompted Cambyses.

Cambyses wrung his hands, confused and anxious.

"Your request? Of the boy?"

Cambyses face registered recognition. "Boy –" he said to Cyrus, "Go help." Then King Cam looked eagerly to Sadeghi like a toddler for praise.

Sadeghi, a smirk on his face, bowed to the king.

In the silence that followed, a feather's fall would have resonated like a bell.

Cyrus turned a desperate, pleading face up to Cambyses. "Father?"

The king looked down at the boy beside him. He blinked hard, as if trying to clear his eyes. It didn't work. King Cambyses adjusted the tarnished golden ring around his head and waved a weak hand for Cyrus to go – take the whip and the spear. Break the horse.

The others watched, horrified, as Cyrus stepped forward and approached Sadeghi. Even Sadeghi appeared suddenly uncertain when Cyrus took the whip and the prodding spear from him. Sadeghi handed them over and took a few quick steps back. But Cyrus turned toward the paddock. His little horse, quivering against the far fence, flicked her ears and stepped anxiously, agitated and pacing, her eyes on the boy. Cyrus walked into the space, the ground churned to dust all around him. He walked across it to the mare. Her eyes rolled as she crushed her body against the fence from which there was no exit. Then, when

Cyrus was mere feet from the terrified animal, he stopped. He turned.

His back to the horse, Cyrus faced his father. Cambyses's mouth hung open. He had watched the boy's every move. He watched him still. Like that – the son's eyes holding his father's; the prince, a king's – Cyrus lifted the whip and the spear. And he let them drop from his hands. In a voice clear as a mountain lake, "No," Cyrus said. "No more."

Sadeghi sputtered with indignation. Everyone else held their breath.

They stood like that, a simple tableau against the backdrop of a broad Parsan sky.

The horse moved first. Slowly, tentatively, on splintered hooves she stepped forward, stepped to the boy, and laid her chin on his shoulder. Cyrus turned his head, his eyes soft, and muttered something to her. She blew warm breath into his face. Then Cyrus turned his eyes, hardened again, back to his father's.

Martiya gasped. The groundsman upped his sputtering indignation, Upadarma shifted his weight to step forward somehow to resume the task; and Nahhunte braced to catch Cam when he fell.

But the king needed no help at all. It was as if someone had pulled back an invisible curtain. Still staring at Cyrus, King Cambyses said, his voice a deeper version of his son's, "The horse is not for plowing."

Then the curtain fell again. But for that one transforming moment, he was the king of old.

CHAPTER 49

*S*adeghi might have failed in his effort not only to steal away from Cyrus but also to destroy altogether the one thing, the one being who gave the boy a modicum of comfort and peace. But that didn't mean the groundsman wouldn't take every opportunity he could find to make life hard for the prince. He increased his efforts to get after Cyrus. Whenever he could, Sadeghi rubbed the boy's face in his father's weaknesses and disinterest. In private, Sadeghi insinuated things about Cyrus's mother -- that she actually knew of his birth, for instance, and simply didn't want him; or that there was something so wrong and strange about him at birth that she killed herself. He suggested to Cyrus, in so many words and ways (without ever needing to come right out and say so), that Cyrus was to blame for Zubaba's murder. And that Cyrus had in some way killed his mother, too.

In addition to these things that cut Cyrus to the quick indeed, Sadeghi was not above assaulting Cyrus with little annoyances -- stirring up the chickens in the middle of the night so that Cyrus couldn't sleep; or planting scorpions in his room, snakes in his wash basin – anything to keep Cyrus on edge. No one could prove these things, of course, but Cyrus knew the groundsman was behind it all. It wore on him, troubled him. And many nights, Cyrus laid sleepless on his bed, rehashing details from his childhood, trying to restore what happiness and security he'd experienced in the cottage with Mit and Spaco, wondering how it all gone wrong. It was useless, of course. And he'd rise raw, even less able against the groundsman's aggressions.

So Cyrus tried to stay out of the man's way as much as he could. The others could help Cyrus only but so much. They scrambled, each in his or her own tasks to keep the palace functioning, even as Anshan and greater Parsa slipped further into a desperate poverty. It was an economy that didn't sustain – not like the groundsman had promised when he gave the people no choice but to put everything – land and labor – into poppies. Cyrus didn't know such dealings. Not yet. Relations with the region's tribes were the purview of Sadeghi.

Neither of Cyrus nor his nemesis recognized that the boy had a special power: His weakness. Cyrus was a child. He couldn't leave. What's more, he had been thrust into an utterly unfamiliar place. In everything he did, wherever he went Cyrus was a beginner. Sure, he had gained skills with Mit and Spaco and again under Harpagus's hard-driving instruction. And he used some of them. He could ride a horse, shoot a bow, shear a sheep, and dress a chicken. But even the details of these – the land where he rode and the game he hunted for their table Cyrus didn't know. What sheep there were had to pasture far away on account of the poppies, and Cook needed help in the kitchen garden beyond dressing a chicken. Some of what he'd learned with Harpagus – techniques of foot combat, for example, or the complex hierarchies of the Median court – was simply irrelevant.

It started with avoiding Sadeghi. Cyrus retreated to the courtyard and the kitchen gardens where Cook's nephew was hard at work. Cyrus stepped in next to him and bent to the soil.

"These..." the young man pulled a plant with small round

leaves from among the tender shoots of chickpea plants, "... don't belong here." He laid it down sideways between bean plants. Cyrus nodded. He set to doing the same. Soon, Cook's nephew had migrated to another part of the garden while Cyrus continued along on his own. Sadeghi had ridden off that morning to check on the progress in planting a field of the Dropici tribe, so Cyrus felt relaxed. He had lost himself in the task – early summer sunshine warm on his back, the twitter of birds a pleasant music in the air... when Cook was suddenly standing over him.

"Stop!"

She flapped her apron at his head, its hem swatting the curly hair.

"These..." Cook lifted the limp remains of what Cyrus had pulled "... are fritillaria!"

Seeing the stricken Cyrus, his face empty of recognition. Cook huffed.

"A flower." She lifted another dying plant with dismay. "And this is a rose."

Cyrus nodded. "A flower. But these are chickpeas. This is where the beans are supposed to be."

Cook looked to her nephew with an accusing glare, pointing to him then to the space next to Cyrus. He returned, chastened, to stay near Cyrus.

"It isn't just about growing one thing," Cook explained. "Here, the flowers feed insects that feed us. And the birds and so on and so on. Some plants produce things other plants need or draw bugs that the ones who move pollen from blossom to blossom, fertilizing fruit, might themselves eat. It's too complicated to explain." She paused, inhaling deeply through her nose, clearly struggling to explain anyway. "It's like this," she said. "A single thing growing over acres and acres..." she cast her arm out at the monoculture of poppies "... without anything else in balance is a sick thing. Everything does better when there are differences all around. Fruits and vegetables and flowers and animals..." She squinted at him. "Everything. Besides..." Calm now, Cook leaned back and looked around with satisfied pleasure. "It's more beautiful this way." And Cyrus remembered with a pang that that was the way in Ecbatana, too. Would he ever feel at home again?

CHAPTER 50

*L*ike the rest of the palace staff, Cyrus learned that there were times in the day when his father was more lucid, more reasonable -- before the groundsman got to him with drink or smoke. But no matter what the king's condition, the boy Cyrus looked so like Mandane that just seeing him set Cam off. So when he wasn't helping Cook in the gardens or Upadarma with their few livestock, Cyrus took to riding his horse away from the palace. Indeed, the older he got, the harder Cyrus found it was to be at the palace, the easier to be away. Cyrus took to leaving for ever longer stretches of time.

In the fall, vast numbers of birds flew overhead to winter in the large saline lakes of Tashk and Bakhtegan south-southeast of the city of Anshan. It was a long ride – days - from Anshan. But because Cyrus's aim was to ride long and far, far from the stress of the palace and bullying of the groundsman, it happened that one day he chanced on this wonderland of wildlife and fowl.

Cyrus set up his primitive camp and settled in. For a while, Cyrus forgot the troubles of Anshan. Long-legged pink flamingos, glossy ibis, and black-and-white avocets waded in the water while quick-darting plovers and stilts skittered along the shore.

Pelicans and gulls glided over, and ducks of all kinds bobbed in flocks on the water's surface.

Examining tracks and scat, Cyrus learned that the woods around were home to bears, wolves, and the long-legged caracal -- wild cats with black fringes on the ends of their ears. Sometimes he even saw them. Panthers hunted black-tailed gazelles and wild goats before disappearing again in their spotted hides, melting into dappled shade. Sheep hundreds of pounds in size with magnificent curling horns watched from the hillsides.

The months passed, and the seasons, too. Cyrus watched the winter snows blanket the high plains of Parsa and took refuge in the wild places and spaces of the Kur River basin. He fished the darting silver forms from there and of the Pulvar River, too. He saw how the flower fields drew water from old irrigation systems and let himself imagine what it had been like and could be again.

And so it was that the shepherd boy who had come from the outskirts of Ecbatana to Cambyses's Anshan by way of the ostentatious palace in Media grew into a young man intimately familiar with the Parsan region. Indeed, with time and experience... with more time and the experience of paying close attention to this place the qualities and proclivities of its fruits such as pomegranates (those orange blossoms!) and quince with its early flower to feed the first pollinators; vegetables such as legumes feeding others such as the savory wheat; and the herbs that drew more bees and butterflies than Cyrus could imagine existed... With more time and experience - paying closing attention also to the region's being – floral and faunal, avian and those that slithered and hopped and swam – the creatures in and around Anshan, without entirely realizing it, Cyrus's own roots began to sink into this place.

* * *

IN LATE SPRING, during one of his long expeditions from the palace, Cyrus watched a falcon fly over his camp following the same path day after day, its *ki-yee* cutting through the soft air like a blade. He followed it to a tree where high up lay a messy bundle of twigs, the abandoned nest of some much larger bird, a buzzard or heron, maybe. Not a week later, he could make out three tiny downy white heads over the edge of the nest.

One day, as soon as the adult had left to hunt, Cyrus led his horse to the base of the tree where he tied her carefully. He stood on her back and before she could bolt, grabbed the lowest branch. He heaved himself up and kicking off his boots to gain a better hold with his feet as well as hands, climbed up to where the nest hung. The adult returned and with a screech, flew at Cyrus. He ducked, feeling her talons graze his skull. He stole a glance at the baby birds before the mother made another pass.

The nearest fledgling fixed its shiny black eyes on Cyrus, a fierce and ancient gaze for such a fluffy little thing. This time when the mother grabbed at the human interloper, Cyrus used the tree to block her attack. Then, keeping his head behind the tree's trunk, he reached over to seize the closest bird. Just as he felt the soft bundle at his fingers, the angry adult caught the top of his hand, scraping and slicing with razor-sharp talons.

Cyrus winced, but he closed his hand over the wriggling, downy mass. He drew it out and quickly tucked the bird into his tunic, even as its mother screamed and dove. Streaks of blood from the back of his hand stained the fabric above his belt. The tiny bird scrambled and fought inside Cyrus's tunic, scratching his belly and chest as he made his way back down the tree, untied the horse, and rode back to his camp.

The first thing he did was to give the little bird scraps from ducks and other fowl that Cyrus shot or caught from the edge of the lakes. Cyrus knew, from watching the adult that the baby birds needed nearly constant feeding. After a few weeks of providing directly from his hand, he encouraged the bird to fend for himself. When the bird began to fly, it was a great pleasure to Cyrus to watch it stream over the grasslands and gorges, a keen hunter and a loyal friend. Cyrus returned to Anshan with a Saker falcon entirely bound to him.

Cyrus could see the groundsman's envy, felt Sadeghi's resentment come off the man in waves. And he knew. One of them would have to go.

PART III

(PARSA, CA. 562 B.C.E.)

CHAPTER 51

Cyrus's horse picked her way along the edge of a rocky outcropping of a region of Anshan that they hadn't yet explored. Suddenly, she stopped up short. The falcon on Cyrus's shoulder swiveled its head. Cyrus could feel its crest against his neck. A wind stirred the trees and moaned in the valley below. Cyrus urged the horse forward again. She agreed, hesitating and slow. Her nostrils flared and her ears flicked forward, fixed in rigid peaks. The falcon straightened and flapped its wings briefly, stamping and clenching its feet. The horse stopped again and clipped the ground with the hoof of her foreleg.

"C'mon, girl," Cyrus urged. His legs had grown in the past years so that, even bent at the knees, they extended the width of her sides. He was lean, much to Cook's chagrin, but his shoulders were filling out, broad and strong. "C'mon." He squeezed her sides and then heard it: a low moaning howl. The horse pawed again, bobbed its head, and snorted.

Cyrus strained to see where the sound was coming from. He reached over his shoulder and released the falcon. It flapped its wings and gave a sharp cry as it lifted and made a wide circle over their heads. The bird disappeared into the trees, then came back around dipping below the outcropping. The horse's ears flicked forward and back. Cyrus hopped down off her back and dropped the reins.

A rough square of linen, streaked with reddish brown and torn along the edges had snagged in the branch of a large, over-hanging shrub. The ground was loose along the edge of the path. A section was shorn clear of pebbles where it dropped off, smooth over the bank. Cyrus gripped the trunk of the shrub and peered over. A man's form – unmoving – lay several yards below. It seemed wedged between a boulder and a pine.

"Stay here," Cyrus said to the mare. She nickered, shifting her feet.

Cyrus stepped and slid his way down the steep bank, catching the limbs of shrubs and trees. The man's leg was bent at an unnatural angle. He lay face down. A robe, pulled up and awkwardly twisted, covered part of the back of his head.

"I'm coming to you," Cyrus called as he dislodged a small river of stones.

The man moaned again with a muddled tone that chilled Cyrus.

Cyrus worked his way around the boulder to the man's head. He drew back the dusty, blood-soaked robe and caught his breath. Blood matted the man's hair. One eye socket was filled with clotted blood where the eyeball should have been. The other was swollen shut. His nose was broken and his jaw askew. Cyrus turned away and took a deep breath. Again, the man garbled a low cry. Cyrus laid his hand on the man's back.

"I'm going to shift your leg to free you from the rock," he said. "Then, we'll get you out of here."

When Cyrus tugged the broken leg around, the man passed out. Cyrus moved quickly then. He got the man onto his back and adjusted his robe. An empty scabbard hung from a broad leather belt embossed with a geometric weave. Blue and red interlaced in laddered blocks against the dark brown background. Suddenly, the man grabbed Cyrus's wrist with a strong grip. He tried to open his mouth but spilled only pink bubbles, no words.

"Don't worry." Cyrus bent over him and said. "I'm from the palace."

At that, the man flinched away, his one eye pulled open as far its swelling would allow. He flung out an arm for his scabbard – empty – and scrambled frantically, crying and groaning as he tried in vain to get his leg underneath him.

"I'm not going to hurt you," Cyrus said. "I just want to get you back to the palace."

But the man tried so hard to distance himself from Cyrus and grew so obviously agitated at his inability to do so that the prince backed away. When the man quieted again, Cyrus approached. He extended his water skin. But the man, trapped by his injuries, shook and moaned. He leaned on one arm. The other he held up as if to ward Cyrus away.

"It's water," Cyrus said, "for you to drink."

The man eyed him warily. He had been baking in the sun for the better part of the morning.

Cyrus reached around the back of the man's head to hold it up. Cyrus touched the man's lips with the flask and let the water trickle into the slit of his mouth. Water and blood dribbled out the side.

"Can you open your mouth just a little?" Cyrus asked. He cringed at the sight of the mangled jaw.

The man winced as he struggled to do so. He couldn't get it open much farther than another quarter of an inch. Cyrus had to bend close. He looked carefully to control the water's flow then gasped and jerked back, sloshing water onto the ground around. The man's tongue had been cut out.

Horrified by the sight, "Can you swallow?" Cyrus asked.

The man shook his head.

When Cyrus lowered the man's head to the ground again, his

hand came away sticky with blood. Cyrus looked back up the hill. It was a long, steep climb. "I'm going to move you into the shade hidden from the road. I will come back for you."

The man tugged Cyrus's wrist. A mud-red tear gathered in the corner of the man's swollen eye and ran in a dirty streak down his cheek.

"This way. Try to relax." Cyrus took the man's shoulders underneath his arms and lifted. The man was heavier than he looked. Then he dragged the whimpering man as gently as he could a few yards over to where a few low pines were clustered, their bottom branches forming a lacey, blue-green cave.

"I'll be back soon," Cyrus said.

The man gripped Cyrus's wrist with the strength of terror.

"Don't worry," Cyrus said. "Not the palace."

The man loosened his grip and let the swelling overtake his eye again.

* * *

BUT WHERE WOULD HE GO? Cyrus wondered as he scrambled back up to his waiting horse. To whom could Cyrus turn for help? As well as Cyrus had come to the know the land of Parsa and its inhabitants, living beings of all kinds, there was one category he didn't know at all. One kind he'd avoided altogether: human. Apart from the few people who still lived in the neglected palace, Cyrus didn't know Parsa's human residents. He'd steered clear of their settlements and avoided interactions of any kind. Since he'd arrived as a child, woefully out of place in everything and everywhere, Cyrus had accepted that it was Sadeghi's job to interact with the region's tribes.

Oh, he knew a little about them, had learned from both Zubaba on their journey south and from Nahhunte too what he, as prince of the region, should. But it was the barest basics and all intellectual. Their names, and maybe a little more. The most noble tribe was easy: the Pasargadae. Other "noble" tribes included the Maraphii and Maspii. They were tribes of indo-Aryan descent, who had migrated down from the cold north that had mixed, in part, with the native Anshanites and Elamites who had occupied the region long before. Beside these, there were the Dai, Dropici, Pantheialaei, Drusaiaei, and Germanii, (which means "attached to the soil," Nahhunte explained). Their names applied also to the territory that each inhabited, and each kin group and territory was governed by its own chief, called a *zapanitu.*

Two others Cyrus considered now, in light of the man's injuries, were the Sagartii ("nomadic"), who had styles of combat all their own, including the use of lassos. This man had suffered a lot but not that. And the Mardians, who had a reputation for being especially warlike and aggressive. But finally, Cyrus dismissed the likelihood that it was any of the Parsan tribes who had so brutally attacked the man he'd come across. The man was clearly terrified of "the palace." So, as uncomfortable as it made him, Cyrus suspected it had to be someone representing the crown, someone speaking for King Cambyses. Sadeghi. Without proof, Cyrus was nevertheless certain that this was the grounds-man's work. And it burned Cyrus to the core.

Finally, Cyrus stepped up and onto the path again where his horse stood waiting. But when he reached out to grab her reins, she threw her head back, eyes white and rolling. She snorted with alarm. Cyrus's hands were covered with blood, human blood. He walked up the path to where a stream trickled out of a hidden spring. He rubbed his hands against the wet rocks, wiped them on his under-tunic, and returned to the horse. He considered.

The path was worn enough to suggest regular use. Occasionally, a narrower trail had crossed theirs – animals, probably. So, when Cyrus heard voices ahead, he slipped off the path and onto one of those trails. He dismounted quietly and led the horse to a thicket at the edge of woods. Out of sight, he crouched, watching the main path. The voices grew louder. He still couldn't make out what they were saying when the first person came into view – partly. The man was turned back in his saddle, talking to whoever was behind him. Cyrus couldn't see his face. He waited. The second rider emerged from the bend, leading a riderless horse behind him. Cyrus didn't recognize the man. But something about that horse…

Suddenly, a hand slapped over his mouth, pulling his head back. Another hand twisted Cyrus's arm painfully behind him. That's when he realized – the horse was Sadeghi's.

CHAPTER 52

$\mathcal{C}$yrus struggled to throw off the grip that had paralyzed him. Finally, he got ahold of his assailant's head. He turned into the grip, freeing himself. Cyrus drew his dagger, an old piece lent by the palace guard that had endured so many sharpenings over the years that it was only about half its original size. With the man under his knee, Cyrus held the mortal tip against the man's throat -- thin and ropey.

"Bartatua," the man whispered.

Cyrus dropped the dagger and with a yelp threw himself on top of Mit – for it was indeed the shepherd who had raised Cyrus – in an awkward embrace.

On the path, the riders stopped. "Did you hear something?" the leader asked.

"What?" It was Sadeghi's voice.

Mit held his finger to his lips. His eyes shone with tears.

"I thought I heard something."

"Like what?"

In the thicket, Mit and Cyrus froze.

"I don't know, just something, something different."

"I wish you'd be more specific," the groundsman said, drawing his bow.

"Maybe just a goat. Sounded big, though." The men sat silent, listening.

Cyrus's horse shifted her feet and sent a small flock of sparrows darting out of the thicket.

Sadeghi scoffed. "Big birds, maybe," the groundsman said with a sneer. He turned to replace his bow and arrow in their quiver when his eyes caught sight of a falcon overhead.

"Wait," he said.

Sadeghi put his hand up to his eyes as the bird flew into the sun. He squinted. In sun and shadow, the bird's colors were lost to white and black. Sadeghi twisted his head this way and that, turning in the saddle to make it out. But the falcon dipped behind the tree line and lifted away.

He shook his head. "Let's go," he said and kicked his horse forward again. The men resumed their conversation, its content masked by the clomp of the horses' hooves.

Cyrus and Mit waited some minutes after the voices had disappeared until they were sure that the riders would continue on.

"Pop!" Cyrus said as he pulled the wiry man to his feet. "I could have killed you!"

"You'd be dead if I hadn't stopped you," Mit replied.

"Wait," Cyrus studied the old man. "How do you know that?" Cyrus asked.

"That man –" Mit shook his head in disgust. Then he grinned. He embraced Cyrus again, long and hard. Cyrus stood still at first, arms stiffly at his sides. Then gave in to his affection and embraced the man that had raised him, the man he'd thought was dead.

When they released one another, "How is it that you're here?" Cyrus asked. "And Mama?"

"Spaco is fine. There is much to talk about."

Cyrus stepped back. "Yes, much," he said. Again, his face clouded with confusion and long-buried hurt.

Mit didn't seem notice. "Look how big you are. And strong." He grinned. "I can vouch for that," Mit said, rubbing his chest. "Come, come." He waved Cyrus to follow him further into the woods. "Spaco will be beside herself."

But Cyrus stopped. "There's a man badly beaten back a way," he said. "I told him I'd help, but I couldn't get him out alone. And..." Cyrus swallowed hard. "He cannot speak. Someone cut out his tongue."

Mit hesitated.

Cyrus frowned. "Is there something..."

Mit inhaled through gritted teeth, then seemed to decide something. "Can we do it," he asked, "Just the two of us?"

"Maybe."

Mit nodded. "Let's go first to the cottage. It's not far. If the man is as bad off as you say, and I've seen..." He stopped himself. "We'll need a stretcher to carry him back. Besides, Spaco can help." Mit strode forward. When Cyrus didn't follow, he turned.

Cyrus stood, considering. His horse nickered her own uncertainty. Cyrus looked at Mit. Could he trust him? There were so many questions Cyrus had, so much unanswered. But – He glanced back toward where he'd left the man. So many new questions, besides. Cyrus retrieved his horse and stepped in behind Mit.

They followed the narrow path, Cyrus leading his horse behind Mit, the falcon circling overhead. Cyrus looked at the man's back, walking ahead, still broad and strong, and felt himself battered by competing emotions. Angry – why hadn't Spaco and Mit told him whose he was? Why hadn't Mit fought to keep him, when the truth came out? Confused – why hadn't the shepherds alerted the palace to report that the prince they thought dead at birth was alive and well, that they hadn't returned him as an infant? And so, so relieved. To find that the pair had not only survived but were well. Cyrus noticed a little stoop in Mit's shoulders, errant gray hairs standing out at the nape of his neck, a stiffness to his gait. Yes, whatever else Cyrus felt about the shepherds' deception -- anger, disappointment, betrayal – he couldn't deny that he was glad to see them again. And after they'd taken care of that man, after the crisis was past, Cyrus would make get all the answers he could from them both.

The meandering trails Cyrus had noticed miles back multi- plied the closer they got. Then Cyrus saw the thatched roof of a tiny cottage in a clearing ahead. One side of a corral peeked out from behind it. Inside, goats snuffled at the dirt. Next to the cottage a garden sported a profusion of color. Cyrus recognized many of its plants. There, her back to them, gray hair tied in a loose braid, an old woman tended the plot. Spaco.

"Woman," Mit called to her, "I've brought a guest."

Spaco turned around, hands on her hips. She squinted. Then, her hands flew to her mouth and she ran toward them, arms outstretched. She hugged Cyrus close and tight, and then pulled him away again to arms' length and looked at him, her eyes shin- ing. "I have waited for this day," she said. "Waited and waited. Now here you are." She ran her hands in wonder over the bristles on Cyrus's cheeks and chin.

"It's my fault," Mit said to Cyrus. "We knew where you were, but I wouldn't let her go to you -- too dangerous for all of us. I knew that the gods would bring you to us in time."

Again, Cyrus stepped away from him. The couple didn't notice his pained bewilderment. They seemed each to be strug- gling themselves with some internal conflict.

"But listen," Mit turned to Spaco, his voice urgent. "There's a man -- the same bad business -- who needs our help right away."

"You've seen this before?" Cyrus asked.

Mit and Spaco exchanged a look.

Without explaining, "Even once would have been too much," Spaco said. She hurried toward the cottage with her basket. "It's an evil thing." She left the vegetables at the door. "That much I can say."

Mit disappeared inside.

"Get the horse settled." Spaco waved toward the corral with its cozy little lean-to. "She'll be no use to us there."

Cyrus walked the mare around back. Just like in Media, the corral was attached to the rear of the cottage. A three-sided lean-to faced into it, and a pail of clear water lay in a shady corner. A few goats and sheep, too, milled about. Cyrus led the horse, nickering softly at the goats, into the corral and hobbled her feet.

"I'll be back for you," Cyrus said and patted her shoulder. As he stepped outside, his falcon swooped down and landed on rail near the horse. "You, too," he said.

Cyrus returned to the cottage and stepped through the doorway. He looked this way and that. The house was identical to the cottage in Media. A flood of memories rushed forward. And a sudden nostalgic longing for that life. If the slaves had come clean with the palace, would he still be there? Could he still be there, tending sheep, hunting in the mountains, foraging in the hills? Cyrus could hear husband and wife talking in hushed voices. He'd confront them later. For now, he simply took the place in.

As with the cottage in Media, the room where he stood served as kitchen, dining, and general living. Off of it, were two rooms. He guessed that the one from where the voices came held miscellaneous supplies. Through the other doorway lay a pallet bed. Just like in Media. Then he saw. Indeed the only difference between this and the cottage in Media was that there, on the rough-hewn table in front of him stood a bouquet of flowers – garden and wild plus mint, flowering oregano, and thyme – all arranged in a painted, if chipped, pot. This was not the cottage of a slave.

"Grab the sheet off the bed," Spaco called to Cyrus. He walked into the empty room, their bedroom indeed. Cyrus stripped the tick and returned to the large room just as Mit and Spaco came through from the other. Spaco carried a small sack. In Mit's hands was a homemade stretcher. They'd done this before. Cyrus followed them out.

Spaco stopped briefly in the garden. From a woody plant – golden-green, tall, and oddly human-looking (Cyrus didn't recognize it) - she snipped some branches. Spaco thrust handfuls of yarrow, its leaves lacey and green into the sack. "Which way?" she asked.

CHAPTER 53

The man was just as Cyrus had left him. Yet now, there was no color in his face. Spaco tipped water into his mouth, just as Cyrus had done, but she kept his head leaning to the side. She let the water run in and out, without the man swallowing any, until it became clearer.

The man's cheeks pinkened. He stirred.

"It's all right," Cyrus said to him. "These are good people."

The man stirred. He groaned. His one eye was still swollen shut but for a tiny slit. It was worse. Spaco and Mit conferred in low voices. The man began to tremble.

"If you can hear me," Spaco said, "I am going to try to stop the bleeding." She took the soft yarrow from her sack, stripped the lacy fronds from their stems, and laid them gently on his mouth, pushing what she could inside, taking care to make space for his breath. "This will help," she said. "But we must move you."

The man stiffened in alarm.

"There is no other way," Spaco said. "We'll mitigate the pain the best we can."

Spaco removed the golden-green twigs and stopped. She murmured to Mit and shook her head. Then, to the man she said,

"In your condition, I can't administer the haoma. It'll take too long to prepare. But it's all right. We've got another way."

While she spoke, Mit busied himself with what supplies they had carried.

Cyrus shuddered to see him produce a small tin disk and shake from the sack a few large granules of the stuff Cyrus hated to recognize: opium.

Mit lit the granules. Quickly, with another thin sheet of tin he formed a cone, which he held over the tiny fire. When a stream of smoke issued out, he put it under the man's nose. But the man gave his head a tiny but obvious shake, No.

"Just breathe."

The man struggled to turn away.

"It can be medicine, too," Mit said.

The man slumped, giving in as he took in the breath he needed. With it went the smoke. Another two or three breaths, and the muscles in his face relaxed. Mit motioned Cyrus to take his shoulders. Mit and Spaco lifted at each thigh, trying not to torque the broken leg. When they hoisted the man onto the linen stretcher, he was completely limp. They took the makeshift stretcher by its corners and slowly worked their way back up the hill. Each slipped more than once, but among the three of them, Cyrus going backward for much of the way, they were able to get the man up to the path and to the cottage.

There he lay, unconscious, while the three stood around him.

"He grew really agitated when I said I was from the palace," Cyrus said.

"Yes," Mit said, not the least surprised.

Spaco merely shook her head.

* * *

OUTSIDE, Cyrus and Mit picked vegetables while Spaco went around back to prepare a chicken for them to eat. Cyrus had tethered his hawk to a tree limb in the front. It tilted its head back and forth.

"Hopefully, he'll recover and be able to explain for himself," Mit said, clipping a heavy purple eggplant from its plant with a small knife. "You should hear it first-hand." Mit gave Cyrus a searching look. Seemingly satisfied that what he looked for wasn't there, he said, "There's been a lot of pressure for farmers to convert their traditional crops -- mostly food, some fodder for animals -- to poppies. I figured you would know. The king's steward has delivered orders from the crown to demand it."

"There is no steward," Cyrus straightened abruptly, one hand still full of mint sprigs.

"What?" Mit asked. "Then who –?"

"There is no steward. There are two guards who share the duty of protecting both the town and the palace. When they're on at the palace, they also aid the king. But a steward? No."

"Out there on the path... when you nearly killed me... If he's not the king's steward, who was the man who rode past us?"

Cyrus nodded, a sardonic smile on his lips. "The groundsman. Sadeghi. He's convinced opium is our future. And he's gotten my fa -" Cyrus stopped. He bent again to the herbs.

"It's okay," Mit said gently. "And it's true. Cambyses is your father."

Cyrus didn't look up. "Well, Sadeghi has gotten the king completely dependent on the stuff." He tore a sprig of mint out by its roots. "It's bad." His voice quieter again, Cyrus said, "Actually, Sadeghi is why I'm here. I can't be there with him around. But what I want to know is --"

Mit shook his head. "I don't--"

"What happened?!" Cyrus threw the mint to the ground. "What happened back there in Media?" he shouted.

Mit considered the young man before him. Finally, he nodded. He took a deep breath. "Over dinner. With Spaco. We'll explain everything."

Cyrus stared hard at the man he'd called Pop. Then he stooped to retrieve the herbs he'd thrown to the ground. His voice level again, "I can't get rid of Sadeghi because my father adores him. Or adores what he brings. Anyway, he's the one you've been calling steward."

"So your father isn't capable at all?"

"You could say that."

Mit sighed. "Some have been saying just that. No one ever sees him."

"Well they're right. My father can hardly do anything. Cook tells me that it was different before, when my mother was alive. But after she died, he lost his will, self-respect, motivation... Then along came Sadeghi, calling himself a groundsman. He'd take care of the lands – everything beyond what the palace staff could do. You can figure out the rest, I guess. Beans, right?" Cyrus said, walking toward the twining plants. Mit nodded, and they began to pick the long pods from their vines.

"I suppose I should have known," Cyrus said. "It's obvious to me now. But - "

"You were a child," Mit said, his voice soft. "And then..." he shrugged, "it was just the way it was."

A squawk from the falcon made them look up. Spaco held up the chicken's entrails. "For your friend?" she asked Cyrus.

Cyrus gave her a small smile. "He'll love it." He nodded. "Just set them on the stump there."

Spaco walked over to a particularly fecund spot where the land rose again into higher hills. A spring, surrounded by lush green, bubbled out of the rocky soil. She drew a bucket of water from the spring and poured it into a deep wooden basin sitting a few feet away. She took a block of soap from a stump and scrubbed her hands, rinsed them in the basin, then dumped the dirty water at the base of a slim almond tree.

"What did you two figure out?" Spaco asked, wiping her hands on a clean but tattered apron.

Mit glanced at Cyrus then back to her. "That it's time to eat," Mit answered.

"Well, get those ready. The chicken's nearly done."

They worked in silence after that. It didn't take long. While Mit sliced the eggplant, Cyrus snipped an end from each bean, drawing it back to pull the string from its spine. Mit brought a heavy metal pan from the house and a stoppered clay jar. Over the fire Spaco had going, he laid the pan, poured oil from the jar. He squashed a few cloves of garlic with the heel of his hand against a flat stone and tossed them in. Then he added the eggplant and beans. Spaco laid a flat metal sheet over the top of that and chopped the mint up fine. She tossed the vegetables, added the mint, and put the sheet back.

Cyrus stepped into the house to check on the man. He was still resting quietly, so Cyrus rejoined the others. They sat and began to eat.

"Until we found the first man, I didn't realize it was so bad," Mit said. "People had been complaining -- there's no justice, no defense like they claim the palace should provide... Spaco and I have stayed clear of a lot of it. It took us a long time to get here from Media. A long time to find where we could live that wouldn't draw attention. From anyone."

Spaco nodded. "We kept our heads down, tried to be inconspicuous. We built up a little herd – you saw the sheep and goats. From them we trade occasionally for things we can't grow or make. But as you can see, we maintain distance. There are a lot of different people around here, people who have been in Parsa for generations. We didn't want trouble. And we hoped..." Spaco gave Cyrus a small smile. "That one day we'd see you again."

"About that." Cyrus pushed his plate aside.

CHAPTER 54

"Why didn't you tell me? Why didn't you tell me who I was? Who I am?" Cyrus's face wrinkled in anger.

Mit and Spaco looked at each other.

"You were so little at first, and seemed happy enough," Mit said gently.

Spaco pushed her plate away and rubbed the tops of her thighs. "Maybe we should have told you."

"Told me?! Told the palace!" Cyrus said. "Right away."

The couple looked at each other, again. Mit hitched his shoulders, still looking at Spaco, and gave his head a single, small shake.

"What are you not telling me?" Cyrus demanded.

Spaco met Cyrus's eyes, her forehead creased. "The palace --"

"Yes," Cyrus said, "the palace, where I was supposed to belong."

Mit said, "But we kept you alive."

"I wasn't dead, if that's what you mean. Not like everybody thought. When you saw that, when I – I don't know, took a breath?! – you should have told the king." Cyrus shook his head. "Maybe then my mother would still be alive."

"What?" Mit stood so quickly that his plate spilled from his lap, forgotten. "It was Astyages who --"

"Maybe we should indeed have told you." Spaco interrupted her husband and gave him a long look. "What did you learn?" she asked Cyrus. "What did they tell you?"

Mit sat down again slowly.

"That everyone thought I was born dead," Cyrus said. "They said that you were supposed to take care of... of my body. And that that's all they knew until Astyages recognized me, that it turned out that I was alive, and only you knew it, and you kept me when you should have told the king and sent me back." Cyrus finished in a rush.

Mit shook his head furiously. "That's not --"

Spaco put her hand on Mit's arm. "We did the best we could for you," she said, silencing them both.

"Then how you could leave me there?" Despite his anger, despite thinking that he had finally put the whole thing behind him, despite all the years that had passed between then and now, Cyrus's voice broke at the recollection of it. Cyrus looked at Mit.

"You just walked out," he said to Mit.

Mit's eyes clouded over. Beside him, Spaco squeezed his hand.

To Cyrus, she said, "Back then, before that awful day, did you trust us?"

Cyrus swallowed hard. He nodded.

"I'm asking you to trust me now when I say that there is more to it than you think."

Cyrus sat still, silent.

Spaco inhaled deeply. She released Mit's hand. "But all that is in the past," she said, brusque again. "You are the rightful heir of Anshan. And we..." She smiled at Mit. "... Have made a life here. One day. Maybe. The rest will be clear."

Mit cleared his throat.

"That's enough for now," Spaco said. "Can you trust us in that?"

Cyrus looked into the clear eyes of the only mother he had ever known, her expression soft in a face lined with experience and age. "I'll try," he said.

Mit nodded. He swiped his cheek against his shoulder. "I'll go check on our guest," he said, his voice gruff with unspent emotion.

Spaco and Cyrus resumed eating.

After a while, Mit returned. "He's resting now. Quiet."

And their talk turned simply to catching up on the years that had passed.

It had taken Mit and Spaco about a year to make the trip from Media to Anshan on foot, traveling wide to the east of the Zagros range. As the miles between them and Ecbatana grew, they became more comfortable meeting inhabitants of the regions through which they passed. Some were friendlier than others. They spent late summer and fall working for a group of people, Judahite immigrants around Isfahan, culling lambs, repairing equipment, and any other odd jobs that the busy season had made short-handed. For their labors, Spaco and Mit not only had earned food and safe lodging, but when it was time to go, they left with five young animals -- two goats and three sheep. They never worked again for anyone else, but they did trade for goods and the opportunity to breed their animals outside the herd. And they kept to themselves.

For his part, Cyrus tried to tell about his life, convey all that had happened since that fateful day when Mit had returned to the cottage without him. But it was hard. Some parts seemed impossible to recount, even had it been a happy tale. The circumstances, the people, the places were all so different than anything they had shared before. How could the shepherds understand what training Cyrus – a Median prince of the highest order – had endured in the grand palace under the harsh demands of an angry Harpagus? It was in itself incongruous. There was the journey with Zubaba. And then these recent years at the palace in

Anshan, its life of immersion and escape... Besides, merely seeing Mit and Spaco again had cracked the casing Cyrus had so laboriously built around his pain to contain and smother it. The pressure of its release strained his heart. That there were still things unspoken, parts of the story they withheld, made Cyrus's telling a halting affair. But he tried.

After a while, they went inside the cottage, the better to be near the man they hoped to save. And Mit and Spaco told Cyrus what else they'd seen. None had been as bad as this. None had put them in quite this position. In some cases, they'd only seen the effects after the victim had recovered. In others, they'd been able to summon help for the wounded person without drawing more attention to themselves Never had they solicited any more information than they either overheard or had been volunteered. Never had they had to retrieve a person and bring him into their house like this. And in such terrible condition.

"At least we know where he's from," Spaco said.

Cyrus and Mit looked at each other. "We do?" Mit said.

"For certain," Spaco said. "Did you see his belt? It's the pattern and colors of the Pasargadae."

"The man belongs to the Achaemenid clan."

Cyrus gulped. The most esteemed family of the most noble of Parsa's many tribes. What did it mean?

CHAPTER 55

A hoarse moan from the bedroom brought the three running.

The swelling in the man's good eye had gone down a little, but he still couldn't lift the lid. When he opened his mouth a crack, clearly trying to speak, Cyrus leaned down over it.

The man labored to make any sound at all. What he got out, in slow bursts across his lips was garbled, incomprehensible. Cyrus looked up at Mit and Spaco. They shook their heads. Still, the man struggled.

Cyrus tried to quiet him. "As soon as you're better, I'll take you back to your home, back to Pasargad." The man squeezed Cyrus's hand. Then he tried again, tugging on Cyrus's arm with each syllable. Finally, exhausted, he dropped his head back down, loosened his grip.

"Rest some more," Spaco said.

When the man let out a low cry, Mit hurried off. He came back with another tincture of opium. Again the man struggled to refuse.

"It can help you rest," Mit said, "spare you some pain."

But the man didn't hear. He was dead.

For a moment, they all froze, each locked in his or her own thoughts. It was Cyrus who asked what each wondered and had been desperately trying to answer.

"What do we do?"

Spaco shook her head. "I don't know."

"What do the stones say?" Cyrus asked.

Both Mit and Spaco sat heavily.

"I have yet to learn the language of spirits here. Or maybe they simply don't wish to speak to me, who came from so far away."

Mit looked at her. "But…" he said meaningfully.

Spaco lifted her shoulders. "There is a place… Sometimes…"

Mit nodded for her to go, to try. From his perch outside, the falcon cried a single piercing note. Approval? Spaco stepped outside and was gone.

* * *

THEY WAITED A LONG TIME.

When she returned, Spaco's face was difficult to read.

"We have to get him back to his people," she said.

Cyrus nodded. "I'll do it."

"No!" Spaco said. "They'll kill you."

"Is that what the sto-… Is that what you heard?"

Spaco shook her head. "It wasn't clear."

Mit nodded. "Better I should go."

"Have you even ever been on a horse?" Cyrus asked.

"I could learn," Mit replied. "Besides, I know the way."

"My horse might let you. She's better with others now. But –" Cyrus shook his head. "No, it's better that I go," Cyrus said. "Tell me the direction. I want to speak to them myself, to learn what I can."

Spaco wrung her hands. "But to them, you – the prince of

Anshan – are the enemy. They'll say that this man's blood is on your hands. Everyone knows it's the palace's doing."

"All the more reason that I should go." Cyrus pulled his shoulders back. "I need to find out what's going on."

Beside him, Mit seemed to shrink. "But we just got you back," he said.

"I'm the prince. You said it yourself."

Mit and Spaco exchanged a look. Mit nodded to Spaco, whose eyes filled with tears.

Cyrus took her hand. "Mama…" he said. With his other, he took Mit's hand. "Pop." Looking from one to other, Cyrus said, "You raised me to take responsibility, to protect what is in my charge, and to do what is right and true. I have some authority. It's time I accept that."

Spaco freed her hand and wiping her eyes impatiently, said, "Get your horse ready. I'll prepare the body and provisions for your journey."

The men walked to the corral, Mit gesturing to the east, Cyrus leaning in to listen. Spaco wrapped the dead man in the linen sheet on which he lay and tied it closed with jute string. She laid her hands on top of the body and closed her eyes. After a minute, she opened them again.

The days were hot, but at least they were dry. Gods willing, Cyrus wouldn't get lost or detoured but make the trip with the body still intact. She took a large bladder flask from the wall and brought it to the spring to fill. She returned to the cottage with heavy steps.

Cyrus and Mit came in, the horse stood saddled and ready outside. Spaco nodded to Mit, who went into the bedroom to collect the body.

"Trust no one on the road. Keep your eyes bright."

"Yes, Mama."

"Be careful when choosing a camp. Keep your fire low."

"Yes, Mama."

"And when you near the village, hold your hands in the air," Spaco said. "Give them no reason to doubt or fear you."

Cyrus nodded. "I know," he said.

"And when you have done your business there…" She bent her head and paused. She wiped her eyes hastily and said, "Find a way to let us know that you're ali - … that you're back."

"I promise I will, just as soon as I can. I'll be fine, Mama." Cyrus only wished he felt as confident of that as he hoped that he sounded.

Mit emerged with the body slung heavily over his shoulder. He walked to the horse.

Cyrus pulled away from Spaco. He and Mit laid the body over his horse's back behind the saddle.

"Shhh," Cyrus said to the mare, when her haunches tightened.

Mit drew the long ends of jute that Spaco had left through loops on the saddle, then looked from Spaco to Cyrus without speaking. He cleared his throat. "Well, you know the way. Remember what I told you about the springs. The gods – Napirisha, Kiririsha – they will nourish you. You shouldn't have any trouble. Now, have you got everything?"

Cyrus fastened the hawk's tether to a shoulder strap. He tugged again at the strap holding quiver and bow onto the saddle. He checked his belt and sword, felt at the full flask of water, and looked to the saddle bag bulging with food that Spaco had packed. He had felt so certain, so strong when he'd insisted on returning the man's body to his people. But Spaco's fears for him were legitimate. And now he was scared. He didn't trust his voice, so Cyrus nodded to them in a way that he hoped conveyed confidence and mounted.

Mit cleared his throat. "Be on your way, then." He jerked his chin toward the path. "You can still make good progress before nightfall."

But sitting atop the mare, Cyrus turned again toward the old couple. He held the horse in place and took a long moment trying to memorize their dear old faces. Life was full of uncertainty and danger. This he knew.

Then he spun the horse, and they were off – into the future, no looking back.

CHAPTER 56

Cyrus followed Mit's directions. He camped near the springs that the shepherd had told him about and made simple prayer offerings to the region's gods. Each night he lay contemplating the stars and the path that he was choosing.

Cyrus had never traveled this far from Anshan. He was struck by the land's beauty. After tracking east, Cyrus met the river Mit told him to follow to approach Pasargad from the north. It took him along a rocky road hugging the edge of the mountain range. He passed through tall stands of pistaka, pine, and oaks. The river was a constant and reassuring presence. Cyrus imagined it to be Anahita herself chattering loudly over steep stones and murmuring amiably in winding stretches, watching his way. More likely, in this region it was Napirisha. He'd have to remember also the priority of Humban, and less Inshushinak to the people of Pasargad. He was still learning the deities of this place.

Midmorning on the third day, Cyrus saw through a pass ahead where the wilderness yielded to a broad plateau. He emerged and saw before him a rich land cultivated in flowing grain, sesame, chickpeas, and lush hay.

No sooner did Cyrus note the absence of the poppies he'd grown accustomed to seeing in a landscape than he spied two riders galloping toward him. They were ostentatiously armed with arrows and spears. Cyrus released the falcon. He held his mare to a walk, put the reins into his teeth, and raised both hands high over his head. As the others neared, his horse stepped high but didn't run.

Cyrus tried not to betray his fear as the men rode up next to him. With effort, he didn't protest when one seized Cyrus's bow and arrows, and the other took the dagger from his scabbard. The falcon screeched overhead. When the men backed off, the bird circled away. The shorter of the two said, "Who are you, and what is your business?" Their horses pranced around Cyrus, eager to be on their way.

Cyrus took the reins from his mouth and held the mare steady. "I am Cyrus, prince of Anshan. I come in sympathy and respect to return a member of your tribe." He gestured to the body bag behind him.

"Prince, you say?" The two looked at each other. The tall one poked at the bag with Cyrus's dagger, attempting to lift a flap; but Spaco had secured it well. The short one shook his head at his companion. "This way," he said to Cyrus. He rode forward into the plain. The taller man gestured to Cyrus to follow and then fell in close behind him.

CHAPTER 57

*R*iding like that, Cyrus closely guarded between the two men, they left the river's course and loped about one kilometer south. There lay a settlement, a collection of large felt tents clustered on a wide plain. Nearby, the surface of a lake shone like the great silver mirror of a vain goddess. Mountains ringed the entire plateau. In the middle, atop a slight rise, a huge stone platform jutted out over the plain. They rode toward that.

As they drew closer, outside the largest of the tents, a young man, strong and handsome stood, hand on hip, in an impeccably fine, embroidered tunic. When they reached him, Cyrus's escorts dismounted.

"Says he's prince of Anshan," the shorter one said.

"Is that so?" The youth took hold of Cyrus's mare's bridle.

Cyrus sat still.

"You may dismount. Now."

Cyrus got down. "I was exploring the region when I came across one of your men, badly injured. He died despite all efforts. I believe Humban directed me to return his body to you."

The youth raised his eyebrows. He motioned to the escorts to untie and remove the body, then handed the mare off to a dusty boy who emerged from a neighboring hut. The boy took the other two horses and led all three out of sight. Cyrus watched them go.

"If you're telling the truth, you'll get her back and your weapons, too." The youth gestured to the door of the tent behind him.

The escorts led, carrying the body carefully, a man at each end. Cyrus followed with the youth close behind. As they entered, two older women met them there. They took the body, laid it out on a mat in the middle of the floor, and unwrapped it with deft fingers. As soon as they revealed the man's battered face, they began a keening cry and backed out of the house invoking the goddess Kiririsha in their grief as they went.

"His weapons," the taller of Cyrus's escorts tossed Cyrus's dagger, bow, and arrows to the floor in front of the youth.

"You say you're the prince of Anshan," the young man said to Cyrus. "Yet *these* are your weapons?" He scuffed them with his foot. The dagger's blade though bright along its edge was a puny partner to its much larger, crudely carved handle. The bow was one that Cyrus had made himself based on recollection of Zumbaba's. The arrows, too, showed the craftsmanship of an amateur at best.

"They have served me as necessary," Cyrus said, keenly aware of the poor quality of his tunic and trousers.

"I can't imagine how."

The escorts chuckled.

"You admit you're from the palace?"

"I do. Of course."

"Do you know who did this to our cousin?"

"I am led to believe that it was someone from the palace."

The young man laughed. "You are some kind of fool!" Then, he drew back his hand and let it fly, smashing against Cyrus's cheek and mouth. The shock of the slap as much as its force knocked Cyrus to one knee.

"Prince? Prince?!" the youth said.

Cyrus stood.

"You are a murderous fool." The young man drew his hand back again.

"Hold." A man's frame blocked the doorway and cast a long shadow into the room.

Cyrus squinted and winced, rubbing his jaw. He wiped away the blood that ran from his lip.

* * *

"FATHER." The young man said, drawing his tall frame even taller. "This man --"

"Will have a chance to speak," the elder said as he walked into the room. He was of medium height; but as the others fell away, height meant nothing. The man seemed to tower.

"Now, what is going on?"

"This man rode into our village carrying one of our own, abused and dead, as you can see," the young man said.

The elder reached down and gently laid the linen cloth back over the dead man's face. "How did you come to run this morbid errand?" he asked Cyrus.

"I was just explaining to your son, Sir..."

"He says 'sir!'" the youth exclaimed, throwing his hand up in the air. "The prince of Anshan?"

"Our guest," the elder growled. "And he does speak now to the zapanitu."

So this was the leader of the most highly regarded clans within the most highly regarded of Parsa's tribes. Cyrus shook off his nervousness and stood a little straighter.

"Go on," the chieftain said to Cyrus.

"I was just telling your son –"

"Prexaspes," the zapanitu said.

"... That I came across this man a few days' journey to the

northwest. He lay in a ditch, badly beaten, his tongue severed. I brought him to the cottage of – to a nearby cottage for help. We couldn't save him. It was they who told me, based on the man's clothing, that he belonged to your clan. And it was they who told me that someone among my own staff has been posing as the king's authority and making threats."

"You are the king's son?" the chieftain asked.

"I am. I didn't know it, though, until a few years ago."

Prexaspes snorted, eliciting chuckles from the two escorts.

"I was born and raised in Media. When I was ten years old, I learned about my lineage and came to live with my father, King Cam of Anshan."

"Then you know that the king has required that we must raise poppies for a trade that the palace promises will support a renewed military for common defense and somehow restore justice."

"No, I didn't know." Cyrus hung his head.

Prexaspes saw Cyrus's weakness and stepped forward. "What kind of a *prince...*"

"Prex!"

At his father's bark, the young man closed his mouth and stepped back.

"In truth," Cyrus said, "I am seldom there."

"Know it or not... prince or no..." the zapanitu said, "the order is real. All of my life I have been a loyal subject of Anshan. But after consulting with elders of the tribe and observing the fate of the tribes who obeyed, I rejected the order.

"This man, now dead, was to carry a message to King Cam: We understand that there is considerable trade in opium. Much of the kingdom is already devoted to its production, and we have seen it destroy communities. Formerly self-sufficient peoples cannot meet basic needs, and always the specter of misuse is present."

"I thought..." Cyrus began. But there was no excuse. Even if the tribes agreed believed Sadeghi's promises about strength and wealth, he should have known it wouldn't work out – a cash crop such as that. And Cyrus thought of his father's glassy stare, inexplicable rages, and long sleepy absences. He nodded.

"This region, as you probably observed, is unusually fertile, thanks to the runoff of rivers many years ago. In a normal year, we can easily exceed our food needs and grow crops for other uses, as well. We have always made a generous tribute of such goods to the palace. Still, we shall not turn even a small square of it over to opium."

"I don't think that your man was ever able to deliver the message," Cyrus said, "not to the king, anyway." He licked his split lip.

"Oh, it was delivered, all right," Prexaspes said.

His father nodded. "It would seem that our intentions were rejected. Not only that, but we should prepare for a violent reprisal."

"But what has it to do with you?" Prexaspes asked Cyrus. He stepped forward, to his father, "This man is an imposter," he said, "at best. Let's take care how we deal with him."

CHAPTER 58

*C*yrus looked at the men in turn. "You might not believe that I am the prince. But consider this: If I were someone from the palace on a tyrannous errand, would I have come alone?"

No one answered.

"Would I have dared deliver a man who had been murdered to people I have never met and identify myself in such a way as to link myself to those suspected of killing him?"

The escorts looked at the floor. Prexaspes narrowed his eyes.

The zapanitu held Cyrus's gaze. "Whoever you are, we do thank you for returning to us one of our own," he said. "Now, if you are indeed the prince of Anshan, deliver the message. I have not changed my mind."

The women's keening grew louder.

"They'll gather and prepare the body for burial this evening, while priests make appropriate sacrifices on his behalf," the elder said to Cyrus, nodding to a square altar atop the central platform. "You will stay the night here in my house. Unmolested." He gave Prexaspes a hard stare. "And leave at first light. Is that your falcon?" he pointed to the bare limb of a tree just outside.

"Yes."

"Well, tether it. We've got all sorts of fowl running around here. Wash if you like at the public bath. Just there." What looked like a low wall turned out to be a broad basin into which water diverted from the river ran and collected. A small piece of the wall could be lifted to let the water spill out. There, it watered a long trellis on which roses, oleander, and jasmine climbed, creating a fragrant and colorful privacy wall between the bath and settlement.

Cyrus secured the falcon to the branch it had chosen. The bird's gullet was full. Cyrus hoped it hadn't already taken one of the tribe's hens. He went next to check on his horse, walking in the direction of the boy who had led them away.

* * *

THE MARE STOOD GRAZING PEACEABLY on hay within a fenced ring. Someone had wiped her down. Cyrus wondered at the courage of the hands that touched her. Well, the horse was exhausted after days of hard riding -- too much to protest, he thought, or maybe she really was gentling with others, finally. When the horse caught sight of him she and trotted over, nickering. He stroked her soft muzzle and admired her deep brown eyes. He ran his hand over her neck.

"We've come a long way, you and I." He patted the mare's shoulder. "Tomorrow we begin again."

A high whinny made him look behind her to the stable tent. A stallion glossy and black as bitumen stomped, throwing its head up and down. A long, wavy forelock hid and revealed, hid and revealed shiny eyes.

"Seems you have an admirer," Cyrus said to the mare. "Though this *is* the time they'd be coming around, isn't it?" She'd been in heat before, of course. But all of the palace's male horses had been gelded. Sadeghi insisted on it. Cyrus suspected he was simply scared of stallions.

Cyrus gave the little mare one more gentle stroke along her forehead, then turned to go, anticipating the bath ahead. He stopped abruptly. Captivated. Approaching the tent nearest the stable tent was a young with the darkest brown hair Cyrus had ever seen. It cascaded in waves over her shoulders. She held a bundle of colored cloth in her arms. Feeling his eyes on her, the young woman looked back. Over round cheeks, her eyes were like almonds and dark as the horse next door. Unapologetic, she studied him right back. Cyrus was the first to drop his eyes. When she turned away and disappeared under the flap, Cyrus exhaled. Just then, a little boy dashed past Cyrus, running toward the door into which the bewitching woman had stepped. Cyrus caught the boy's arm, spinning him around.

"Who is the girl, the one who just went into that tent?"

"My sister?" the boy said. He looked up. "Sir."

"And who are you?" Cyrus asked.

The little boy squared his shoulders. "I am Otanes, son of Pharnaspes, of the clan Achaemenid." Then, seeing Cyrus glance back at the tent, he added brightly, "That's Sanda -- Cassandane."

Cyrus released him, and the boy ran off.

Sanda, Cyrus thought. Sanda. Daughter of Pharnaspes, Sanda.

The sense that someone was watching him broke Cyrus's reverie. He turned to see the youth who nearly broken his jaw looking at Cyrus as though he'd like to try again.

Prexaspes walked over. "I thought you were leaving, back to Anshan... to the palace." He curled his lip.

"I am. Your father said I'm to go tomorrow, at first light."

Prexaspes made a show of stepping between Cyrus and Sanda's family tent, directly into Cyrus's line of sight. There he stood, his feet shoulder width apart.

"You should probably get some sleep then."

"First a bath, as your father suggested."

"Make it quick, prince. My mother's dinner is waiting."

* * *

THE EVENING WAS A BLUR. Sure, Cyrus recognized when he stepped inside the chieftain's tent that it was more house than hovel. It was the luxurious accommodations of someone with comfortable means and no need to be ostentatious about it. Temporary, a tent might be by definition; but there was nothing wanting about this one. The furnishings, the food – all were of the finest quality. Yet Cyrus hardly noticed. Its details were lost on him, except for the sword – its handle forged of iron and bronze twisted into a braid – that hung in a leather scabbard from one of the tent's supports, an arm's reach from the zapanitu. The hostility Prexaspes bore toward Cyrus emanated from the tall young man in waves. And Cyrus knew that Prexaspes's father shared it. Despite their hospitality – they'd never hurt Cyrus, not here, that would be to break a code of conduct that transcended all else – it was easy to see that the zapanitu reserved suspicions of his own. As for the women, to a person they glared at Cyrus as if he had indeed been the assailant who brutalized their kin, tortured to death. So, as soon as he could excuse himself, Cyrus did.

While the others slept, he lifted the flap of the tent, and slipped out. He walked past his falcon, hooded and quietly tethered at her post. Under a cloudy night sky, Cyrus walked to the settlement's outskirts and beyond, past the pens of livestock quiet for the night, the coops for fowl all tucked in, and the corrals where mules shuffled in dreams. He walked northeast and then seeing an elevated area, he walked there. On one edge of the sprawling mud-brick terrace, two stone plinths, like massive eternal witnesses behind him, Cyrus sat. Overhead, the clouds broke apart, came and went across the face of the moon. The air felt clean, cold. Winter was coming on. The nutty smell of cut grain stalks drying in the late autumn air brought to mind the alfalfa fields of Media. He lay back against the cool bricks, grateful for the old pelt Cook had insisted he wear.

"Room enough for another?"

A woman's voice startled Cyrus to sitting again. He brushed his hands across his eyes. Cassandane. Her figure, standing there before him and round in all the right places blocked and merged with the mountains behind her. Cyrus grinned. He slid over and patted the place where he'd been.

"Now there is," he said.

She smelled good – something herb-y, earthy, and vaguely floral, like the linens after hanging through a hot summer day.

Suddenly, something scurried behind them. Cyrus turned to look. Sanda didn't.

"Probably jirds, cleaning up the last bits of grain from the shiyip."

Cyrus knew of the feasts but as Cook had regularly complained, what he'd seen was a pale thing of past events.

"So what do you think of our place?" Sanda asked.

All the answers that occurred to Cyrus in that moment had to do with her. So he simply said, "It's wonderful."

That seemed to be the right answer. And enough. Because Cassandane settled back on her hands. And when she spoke, Cyrus could hear the smile in her voice. She talked of growing up there, the delights of every season, the different regions they occupied throughout a year with their animals, the diverse crops, and that great big sky. They talked about the pleasures of the rivers, the singular feel of catching a fish and eating it right there. Stretching their arms out his way and the other, they talked of how the land lay in just such a way as to feel... "Cozy," Sanda said. "I cannot imagine ever wanting to live anywhere else," she said with a happy sigh. And finally, before the sun began to brighten the eastern ridge, they stood and walked back toward the tents. Neither said anything more about the other. Sanda never asked

Cyrus about the man who'd been killed or who exactly Cyrus really was. They simply walked companionably under a sky nearly clear now. Just before they got to her tent, when Sanda turned to say goodbye, she suddenly reached her hand up.

Pointing to the sky behind her, she said, "Look. There."

Cyrus did. A star, low in the sky shone with hue of rusted iron. He'd never seen it look so big before.

"Shimut," Cassandane said.

Cyrus waited for more, some explanation, some interpretation of its significance for her. But she simply raised her eyebrows high and with a little smile, disappeared inside her tent.

When Cyrus returned to the zapanitu's tent, he was so enchanted by how Sanda had transformed the evening, the night, indeed the whole place for him that he didn't notice that among the sleeping forms, one was not but watched Cyrus enter, quiet and late.

CHAPTER 59

*C*yrus woke to a chilly morning. When he stepped outside, the plain glittered as if filled with millions of stars. Everywhere shimmered with a frost of thinnest glass. The sun just rising lit the trees yellow, umber, and deep red. The mountains wore robes of violet, blue, and peach-orange. For the first time in his life, Cyrus thought, I could stay here forever. But his horse was already saddled and loosely tied to a post at the corral's door. Cyrus looked around but saw no one.

Cyrus collected his falcon, mounted the mare, and with a sigh turned his back on Pasargad. There were two routes back to the palace in Anshan one faster and more direct than the other. The horse moved more freely without the burden of an additional man on her back. They made good time. Since Cyrus was hardly in a hurry to get back to the palace, he directed the mare north. He'd take a longer route and a detour too.

The chieftain's son tracked Cyrus by his horse's footprints and droppings. It didn't take much convincing for the zapanitu to agree to his son's following the young man who had so boldly declared himself prince but seemed anything but. Prexaspes insisted he was a fake; the chieftain said they'd need proof. Prexaspes camped carefully, without fire, grateful that the falcon that followed Cyrus from the sky when it wasn't on his shoulder couldn't report the man who tracked them. When Cyrus departed from one of the only two direct routes to Anshan, and rode into the hills where only bandits and poor shepherds lived, Prexaspes nodded smugly to himself.

* * *

CYRUS DISMOUNTED at the cottage and looked around. He called, "Pop, Mama?"

Prexaspes heard it all. Well behind, he dismounted, tied his horse to a tree, and walked forward in mincing steps, keeping to the underbrush. From there, he saw an old woman in a dirt-soiled apron step out of the far forest into the clearing.

"Hello-o, Mama! Pop!" Cyrus called again.

Prexaspes watched Cyrus remove his horse's saddle, lead her into the empty corral, throw in a pile of hay, and walk into the house.

Spaco returned first. She saw the horse and ran into the house.

Peering out from underbrush near the spring, Prexaspes could hear the excited tone of a happy reunion.

Then the two walked out. Spaco held a pail. She and Cyrus moved their heads as they spoke, making it difficult for the young man hiding to hear everything. "Except for... when I first arrived, I think they...prince..."

Spaco began to walk toward the spring, Cyrus with her. Prexaspes caught snippets of Cyrus's words. "...chief, anyway. And he ... that matters." When they got too close, Prexaspes withdrew a safe distance and crouched down again.

"How's our pretty little horse?" Spaco asked, watching the mare munch the green hay.

"Well. Surprisingly well. Someone in Pasargad treated her

with kindness. And she accepted it," Cyrus said. "And there's more."

"Save it for your pop. He'll want to hear everything, too."

"Where *is* Pop?" Cyrus took the pail of water from Spaco's hand.

"He should be bringing the flocks in any time now."

Prexaspes watched the older woman take Cyrus's arm and walk back into the cottage, her head on his shoulder as he chattered.

Inside the cottage, Cyrus resisted Spaco's pleas that he spend the night. He was determined to be on his way, to return to the palace as quickly as possible. He'd explained enough for her to understand. Cyrus accepted another sack of food from Spaco and filled his water flask and left before Mit got home.

But Prexaspes was already gone. He'd seen everything he needed to see, everything he'd expected. Prexaspes mounted his horse and rode away, prepared to report that he had proof. Cyrus was the son not of a king but of a commonplace shepherd couple.

CHAPTER 60

*a*s Cyrus drew closer to the palace, he slowed the mare. What determination he'd felt finally to fix things at the palace became riddled with doubt. How could he possibly reverse the years of neglect and his father's deterioration? The king couldn't see his own shortcomings, the groundsman was Cam's only trusted confidant, and the argument for financial gain from opium production was a strong one. There were definitely people on the groundsman's side and in his pay who wouldn't take kindly to meddling from the prince.

Yet, many people, people Cyrus hadn't even known existed before (an image of Sanda's deep eyes and dark tresses flashed in his mind), wanted something different. And there were a lot of people suffering for lack of justice from the palace. No, he had to do something. Also nagging, something he wished he'd asked the Pasargad chieftain to explain: what was it that the groundsman had promised with gain from opium trade -- defense, military weapons? Against whom?

Cyrus released his falcon. Its energetic flight, casting off the fetters of land, flapping and soaring, could transform any day. It was as if the bird pulled Cyrus's troubles from him and flew them away. He watched, and his thoughts turned again to Sanda. Sitting next to her on that high plain under the night sky, the sound of her voice – its rise and fall like balm in his mind, the mountains rising behind her as if she and they were one... Another time. He would go back.

Cyrus watched the Saker swiftly gain critical altitude and then dive, fearless in a descent so fast that his eyes could hardly follow. The falcon dropped straight down until mid-air it hit with lethal force another bird, slamming its prey against the ground and then breaking the other bird's neck with the little protrusion on its beak. Cyrus jogged over. The bird that his falcon had dispatched was a houbara. Cyrus grinned. Cook would tease him. The meat was prized as an aphrodisiac. He'd take it as a sign, a sign from Pinikir or whoever was the goddess of love around here, that there was something there, someone back in Pasargad for him. Cyrus gave his falcon the choicest entrails, fastened the bird again to his wrist, and rode back to the palace such as it was.

Sadeghi was nowhere to be seen when Cyrus arrived.

"Not expected for a time," the old groom told him.

Cyrus hated to admit his relief, but the absence of Sadeghi bolstered his confidence.

"Look the girl over carefully," he said turning his horse over to the groom's care. "It's been a long ride. But she'll have plenty of time to rest."

Upadarma nodded. "So you'll be leaving again soon." There was no question in the tone, only weary resignation. He turned the mare's head toward the stable.

Cyrus stopped him with a hand on the old groom's arm. "Actually," he said, "I intend to stay."

Upadarma nodded a quick smile.

* * *

NAHHUNTE, who had been on duty when Cyrus had first arrived in Anshan was on duty again when he returned. Over the years, the two had become friends, despite Cyrus's long absences and surliness in the face of the taut palace atmosphere. They were the same height now.

"Nice to have you back," Nahhunte said.

"I'm here for good this time," Cyrus said.

The guard raised his eyebrows as if to say, We'll see about that.

What he said was, "Your father is in there." Nahhunte gestured to the audience hall where Cyrus and Zubaba had waited on their first day.

Cyrus walked to the doorway and looked in. Hard as it was, he made himself see it all, really see it. The room was empty but for Cam, sitting on an old throne, cobwebs clinging to the back bars under the seat. Cyrus studied his father. Twice, the frail king brought his hand down on the armrest and muttered something. He'd nod, then sit still again, seemingly as alert as if he were attending on some serious matter of state. Though there was no one there. Cyrus stepped into the room.

When Cambyses saw Cyrus's shape in the doorway, "An audience with the king?" he asked with a quavering voice.

"Hello, Father," Cyrus said.

The king gripped the armrests leaned forward, craning his neck and squinting to see.

"It's me, Cyrus."

The king sat back. In the past year or so, King Cam seemed to have grown more accustomed to the boy himself, less agitated around him. Besides, as Cyrus grew, he looked more and more the strong young man he was becoming and less like the waifish mother who had taken her own life some sixteen years ago.

Still, it was rare that Cyrus would elect to visit King Cam, choose to be with his father.

Now, Cyrus walked up to the pale king. He laid his hand on top of his father's.

Cambyses flinched, but he didn't pull away.

"I want to talk about the future," Cyrus said. "I was thinking that you and I could talk together about plans for the welfare of the kingdom."

The king looked at Cyrus then. But his eyes quickly clouded. "I'm tired," he said. "Such a long audience today." He furrowed his already lined brow. "I need lie down, time for me to have a smoke to relax." The king put a skinny hand to his head, nudging the golden ring askew. "All too much," he muttered as he hobbled out.

Cyrus watched him go. The monarch was no older than Mit but so decrepit that he seemed ancient. Hatred for the groundsman welled like acrid rot in Cyrus's gut. Suddenly, without thought except for rage at his own impotence, Cyrus swung his arm against the simple throne. The force of it flung the chair across the room. Its legs splintered against the far wall.

"My lord."

Cyrus spun, his face red, his eyes still glinting. "What!" he yelled.

Nahhunte looked from Cyrus to the broken throne. "It's nothing."

"It better be," Cyrus raged, "because I can do nothing. I *am* nothing!"

The guard stood silent.

"I can do nothing," Cyrus said again, holding his palms out. His voice was quiet, broken.

Nahhunte held his gaze. After a moment, he said, "You'd be surprised."

Cyrus hung his head. The guard left.

* * *

CYRUS RETURNED to his room and began to pack. It was the same churning, same burning in his chest and gut that drove him out every time. Reflexive. Self-defense. Self-preservation. But this time, Cyrus suddenly saw his hands as they moved – swift and rough – to gather the things he'd need. Really saw them. He saw his arms, looked at them as if they were on someone else's shoulders. These were the limbs of a man. And Cyrus heard in his mind, as clearly as if Prexaspes were sneering over his shoulder, "... what kind of *prince* ..." Cyrus stopped.

He looked around the room he'd known for years now, as if seeing it for the first time. It was exactly as it had been when he and Zubaba first arrived. The fruit changed with the seasons and the linens were sometimes those with the hint of an old dye, but there was always rosemary and the space was clean and fresh. Cook insisted that no matter how often Cyrus left and for how long, each time longer than the last, his room would be ready for his return. Cyrus picked up a sprig of rosemary, its spiky green leaves offset by the palest tiny blue flowers. Loyalty. To what? To whom?

Cyrus crushed the herb in a fist, feeling the woody stem dig into his skin, the leaves like needles crumble in his hand. When he opened his palm, its scent rose more powerful than before. Cyrus threw it back into the dish. He'd finish packing later. Cyrus tossed water from the basin against his face. Again, and again. Each time, the smell of rosemary. And again, "What kind of *prince*...?" Through the window, Cyrus saw Cook's garden, a riot of colors and shapes all of which he now knew.

He left the room, left his things just as they were. And Cyrus wandered through the palace. He had never really studied it. He'd said he would stay. He would try. As he walked, he reflected how little interest he'd taken in the place. Nothing about Ashan's palace attracted him. Not even the fact of its former reach, its former greatness. If he wasn't outside, tending the garden or the animals... and even then, he had wanted only to leave, always to leave. The land around -- the mountains, wild gorges, and fields -- felt far better to him than these old rooms, so stale these days.

Besides, Sadeghi seemed ever present, sneering at him, threatening him with vague punishments for troubling his father or for some misstep imagined or real. Even when the groundsman was gone, he was there - in the vacancy in King Cam's eyes, in the anxious eyes of Cook's nephew, in the nervousness his little mare still showed every time she crossed the threshold of the stables... So Cyrus would leave. Well, Sadeghi wasn't here now. So, yes, Cyrus would try.

In his wandering, lost in thought, Cyrus found himself near the king's quarters. Despite his long absences, Cyrus knew that Cambyses left his rooms less and less often. Now, unless someone brought King Cam to the audience hall or in for dinner, the king lived in less and less space. Nahhunte would coax him out into the greater palace sometimes, to the audience hall or courtyard. And of course Cook still required his presence for dinner. But even that it didn't always happen. King Cam didn't want to leave his rooms at all. Finally, he wanted only the cot where he smoked his opium. And he wanted the man who gave it to him. No one questioned when Sadeghi moved into the king's quarters with him.

It was the voices that broke through Cyrus's ruminating, voices raised in agitation, in anger. But Sadeghi was away from the palace now.

So who was it with the king? Cyrus froze.

CHAPTER 61

Sadeghi rode toward the palace deeply satisfied. He had closed another deal with the ironsmiths of the central highlands - his stash of weapons had grown almost to what he figured they'd need. And he still had enough money for his strongmen to teach the last holdouts exactly who would determine the fate these of these lands. They didn't think the palace would protect them? Well, he'd prove it. He savored the image of that hoard – swords, bows, spears,... - in the cave. And more like it all over Parsa. And a good thing, too. The geopolitical situation had made his plans yet more urgent.

Sadeghi grinned. The news troubled him, but at least it was his alone. He knew what the others in the palace didn't. Not yet. But why would they? Over the years they'd become so insular, diminished in their protection of the king. They were so concerned that no one see the king in his pathetic incompetency – and so caught up in all their little jobs that they'd heard nothing of the outside world... Well he did. And it made him nervous: Cyrus's cousin had become king of Babylonia.

Amel-Markduk, the young man called himself, clearly a desperate move to show loyalty to Babylonia over his mother's

Media, Sadeghi thought. Following Amel-Marduk's fortunes was whiplash: from the nothing-son of a foreign wife, to crown prince of Babylonia, to death-row imprisonment, to acquittal and now king of the world's most powerful empire was blisteringly erratic. That young man, once called Bushu was now "servant of Marduk" and sitting on the most powerful throne in all the world. And his mother Amytis, the queen mother was back in Media more powerful than ever. Amytis: sister of Parsa's late queen Mandane. Mandane: Cyrus's mother.

Sadeghi feared that it was only a matter of time that the two of them (Amytis and Amel-Marduk) could leverage more support than Sadeghi could counter. And they'd throw that power behind Cyrus. Cyrus, who'd grown into a strong young man with an even stronger mind, damn him. Better to get ahead of the problem, Sadeghi thought. Better to get rid of Anshan's royal family altogether. No, better to install a new one. Sadeghi could almost feel the weight of the crown he'd wear. His hard work was paying off. It was all coming together for him, and just in time.

To top it all off, he had seen the red planet so close to the earth the night before, close enough to speak into Sadeghi's ear. Mighty one, herald of the gods, indeed. Sadeghi wondered what it would feel like, the *kitin* of the gods. Perhaps Humban himself would bestow it. Well, never mind. Sadeghi already felt invincible. Only few more days of travel, and he would be. Invincible.

CHAPTER 62

"*N*ow!" Cam yelled, "I must have it now!"

Outside the king's quarters, Cyrus stepped up to the closed door.

Another voice, a man's, murmured too quietly to understand.

"Please, help," Cam's voice had changed to a child's wheedling tone.

His ear against the paneling, it chilled Cyrus to the marrow.

"You have to help me. Help."

The other voice again, and then – Cyrus ducked back – footsteps getting louder. Cyrus's fingers clenched to fists.

"Don't leave me!" Cam yelled.

When the door opened, Cyrus flattened himself against the wall.

Nahhunte. As the guard pulled the door shut behind him, Cyrus leapt at him. With all his might, Cyrus smashed the guard against the wall. Despite the man's brawn, Cyrus held him in place, held him by the throat, just like Harpagus taught him. Just like Harpagus taught him – learned well and hard – those combat skills turned to instinct. His face inches from Nahhunte's, Cyrus spat, "What are you doing to my father?"

The guard wrested Cyrus's hand from his neck. He bent over, coughing. When he'd recovered enough Nahhunte scowled at Cyrus. "I'm trying to help him."

"What kind of help is that?"

Nahhunte opened his hand. There lay the paraphernalia - unused. "I withheld his opium," he said, turning his head back and forth, his hand on his neck. "Gods, you're strong." He coughed. "Come here." The guard gestured to follow him down the hall. When they reached the courtyard, they found a shady spot and sat. Chickens clucking and scratching in the dust around their feet. "The stuff is destroying him," the guard said. "Maybe it has already. I don't know. But when you came back, determined to stay this time, I knew I had to try. Seeing him like that... Seeing you like that.... It's got to change." Nahhunte bent, tossed a pebble at the trunk of a little tree, missed. "I've tried before -- Cook, Martiya, me... -- but it's hard. And when the groundsman is around, well, then it's impossible."

"But he's so desperate."

"I know. It's tough to watch. But I've also seen his lucid moments. You've seen them, too. When you're here."

Cyrus couldn't miss the subtle dig.

Nahhunte shrugged. "Infrequent, I'll grant you that. But every so often, he's almost like he was. The king we remember is still in there somewhere. It's an evil business, this opium, a kitten that turns into some panther-demon from the underworld. He has to fight that monster." The guard looked hard at Cyrus. "When he's weak enough, he just might win."

They sat like that a moment.

"Listen," the guard said. "The good news is that right now, he's just angry. So, if you had come here to talk to him, it might be all right. He's not delusional. The bad news is the worst fight is still ahead." Nahhunte stood. "As for me, I've got some furniture to repair." He shot Cyrus a forgiving grin.

The thought of going back anywhere near Cam's recent outburst made Cyrus want to saddle the mare. But. He remembered Prexaspes's challenge: What kind of *prince*...?! So, he took a deep breath and stood. At his father's door, Cyrus stopped and listened. Then Cyrus walked on. To the next door.

CHAPTER 63

Outside the room that he'd never entered before, the room that had been closed off to anyone – except Sadeghi, didn't need saying – since Cambyses's beloved wife, Cyrus's mother Mandane had died, Cyrus hesitated. He was unsure what it might hold for him. But he was curious, too. And if he were going to stay, really stay… Cyrus tried the handle. Surprised to find the door unlocked, he opened it slowly and peered around. Only one small window up high let in the sun. A beetle skittled across the floor. Cyrus stepped inside quietly and closed the door, leaving just a crack for more light and, he admitted, the reminder of an exit.

Cyrus stood against the wall next to the door for a while and let his eyes adjust. The room was small, smaller than he expected. In the center was a rectangular table with short benches that had been pushed neatly underneath. Ringing three sides of the room were waist-high wooden countertops. They rested on braces attached to the walls and legs further supported by cross-beams. He walked to the nearest. On top was an assortment of colored glass bottles and glazed clay jars, some with designs that Cyrus recognized from Ecbatana, some in foreign shapes and with decorative patterns he had never seen before. There wasn't anything of particular value.

On the countertop against the wall were a woman's make-up set, hair ornaments, and jewelry of only the simplest, cheapest kind. Cyrus lifted a clip and teased from it a strand of long light hair. He wound it around his finger. Mandane, my mother. Mandane, whose death had so completely undone the king that he not only closed off this room from the palace but also the whole palace from the world. With Sadeghi's help, the king had closed himself from life. Cyrus ran his finger along the tabletop, leaving a long dark streak through pale red dust. Cambyses had loved Mandane beyond imagining, people said. Now, Cyrus could imagine.

As the sun moved across the window, its light suddenly illuminated a small wooden box.

Through the dancing motes of dust, Cyrus tilted his head with interest. He unlatched its tiny bronze clasp. A soft woolen weave dyed with purple and red stripes lined the inside. On top lay a small bundle of darkest blue velvet. But just when Cyrus reached inside to retrieve it, the trembling grip of a hand seized his wrist and yanked him around.

"Give it!" Cambyses stepped in front of Cyrus, still gripping his wrist. "Thief!" he called loudly. "Guards! Thief!" His voice was tremulous, shrill.

Cyrus stood still, paralyzed by his father's wrath and acutely aware of the man's frailty. If Cyrus wrenched his hand – still holding the blue velvet bundle – away from Cambyses, the king might fall.

King Cam swayed on his feet. Cyrus wanted to run. He was eager to run. Instead, Cyrus caught Cambyses with his free hand, steadied his father.

The exertion had caused the slim band of a crown around the king's brow to slip. He glared at Cyrus. "What are you doing here?" he hissed. Cambyses tugged Cyrus closer to his face. He snatched the fabric from his son's palm. Suddenly, he stopped, arrested by some thought or image only he could see. Rather than inspect the fabric, he grabbed Cyrus's hand again. Ever so slowly, he brought it to his nose. Cyrus let him. Holding Cyrus's palm there, Cambyses closed his eyes and inhaled deeply. Rosemary. When he opened them again, they shone.

"Mandane," he said. "Why are you here?" the king asked. His voice was weak but clear, demanding.

"I was just looking around," Cyrus said.

"Yes, but why are you here?" Cam asked again.

Cyrus furrowed his brow and pulled his head back, looking down at Cam through narrow eyes. "Because I am her son," Cyrus said.

Cambyses's eyes swam. He released Cyrus's hand.

"I am your son," Cyrus said. He reached out and straightened his father's crown, "And this is where I live."

Cam's eyes overflowed. He pushed the fabric back into Cyrus's hand and gripped his wrist again. "Our son." His whisper stirred the motes of dust caught in the window's fading light.

Cyrus felt a tremor through the king's bony fingers. Cam began to shake. Cyrus's eyes grew wide with fear and the uncertainty of what to do. With great relief that he watched Nahhunte rush in. The guard stepped up behind the king just as Cam slumped unconscious.

"Father!" Cyrus said lunging to catch him from the front while Nahhunte caught him from the back.

"Let him lie on the floor a moment," Nahhunte said, lowering Cam gently to the ground. "He'll come around soon."

Cyrus watched Cambyses's chest rise and fall with shallow breath.

Nahhunte nodded to the scrap of fabric Cyrus still clutched in his hand. He raised his eyebrows, inquiring.

Cyrus had forgotten all about it. He opened the fine cloth. There was nothing inside.

Nahhunte exhaled and nodded, resigned. "It held the king's seal," he said. "Gone. The official mark of Parsa's crown." He shook his head. "As you can see," Nahhunte waved his arm to take in the room, "Sadeghi cleaned out everything of any value – kept or sold." He laughed a wry laugh. "But that seal... even Sadeghi doesn't have it. Oh, he was so furious. He questioned everyone over and over again for months." His smile died away. "And in the worst ways. But it's as if Mandane took it to her grave. We've never seen it since." He shrugged. Then Nahhunte looked back down at Cambyses lying there. He sighed again, resigned. But his voice was tender. "I can get him to his bed. Why don't you fetch some wine from Cook?"

"Be sure it's diluted with plenty of water," Nahhunte called to him. "We have to do this gradually."

* * *

CYRUS DID as Nahhunte had asked. And he came back. He returned to the king's quarters. There, he and Nahhunte agreed that they would do everything they could to bring Cam through the trauma of detoxification together. Cyrus insisted that he would hold vigil through that first night. It was a good thing because – Cyrus would learn the next day – in the guard's own weariness, Nahhunte had collapsed in the courtyard. He wrenched his shoulder in the fall.

Cyrus sat by the bed and tried to find in his father's ravaged face and manic eyes the man who had recognized him, if only for a moment, just hours before. But that king was gone, replaced by a ranting madman singularly intent on a desperate desire.

Cyrus ordered that ropes be brought. With stinging eyes, he and the guard bound the king to his bed. The prince spent the sleepless night studying Elamite cuneiform, relieved to find that its script was simpler than the written language that he had seen in Media.

Near morning, Cam finally slept, his body soaked in sweat, his wrists and ankles chaffed from the ropes. Strips of silk that Cyrus had torn from an old tunic and placed between rope and skin minimized the damage. Still, the king bled from sore spots. When morning came, Cyrus emerged from the room, his face puffy and worn.

Cyrus left his father in the care of the guard and of Cook who tended the king's injuries and went to his rooms, stripped and fell into bed.

He slept fitfully, tormented by his father's hateful raging and dreading the altercation with the groundsman. Images of monstrous demons from childhood stories in Media troubled his dreams. He woke from battling a being part lion, part man that had the head of a slit-eyed eagle and long talons where its hands should have been. The fight was unresolved. Cyrus woke, sweating profusely.

Cyrus got up, naked from the bed, and went into the wash-room. He soaked a linen in cool water and ran it over his entire body. He dipped the cloth again and wrung it out over his head, letting the water find rivulets through his hair to run over his eyes and mouth, neck, and chest.

Cyrus reached for a towel.

"Sadeghi! He's coming!" Hurried footsteps through the court-yard grew louder. "From the north!" Martiya called as he rushed into the prince's room. Seeing Cyrus standing bare, he turned away. "I'm sorry, my lord."

"Saddle the mare," Cyrus said, and Martiya was gone.

His heart pounding, Cyrus dressed. He tried to steady trem-bling fingers as he fastened his belt, drew the dagger from its sheath and returned it again, flat against his side. He grabbed the bow he had fashioned and the arrows, which looked to him now like a child's playthings, sighed and threw the holding strap over his shoulder. He tied a twisted cord around his head, pulling his long hair back behind his ears, and walked swiftly to the stable, scattering chickens as he went.

* * *

THE MARE WHINNIED when she saw him. Upadarma held the horse loosely as she pranced this way and that. She felt the excitement, felt the fear. She reared, resisting the constraint of the lead but came down again carefully to avoid the crippled man. Nevertheless, Martiya took the reins from his father.

Cook's nephew waited with the falcon, hooded and tethered. Sensing Cyrus's proximity, the bird darted her head this way and that.

Cook was frantic. "Where's Nahhunte?" She twisted her apron in her hands. "Cyrus really should have a guard!"

"I can't wait," Cyrus said.

Cook's nephew shook his head as Nahhunte appeared. Clinging tightly to one arm, Cambyses walked with fragile steps. Nahhunte's other arm, his good arm, was in a sling. He'd be no help.

"Martiya, then," Cook said, spinning on the young man.

Martiya nodded eagerly, "Yes, but –"

"He could ride Ochre," Cook's voice rose into a question hearing its absurdity even as it left her mouth. The old horse could hardly lift its head anymore. Any other horses the palace had were those that Sadeghi brought. They came and went at his pleasure. All were gone.

Cyrus shook his head. "He has to stay." Cyrus took the mare from him. "If it happens that –" He stopped himself. He looked straight at Martiya. "Someone will need to seize Sadeghi when he comes back here. By then he will know the terms, the charges. He has no place here. "

Martiya straightened his back and nodded.

Cyrus took one precious minute to look at the faces of the

each of the people gathered. So few, and only a fraction of those whose welfare teetered on the battle ahead.

Cyrus swung up into the saddle and gestured to Cook's nephew to bring the falcon.

As he reached up, the boy's sleeve fell back, revealing a broad bruise on his bicep. Its color made Cyrus yet more determined that it would be the last wound Sadeghi inflicted in this place. The boy quickly tugged it down and shook his head, eyes begging Cyrus not to say anything. Cyrus gritted his teeth. The last shame.

"Be careful," Cook said, her eyes finding Cyrus again. "He won't stop, you know."

Cyrus looked at Martiya beside her. He knew the back of the young man's neck was deeply scarred from a brand the groundsman had given him years ago when little Martiya, not yet grown had refused to drive Ochre harder in the field. Cook's face, so plump and soft, given as quickly to laughter as to scolding, was tight with anxiety. And Cambyses – the king. Gaunt and trembling with weakness. He wore his best robe... frayed at the hems and stained beyond cleaning. Cyrus tore his eyes away.

"Did you see it?" Upadarma asked as Cyrus took the reins. "For several nights now, still he shines - Shimut, red as rust in the sky." That star. Pasargadae.

In his mind's eye, Cyrus saw Cassandane, her head turned, looking just over his shoulder. Cyrus nodded. With her, he'd seen the star. And he knew: herald of the gods; some time bestower of *kitin*. Cyrus knew the stories – that god a warrior, too.

From the hawk on Cyrus's shoulder, he removed the hood and tossed the tether, too.

Well, Cyrus didn't need a god to tell him he was in for a fight.

The bird shrieked its shrill cry. As the horse lunged forward, the bird alit for the sky.

What Cyrus didn't know was just how big a fight it would be.

CHAPTER 64

*C*yrus scanned the horizon to the north. A horse stood, saddled but riderless, on the edge of a field of poppies. Cyrus cantered the mare toward it. The horse's bridle glinted with silver lozenges along its cheek and forehead pieces. Cyrus didn't have to look closely to know that its bronze bit was decorated with striding stag. This was the bridle Upadarma had told him that one of the northern tribes had gifted to his grandfather some decades ago. Sadeghi "used it" now.

So intent was Cyrus on closing in on Sadeghi, so intent was he every sense and all attention lasering to focus this singular foe that Cyrus didn't notice the fierce band of riders crest the eastern ridge. From the horse's bridle, Cyrus moved his eyes to the long stave that hung parallel to the ground under a stirrup strap. No wonder the dead man's face had looked like it did. Still some ways from the man, Cyrus slowed the mare to a trot, to a walk. From there, the horse moved and her rider with her like inexorable time through the flowers, pollen speckling yellow among the red that splashed across her shoulders. Out of the sky, the falcon banked and without a sound dropped to Cyrus's shoulder.

Still the man on the ground bent to his task. So intent was the man on it, seeing not only the sticky stuff of each seedpod he scraped but the castles he would have, the women, the drink, and the masses of fawning subject, that he also didn't see upon the riders the colorful robes of the Parsan highlands or the mounts that only the most noble of the tribes - and most resistant to the palace - could afford to keep. And neither Cyrus nor Sadeghi saw when the zapanitu stopped his group's advance, could not hear the chieftain say to his son, "Wait. The man will finish the boy, send him back to his peasant home. When he's done, we will deliver the message ourselves." And so their horses stamped with impatience and the hands of their riders went to their swords over and over again. Waiting.

Not long. The mare called out with a piercing whinny, and it began. Cyrus watched the groundsman's head pop up in the midst of the field. He saw Sadeghi see Cyrus, and he watched the groundsman run toward his horse, legs swinging over and around the flowers until he reached the bay, swung up, and kicked his mount into a gallop, closing the ground between them.

"Harvesting the royal fields, I see," Cyrus said as the groundsman pulled up his horse. Cyrus nodded to the pouch attached to the groundsman's belt. A silk cord tied off the fabric at the top out of which the handle of a sharp-edged spatula caught the light.

From the side of his eyes, the groundsman studied Cyrus. Never had the boy spoken like this. A new normal? He'd deal. "You can thank me for it later. I'm famished," the groundsman said. He narrowed his eyes at Cyrus. "Ride back and tell that mealy-mouthed n-n-n-nephew of Cook's to have something good ready for me."

Cyrus's blood thickened at Sadeghi's easy ridicule. "There is no later," Cyrus said. "And there's nothing for you at the palace." Cyrus nodded to the pouch on the groundsman's belt. "I'll let you keep that. But your time in Anshan, in all of Parsa, is over."

The groundsman looked at his hip, threw back his head, and laughed an ugly bray with no mirth in it. "Say what, boy?"

"You can keep the opium you've harvested into that pouch of yours." Cyrus spoke as if to a slow-witted toddler. "And I will let you go without harm." Then, his eyes steely, Cyrus said, "Provided I never see you here again." The falcon swiveled its head.

The man's face clouded with anger. "You will Let. Me. Go?! You impertinent fool. I have everything you need, everything the *king* needs. Step aside. The king of Anshan requires my service."

Cyrus angled the mare directly in the man's path, directly between Sadeghi and Anshan.

Sadeghi narrowed his eyes. "You. You're nothing but a bastard. Your mother was a whore who bore you in shame and killed herself, hating you, you filthy son of a slave."

Cyrus's jaw clenched. His nostrils flared. He hands shook, itching for the dagger. At the flex of his shoulders tensed, ready, the falcon took off. But Cyrus contained himself. Besides all that Harpagus had taught him, it was by accident that Cyrus had learned even in the face of a raging insult, restraint.

"Go ahead," the groundsman said, nodding to Cyrus's dagger.

"Not today," Cyrus said.

On the ridge, Prexaspes said, "What are they doing?"

"Talking," his father answered. He didn't need to hear Cyrus say, I will kill you. The zapanitu added, "But not for long."

"How dare you!" The groundsman pulled the long stave out from under his thigh and swung it hard. But Cyrus's horse had already bolted aside, carrying him out of range. She'd seen such sticks, knew their pain. Yet when Cyrus turned her back to the man, she went. By then, Sadeghi had already recovered for another swing. The next blow clipped Cyrus across his ribs. Sadeghi had learned to fight even earlier than Cyrus had, learned to fight for his life with whatever it took. Cyrus heard the crack, caught a painful breath, and spun back, dagger in hand.

The battle was short, the battle was long. It seemed suspended outside of time each thrust, each parry, each blow. Different than any kind of fighting that Cyrus had done during those short but intense weeks in Ecbatana. There was no mistaking, this was to the death. The mare shrieked and spun and reared and bit, but she bled from wounds ear to tail. Cyrus hated that. It was her he thought of when he asked her to shift left. So it was he who caught the full force of the blow. And it flung him from the saddle.

Sadeghi grinned through bloody teeth and gunned his horse toward the prone young man. Just then, from out of the sky, Cyrus's falcon let loose a shrieking cry. He dove and with razor talons and wings flapping swiped the man's cheek, his neck, his scalp. Sadeghi brought his fists up to shield his eyes, the stave under his shoulder. As his mount shimmied in terror from the screeching bird, the falling stave caught in the ground inches from where Cyrus had rolled to his knees, dagger in hand. Cyrus seized the end and with a mighty thrust catapulted the groundsman out of his saddle and over his horse's head. Sadeghi landed on his back with a thud, knocking the air out his lungs.

Cyrus brought his knee down hard on the man's chest. It was over. Sadeghi knew it. Cyrus knew it. Cyrus held the tip of his dagger against the groundsman's throat. The man gasped for air, a fish wanting water. His eyes wide, rolled past his pitted nose at the dagger. Blood at the tip pearled like some grim jewel.

Cyrus said, his voice low and menacing, "You are not welcome in Anshan, nor anywhere in my kingdom." One hand on the man's throat, Cyrus moved the dagger to his eye. Sadeghi flinched. Cold steel lay against the soft flesh at its edge. "I've a mind to pluck this nasty little orb. Or better I should cut out that tongue, good for nothing but lies."

The man winced. Under Cyrus's hand, he couldn't speak. But his eyes begged miserably.

"But," Cyrus brought the dagger back to the man's neck, to the slaughtering strip, the vein that would drain Sadeghi's blood in an instant. "I am not like you." The falcon circled overhead. "I am Prince Kurash, grandson of Kurash, ruler of Anshan. I will spare your rotten life this one time. Cyrus slowly pulled his knife away across the groundsman's throat. The man gulped as a line of red leapt to his skin.

"But do not mistake my generosity for weakness. And so that you don't forget," Cyrus said, "what you've seen and heard from me today..." Before the man could protest, Cyrus swiftly cut a bleeding swath from the corner of the groundsman's eye to his ear. On each side. "Count yourself lucky." With the groundsman's blood running into his tears, Cyrus released him, easing the pressure from his knee slowly. "Take the horse and your things..." Cyrus stood. "And ride directly from this kingdom."

The man sucked air as he scrambled to get his legs back under him.

"If I see you again," Cyrus said, "I will kill you."

The skin flapping down off his cheeks, Sadeghi mounted his skittery horse. He spat on the ground at Cyrus's feet. "Hah!" he called to the horse and galloped back in the direction from which he had come. Cyrus watched until his form was lost in its private cloud of dust and still longer until even the dust had disappeared into a mountain pass.

And that's when he saw the Pasargadae descend.

CHAPTER 65

hey galloped toward Cyrus, the zapanitu at their head, Prexaspes tall and broad beside him. For his part, Cyrus, suddenly exhausted simply waited. He checked the horse, relieved to find that except for cuts – some longer and deeper than most – the blows she'd taken didn't risk her life. She stepped high around him, nervous energy still quivering her hide. Cyrus remounted.

"Imposter!" Prexaspes called as soon as they were within shouting distance.

Cyrus gingerly prodded his side. Yes, broken. At least a couple of ribs. He experimented turning a few degrees in each direction and forced breath into his lungs, despite the pain. The falcon dropped to his shoulder as the men pulled up.

Prexaspes sputtered. Clearly the zapanitu had ordered him to silence. "Come with us," was all the chieftain said.

And so Cyrus returned to the palace not a conquering hero, but under suspicion of treason and in the control of the one tribe who had kept the faith of Anshan, of Parsa. To Cyrus's relief, they rode slowly. The tribesmen had already come a long way. And with Cyrus, clearly exhausted, wounded in more ways than one, and so escorted as to be at no risk of escape, they took their time.

As they approached, Cyrus noticed again what he had those half dozen years earlier, when he'd first arrived: how abandoned the city felt and in such obvious disrepair. Prexaspes had stopped sputtering. The others had stopped murmuring amongst themselves. Cyrus saw their heads turn, taking in the dry weeds blowing through the narrow streets, the skittering retreat of feral animals and what few children the environs supported. He saw again the impoverishment of those few who remained. He was ashamed to see that Anshan had gotten worse, if anything, over the years since he'd arrived. Cyrus felt his captors take it all in. Cyrus didn't have the energy to explain, didn't even know where to start. And how could they understand, anyway, that everything was different now, that Cyrus was here to stay? How could they know that Cyrus was determined to rebuild, to do whatever he could to restore Anshan to her former strength and glory? Cyrus slumped further in his saddle. It was all just words. And it hurt to speak.

Then, when they crossed into the palace complex, such as it was, when Cyrus saw Cook's nephew rush from atop the crumbling gate, Cyrus wondered, Was such restoration even possible? They stopped in the courtyard, met by the few souls who had kept the place functioning. But it was when Cambyses shuffled up, born up only by the solid arm of a single injured guard, with the slim and tarnished band of kingship, and wearing that robe – its embroidery faded, stained front and back with the waste of a man long ill, frayed thin and torn – that Cyrus knew there was no hiding it. Sadeghi might be gone, but Anshan was defeated.

The zapanitu's voice rang with conviction as he told the story of Cyrus's coming to them, of Cyrus's claims, and of Cyrus's return to his parents' hovel in the mountains. When the chieftain had finished – "I saw it with my own eyes," Prexaspes proclaimed. "He is those peasants' son!"

The charge hung in the air. Cambyses wavered on his feet. Nahhunte led the king to a bench, where he sat unsteadily. When King Cam spoke, his voice was thin. But it was clear.

"He belongs here," Cambyses said.

Cyrus's eyes smarted. Then someone told the tale. He wouldn't remember who it was from among the staff, his friends who had gathered. But someone told the story of Mit and Spaco, the story that Cyrus had heard, the story that Spaco had warned might itself not be complete though for now, it told enough... Who it was that told the story didn't matter. And maybe it was each, adding a detail. At any rate, it didn't take long. But although Cyrus's visage, that swoop in the lower lip and so much more, told it true enough, each would vouch for Cyrus: he was indeed Mandane's child returned.

When it was done, Cyrus saw out the corner of his eye, Cook's nephew dart out from behind Martiya. The boy had disappeared after delivering the news of Cyrus's return and the Pasargadae's arrival. At the story's conclusion, Cook's nephew got back. Breathing hard from his running, the boy stopped in front of the king. He bent before the old man, took the king's hand in his own and opened Cambyses's palm. Into it, he laid a tiny object. Cambyses stared down at it. He stared and stared. And then he stood. Nahhunte rushed forward to support him, but Cambyses waved it off.

"Come here," the king said to Cyrus.

Cyrus dismounted, wincing at the pain from multiple injuries. He walked to his father as Upadarma led the mare away. Cyrus crouched carefully to be level with the king.

While the others watched, "This is yours," Cambyses said. Cyrus looked down at the cylinder of stone, only about half the size in width and length of his little finger. Carved indentations – an image and script - ran all around it.

To her nephew, Cook said, "Run fetch a bit of writing clay." He grinned through crooked teeth and produced it immediately.

Cook laughed, threw an arm around his shoulders and hugged him quickly, proudly against her wide hip. The boy set the sheet down on the bench next to Cambyses. Behind Cyrus, the Pasargadae stirred, murmuring amongst themselves. They'd delivered a message, a criminal. This was the king – pathetic, yes; but king nonetheless and capable enough... What was happening?

Cyrus turned the piece over in his hand. The writing was backward.

"Go ahead," Cambyses said to Cyrus, nodding to the clay.

Cyrus picked up the seal and laid it gently on top of the clay. He pushed it forward with his finger. Impatient, Cambyses pushed his finger on top of Cyrus's. "Press on it, now," Cambyses said. "Don't be scared. You're not going to break it." Cyrus nodded. Together, they rolled it across the surface of the clay, rolled it until the image began to repeat. Cambyses sat back again.

"Can you see it?" he asked.

Staring at the image, Cyrus nodded. Holding the clay, he explained as he showed it around, "There's a man, depicted in simple lines, astride a charging horse. The man controls his mount with one hand. In the other he holds a javelin aloft as if to strike. Two men lay prostrate beneath the horse, just beginning to jump over them in pursuit of another man fleeing on foot. A spear stuck through his belly, the running man looks back holding a broken bow up to the victorious rider. In the writing, it says –"

Cambyses recited from memory as Cyrus read aloud, "Kurash of Anshan, son of Teispes."

Cambyses reached for Cyrus's arm. He said, "This is my son, son of Cambyses, son of Kurash, son of Teispes. That is his seal now. He will be king."

Before the Pasargadae could dismount, Prexaspes said, "It doesn't say anything about a king."

Even the zapanitu stopped. They looked at Prexaspes.

"There's no king there," Prexaspes repeated.

Cambyses shrugged. "There is one here. My son."

The chieftain of the Pasargadae dismounted and bowed to Cambyses. Seeing him, the others followed suit - Prexaspes last and reluctantly but he showed his respect. None of them bowed to Cyrus, but neither did they try to press the suit. All except Prexaspes nodded acknowledgment and acceptance. Then they left.

Except for one man. One held back as they others rode out. He stepped his horse up to Cyrus. "I've heard about you," the man said. He wasn't old; he wasn't young. And his expression was hard to read. "Prexaspes rightly said, the seal mentions no king." He nodded slowly. Then he said, "Teispes knew it. Kurash knew it. The king is in the doing."

With that, he kicked his horse forward and out the gate.

CHAPTER 66

$\mathcal{T}$he next days were tense at the palace. The staff watched and waited anxiously for the groundsman's return, likely accompanied by a brutal posse. At the same time, the ordeal of Cam's withdrawal from the opium he'd depended on unsettled everyone.

More than once, either Cyrus or Nahhunte approached the other to ask about the wisdom of their decision to withhold the drug. Could the king even survive this? Then again, the other would remind: what kind of survival was it, in the grasp of such ruinous addiction? The groundsman did not return, and Cam pulled through.

One morning, as Cyrus passed his quarters, King Cam emerged. He was barefoot, his birdlike ankles visible beneath a rumpled robe. Gray hair, what there was of it on top of his skull, stood up and out at awkward intervals. Cyrus stopped before him. With thin hands, Cam grasped Cyrus's shoulders. The king had shrunken with the years even as Cyrus had grown. Now, the king's frail body was a diminutive mirror of Cyrus's strong frame. But Cam's voice was strong. "You look like him. Kurash. What I can remember, anyway." Then the old man smiled. What teeth remained were cracked and stained. "It's a good name, 'Bestower of Care.' May you continue to live into it."

* * *

CYRUS HEARD HIS FATHER. And in the months that followed, he began to try to set things in the kingdom back to rights. King Cam helped, but he tired easily. Among the first things they did, on Cyrus's initiative was to compose and to send messages to each of the region's tribes. Sealed with the stamp of kingship, such as it was, they told the different peoples of Anshan, tribes of the kingdom of Parsa and former Parsumash that the palace wished for them to manage the lands of their place as they best saw fit. Most importantly, they made clear: no more would the palace demand poppies at the expense of all other things.

In those months, Cyrus became acquainted with people nearby whom the groundsman had employed, those who lived in the city or worked the palace fields. Cyrus visited each one, promising fair pay for honest work. And he instructed that all of the poppies, acres and acres of palace land were to be replanted with food crops, flax, or seeded for grazing. For their service, he offered a choice: he would certify double pay when the harvest came in, or if they insisted on something up-front, he could pay an advance from the royal treasury.

Because as it happened, Cook's nephew had learned early for himself what others came to know late: among those who simply cannot do a thing others take for granted of themselves, some become extraordinary adept at skills others can never master. Cook's nephew had suffered a stutter for as long as he could speak, and it worsened with nerves. If he were nervous enough, the boy's speech no matter how hard he might try was virtually unintelligible. And Sadeghi had made him nervous. He had barely learned to walk before he learned that some people say one thing but think another. He saw that some people talk so smoothly that others do not notice what they are meanwhile doing. Cook's nephew heard Sadeghi's speech. And he saw what the man did. So, the little boy, barely older than a toddler, began to squirrel away into a hole he had dug under the kitchen floor, the things he saw adults, especially Sadeghi, value.

From out behind his aunt's stout legs, Cook's nephew saw that Sadeghi had come to the palace with no silver but his tongue. And he saw Sadeghi take whatever the groundsman wanted out of what was around. Even from before the man first cuffed his ear and sent the boy, head ringing, across the courtyard, Cook's nephew was afraid of him. And he knew that because of that fear, he could not force his mouth to form any kinds of words. And under those circumstance, the child secreted away more than the royal seal.

So, when Sadeghi came around wheedling or demanding or brutally "just asking" of each person where might be gold pieces "to pay the laborers" or silver "that I might shine it for the king..." When he asked and asked and asked for the royal seal "so that the far tribes understand that these are indeed palace orders," Cook's nephew could only stammer and stutter.

Now, with Sadeghi finally gone, and the king restored to himself, no one could have been more proud to set out the silver drinking vessels or polish the king's golden bracteates than Cook herself. Her nephew revealed what he had hidden away and together they returned them to King Cam. Besides these and the precious seal, there were ingots of gold and to King Cambyses's greatest joy - a nostalgic pleasure – fine jewelry, the things that he had given to Mandane when she, a waifish stranger, first came to Anshan.

* * *

As for Cyrus, in everything he did, he thought of Sanda, the woman of Pasargad. And he couldn't help but hope that he'd hear something, receive some kind of message if not invitation in response to his efforts. It wasn't a baseless hope. Indeed, little by little, the palace received reply from the region's tribes. One by one, they reported – some in great detail, some with only the barest wedge-markings necessary – gratitude for Cyrus's message and compliance in replacing poppies with crops, rewilding or a combination such as their wisdom traditions dictated. More than one reported knowledge of weapons stashed by Sadeghi's thugs in the mountains and hills and around. From the palace in Anshan, Cyrus told them to keep the weapons. They'd earned them themselves, after all. And, he reiterated: each of the tribes was a part of greater Parsa.

As the townspeople worked side by side with Cyrus to replace the poppies with annual food crops, young trees, and pasture, the region came alive. Cyrus thanked the gods for sending good weather that promised a strong harvest. Flocks and herds prospered. Cyrus had solicited help from elders in the town in determining optimal planting times and allocation of the fields. They felt honored and respected for their wisdom, and Cyrus genuinely valued what they offered.

He also began to talk with both elders and youth, women and men, about improving the nation's defense with a trained army composed of men drawn from the region itself. He revealed that the groundsman had been gathering high quality weapons, and he said that he would gladly distribute to those who submitted to hard training. Cyrus accepted a verbal commitment to serve should the need or opportunity arise. He won the people's trust by degrees. With honesty and a candid transparency about his aims and goals for the nation, Cyrus discovered that the people were eager for strong leadership.

After six months or so, King Cam had emerged weak and frail but mentally competent. He heard disputes and administered justice again, now with Cyrus beside him. The two discussed daily how best to proceed for the welfare of greater Anshan. Crops and herds flourished, and the palace hired more staff. The king made Nahhunte his steward, the courtyard was beautifully replanted, and the chickens moved to a coop outside. Martiya was promoted to military adviser and was already training three, new, young guards.

With such improvements, with this public acknowledgment of a crown prince in Anshan, and capable besides, some of the region's leaders began to approach Cambyses with this or that eligible daughter or granddaughter or niece. They talked of marriage. Cambyses talked to Cyrus. And Cyrus kept to himself the memory of Sanda and the hope that lingered.

"You do know I'll die," Cambyses said. "The gods do what they will. And I'd like to know that this family will continue."

"I'll find a wife in my own time," Cyrus said. "Who knows? Maybe the *gods* have already found her for me."

But there was no word from Pasargad.

When it came time to bring in the grain, pick the fruit from limbs drooping with the weight, time to cull animals for the winter, when their public audience had concluded, King Cam said to Cyrus, "The harvest this year was good."

Cyrus nodded. It wasn't news to him.

"I reviewed replies from the tribes of our people, near and outlying. Each one has confirmed receipt of the instruction, each complied. Except one."

Again, Cyrus knew. He nodded. Ever since the first – the Dropici – had said that they received the message, welcome indeed, Cyrus had waited. He had counted every one, had reread every missive just in case he'd missed any. One was unaccounted for.

"The Pasargadae," Cyrus said.

Despite all the work of all the days, despite the attention and concentration it had required of him, his mind was never far from the woman with the almond eyes. Cassandane.

"I was thinking..." Cyrus began. "Maybe I should visit, go there and ask –"

Cambyses suddenly laughed. "She's there, isn't she? The woman."

Cyrus didn't laugh.

Serious, King Cam said, "Yes, whatever the case, you should go."

CHAPTER 67

*C*yrus left Anshan for Pasargad the following day. Cambyses met him at the stable door.

"For her," the king said.

He held out to Cyrus a purple silk purse, tied with a golden cord. It jangled in Cyrus's hand. He loosened the tie and reached inside. A heavy silver bracelet studded with lapis lazuli hung from his fingers. But there was more. Cyrus withdrew a necklace strung of pure white beads among which hung leaves of beaten gold. The webbed veins looked so real that they might have come from autumn aspen but for the fact that they were solid gold. In the rising sun, Cyrus turned it this way and that, saw how it caught the light and sent it back out in golden pools on the ground. Careful to drop nothing, he poured the rest of its contents into his palm. Thimble sized cylinders of beaten gold hung with tiny gold pendants -- a woman's hair ties. He didn't need to ask, didn't need to be told. These had been his mother's. These, gifts from King Cam, had belonged to Mandane. And already Cyrus saw them – stars in Sanda's long dark hair.

Eyes shining, Cyrus said, "Thank you."

* * *

DESPITE THE DISTANCE TO PASARGAD, time flew. Cyrus's mind was full of Cassandane. He rehashed not only every detail of their evening under the stars but also every detail about her family. Otanes, he remembered. That's the name of her little brother, the one who first told him her name. Sanda, he had called her. Affectionate. It was easy to tell that she was fond of him, too – the affection went both ways – and tender. Her name sounded happy in Otanes's mouth. Pharnaspes, her father. Cyrus had had to work hard to bring it to mind. It was like the name Prexaspes but not quite. Cyrus hoped the same could be said of its bearer. Cyrus had yet to meet him. Whatever the case, it wasn't Prexaspes he would have to deal with as Cassandane's father, but Pharnaspes.

So, Cyrus was eager to get there, eager to complete the official errand – to confirm the palace's respect and generosity that like the other tribes, Pasargad would be expected to manage their lands only as they determined was best. Important it was. But he wouldn't pretend. That's not what drove him on so hard. His hand went to the doeskin pouch closest on his saddle. The jewelry made a satisfying susurration there.

The final day was long. Had he not been in such a hurry, Cyrus would have stopped for the night still shy of Pasargad. Had he been an ordinary traveler, he would have camped somewhere in the nearby hills and enjoyed well-deserved rest, before finishing his journey in the morning. But Cyrus was no ordinary traveler today. So, he pressed on into the late afternoon, into the evening. Despite Cyrus's eagerness to arrive, the closer he got, the more captivated he became by the place itself. All the things that Cassandane had talked about with such reverie and delight, he had seen for himself and saw again now. The clear babbling river, and by its side the willows, reeds, and oleander. And oh the color! The trees yellow-orange to carmine-red, the sky in bright turquoise, the mountains violet, blue, red, yellow.

It was indeed near-dark when Cyrus entered the plain. But – he pulled the horse up short. The northeastern part of the plain, the place where Cyrus had sat with Cassandane those months ago, was alight with fire. The whole place hummed with the activity of a feast. Cyrus urged his horse on but held her to a walk. The *šip*, of course. Cyrus should have known. Cook had talked about the old festivals, the great offerings kings would make to the gods of Parsa – Humban chief among them, but also Zizkurra, Napiriša, Mišdušiš, and more. She'd said they could be grand. And yes, the palace had tried to honor them with what paltry things they had. But this, this Cyrus had never seen, not even in his imagination.

* * *

THE BRICK PLATFORM that had seemed so enormous, so expansive that evening was packed with people, revelers seated and standing, milling about with sloshing cups. Tables bent under the weight of the food there. Musicians played on harps and drums. And there, in the middle, where those massive stone plinths had stood quiet and bare, atop them fires reached their flames to the sky. Even from this distance, Cyrus could see the zapanitu mount the stairs of one and lay on the fire armfuls of bread, then platters of meat. Wind carried the aroma, and Cyrus's stomach pinched reminding him how little he'd eaten since leaving Anshan. The zapanitu, dwarfed by the plinth on which he stood, raised carafes high above his head and from them poured wine and beer all around the burnt offerings that sizzled on the fire. While the people in their finest clothes ringed the altars below him, the chief of the Pasargadae called on all the gods of Parsa with praise and thanks for the year's bounty, adulation for their greatness, and prayers that they bless the year to come. Then, he directed a team of people to disperse provisions to the tables that filled the place. People roared and cheered, the music grew faster, the flames reached higher. From the outskirts and the edge, Cyrus watched it all.

Finally, after the zapanitu had descended, and the crowds settled into their revelry, Cyrus approached. Those who noticed him coming saw a man alone. So they gestured him forward, waved him to have some food here, food there. Someone shoved a cup into his hand – a fine cup of wrought silver with engravings all around its sides – and then was gone. A woman – old enough to be his grandmother, bracelets jangling on stout wrists, Thrust cheese-stuffed figs into his hand and then shoved him lightly toward another, a girl who took his hand, spun him around, and danced away again, her hair clips glinting in the firelight. Cyrus watched men in clothes as fine as Cam's must have been before accept with pleasure cuts of meat and sacks of grain, baskets of choice fruits with the gracious demeanor of self-respect. And he looked for Cassandane.

It was Prexaspes who found him, the chieftain's son who was suddenly beside him.

"Prince of Anshan," Prexaspes said. He slurred his words. A cup of wine in his hand, the tall young man swayed on his feet as leaned back to run his eyes up and down the traveler.

Cyrus kept his head up with effort, painfully aware that not only did he show the miles he'd come, but even starting out, in the best he had he was a dim thing beside the grandeur of Prexaspes, beside any of the Pasargadae here. His hand went to the purple silk purse with the jewels that were the most precious to his family, his mother's wedding jewelry. And his hand fell away. The jewelry he carried paled in comparison to what the women here wore. Each of them.

"What brings you back to our humble settlement?" Prexaspes narrowed his eyes, then. "Or can I guess." He leaned in, his breath sour with wine. "I saw you, you know," he said conspiratorially, and bumped Cyrus's shoulder. Wine sloshed over his cup's rim. Prexaspes didn't wait for an answer. "Or are you merely hungry in the belly?" He nodded to Cyrus's hand, reminding Cyrus of the figs that lay there. "Thirsty?" Prexaspes poured from his cup into Cyrus's... what didn't spill to the ground.

At a break in the river of people flooding past and all around, Cyrus set the figs down on a nearby table.

"I came here," Cyrus said, "for two reasons. Neither of them has to do with you."

Prexaspes widened his eyes in mock amazement.

"But if you could tell me where I might find your father –"

"Whatever you have to say to my father, you can say to me." Prexaspes threw back his shoulders and stood yet taller. His chin would skim the top of Cyrus's head. Prexaspes was impressive. He didn't even need to try.

Cyrus took a sip of the wine. It was good. He looked up at the chieftain's son. "I ask a simple confirmation of receipt of our message from the palace. Each of the other tribes responded –"

Suddenly indignant, "What need have we to respond?" Prexaspes demanded. He might be drunk, but his message was clear. "We were never going to comply with that groundsman's demands, palace or no. Your message changes nothing. And as you can see..." He let his hand invite Cyrus to take in the grand spectacle. He didn't need to finish the thought. On display was clear demonstration of all that Pasargad had done for its people in the absence of palace oversight, in defiance of Sadeghi's orders.

Cyrus took it all in – the bounty, the comfortable happiness of people who had all that they needed, all that they wanted. And he thought about Cassandane.

"And the other?" Prexaspes asked.

"Excuse me?"

"The other reason?"

What could Cyrus possibly give her to compare to this? Again, his hand went to the purse at his side. Again it fell away.

"It's nothing," Cyrus said. "Never mind."

Prexaspes smirked, shrugged, then disappeared again.

Cyrus stood, rooted to his place on the edges of the crowd. He heard the singing, felt the shudder of earth under hundreds of happy feet. He picked up one of the figs, nibbled at its sweetness but tasted only dust. And then he saw her, close the crowd's center, a swirl of color and laughter and joy. Just beneath the massive plinths, in the areas reserved for the most prestigious of the tribes people, Cassandane danced. She flung her shoulders to and fro, swayed with her hips, turned and turned again, her head tipped back in delight.

"Lovely, isn't she?"

A voice beside Cyrus startled him from the sight. He turned. The speaker was the same as the last man to leave Anshan, the man who had spoken so enigmatically of kingship.

The man smiled. He dipped his head in recognition of Cyrus then joined him in appreciating the dips and turns, the grace and light steps of the woman so far away.

"Then again, of course I would say such a thing. She's my daughter."

And they watched, each with different eyes, a man join her there. Prexaspes stepped into the dance, moving with Cassandane, smiling and turning, his body a complement to hers. When the chieftain's son looked their way, Pharnaspes raised a hand in greeting.

"Would you like to speak with her?" Pharnaspes asked.

Cyrus startled again. "No, no," he said quickly. "I – should be getting back."

At his side, the purple silk pouch, small as it was felt as heavy as life itself.

CHAPTER 68

Cyrus camped that night next to the Pulvar River. The exhaustion of his travels, the terrible disappointment made going any farther anywhere impossible. Only with the horse's help could he remove himself far enough away to lose the sounds of celebration, though light from the great fires still lit a wedge of sky overhead. Sleep was poor rest. But in the morning, a frosty one like the one he'd seen on this land before, the colors of the sun against the mountains and the babble of the river were as beautiful as when he'd first met Cassandane. But instead of the bright energy of a happy hope, it was grief that bore Cyrus on his way again.

He rode slowly, letting the horse pick its way until Cyrus came to the wadi where he could turn either continue angling west to Anshan or turn north back into the mountain cottage where Mit and Spaco lived. He stopped. What was there for him in Anshan? At the palace, Cambyses expected a woman who would bring new life to the kingdom. And not only King Cam but all the staff. It was a happier place now and their anticipation bore not a tinge of doubt that Cyrus would return with a bride. For Cyrus, though, returning alone, what was there in Anshan for him? What to satisfy the deep yearning that had settled in his soul those years ago, the terrible deficit that bore a hole in his heart ever since Astyages took him from the shepherd slaves?

Cyrus turned the horse north. Mit and Spaco were delighted to see Cyrus coming. But even before he'd dismounted, before he handed the horse off to Mit to settle at the little lean-to in the corral, they could tell that something was wrong.

"I don't want to talk about it," Cyrus said, when they were seated at the table, a stew of greens, roots, and lamb before each one. "My mind invited me into a future. Too good to be true, a future that cannot happen, and I nevertheless went along." The soft rap of wooden spoons against the pottery bowls was all the sound there was. "I thought I could live in it," Cyrus said. He lifted his spoon. "I was wrong."

They ate silently for a while. Cyrus finished his bowl long after the others had sat back from theirs. He smiled. "I remember this," he said.

Spaco patted his hand. "With time… and open hearts, we've learned how to make what was strange familiar." Spaco stood.

"I've missed you," Cyrus said.

Spaco gathered the bowls while Mit tapped dried herbs out onto a shallow clay dish. Cyrus watched Spaco light it, watched her pull the smoke that rose with cupped hands toward herself, watched her brush the smoke toward him, toward Mit, and toward the door.

Seeing Cyrus's bewilderment, Mit said, "We saw something like it among the folks in Isfahan."

Spaco sat again and smiled. "It's nice," was all she said.

Cyrus slept under the table that night on a pallet they'd constructed of scrap lumber, delicate pine branches, and fresh linen. A rough wool blanket kept him warm, as did low voices of the old couple in the adjacent room. After checking on the animals together, just as he had done with Mit in the cottage that had been such an easy home, after they had cleaned their mouths and faces and laid up the clothes of the day, Cyrus listened idly to the old couple murmuring together from the adjacent room. He fell asleep to the sound of their gentle snoring, just as he had when he was a boy. When he was their boy.

So, in the morning, after Cyrus had put on his clothes - "Such fine things!" Spaco said – Cyrus sat them down at the table. They smiled at the brightness in the young man's face, a happy optimism returned.

"I was thinking..." Cyrus began. "I have so much now. And every year there will be more. I told you about the things we're doing... And Anshan used to be really quite grand, not long ago... Anyway –" He took their hands in his – Spaco's in one and Mit's in the other. "Come back to the palace with me," he said, his voice full of eager excitement. "You can make it your home!" Seeing Mit and Spaco look at each other, Cyrus said, "Just think about it. We could all be together again..." His voice trailed off.

Spaco gently removed her hand from his. Mit, too, gave Cyrus's hand a little squeeze and extricated it from Cyrus's loose grip.

Spaco, her eyes moist, nodded for Mit to speak.

"Your mama and I..." He took a deep breath. "We've had enough of palaces and kings."

"Though we're sure you'll be a good one," Spaco added quickly.

The rest of what they said was lost on Cyrus. He felt as if he'd been laid out – an infant alone - on that forsaken mountain peak, after all. The couple's tender kindnesses as Cyrus packed his few things, saddled and mounted his horse were lost on him. The words of goodbye, of good wishes, even "The gods guard your way"... all lost. He looked back only once. Mit and Spaco stood side-by-side, arms around one another, in front of the simple cottage, its garden a mass of dead and dying plants, turning itself inward for winter.

As Cyrus made his way back to Anshan, each of the horse's

thud-thudding footsteps taking him closer, all he could think of was all that he lacked. He too had had enough of palaces and kings. Yet. Here he was, a man who lived in a palace, a man who would be king. And all he wanted was what it seemed he'd never have: home.

CHAPTER 69

The palace and its environs, the city of Anshan and the land around flourished. It would take time but the improvements reminded people of what Anshan had been. And what it could be again. With the harvest over but winter not yet here, the market was a lively place. It was a place where Cyrus liked to wander. Among the foreign merchants and general crowds, Cyrus could be anonymous. He was simply another a man of the area and nothing more.

One day, a particular foreigner caught Cyrus's eye. Until recently, it had been rare to see anyone from as far away as Babylon. Yet the man who brought fabric woven from the fine wool of Mesopotamian sheep, dyed in delicious colors, and crafted by skilled weavers was unmistakably Babylonian. And familiar. The merchant, maybe twenty years old, didn't look much older than Cyrus. As Cyrus looked over the merchandise, he watched the man work. He was a cocky young man, confident in himself, comfortable even self-congratulatory in his position. The young man would adjust his belt and tunic whenever he felt an admiring gaze and drew his golden bracelet down his wrist as far as possible from under his sleeve, all while talking with confident animation.

When the man approached, "You're from Babylon?" Cyrus asked.

"You could tell!" The man put out his hand. "Itti-Marduk-balatu, eldest son of Nabu-ahhe-iddin, of the Egibi family." Cyrus took his hand and the man seized him by the elbow. "But they call me Iddina." He released Cyrus again and rearranged a stack of whisper weight scarves. "Folks call my father Khai," he said. "Perhaps you've heard of us. Not citizenry, but our business has earned a reputation."

"Sorry, no," Cyrus said, "I haven't heard of your family." He added quickly, "I spent my childhood in Ecbatana –"

The man raised his head sharply at that, raised his eyebrows in admiring acknowledgment. If there were a capital city of foreign trade, it would be Ecbatana.

"But I haven't been out of this area," Cyrus gestured with a smile, "for many years."

Iddina gestured to a tea-man to pour them cups. "That's a shame." He handed one minty cup to Cyrus, sipped from the other. "No offense, of course, but Babylon is wonderful." He returned his cup to the vendor. "'Media,' you say? Our queen mother, the lady Amytis, is from Media. She was married to King Nebuchadnezzar."

"Was?" Cyrus asked.

"The great king just died." Iddina glanced around. I don't suppose it's easy to get the news here. "What a send-off. You should have seen the funeral."

A woman held up a bolt of fabric, indigo blue, and cleared her throat.

"Amel-Marduk, Nebuchadnezzar's son is king now." Iddina hurried to assist the woman. Over his shoulder, he added, You're a merchant, too?"

"Something like that," Cyrus said.

* * *

CYRUS SAW IDDINA AGAIN LATER, the bulge of a full purse hanging from the merchant's side. Iddina greeted him then bobbed his head, looking all around. "Say, where's that man... the one with all the opium... He said something to me last time..."

Cyrus's stomach dropped. He simply shook his head.

Iddina shrugged. "Join me in the slave tent?"

Cyrus fell into step beside him. He hoped he wouldn't have to ask in order to learn what it was that Sadeghi had told the Babylonian.

"I hope to leave tomorrow but must first do some buying. It's much easier to return with slaves, who can put up at least some kind of resistance against bandits, than to carry our profits in a purse. Besides, I've heard that there are beautiful girls for sale around here."

Sadeghi's legacy of impoverishing the tribes even while they tried to comply with what they thought were palace orders, even when they thought they'd see even greater return than with the crops and subsistence lifestyle they'd had before, hung on in bits and pieces throughout Parsa. Cyrus knew that one of the ways to manage was to reduce the number of dependents, move them away. No one knew how many of those ended up here.

"My father instructed me to buy some boys that we can train up for the business -- to become scribes, financial managers, agricultural officers, you know. But I'm especially interested in the girls. Some will be laundresses and weavers and the like, but..." he turned to Cyrus, "what man can do without the pleasure their soft bodies bring?

"There's profit to be made there, too. Unless you're the king, we Babylonians have only one wife, so it's nice to have diversion, if you know what I mean. Besides train a girl right, keep her healthy, lease her judiciously, and she can make as much in those first years as a laundress would in a lifetime. Some even gain enough business sense to have their own enterprises, in time."

Cyrus was grateful for the man's garrulous nature, his liberty with talk. How could Cyrus explain that he'd been enslaved himself? And overnight became a prince. How could he explain how horrible it was for one's life to be so completely in the power of someone else, someone with the power to steal you from family, to steal a child from his parents no matter what the destination?

"I do want to hurry back. My father has become the business agent for the new king's brother-in-law, Igliss, who comes from a prominent family in Puqudu. The man is as shrewd a politician as he is a businessman. Igliss, I mean."

"Listen." He leaned in close to Cyrus. "I'm not saying that he married Cassiya, Nebuchadnezzar's daughter, out of sheer ambition. She's lovely if a bit boring, and she gave him a son -- a spoiled little tyrant, if you ask me. But it hasn't hurt his career, either. That's for sure. Igliss is now *qipu* of the Ebabbar temple in Sippar. Not bad, to have such a high administrative position." Iddina stepped back again, his hands on his hips. "A lot of people think highly of him. I don't envy the court life, though. Full of back-biting, deceit, and scrupulous ambition. At least with business, you know where you stand. Did you know that the present king was imprisoned himself by Nebuchadnezzar, his own father, for a time?! Tea?" he asked, grabbing a cup from the hawker passing through the tent and dropping a shekel into the boy's apron pocket. Iddina didn't wait for an answer but handed the cup to Cyrus and grabbed another. Iddina nodded to the makeshift stage as another old woman shuffled onto it. "I hope I'm not wasting my time."

As they sipped the minty brew, Iddina one eye on the stage, went on, "Turned out to be twisted half-truths and lies that landed him there. I for one think Igliss was behind it. My father, though, won't hear me say it. Run a clean business, he says, judge fairly when called up by the courts, and leave matters of state to the politicians.

"Oh, please!" Iddina gestured to the stage, Decrepit old men, now?" He turned back to Cyrus, "With skills and ambition, they actually can be quite valuable. Now, where was I?" Before Cyrus could answer, he went on, "Right. Amel-Marduk, the ex-con king. When he was thrown into prison, his poor mother was beside herself."

Seeing Cyrus's blank look, he said, "Amytis. His mother."

Cyrus tried to keep his face blank.

"Median by birth," Iddina went on. "So, she had reasons for being anxious. The Medes call themselves our friends; but nobody fully trusts Astyages, not even his own people, I hear. But now, her son is Babylonia's king. And she's back in Media." Iddina stopped talking then, and for the first time looked full on at Cyrus, thinking.

Seeking nonchalance, Cyrus said, "So what was it that that merchant... the one with the opium said?"

Iddina's face brightened to recall. "When he learned how Amytis's son went from a nobody half-breed prince to crown prince to prison and then to the throne, the *Babylonian* throne, he'd said it was enough to give a person whiplash." Iddina laughed. "*And* he'd said, deadly serious, 'Who's to say that his fortune won't change again?'" Iddina shook his head in wonder. "What did you say was your connection to Media?" Then Iddina saw a boy on the stage, "Much better." He threw his hand into the air with interest.

And Cyrus slipped out.

CHAPTER 70

*L*ate winter. Another month or so, and they would be back into the business of planting and all that. In a few months, it would a year since Cyrus first saw Cassandane. Cyrus threw himself with hard energy into the many and diverse tasks of leading the country out of its former trouble. He focused all his attention there and tried to think of nothing else. If this were his life, the whole of it, then so be it. Among the projects he saw to do was this: to strengthen relationships beyond Anshan's borders. Remembering Zubaba's lessons when the old veteran had accompanied Cyrus to Anshan, Cyrus began to look into how they might reinvigorate their relationship to Susa, recall their commonalty in an Elam of the past.

"I've been thinking about setting up diplomatic relations with King Bahuri," Cyrus said. Seeing Cambyses's blank look, Cyrus added, "In Susa. I'm hoping that we might find in them again the same strong allies they were in the past. Have you got any thoughts on where to start?" Cyrus always deferred to his father. Cambyses was king, after all. And his elder. But as usual, Cambyses shook his head.

Cyrus shrugged. "I'll figure it out."

Cam's shoulders slumped. "I suppose you will." He eased to the front of his throne, prepared to rise, and hung his head. "I'll go to bed."

Cyrus took his father's elbow to help him to his feet. The king weighed little more than a girl now. Cam leaned against Cyrus, halting every so often to catch his shallow breath. In the courtyard, Cam stopped. He gestured that he wished to sit. Cyrus lowered him gently then sat quietly beside him. Where chickens had pecked leggy weeds and algae bubbled across the small pond, tidy shrubs encircled clear water animated by bright tiny fish.

"I'm of no use to you," Cam's voice was flat, weary with the saying.

Cyrus bit back a reflexive denial. Then he said, "You're wrong," Cyrus said. He took a deep breath. "You don't know what it is to grow up thinking you're one thing and then to learn that it's all been a lie. You are real to me, and now this place, my place in it..."

"It's not enough." Cam shook his head impatiently. He was too old for pretending. He sighed. "But I suppose... in this too, you'll figure it out." Cam leaned his head against Cyrus's shoulder. After a time, the king's rasping breath steadied in sleep.

Cyrus felt the cold band of Cam's crown against his shoulder. Even after Cook's nephew revealed the stash of valuables that he'd saved, the king had never wanted another crown. And its simplicity suited him. Cyrus knew – and it warmed him – that to Cambyses, Cyrus was enough. Cyrus prayed a silent prayer that Humban be kind to the king who had suffered so much and that what time remained to him would be in peace. Then Cyrus eased Cambyses into his arms and carried the sleeping king into his quarters and laid him on the bed. Cyrus took off his father's crown, turned its slim shape around in the moonlight, and set it on the nightstand. He removed his father's shoes and drew a light woolen sheet over his legs.

"Good night, father," he whispered into the dark and left.

* * *

THE NEXT MORNING, the normally laconic groom surprised Cyrus by telling the prince that he'd like to talk to him about something. Cyrus followed Upadarma's limping form to the stable. He greeted the falcon on her perch outside, promising her a good hunt later, and walked beside Upadarama to the mare's stall. Cyrus hadn't ridden her months, had visited seldom since he'd last returned to Anshan. Upadarma laid a hand across the rail and looked over to where the horse slept. He stepped back and gestured that Cyrus take a look. Cyrus peered over. Old Avery, curled against her belly as usual, moved with her inhalations and exhalations. A tableau of contentment.

"Notice anything different?"

Cyrus looked again. She had filled out nicely, something Cyrus attributed to a less stressful environment and improved pasturage. "She's whiter now, almost fully," he said. But they'd remarked on that before. The red splotches along her shoulders had faded recently to nearly invisible but for some striking speckles.

Upadarma smiled at him, waiting.

"She sleeps a lot, eats like crazy... Her nose is still as concave as the Nisean horses are rounded... All the same things." He shrugged. "Why? What do you see?"

Upadarma opened the stall door. He rattled the feed bucket, pouring some more sweet grain against its empty sides. At the sound, the horse stood. Old Avery shifted to sleep in a corner. Cyrus followed Upadarma inside. While the mare gobbled the grain, the groom bent stiffly to her belly. With a gnarled hand on the horse's hip, he gestured for Cyrus to do the same. Cyrus looked up in alarm. The mare's udder was distended.

Cyrus drew back quickly. "Is she ok?"

The groom straightened chuckled. "Just pregnant."

"Pregnant?!"

"Probably about ten months along," Upadarma said.

"But --" Cyrus stammered trying to figure... They'd introduced several new horses into the palace stable. But the stallion had come in only a month or two earlier.

"How?" Cyrus asked.

"I don't know. You tell me."

"I can't... I don't..." Cyrus shook his head. "Ochre?"

"Couldn't be. You know the groundsman had him gelded."

"If all goes well, she'll deliver in a month or so."

"I just can't imagine..." Cyrus shook his head again. Then he did the math. "About ten months, you say?" His expression was hard to read.

"Give or take."

"Pasargad," Cyrus said.

CHAPTER 71

𝓘t was as if Cyrus's realization, his putting together the timing of his mare's pregnancy with his visit to Pasargadae that very first time – the bitumen-black stallion and the almond-eyed girl, flashing-smart – summoned the Achaemenid band. It was as if his speaking aloud, there in the stable with his horse and companions "Pasargad" brought them forth.

Martiya led the guards to inquire their intentions... and to let them know that the palace had defense now – modest, but better than when they'd seen it last.

In truth, Cyrus felt a flash of pride in watching Prexaspes and the zapanitu at the fore approach a repaired city gate. He noticed their respect for the armed guards who cordially and demonstrably ushered them toward the palace. Cyrus watched from atop the wall's new height. He recognized Pharnaspes there and one of royal muleteers, early recipients of the *šip* feast's honorary gifts. They weren't many in total. Among the riders, men in the colorful robes Cyrus recognized, patterned belts indicating their tribe and clan, was one draped in a hooded robe the color of the iron gray stallion he rode. Cyrus recalled Sadeghi's fury, thought about the stashes of weapons... and summoned Nahhunte. The steward could identify the person no better than Cyrus. From the way his shoulders stiffened and his voice clipped, Cyrus knew Nahhunte shared his concern.

When they reached the palace gate, Cyrus prepared to meet them. And stopped. He saw Martiya gesture them forward, invite them to enter. But they demurred. Martiya spoke with the zapanitu and then rode in himself.

"They wish to meet you at the stable, sir," he said to Cyrus.

* * *

CYRUS ACCEPTED the sword Martiya handed to him. He buckled it around his waist. "Release the falcon," Cyrus said. "All these people will make him nervous." He shook his head. "Besides, I think he's hungry." Nahhunte confirmed that he'd keep Cambyses occupied – and safe – inside until further notice. Cyrus took a deep breath and went to meet the visitors.

They kept a tight group, the hooded figure well to the back. Cyrus nodded to the zapanitu and to Prexaspes beside him.

Martiya and the young guards he had trained flanked Cyrus one on either side, one to the back.

To Cyrus's surprise, it was Pharnaspes who stepped forward, "You have something of ours," he said. His face was stern, uncompromising.

Cyrus looked at Upadarma then back at them. "I don't understand –"

It happened in a fraction of a moment – the Pasargadae dropping their fierce demeanor; Cyrus's shocked disbelief; Martiya and his men leaping to defense and back again, confused; and the hooded figure suddenly revealed, her head tipped back in bright laughter. Cyrus's heart leapt in his chest. It was none other than Sanda, Cassandane.

* * *

As THEY WALKED into the stable, Cassandane beside Cyrus, he asked, "So where is he? The stallion?" She looked behind them to the iron gray horse she'd ridden there.

"Seems black didn't suit him."

Cyrus smiled. "My mare changed, too." He pointed to the stall where his mare rolled her eyes in concern. Upadarma stroked her muzzle, and she remained calm. "And yes, she's carrying the foal –"

"That belongs to me," Cassandane finished with a mock serious expression on her face.

Pharnaspes watched, his face as soft with pride and affection for his daughter as when Cyrus had last seen him. "She set it up," he said.

Cyrus pulled Martiya to him and whispered in his ear. He dashed to the palace.

From the fringes, Prexaspes stepped up next to Cyrus and Cassandane. They quieted. He nodded toward the little mare then back at Cyrus. His dark eyes were deep, unreadable, as they stared at the prince. Yet for the first time, the bore no hint of hostility. "Seems she saw..." he began. "She chose you," he said. Then a smile played at the corner of his lips. "And you look happy."

Just then, Martiya returned. He slid to a stop. In his hand was the purple silk pouch that held Mandane's wedding jewels. Cyrus accepted it. They waited as King Cam made his way across the yard, Nahhunte steading his steps, Cook and her nephew both of them bouncing – one heavy, one light – behind. When they'd assembled, Cyrus turned to Cassandane.

"For the foal," Cyrus said, "an exchange." And he handed the purse to Cassandane.

She opened it and with a soft smile withdrew and examined

each item. Her eyes were warm when she looked back at Cyrus. "I accept," she said.

* * *

THEY WOULD MARRY in the spring. For King Cam and the Anshanites it was a bittersweet time. Some spoke softly among themselves of the late queen Mandane. The dip in Cyrus's lower lip remained the most striking reminder of her. And they remarked on how different that princess from Media, groomed for Babylonian life and luxury who'd arrived nearly two decades ago, was from the strong and confident woman of the Pasargadae who stood before them now. Different, too: the aura of happy hopefulness and buzzing love that hung unmistakably around Cyrus and Cassandane and had come only later for Cambyses and Mandane. But come it had. The heady mix of joy and sadness that illuminated the old king's face told all these things and hinted of things only he knew. Mit and Spaco declined the invitation to attend. So Cyrus and Cassandane went to them. With customary candor, the couple Cyrus knew first as his parents made clear that they were quite simply happy for Cyrus and his bride.

With Cook's oversight, official and otherwise, the palace at Anshan was transformed. Cyrus and Cambyses had already undertaken the kind of capital improvements that had made it serviceable, respectable again. In advance of Cassandane's arrival, Cook made it beautiful. It had taken all of spring and into the summer. It was she who had convinced them to wait, to hold off the months until then. Oleander hung from trellises and walls. Tulip petals that Cook had saved and dried from the spring lined the walkways. Among the dusty purple and thick green rosemary bushes, blooming lilium ledebourii rolled their white petals in a shameless display. Hanging over them, on pomegranate trees, Gulnar exploded in brightest orange. There were roses everywhere. And scattered betwixt and between the bright colors and fragrant flowers, visible only to those who might bend and look were fritillaria, which she had coaxed to bloom at just the right time. Its muted bells dropped tears for Mandane.

The Achaemenids were a modest but illustrious contingent. Besides the elder priests of the Pasargadae as well as the chieftain and his son, were of course the bride and her father Pharnaspes. Pharnaspes had not remarried after Cassandane's mother died. But little Otanes skipped and grinned around his father, shy one minute and bold the next. Also present were the chieftain's wife Šeraš and her sister Udusana. Cyrus tried to keep them straight from the cousins who accompanied Cassandane, Rašda and Irdabama, whose bright smiles captivated Martiya and distracted the new palace guards – dangerously, had there been any such danger. There wasn't. The Achaemenids graciously accepted every gesture of hospitality the Anshanites could offer. Cyrus might have been the only one to notice that although the Achaemenids wore such things as reflected their status – long the most noble of the Parsa's tribes – it was understated. He had seen the *šip* and their festival finery. Most striking was the near-absence of jewelry on the women. These things registered for him as unexpected. But in truth his eyes and attention were all for Cassandane. She was radiant. And the wedding jewelry that she wore, the hair clips, bracelet, and necklace that had been Mandane's stood out among all who gathered as the finest, most beautiful of all.

After the wedding, long only for the sheer number of deities – gods and goddesses alike - invoked and honored, from Humban and Zizkurra, Napirisha, Kiririsha, and Tepti. Šimut won a glance between the couple recalling that night talking under the stars, …to Mišdušiš and Hutran. The list was long and offerings granted in each direction, to the heavens and the earth, water, and by fire. It took a while. But few noticed. A breeze swept gently across the plain bringing fresh air from the mountains, water trickled along the newly repaired canals, and the sun made of everything gold. As the priest turned to the couple finally to conclude the religious formalities, Cyrus's falcon threw a shadow across the ground. When Cyrus looked up, so did the gathered crowd. They watched the bird bank lower in the sky revealing in her talons a bird, limp - killed no doubt on impact. When she was nearly overhead the wedding couple, the falcon screamed one piercing cry and loosed her prey. They all watched it fall as the falcon spun away. With a soft thud, the falcon's gift dropped between the feet of Cyrus and Cassandane. Cassandane grinned. She took Cyrus's hand and together they raised it high. A houbara bird. At the sight, a happy shout went up, and the feasting began.

Cook was thrilled to see the sacred precinct with its festival square full again. When she was there, that is. She was a dervish of officious energy, ordering around even ordinary Anshanites who had wandered into the festivities to keep the food coming, the wine and beer flowing, and the music peppy. Her nephew had been deputized but was rarely unsupervised as Cook seemed to be everywhere at once. And everything was better for it. The feast itself was a spectacle. Even the Achaemenids were impressed. They couldn't hide their pleased surprise. Cook had made countless diverse pasta dishes – an amazement – and roasted lamb and goats, *basbas*, chickens, and beef with all kinds of different spices and herbs, flowers and fruit. Fish and wild game, berries and stone-fruits, pomegranates, figs, and cheeses young and old. Barley, bread, tubers ground to a paste and fried, all of this and more Cook had overseen, much of it made with her own hands. And with her own hands, she prepared and served to Cyrus and Cassandane the meat of the houbara bird.

Prexaspes celebrated on the fringes. Cyrus's eyes found him every so often during the hours of celebration that followed. And always, his eyes were on Cyrus. And each time, they were still inscrutable.

Cyrus's mare dropped her foal on the last night of the wedding celebrations. The colt was as black as the pools of the bride's eyes that night. In the morning, Cyrus made of the newborn horse a gift to his bride.

They saw the Achaeamenids off in the following afternoon. Despite his happiness, Cyrus watched Cassandane carefully for any sign of sadness, any sign of regret as these people of her clan prepared to depart back to Pasargadae, the place that she'd so unreservedly told him she loved. He could find none. She seemed as happy as he was simply to be there. And to his relief, she said so, too.

So, they prepared to meet the Achaemenids, clustered with their horses just inside the palace gates. There, the royal family of Anshan – King Cambyses, Prince Cyrus and his wife Cassandane – would bid the clan from Pasargad farewell. But just as Cyrus stepped up next to Cassandane to walk beside her there, he felt a hand on his arm.

"Prexaspes!" Cyrus exclaimed in surprise.

Cassandane urged Cyrus to go, talk with Prexaspes privately, since it was obvious that that's what the zapanitu's son wished.

When they were alone, well enough aside not to be overheard, Prexaspes said, "There's something I'd like to ask."

Nervous? Cyrus was surprised to detect a kind of nervousness in Prexaspes's demeanor and voice.

"Ask it," Cyrus said. "I'm of a mind and mood to give you whatever is in my power to bestow."

"That I stay on," Prexaspes said.

Cyrus's eyes shot open in surprise. "Here?"

"As your steward," Prexaspes finished.

Cyrus couldn't hide his shock. "But –" he stammered, "... Pasargadae... Your position there..." Prexaspes stood his ground. But across his face a cloud, disappointment. Cyrus gathered himself together and said, "Honestly, I thought you didn't like me."

"If you don't wish it —"

"No," Cyrus said. He smiled. "Yes, I... didn't have one. Thank you."

Prexaspes didn't smile. He didn't ease the wary stiffness in his shoulders, merely gave a quick nod and fell into step beside Cyrus to return to Cassandane and the king.

CHAPTER 72

*P*artly in preparation for the wedding but also because King Cam requested it – and it made sense – Cambyses and Cyrus switched rooms. King Cam moved into the room Cyrus had had from the day he arrived; his steady caretaker Nahhunte would have the room adjacent, the room where Zubaba had slept before his fateful return. And Cyrus moved into the king's quarters. It remained Cyrus's with Cassandane after they married. And the room next to it, the room that had been so long shuttered was opened, aired, cleaned and refurnished. Cassandane loved it. As for Prexaspes, he took over a spacious utility closet on the other side. Within days, it was as tidy as a monk's cell.

After the last of the Pasargadae returned home, Cam showered on Sanda all the fondness of a father for his daughter. And Cassandane settled into Anshan as if she had been there all along. Except, that is, in her dealings with Cook. It went both ways.

With the passing weeks, both Cook and Cassandane grew increasingly exasperated with each other until it became clear: Cook did her level best to be deferential, to ask rather than declare, invite suggestions rather than dictate judgments. And

Cassandane did her best to take interest, have opinions, to answer and to direct. Both were uncomfortable with the other, and it set everyone in the palace on edge until one day, somewhere between the courtyard and the kitchen, Cook exploded.

"But if we use all the shallow bowls for decorative aromatics, how will we eat the pasta pouches with the walnuts, peas, and mint?"

Cassandane came back with equal fire. "But you said, 'Don't you think it's nice to have dishes of dried spice and flowers scattered throughout the palace?' *I* don't know what bowls we need for what food..."

Cook's face was a volatile mix of anger, surprise, anxiety, and remorse.

But when Cassandane finished by throwing up her hands and saying, "And I don't care!" It silenced them both.

The two women – one stout, the other tall, both strong in arms and legs and temperament – stared at each other, the air clear as clean between them as a lightning strike. And then they laughed. And that was the end of it. Cook resumed her dictatorship, leaving Cassandane to relax into the business of managing with Cyrus decisions about the land, the palace, and the peoples around. Cassandane was quieter than anyone expected but it was a comfortable, peaceful thing – the quiet of a person settled into the moments of her days with a clear face and an easy way.

TIME PASSED. Whatever was the trouble Amytis in Media and her son the king of Babylon faced in lands so far away – was swiftly lost in the happy news that Cassandane was pregnant. Hopeful anticipation of a better future for Anshan and Parsa under the leadership of Cyrus and his family, overtook vague anxieties about political trouble far away. Cassandane was most definitely pregnant. The bulge that started with remarks about the irresistibility of Cook's food turned into a definite bump and the bump had life of its own. Any talk of the royal family, of the palace at Anshan was talk of that. The excitement was palpable. Concern, too.

King Cam doted on his daughter-in-law with near over-bearing anxiety. He would let her out of his sight only to be with Cyrus and went to great trouble to line up a team of midwives to assist with the birth. He vetted them himself, which was preposterous, since he knew nothing about childbirth. Still, the women he gathered to attend Cassandane were indeed those with the greatest experience and highest recommendations.

There are some who say that Sanda's condition was finally old Cam's undoing. If so, it was happiness that killed him. The labor of birth, an ordinary labor – not long, not short – carefully monitored and supported, nevertheless was labor. And Cassandane screamed through gritted teeth. "She is determined. She is strong," one midwife after another told the anxious husband and father-in-law. "The baby is in the right position and moving just like it should." But Cambyses was beside himself. When the baby was finally born – a boy – the old king fell back, as exhausted as if it had been he pushing that infant from water into air.

When the newborn had been cleaned, after he had suckled at Cassandane's breast and fallen fast asleep (his mother, too), Cyrus laid the warm bundle of his son into King Cam's hands. Arms trembling, Cambyses raised the baby to his face and kissed the downy brow. He handed the baby back to Cyrus, stroked the sleeping Cassandane's hair, and – faithful Nahhunte at his side – left the room.

They walked slowly, the steady guard and the wavering king out into the light of a new day. As per King Cam's request, Nahhunte settled in the old king on a bench in the courtyard, where trees freshly planted had already begun to flourish along with flowers and fragrant herbs. King Cam turned his face to the sun, pushed his toes into the dirt, and smiled. Nahhunte left the old man to his simple pleasure. When Nahhunte returned, lengthening shade from a slender tree covered the bench where the old man lay on his side. King Cam was dead.

The region mourned the death of their monarch, grateful that he'd lived his last years free of the torment that had so long plagued him. Cyrus and Sanda, now King and Queen of Anshan and Parsa, named their newborn baby after the old king. That boy, Anshan's newest crown prince, would be called Cambyses.

CHAPTER 73

*B*ack at the palace, the baby Cambyses faced a battle of his own. Sanda happened to be alone with him. She relished the serenity of such solitude, the peace of watching her child sleep. She was sitting like that, daydreaming sweet futures for her son when the tiny Cambyses suddenly began to stick his tongue out repeatedly. His legs and arms jerked about. Sanda leapt forward but hesitated unsure what if anything to do. The baby's eyelids were fluttering. A stimulating dream? But then Cambyses opened his eyes. They darted back and forth without focus or purpose. When he stopped breathing, she screamed. It had all happened in a mere instant.

"Help!" Sanda cried. She grabbed Cambyses up into her arms. "Someone help!" Frantic, Sanda patted his little back, then pushed her own air into his mouth.

The baby drew a ragged breath. Sanda scoured his face. She watched in horror as his eyes fixed in long stares before dashing randomly about again.

Sanda bounced him up and down. "Help!"

The time between Cambyses's breaths was excruciatingly long even as the infant paddled his arms and legs wildly.

Cook flew into the room. Behind her, Nahhunte and Martiya slid panting to a stop. Just as suddenly as he'd behaved erratically, the baby relaxed, his breathing regular again. Cambyses looked around, rolling his head, as if nothing had happened. Cook laid her hand on the baby's forehead. The infant was sweating but otherwise every bit an ordinary infant again. Sanda put him to her breast.

"I don't know what happened," Sanda said, wiping away a tear. "I thought that I had lost him."

Cook put her arm around Sanda's shoulder and looked down at the peaceful little boy. "He certainly seems fine now. Maybe he just had a belly ache."

Martiya said in a low voice, "Maybe Lilith tried to take him."

"Shush!" Cook said. She slapped him on the shoulder. "No such thing. The boy is protected by all the good gods of Anshan, of Elam, and Pasargad." She slapped him again.

"All right, all right," Martiya said, raising his hands in surrender.

Sanda burped the now sleepy baby and bent to lay him back into his cradle.

"Maybe the gods gave him a vision," Nahhunte said, his voice quiet.

To a person, they stared at the little boy, sleeping as quietly as if it had all been a dream.

Sanda gathered him into her arms again. Cambyses's head lolled; but his eyes remained closed, his breath steady, resting normally. "It doesn't seem like there's anything wrong. I can't understand it." Sanda swayed, soothing, from side to side.

The men shrugged, helpless.

"Babies are a mystery," Cook said, nodding.

"Thank you for coming." Sanda said to them all. She hugged Cambyses tighter. "He seems fine now. Before all this happened, I sent the girl out to the orchard to gather some of the apricots that are just ripening. She should be back soon. I'm sure you have other things to do. We'll be fine."

"Call if you need anything?" Nahhunte said.

Sanda nodded.

The two men left.

"Are you sure?" Cook asked. "I hate to leave you alone."

"Yes," Sanda said with a crooked smile. "He seems fine, and I know you're busy."

"No." Cook settled into a chair like a boulder come to rest at the bottom of hill. "I believe I'll stay at least until the girl comes back."

"Thank you," Sanda said, her eyes filling up with tears of gratitude and relief. "Thank you."

* * *

WHEN CYRUS RETURNED, Sanda still held the sleeping Cambyses. She tried to explain what she had seen.

"I know it sounds absurd. I've just never seen anything like this. If I hadn't been there, would he have died?" From over the baby's head, she looked at Cyrus with wild eyes.

In that instant, Cyrus knew that he'd do anything, anything to make her happy, anything to keep his child safe from harm. Cyrus gathered Sanda into his arms and the baby with her. Now he understood how his father, after Mandane's death and the presumed death of *their* baby could come so completely undone. Well, he thought, he was not his father. To Sanda, Cyrus said, "We have each other. Together we can face anything."

CHAPTER 74

The season's last market day in Anshan. Cyrus and Cassandane had little Cambyses, just the three of them, to wander among the stalls, to enjoy the bustle of trade and all the pretty things. Just the three... and Prexaspes, of course. Prexaspes insisted that he accompany Cyrus anywhere beyond the palace walls. The young king relished passing unrecognized, and Prexaspes drew heads. But it was useless to argue with the Achaemenid steward and self-declared body-guard. So Cyrus asked him to keep a discreet distance.

Cyrus recognized the Babylonian Iddina's voice before he ever saw him. When Cassandane and the baby went one way, enchanted by some twirling paper decorations and Cyrus another, Prexaspes – taller than everyone else – gave a nod to one of Martiya's trainees to keep a protective eye on the queen and baby Cambyses while he followed Cyrus.

In the thick of negotiating with an elderly matron, the merchant's voice rang through at once reassuring and informative, never missing an opportunity to praise her good taste. When Iddina caught sight of Cyrus approaching, his face lit with recognition. He passed the woman's business to an associate - quickly instructing the young man, "Treat her well," and stepped up to Cyrus. Prexaspes angled close, but when Cyrus gave him a side-eye, Prexaspes pretended interest in the goods on a table nearby.

Iddina clapped Cyrus on the shoulder in enthusiastic greeting.

Cyrus asked after things in Babylon.

"Touchy these days. But what's new?" Iddina shrugged. "Ever since Nebuchadnezzar died and Amel-Marduk took the throne, old tensions – who's Babylonian and who's not – have only gotten worse. Name not-with-standing, no one forgets that this king is half-Median. At least his mother had the good sense to go back there."

Amytis. His mother's sister, his own aunt. Cyrus turned his face to the side and coughed into his shoulder to hide – he hoped – his unique interest in it all.

Iddina didn't seem to notice. "My father is forever trying to steer clear of politics. It's tough in our business, though. He actually works for the very man who has always had his eye on the throne, Neriglissar - Igliss. Lately..." Iddina lowered his voice and bent his head to Cyrus's, "Igliss has been assigning the dates of business in Sippar not to the reign of Amel-Marduk but instead to the reign – "

"Of Igliss," Cyrus finished for him.

Iddina's stepped back and laughed. "You catch on quick."

"I was just guessing," Cyrus said.

"And here I thought you wouldn't really care."

"You're right," Cyrus said. But he couldn't help thinking how grateful he was that despite his relationship to Amel-Marduk and to Amytis, he wasn't embroiled in the conflict of empires. All he wanted was a quiet life in Parsa with Cassandane and the family they were growing.

"One of the prophets actually had the nerve to predict yet another change in rule," Iddina said with a laugh. "You know, I'd have thought he'd say the threats would come from the north. It's far more likely, and these prophets, they do a whole lot better when what they say actually comes to pass." Iddina rearranged a set of beaten bronze cymbals on blue velvet. He stepped back to appraise, then seemingly satisfied, shrugged. "You've probably heard. Up north, a new king of Lydia, Croesus, has been snapping up Greek settlements along the Mediterranean coast and getting really rich. You'd think it would be him causing trouble. But –" Iddina grinned. "Funny thing. The prophecy had to do with your general region," he said. "Elam!"

Cyrus started in surprise. Again, Iddina didn't seem to notice but looked at Cyrus, grinning, his eyebrows raised, inviting Cyrus to share the absurd unlikelihood that anyone from this region would be of concern to Babylonia.

"Do you remember what he said, the prophet?" Cyrus asked.

Iddina put a hand to his chin and raised his eyes to the distance, thinking... "I can't remember the whole thing," he said, glancing back at Cyrus. "But it goes something like..." He looked up again, recalling. "'A king of Elam will arise, the scepter... something-or-other. He will remove the preceding king from his throne and... Um." He looked past Cyrus's head as if searching for the words, "Sorry. Well, a little later it goes, 'He will take the throne, and the king he removed... that king the king of Elam will settle in another land.'" Iddina looked back at Cyrus with a grin. "Inscrutable. As usual." He shrugged. "Anyway, that's it. As well as I can remember."

They exchanged parting pleasantries and Cyrus stepped away, down the row of booths, Prexaspes trailing a few yards behind. Cyrus saw little after that but walked on in a daze.

* * *

"Who was that?" Sanda asked, stepping up to Cyrus's side. In her arms, Cambyses grew restless. Cassandane shifted him to the other shoulder.

Cyrus, grounded again, smiled to see them. "Oh, just a merchant I met some time ago."

Cyrus took the baby, kissed Cassandane's cheek, and lifted Cambyses high, jiggling his chubby limbs gently.

"What did he say?" Cassandane asked.

The baby chuckled, and Cyrus tucked him into the crook of his arm.

"Who?" Cyrus asked.

"That man, the merchant."

For a brief moment, Cyrus's face was like stone. Just as quickly, he brightened. He tickled the baby and gave Cassandane a pleasant grin.

"Nothing that concerns us," he said.

Cassandane studied his face. Apparently satisfied, she lengthened her stride and began to tell him about all the things they'd seen, the little adventures and so on. Cyrus listened with half an ear. In the other rang the words Iddina had said. "A king of Elam will arise…"

CHAPTER 75

*K*ing Cyrus folded the scrap of parchment along its old creases and looked up.

But his eyes weren't on the gleaming tiles of this palace addition, neither the tidy courtyard ahead nor the fields beyond, where grain waved green in the spring's mid-morning. He didn't see the flocks that freckled the surrounding hills, not even his wife -- her hair the color of burnished mahogany pulled loosely, here and there, into the tiny clasps of a dozen golden hair rings from the crown of her head halfway down her back -- standing in the doorway.

From his simple throne in Anshan, he saw instead the face of an old friend, the guide who had escorted him years earlier from the snowy mountains of elegant Ecbatana south to this plateau. Cyrus ran a finger over the parchment's ragged edge, bowed his head, and groaned, recalling how that very face was shredded and the man killed for Cyrus's own ten-year-old folly.

Cyrus jumped under the hand laid gently on his shoulder. He looked up, clasped it with his own, and smiled apologetically into Sanda's face. Her eye caught the parchment between Cyrus's fingers. "Some trouble?"

"No, no trouble." Cyrus drew Sanda around to stand in front of him. "I've told you about my journey from Media -- a slave, to this place -- a prince."

Sanda nodded.

"And I've told you about Zubaba, who brought me here and alone witnessed that moment – no joyful reunion, but loneliness and despair."

She nodded again.

"Zubaba told me, during our travels, about how his own family came from Susa. And he told me about ancient connections between our people here and his there. Before he left, he gave me this note." Cyrus handed it to her. "It's the name of a man he knew, someone who lives in the town of Shugalli. In Elam."

Sanda opened the parchment.

"He said that if I were ever there... The man is, or was, one of the elite elders."

Sanda read its few words and handed the worn scrap back to Cyrus. "Maybe my father knows him, or the town, at least."

"I think about it, sometimes -- Elam in the old days. Glorious, as Zubaba described it. And that we were once the closest of allies, Anshan and Susa, that many of us share blood. We do share gods."

Sanda watched the lines in Cyrus's face drop away, his long-lashed eyes fix on some distant idea. A flock of migrating ducks flapped across a long streak of clouds. She traced the swoop of his lower lip with a light finger.

Cyrus grinned. "I might have uncles and cousins just over those hills and all the way to Susa."

"Maybe you do."

Cyrus drew her down to his lap.

"What's this?" she said, laughing.

Cyrus wrapped his arms around her. "Why should I care, when you have brought to me all the family I ever need, all I could ever hope for?"

They both grinned as sound of baby Cambyses's hungry wail reached them. "Speaking of..." Cassandane rose.

"There's something else."

"What is it?"

"I know that Anshan has always been the site of Parsa's palace and of the throne that I've inherited..."

"But?" she gently prompted.

"I'm thinking of moving it. To Pasargad."

Cassandane's eyes opened wide. She clapped her hands over her mouth, then with a happy squeal, took his head in her hands and buried her face in his curly hair. She shut her eyes and kissed the top of his head. "Don't make this move for me," she said, leaning over, her brown eyes finding his. "Don't do it for my father or for my brother."

"It's for me. Pasargad is the first place I have ever felt at home since leaving the cottage in Media." He took her hands and, squeezing them, smiled into her eyes. "It's for us. Pasargad -- you, your family -- is the only true home I could ever have. Besides, it's not so far and still within greater Parsa. I could renew our ties with Elam. Peace and strength. We'd never have to leave."

The sun itself couldn't have been brighter than Sanda's smile. "Promise? Our home forever?" she asked.

"I promise," Cyrus said. "Forever."

THE END

CAST OF CHARACTERS

A few things to note: Even for historical characters, there may be some question or disagreement regarding specific details. I do not provide here dates of death or other details that don't transpire during the course of this particular narrative. With the exception of Iddina and Coniah, nicknames are my own. An asterisk (*) denotes non-historical characters, i.e. people that I've totally made up.

Adad-guppi: Aramean (from the defeated Harran); attendant in the Babylonian courts of Nebuchadnezzar and Amel-Marduk; mother of Nabonidus, grandmother of Belshazzar.

Amel-Marduk (Bushu): son of Amytis and Nebuchadnezzar II; born Nabu-shuma-ukin; becomes King of Babylon in 562 B.C.E. In the Bible, his name appears as Evil-Merodach.

Amytis: daughter of Astyages, king of Media; sister of Mandane; wife of Nebuchadnezzar (and according to legend, the woman for whom he built the Hanging Gardens of Babylon because she missed her mountain home so much); mother of Amel-Marduk; aunt of Cyrus II.

Astyages: son of Cyaxares; king of Media; father of Amytis and Mandane; grandfather of Cyrus II.

Bariki-ili: Hebrew slave who (historically) earned a reputation for seeking his freedom, running away and getting caught over and over again.

Belshazzar: son of Nabonidus and Nitocris and so the (illegitimate, I imagine) grandson of Nebuchadnezzar.

Cambyses I (King Cam): King of Anshan (Parsa); husband of Mandane; father of Cyrus II.

Cassandane (Sanda): of the Pasargadae, Achaemenid clan; daughter of Pharnaspes; sister of Otanes; wife of Cyrus II, mother of Cambyses II.

Cassiya/Kassiya: daughter of Nebuchadnezzar; wife of Neriglissar; mother of Labashi-Marduk; (half-, I imagine) sister of Nitocris and Eanna-sharra-utsur (sharing the father Nebuchadnezzar).

Cyaxares: (d. 585 B.C.E.) king of the Medes; father of Astyages; grandfather of Amytis and Mandane. (Some say he was the father of Amytis).

Cyrus II: son of Cambyses I and Mandane; niece of Amytis; grandson of Astyages; raised by Median slaves Spaco and *Mit(hradates) who called him Bartatua until he was ten years old, then returned to Parsa.

Eanna-šarra-utsur (Ean): son (I imagine eldest) of Nebuchadnezzar with his first wife; in 587 B.C. receives rations in a sick-house in Uruk (historical). I imagine he suffers schizophrenia.

Egibi: family name of Babylonian entrepreneurial family that becomes a powerful corporation beginning with **Nabu-ahhe-iddin (Khai)** and endures for several generations.

Harpagus: palace steward to King Astyages.

Itti-Marduk-balatu (Iddina -- this nickname is historical): eldest son of Nabu-ahhe-iddin (Khai) and Qudashu; heir to the Egibi estate.

Jehoiachin (historically also Jeconiah/Coniah): King of Judah removed by Nebuchadnezzar in the first deportation mid-

March, 597 B.C.E. and imprisoned in Babylon. He was eighteen years old at the time and had been king for only three months.

*Karadara (Kara): Aramean commoner from the defeated Harran; slave in Astyages's court; wet nurse to Amytis; slave to Amytis in Babylon; finally revealed (spoiler alert!) to be Amytis's mother.

Mithradates (Mit): Shepherd slave to Astyages's palace who with his wife Spaco raised Cyrus II (whom they called Bartatua) from infancy until Cyrus was ten years old.

Mandane: (legitimate) daughter of Astyages, hence princess of Media; half-sister of Amytis; wife of Cambyses I; mother of Cyrus II; I imagine that she commits suicide upon being told of her newborn's (Cyrus's) death.

*Martiya: son of Upadarma the groom, head of the stables in Anshan

Nabonidus: Aramean from defeated Harran; son of Adad-guppi; courtier in the Babylonian courts of Nebuchadnezzar and Amel-Marduk; husband of Nitocris; father of Belshazzar.

*Nahhunte: head of the palace in Anshan.

*Nathan: from Nippur, Jewish scribe for Nebuchadnezzar; son of *Rabbi Yakov ben-Isaiah and *Michal; moves with Amytis to Media.

Nabu-ahhe-iddin (Khai): son of Babylonian farmer Shula Egibi; scribe, entrepreneur; husband of Qudashu; father of Itti-Marduk-balatu (Iddina); founder of the Egibi family corporation.

Nebuchadnezzar II: (634 -- Oct. 8, 562) son of Nabopolassar, king of Babylon/Babylonia; husband of Amytis; father of Nitocris (illegit, I imagine), Eanna-sharra-utsur (Ean), and Cassiya by an Ishtar temple slave from Uruk (I made up this unnamed earlier woman/wife). Father of Amel-Marduk by Amytis.

Neriglissar (Igliss): probably served with Nebuchadnezzar on campaign against Jerusalem in 587 B.C.; husband of Cassiya (so, Nebuchadnezzar's son-in-law); father of Labashi-Marduk.

Otanes: Achaemenid; son of Pharnaspes; younger brother of Cassandane; brother-in-law of Cyrus.

Pharnaspes: Achaemenid; father of Otanes and Cassandane; father-in-law of Cyrus

Prexaspes: son of the chief (zapanitu) of the Pasargadae.

*Rachel: Jewish wet nurse in Babylon for the baby Amel-Marduk (Bushu).

Rdiya: head of Amytis's Babylonian household; based on the historical Ardiya of Nebuchadnezzar's court staff.

*Sadeghi: the evil groundsman of Cambyses I's Anshan.

Spaco (probably itself a nickname; means simply "Dog"): Shepherd slave to Astyages's palace who with her husband *Mit(hradates) raised Cyrus II (whom they called Bartatua) from infancy until Cyrus was ten years old.

*Upadarma: head of the stables in Anshan.

*Zubaba Median with family roots in Susa/Elam; he escorts the boy Cyrus from Ecbatana, Media to Anshan in Parsa.

CITATIONS OF QUOTES

p. 10 "**A good man his advisors had said...**" Herodotus calls Cyrus's father Cambyses (I) "a man of good family and quiet habits" (I. 107).

p. 10 "**It was said that the people there ate wild fruits and *pistaka* nuts.**" Nicolaus of Damascus probably following Ctesias *FGH* 90 F66.34. Astyages calls them "terebinth-eaters," but the word translated "terebinth" likely refers to a nut very like but not identical to pistachios (Heleen Sancisi-Weerdenburg, "Persian Food and Political Identity," in *Food in Antiquity* - J. Wilkins et al. eds. - Exeter, 1995). According to the Greeks, it was associated with masculinity and wild nature.

p. 36 "**An exceptionally large breed called Nisean...**" Strabo, XI 13.7 cited by Amélie Kuhrt, *The Persian Empire: A Corpus of Sources from the Achaemenid Period,* vol. 2, 2007, Routledge, 714.

p. 71 "**Pleasure and luxury...**" See Athenaeus XII.512a-b, quoted in Pierre Briant, *From Cyrus to Alexander: A History of the Persian Empire,* translated by Peter T. Daniels; 2002, Eisenbrauns, 300. It was a theory applied to the Persians and Medes.

p. 108 "**It was widely said that they lived in caves...**" This is how Diodorus describes them (calling them Cosseans) and "independent from ancient times" (XIX.19.3-4, 8; cited by Pierre Briant, *From Cyrus to Alexander: A History of the Persian Empire,* translated by Peter T. Daniels; 2002, Eisenbrauns, 729).

p. 124 "He also sent his son -- his eldest, Arukku..." From Ashurbanipal's prism annal of 639 (Amélie Kuhrt, *The Persian Empire: A Corpus of Sources from the Achaemenid Period,* vol. 1; 2007, Routledge, 53-54). It tells that when Ashurbanipal triumphed over Elam, "Kurash, king of Parsumash sent Arukku, his eldest son, together with his tribute, as hostage to Nineveh, my lordly city, and implored my lordship."

p. 135 "He plundered Susa's great wealth..." Adapted From Ashurbanipal's prism annals: Prism A V.126-VI.76 ~ F IV.67-v.54 (cited by Wouter Henkelman *The Other Gods Who Are: Studies in Elamite-Iranian Acculturation Based on the Persepolis Fortification Texts,* 2008 Nederlands Instituut voor het Nabije Oosten, 32).

p. 135 "Ashurbanipal claimed that from Susa he took..." Adapted from D.D. Luckenbill, *Ancient Records of Assyria and Babylonia,* 1927, parag. 811.

p. 135 "'Susa's queen,' Zubaba said..." See Javier Alvarez-Mon, "Ashurbanipal's Feast: A View from Elam," 2009, *Iranica Antiqua* 44: 131-180 for a full description of Elamite representation on Nineveh's palace walls and of the historical circumstances behind in it. The precise identification of the female figure continues to be debated. That she is an Elamite queen is one, quite good, possibility.

p. 136 "He said the king settled 'in grief..." Adapted from D. D. Luckenbill 1926-7, II, parag. 815.

p. 137 "Seventy years ago, when Ashurbanipal assaulted Susa..." Wouter Henkelman, *The Other Gods Who Are: Studies in Elamite-Iranian Acculturation Based on the Persepolis Fortification Texts,* 2008 Nederlands Instituut voor het Nabije Oosten, 17-18.

p. 137-138 "They tore open the secret places...ghosts." This also (adapted) comes from Ashurbanipal's annals (cited by Amélie

Kuhrt, *The Ancient Near East, c. 3000-330 BC*, 2 vols., 1997, Rout-ledge, 500).

p. 294 "Cyrus looked down at the cylinder of stone..." This seal (PFS 0093) was discovered at Persepolis, an heirloom that has lasted until today. Whether or not the Elamite Kurash on this cylinder is the same as the Kurash called "king" In the Assyrian annals continues to be debated. I believe with many scholars that the image depicts Cyrus II's grandfather, the first Cyrus. It reads "Kurash the Anshanite, son of Shishpish (Teispes)." See Daniel Potts, "Cyrus the Great and the Kingdom of Anshan" in *Birth of the Persian Empire*, 2005, British Museum, 18. It might come from a time before he was king (Matt Waters, *"Parsumaš, Anšan, and Cyrus,"* in *Elam and Persia*, 2003, Eisenbrauns, 292).

p. 266 "When he stepped outside, the plain glittered as if filled with millions of stars..." and **"The trees yellow-orange to carmine-red..."** This paragraph's description of Pasargad is informed by the poetic description of modern archaeologist Ernst Herzfeld, which he composed from the site of Pasargadae on Nov 19, 1923. From Herzfeld Archives, Free Sackler Museum, translated by Alex Nagel, personal communication: "The morning was just gorgeous: the plain glittered like it would have been filled with millions of stars; everywhere was a hoarfrost of crystals. After the marvelous last sunset I slept the last moonlit night by the Tomb of Cyrus's (minus 4 degree Celsius). The whole day just beautiful: the narrow valley of the Pulvar River.... By the water there were willows, reeds, oleander,.. The colors of the Fall: the trees yellow-orange to carmine-red, the sky in bright turquoise, the mountains violet, blue, red, yellow. Just gorgeous! I only wish I could send something of the beauty of these days back home."

p. 339, 340 "A king of Elam will arise... in another land" From the Dynastic Prophecy Col. II, 17-21 (Paul-Alain Beaulieu, *The Reign of Nabonidus, King of Babylon, 556-539 BC*, 1989, Yale, 231). The parts that I attribute to Iddina's failure in memory are lost to us -- parts of the text that we no longer have or can make out.

p. 347 "***Karadara (Kara)**" The ancient Iranian Kāradārā means "having work," which Tavernier observes is "a good name for a slave." See Tavernier, *Iranica in the Achaemenid Period (ca. 550-330 BC): Lexicon of Old Iranian Proper Names and Loanwords, Attested in Non-Iranian Texts*, 2007, Peeters, 226. The Indo-Aryan influence in Media at this time makes it feasible that such a name might be given to an acquired slave. A child might shorten it to "Kara." The word *kāra* in Old Persian means "the people, army" (Prods Oktor Skjærvø, *An Introduction to Old Persian,* 2005, online pdf, 25), which I also find provocative.

Details of the feast at Pasargad that Cyrus happens upon borrow heavily from information in Wouter Henkelman's "Parnakka's Feast: Šip in Parsa and Elam" in *Elam and Persia,* 2011, Eisenbrauns, 89-166.

SOME OF MY SOURCES FOR INFORMATION

I am tremendously grateful to those scholars of ancient Near Eastern history and literature who have made troves of information available and keep adding to what we know and how we think about the people, the places, and times that these narratives so lightly brush. I'm deeply sorry not to provide exhaustive documentation for all the research that informs these books. In lieu of even a bibliography, here is a list (itself incomplete) of some of the hundreds of scholars, past and present, whose work informed the story I tell.

Abraham, Kathleen
    Abusch, Tzvi
    Ackerman, Susan
    Ackroyd, Peter
    Adams, Robert McCormick
    Ahn, J. J.
    Aiken Littauer, M.
    Albenda, Pauline
    Albertz, Rainer
    Albright, William F.

Alexander, Robert L.

Algaze, Guillermo

Allen, Lindsay

Al-Rawi, F. N. H.

Álvarez-Mon, Javier

Amiet, P.

Aminzadeh, B.

Anthony, David W.

Ataç, M. A.

Austin, M. M.

Avigad, N.

Axworthy, Michael

Bahrami, B.

Bahrani, Zainab

Baker, H. D.

Balcer, Jack Martin

Bandstra, Andrew J.

Barkworth, P. R.

Barnett, R. D.

Barr, James

Basham, A. L.

Basirov, Oric

Beach, Eleanor F.

Beaulieu, Paul-Alain

Beckwith, Christopher I.

Bedford, Peter Ross

Berman, Joshua

Betlyon, John W.

Bidmead, J.

Bivar, A. D. H.

Black, Jeremy A.

Boardman, John

Boda, Mark J.

Bodi, Daniel

Bongenaar, A.

Bottéro, J.

Boucharlat, Remy

Boyce, Mary

Pierre Briant

Brosius, Maria

Browne, Edward Granville

Calmeyer, P.

Cameron, G. G.

Carter, C. E.

Castle, W. E.

Chalmers, C.

Choksy, Jamsheed K.

Cohen, Andrew C.

Crowell, Bradley L.

Curtis, John

Curtis, Vesta Sarkhosh

Dalley, Stephanie

Dandamaev, M. A.

Davies, Malcolm

Davies, W. D.

de Miroschedji, Pierre

De Souza, Philip

Dever, William

Dick, Michael B.

Dillery, John

Dougherty, Raymond P.

Draycott, Catherine M.

Drews, Robert

Dubberstein, Waldo H.

Dusinberre, Elspeth R. M.

Dvornik, Francis

Eilers, W.

Elgood, C.

Errington, Elizabeth
Eshel, Esther
Eskenazi, Tamara Cohn
Farazmand, Ali
Farrokh, Kaveh
Finkel, Irving L.
Flattery, David Stophlet
Fleming, D. E.
Foltz, Richard
Forsyth, Neil
Foster, Benjamin R.
Foster, Karen Polinger
Fried, Lisbeth S.
Frye, Richard N.
Fuchs, Esther
Gabrielli, Marcel
Galil, Gershon
Garrison, Mark B.
George, A. R.
Gese, Hartmut
Gopnik, Hilary
Goulder, M.
Grabbe, Lester L.
Gray, Louis H.
Grayson, Albert Kirk
Green, Anthony
Green, Jack
Griffiths, A.
Guliaev, Valeri I.
Gurney, O. R.
Hallo, William W.
Handley, Morrison
Harmatta, J.
Harris, Rivka

Harrison, Thomas
Harvey, D.
Head, Duncan
Hedrick, Larry
Henkelman, Wouter
Hirsch, Steven W.
Hoglund, Kenneth G.
Holtz, Shalom E.
Horsley, Richard A.
Houston, Mary G.
Huff, Dietrich
Ibrāmī, Hūshang
Ivantchik, Askold I.
Jackson, A. V. Williams
Jacobs, Bruno
Japhet, Sara
Jawad, Laith A.
Jennings, Justin
Joannes, F.
Jong, Albert de
Jordana, Xavier
Jursa, M.
Kaptan, D.
Katz, Steven T.
Katzenstein, H. Jacob
Kawami, Trudy S.
Kessler, K.
Kessler, John
Killick, R. G.
Kleber, Kristin
Knapton, Peter
Knoppers, Gary N
Knowles, Melody D.
Kratz, Reinhard

Kriwaczek, Paul
Kuhrt, Amélie
Lacocque, André
Lambert, W. G.
Landes, David S.
Lang, Mabel L.
Langdon, S.
Lavī, Ḥabīb
Leach, E. R.
Leiden, W. H. C.
Leloux, Kevin
Lemaire, André
Lerner, G.
Lincoln, Bruce
Linssen, M. J. H.
Lipiński, Edward
Littman, Robert J.
Liverani, Mario
Lloyd, Alan B.
Lloyd, Seton
Lucas, C. J.
Luckenbill, Daniel David
Lukonin, Vladimir G.
MacGinnis, John
Machinist, Peter
Malandra, William W.
Malbran-Labat, F.
Marzhan, Joachim
Master, Daniel M.
Matsushima, E.
Mattila, R.
McGovern, Patrick E.
Meier, S. A.
Middlemas, Jill

Miller, M. C.
Mills, Lawrence Heyworth
Mierhoop,
Miroschedji, P.
Moorey, P. R. S.
Muscarella, O. W.
Mukherjee, Siddhartha
Nashef, Khaled
Nefiodkin, Alexander K.
Nejad, Hadi
Nesbitt, M.
Neumann, C.
Neusner, Jacob
Newman, Judith H.
Nodet, Etienne
Noll, K. L.
Novotny, Jamie
Nylan, M.
Nylander, Carl
Ogden, Graham S.
Olson, J. S.
Oppenheim, A. L.
Page, Hugh R., Jr
Pallis, Svend Aage
Parpola, Simo
Parker, Richard A.
Panaino, Antonio
Paspalas, Stavros A.
Pearce, Laurie E.
Pedersen, O.
Pelikan, Jaroslav
Peradotto, John
Pettinato, Giovanni
Pham, Xuan Huong Thi

Pinches, T. G.
Poebel, A.
Polosmak, Natalya
Pongratz-Leisten, B.
Potts, Daniel T.
Powell, Marvin A.
Pritchard, James B.
Oeming, Manfred
Rainey, A. F.
Reiner, Erica
Rolle, Renate
Röllig, W.
Rollinger, Robert
Root, Margaret Cool
Roth, Martha T.
Sack, Ronald H.
Salonen, A.
Sancisi-Weerdenburg, Heleen
Sanders-Goebel, P.
Sandison, AT
Sarraf, M. R.
Sarshar, Houman
Sasson, J. M.
Schaudig, Hanspeter
Schauensee, D.E.
Schmid, H.
Schmidt, H. P.
Schwartz, Martin
Schwemer, Daniel
Scurlock, Joann
Seymour, M. J.
Shahgolzari, SM
Shea, William H.
Shiff, L. B.

Simpson, St John
Skjærvø, P. O.
Soudavar, A.
Stadter, P. A.
Stausberg, Michael
Stein, Gil J.
Stevens, Marty E.
Stol, Martin
Stolper, Matthew W.
Stott, Katherine
Stronach, David B.
Sumner, William M.
Suter, David W.
Tavernier, J.
Thomas, D. R. A.
Thureau-Dangin, F.
Trotter, James M.
Tuplin, Christopher
Ulansey, David
Ungnad, A.
Vallat, F.
Van de Mieroop, Marc
Van Driel, G.
Vargyas, P.
Vaughn, Andrew G.
Veen, J. E. van der
Vogelsang, W. J.
Waerzeggers, C.
Waters, Matthew W.
Watts, James W.
Weiershauser, Frauke
Weinfeld, M.
Weisberg, David B.
Weiss, L.

Weitzman, Steven
Widengren, G.
Wiesehöfer, J.
Wiggermann, F. A. M.
Williamson, H. G. M.
Winter, Irene J.
Wiseman, D. J.
Wunsch, C.
Yamauchi, E.
Yavari, A.
Younger, K. Lawson
Zaccagnini, Carlo
Zadok, Ran
Zawadzki, S.
Zevit, Z.
Zimansky, Paul E.
Zimmern, H.

AUTHOR'S NOTE

Cyrus's Persian Empire is also called the Achaemenid (or Achaemenian) Empire. That alone, is intriguing. After all, it was his wife Cassandane who was of the Achaemenid clan of the Pasargad tribe. And it is Cassandane's Pasargad that became the capital of Cyrus's empire and is the place where a person still today can visit their tombs. (It is only with Darius – who was not a blood descendant of Cyrus's but rather married Cyrus's daughters – that the designation Achaemenid is applied; before Darius, they identified as kings of Anshan).

Between the uncertainty about Cyrus's birth – how fraught his parentage, how riddled with conflict – and the certainty of his wife's Pasargad as the chosen site of his palace and his eternal resting place, it doesn't seem such a big step to imagine Cyrus driven by the very human hunger for family and home that is central to this story.

This book – and the others in what has become a multi-volume (and could be more) saga – happened (over fifteen years ago) because I started making things up. I had intended to write a nonfiction tome about a momentous period in human history (the transition from Babylonian to Persian rule) and the figure who stands at its center (Cyrus II, a.k.a. Cyrus the Great). But the more I learned, the more intriguing the women became. And the more I learned, the more I was forced to accept what all the experts say: we know very little... concretely, that is. But oh, so much was possible.

I threw myself into the research. At some point, what I was learning reached a critical mass and slipped its academic bonds. Turns out, the research had been seducing my imagination all along. Finally, I had to face it: they'd eloped. I found myself filling in the long blanks between certainties with imagining what might have been. Ancient characters had become real people. Events and places began to take the shape of a novel. Also, I have a terrible memory. In all that research, I was finding associations and connections that no one seemed to have made before, and I didn't want to forget them. My best vehicle for keeping track was story.

I agonized. My agent at the time pointed out the cold truth. We simply could not sell a book of nonfiction with, er, fictional elements no matter how extensive the disclaimers. So, I ordered the facts back into their house, and tried to send my imagination packing. Alas, the two would not be parted. Finally, a friend of mine who had herself recently made a shift from nonfiction to historical fiction confronted me. "Why are clinging to nonfiction?!" she said. "Accept it. It's a novel."

The novel became a multi-volume saga. That said, each book stands (or falls) on its own. In this case, I focus on Cyrus, specifically, the young Cyrus – from his birth (following especially Herodotus's telling) through his marriage to Cassandane, the woman who by all accounts Cyrus loved beyond life itself. It was her Pasargad where a person today still can see the modest tombs of Cyrus and Cassandane, still witness the outlines of their marvelous palace defined as much by beautifully ordered gardens (from which we get our word "paradise") as by any architecture.

How much of the book is true? I understand the question, I

do. And my best short answer is: all of it and none of it. This is a work of fiction. I made it up. That said, it is based on huge amounts of hard-core research undertaken over the many years that this particular project has demanded and over decades before that as a student of the history and literature of the ancient Near East (what today we call the Middle East), earning a Ph.D. on the topic and a tenured appointment as a professor of it.

The question deserves a longer answer. First, a warning: the information here is best read *after* the novel itself for a couple of reasons. Most obviously, it will spoil the suspense. Equally serious, your brain might break. There are so many odd names and potentially unfamiliar references below that without having a story to hang them on... well, consider yourself warned.

Second, a quick note about sources. This story takes place 2500 years ago. Many relevant records, such as they ever were, are long gone. But many remain. Sources for modern researchers are wildly diverse, some primary and many derivatives. They range from the ancient histories of such as Herodotus, Xenophon, Ctesias, Nabonidus, and the business records of the Babylonian Egibi family to modern archaeological excavation reports, from the list of wages due to workers in a Babylonian temple to the Bible's Psalm 137, from an ancient world map drawn on clay (now housed in the British Museum) to a palace gate in stunningly beautiful tile (now housed in Berlin).

No one knows it all. Much about the period and its people is still in question. Hints and rumors abound. Ancient histories followed different rules than what we might wish. For such as Herodotus, one of our most important sources, reporting absolute fact was not always as important as telling a good story. And not all of the sources, ancient and otherwise, agree with each other.

Take Cyrus himself. Ancient sources disagree about the etymology of his name. From where does it come, and what does it mean? (I throw in my lot with an Elamite origin.) We don't know exactly when Cyrus was born or how much of Herodotus's tale (which this reflects) is true. We have no evidence that he ever called himself a king of Persia. Neither did he identify as Achaemenid. He called himself "king of Anshan" and seems indeed to have been the son of Cambyses I and grandson of a certain Teispes. As for the designation Persian, even that is slippery. One thing we do know is that it was in the year 559 B.C.E. that he succeeded Cambyses I as king of Anshan.

In earlier versions of these novels, I included footnotes citing sources, adding more information, and sometimes recording my own thinking about what I was learning. I did it mainly to help myself remember what led me to make the narrative decisions I'd made – from details about food and clothing and particular items such as the seal that Cyrus inherits (extant, discovered with the Persepolis Fortification Tablets), the Elamite bow, and intricate equestrian paraphernalia, to matters such as the production of opium in Cambyses II's Anshan (no evidence) and Cyrus's apparent devotion to Cassandane's Pasargad. I've had illusions of making those footnotes available to readers. But they're terribly unwieldy (in the hundreds), and the research keeps coming. So, apart from the few direct citations that I list below, I return simply to what drove me in the first place: to create a story-vehicle to keep track of a possible history, a drama of love and place and religion and ambition. And I admit to the same truth, which is both exhilarating and exasperating: there's always more to the story.

SOME OF MY SOURCES FOR INFORMATION

I am tremendously grateful to those scholars of ancient Near Eastern history and literature who have made troves of information available and keep adding to what we know and how we think about the people, the places, and times that these narratives so lightly brush. I'm deeply sorry not to provide exhaustive documentation for all the research that informs these books. In lieu of even a bibliography, here is a list (itself incomplete) of some of the hundreds of scholars, past and present, whose work informed the story I tell.

Abraham, Kathleen
   Abusch, Tzvi
   Ackerman, Susan
   Ackroyd, Peter
   Adams, Robert McCormick
   Ahn, J. J.
   Aiken Littauer, M.
   Albenda, Pauline
   Albertz, Rainer
   Albright, William F.

Alexander, Robert L.
Algaze, Guillermo
Allen, Lindsay
Al-Rawi, F. N. H.
Álvarez-Mon, Javier
Amiet, P.
Aminzadeh, B.
Anthony, David W.
Ataç, M. A.
Austin, M. M.
Avigad, N.
Axworthy, Michael
Bahrami, B.
Bahrani, Zainab
Baker, H. D.
Balcer, Jack Martin
Bandstra, Andrew J.
Barkworth, P. R.
Barnett, R. D.
Barr, James
Basham, A. L.
Basirov, Oric
Beach, Eleanor F.
Beaulieu, Paul-Alain
Beckwith, Christopher I.
Bedford, Peter Ross
Berman, Joshua
Betlyon, John W.
Bidmead, J.
Bivar, A. D. H.
Black, Jeremy A.
Boardman, John
Boda, Mark J.
Bodi, Daniel

Bongenaar, A.

Bottéro, J.

Boucharlat, Remy

Boyce, Mary

Pierre Briant

Brosius, Maria

Browne, Edward Granville

Calmeyer, P.

Cameron, G. G.

Carter, C. E.

Castle, W. E.

Chalmers, C.

Choksy, Jamsheed K.

Cohen, Andrew C.

Crowell, Bradley L.

Curtis, John

Curtis, Vesta Sarkhosh

Dalley, Stephanie

Dandamaev, M. A.

Davies, Malcolm

Davies, W. D.

de Miroschedji, Pierre

De Souza, Philip

Dever, William

Dick, Michael B.

Dillery, John

Dougherty, Raymond P.

Draycott, Catherine M.

Drews, Robert

Dubberstein, Waldo H.

Dusinberre, Elspeth R. M.

Dvornik, Francis

Eilers, W.

Elgood, C.

Errington, Elizabeth
Eshel, Esther
Eskenazi, Tamara Cohn
Farazmand, Ali
Farrokh, Kaveh
Finkel, Irving L.
Flattery, David Stophlet
Fleming, D. E.
Foltz, Richard
Forsyth, Neil
Foster, Benjamin R.
Foster, Karen Polinger
Fried, Lisbeth S.
Frye, Richard N.
Fuchs, Esther
Gabrielli, Marcel
Galil, Gershon
Garrison, Mark B.
George, A. R.
Gese, Hartmut
Gopnik, Hilary
Goulder, M.
Grabbe, Lester L.
Gray, Louis H.
Grayson, Albert Kirk
Green, Anthony
Green, Jack
Griffiths, A.
Guliaev, Valeri I.
Gurney, O. R.
Hallo, William W.
Handley, Morrison
Harmatta, J.
Harris, Rivka

Harrison, Thomas
Harvey, D.
Head, Duncan
Hedrick, Larry
Henkelman, Wouter
Hirsch, Steven W.
Hoglund, Kenneth G.
Holtz, Shalom E.
Horsley, Richard A.
Houston, Mary G.
Huff, Dietrich
Ibrāmī, Hūshang
Ivantchik, Askold I.
Jackson, A. V. Williams
Jacobs, Bruno
Japhet, Sara
Jawad, Laith A.
Jennings, Justin
Joannes, F.
Jong, Albert de
Jordana, Xavier
Jursa, M.
Kaptan, D.
Katz, Steven T.
Katzenstein, H. Jacob
Kawami, Trudy S.
Kessler, K.
Kessler, John
Killick, R. G.
Kleber, Kristin
Knapton, Peter
Knoppers, Gary N
Knowles, Melody D.
Kratz, Reinhard

Kriwaczek, Paul
Kuhrt, Amélie
Lacocque, André
Lambert, W. G.
Landes, David S.
Lang, Mabel L.
Langdon, S.
Lavī, Ḥabīb
Leach, E. R.
Leiden, W. H. C.
Leloux, Kevin
Lemaire, André
Lerner, G.
Lincoln, Bruce
Linssen, M. J. H.
Lipiński, Edward
Littman, Robert J.
Liverani, Mario
Lloyd, Alan B.
Lloyd, Seton
Lucas, C. J.
Luckenbill, Daniel David
Lukonin, Vladimir G.
MacGinnis, John
Machinist, Peter
Malandra, William W.
Malbran-Labat, F.
Marzhan, Joachim
Master, Daniel M.
Matsushima, E.
Mattila, R.
McGovern, Patrick E.
Meier, S. A.
Middlemas, Jill

Miller, M. C.

Mills, Lawrence Heyworth

Mierhoop,

Miroschedji, P.

Moorey, P. R. S.

Muscarella, O. W.

Mukherjee, Siddhartha

Nashef, Khaled

Nefiodkin, Alexander K.

Nejad, Hadi

Nesbitt, M.

Neumann, C.

Neusner, Jacob

Newman, Judith H.

Nodet, Etienne

Noll, K. L.

Novotny, Jamie

Nylan, M.

Nylander, Carl

Ogden, Graham S.

Olson, J. S.

Oppenheim, A. L.

Page,Hugh R.,Jr

Pallis, Svend Aage

Parpola, Simo

Parker, Richard A.

Panaino, Antonio

Paspalas, Stavros A.

Pearce, Laurie E.

Pedersen, O.

Pelikan, Jaroslav

Peradotto, John

Pettinato, Giovanni

Pham, Xuan Huong Thi

Pinches, T. G.

Poebel, A.

Polosmak, Natalya

Pongratz-Leisten, B.

Potts, Daniel T.

Powell, Marvin A.

Pritchard, James B.

Oeming, Manfred

Rainey, A. F.

Reiner, Erica

Rolle, Renate

Röllig, W.

Rollinger, Robert

Root, Margaret Cool

Roth, Martha T.

Sack, Ronald H.

Salonen, A.

Sancisi-Weerdenburg, Heleen

Sanders-Goebel, P.

Sandison, AT

Sarraf, M. R.

Sarshar, Houman

Sasson, J. M.

Schaudig, Hanspeter

Schauensee, D.E.

Schmid, H.

Schmidt, H. P.

Schwartz, Martin

Schwemer, Daniel

Scurlock, Joann

Seymour, M. J.

Shahgolzari, SM

Shea, William H.

Shiff, L. B.

Simpson, St John
Skjærvø, P. O.
Soudavar, A.
Stadter, P. A.
Stausberg, Michael
Stein, Gil J.
Stevens, Marty E.
Stol, Martin
Stolper, Matthew W.
Stott, Katherine
Stronach, David B.
Sumner, William M.
Suter, David W.
Tavernier, J.
Thomas, D. R. A.
Thureau-Dangin, F.
Trotter, James M.
Tuplin, Christopher
Ulansey, David
Ungnad, A.
Vallat, F.
Van de Mieroop, Marc
Van Driel, G.
Vargyas, P.
Vaughn, Andrew G.
Veen, J. E. van der
Vogelsang, W. J.
Waerzeggers, C.
Waters, Matthew W.
Watts, James W.
Weiershauser, Frauke
Weinfeld, M.
Weisberg, David B.
Weiss, L.

Weitzman, Steven
Widengren, G.
Wiesehöfer, J.
Wiggermann, F. A. M.
Williamson, H. G. M.
Winter, Irene J.
Wiseman, D. J.
Wunsch, C.
Yamauchi, E.
Yavari, A.
Younger, K. Lawson
Zaccagnini, Carlo
Zadok, Ran
Zawadzki, S.
Zevit, Z.
Zimansky, Paul E.
Zimmern, H.

ACKNOWLEDGMENTS

I'm guessing that any project that spans more than a decade from inception to completion represents the support, goodwill, and contributions of all kinds from more people than a book's "Acknowledgments" can cover, no matter its author's efforts to be exhaustive. That's certainly true here. My apologies to those I've missed. Thank you.

And thank you, each and every named below. I've had illusions of providing detail to describe the nature of the contributions each person or group (libraries! my students! professional organizations!). But just as I bailed on providing an exhaustive list of specific sources and a more exhaustive Author's Note, finally I provide only the barest list here. Its notice – meager – is inverse to my gratitude – great. Thank you.

Finally, a special thanks to my dad, Richard Swenson, and my (late) mom, L. Cecile Swenson whose support of my work has been so unqualified that I might almost take it for granted. I don't. And to my husband, Craig L. Slingluff, Jr., a huge thanks for being so ceaseless a cheerleader of this project. I'm not sure I ever would have sent these books out into the world without your unflagging enthusiasm for the saga and the needling to publish it, such as only a person sharing one's life, day in and day out, can do.

Thank you sincerely also to the following, in order simply by alphabet: Richard Abate, Khooshe Aiken, Lindsay Allen, Hanadi Al-Samman, Gigi Amateau, American Academy of Religion, American Schools of Oriental Research, Willis Barnstone, Bennington Book Club, Biographers International Organization,

Bodleian Libraries of Oxford University, Christiana Brenin, Laura Browder, Ellen Brown, McKenna Brown, Theo Calderara, Bethany Carlson, Jamsheed Choksy, Susann Cokal, Meredith Cole, Jonathan Coleman, Michael Cordell, Rob Crawford, the cadre of Cville Women Writers, Stephanie Dalley, Cliff Edwards, Robin Farmer, Louise Finger, Greg Fontana, Jeannie Fontana, Donna Freitas, Shirley French, Kathleen Gacek, Brad Graff, Martien Halvorson-Taylor, Kate Hamilton, Sandy Hausman, Stacy Hawkins, Paul Hilding, Stephani Hilding, Historical Novel Society, Doug Hoffman, Denise Honeycutt, Kate Hunter, Molly Ill, James River Writers, Eric Jarrard, Gretchen Kainz, Andrew King, Dean King, Chris Park, Eva-Marie King, Amelie Kuhrt, John Kutsko, (late) "Boots" Mead, Meg Medina, Manny Mendez, Alex Nagel, Jen Pearson, Stephanie Pearson, The Porches (Trudy Hale), Debby Prum, Ginny Pye, Emilie Raymond, Dianna Rostad, Charles Shields, Guadalupe Shields, Society of Biblical Literature, Maya Smart, Patty Smith, Jack Spiro, Devon Sproule, Beth Stefanik, Matthew Stolper, Jon Swenson Tellekson, Linnea Swenson Tellekson, Deb Swenson, Nigel Tallis, Sandra Treadway, University of Virginia library, Rachel Unkefer, Virginia Commonwealth University library, Virginia (Foundation for the) Humanities, Claire Wachtel, Pat Watkins, Jon Waybright, Anne Westrick, Vera Wilde, Mark Wood, Women's International Study Center, Writer House, and Irene Ziegler.

MAP

This is a map of the Median Empire, Egypt, Lydian Empire and Neo-Babylonian Empire in the 6th century BC (1024 px; there are other sizes available).

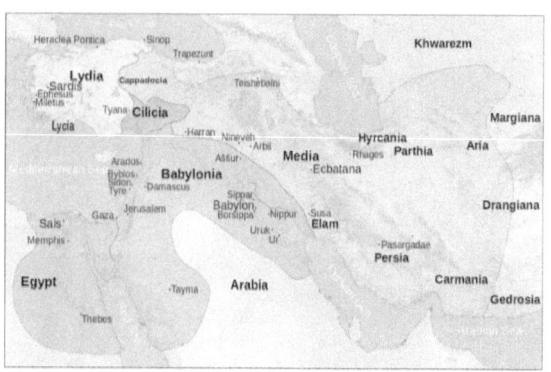

Date: 30 April 2013.
Source: File:Median Empire-hu.svg
ETOPO1 topographic data from NGDC (http://www.ngdc. noaa.gov/mgg/global/global.html).
Author: Original: User:Szajci; English: User:WillemBK

(page URL) https://commons.wikimedia.org/wiki/File:Medi
an_Empire-en.svg

(file   URL)   https://upload.wikimedia.org/wikipedia/
commons/b/bd/Median_Empire-en.svg

Attribution: Original: User:SzajciEnglish: User:WillemBK, CC
BY-SA 3.0 <https://creativecommons.org/licenses/by-sa/3.0>,
via Wikimedia Commons

ABOUT THE AUTHOR

Kristin Swenson, Ph.D. writes across genres. Tenured professor of religious studies with speciality in the history and literature of ancient Israel (Hebrew Bible), she is passionate about the natural world and loves a good story. All the better if a story connects the disparate threads of women and lesser known persons with what history we have. In addition to her writing, Swenson has developed an eco-grief practice to help people continue to advocate for the wild with equanimity and joy. She also maintains a website celebrating (and advising for) the eco-friendly kitchen. Swenson lives and works in Charlottesville Virginia and Duluth, Minnesota.

ALSO BY KRISTIN SWENSON

FICTION

In the Kitchen with Gracie May (PGB)

Let It Out at the Seams (PGB)

Genie of Pasargad (a Babylon/Persia novel; PGB)

Beat the Kettledrum (a Babylon/Persia novel; PGB)

A Falcon Takes Flight (a Babylon/Persia novel; PGB)

Howl of the Golden Jackal (a Babylon/Persia novel; PGB)

NONFICTION

A Most Peculiar Book: The Inherent Strangeness of the Bible (Oxford University)

God of Earth: Discovering a Radically Ecological Christianity (Westminster John Knox)

Bible Babel: Making Sense of the Most Talked About Book of All Time (Harper)

Living through Pain: Psalms and the Search for Wholeness (Baylor University)

What is Religious Studies?: A Journey of Inquiry (with Esther R. Nelson, Kendall Hunt)

POETRY

Haiku 365 at www.kristinswenson.com